PENGUIN BOOKS

THE PALACE OF WISDOM

Robert Marshall-Andrews was born in London in 1944. He was educated at Mill Hill School and the University of Bristol before being called to the Bar in 1967. He was appointed a Recorder of the Midland and Oxford Circuit in 1982 and Queen's Counsel in 1987. He lives in Richmond with his wife and two children. *The Palace of Wisdom* is his first novel.

The Palace of Wisdom

ROBERT MARSHALL-ANDREWS

'The road of excess leads to
the palace of wisdom.'

William Blake

PENGUIN BOOKS

PENGUIN BOOKS

Published by the Penguin Group
27 Wrights Lane, London W8 5TZ, England
Viking Penguin Inc., 40 West 23rd Street, New York, New York 10010, USA
Penguin Books Australia Ltd, Ringwood, Victoria, Australia
Penguin Books Canada Ltd, 2801 John Street, Markham, Ontario, Canada L3R 1B4
Penguin Books (NZ) Ltd, 182–190 Wairau Road, Auckland 10, New Zealand

Penguin Books Ltd, Registered Offices: Harmondsworth, Middlesex, England

First published in Great Britain by Hamish Hamilton 1989
Published in Penguin Books 1990
1 3 5 7 9 10 8 6 4 2

Made and printed in Great Britain by
Cox & Wyman Ltd, Reading, Berks.

Contents

For Brinsley

BOOK ONE

San Casciano

Chapter One

My master beat Galileo at marbles. True, the great apostate was dying and my master no more than eight years of age, the very best age for marbles. Thereafter it entitled him to say with some justification that, for a moment, he knew more about the movement of spheres than any man alive. Not a bad story. Furthermore, considering he had told it to me whilst sitting in chains on the floor of a dungeon in the Bargello prison, waiting to be placed on the rack, it says a lot for his sang-froid. But then he was always a name-dropper. He'd met them all, of course; Pascal, Racine, Voltaire, Vivaldi — even Baruch Spinoza, the great Dutch spectacle-maker, Pantheist and shit-stirrer. It makes for an interesting life being a bibliophile, or at least it did in the seventeenth century.

It's all changed now, of course.

Tolerance abounds; reason is rife. The printing presses of Europe are red-hot from the reproduction of heresies that, sixty years ago, would have left their authors charred on a stake. It's forty years since a Jew was baited in Florence. In the Bargello the hot pincers cannot be prised apart for rust and the unlit coals of the tormentors' fire are covered in greying dust. As always at such times dissent has become vulgar, science reduced to indulgent introspection.

In France, I am told, the well-known gourmet, atheist and Abbot, Etienne Condillac, maintains that all human pre-occupations, thoughts and concentrations are merely 'Pyramids of Sensations'. I daresay, however, that the Abbé Condillac never develops eye-strain copying the *Tractatus Theologico-Politicus* on paper no bigger than his scrotum to hide it from the Inquisition. I daresay *he* never spent days and nights in a haystack with a copy of *Dialogo die due massimi sistemi del mondo* beneath his heaving, adolescent loins. He has never been searched by Medici guardsmen with Descartes' *Meditations* wedged into his rectum. If he had he'd know something about *sensations* all right *and* about

3

concentrating the mind, wonderfully.

As you may have gathered, I have become a little bitter. It has all arrived far too late for me to enjoy it, this cloudburst of tolerance and reason. At the age of seventy-five I am too old for intellectual excitement or much other excitement for that matter. Above all, as a life-long lexicographer I have come to loathe words as a horse detests flies. I would finally have done with them, I would swipe them from my sweating rump. All my life they have swarmed over me, tickling and irritating me with their insect nuances, pricking me with their resonances and crawling into my private crevices to lay nests of new coinages and litters of derivations. Too often they have failed me. Perpetually I write sentences which suddenly bulge and erupt in quite the wrong places like plaster in a Sienese whore-house. Above all I detest their coy alliterations and sinuous similacra. Given the choice I would never come near them again. I would have silence, sun, olives, Tuscan wine, a cool breeze and regular, soothing octogenarian coitus. I deserve it. I've had a hard life in the service of these flies, catching them, arranging them, displaying them in their multitudes, in orderly array whilst all around they buzz and prick and multiply in an ever-increasing vernacular of ever-decreasing sense.

But now I am forced to sit and write this chronology. Just when I was really beginning to enjoy myself for the first time in sixty years.

I have at last returned to my beloved San Casciano and purchased the biggest villa in the town, surrounded by olive groves and hung about with vines. On most days I can't see Florence at all. I have a housekeeper, forty years younger than myself, coarse and sluttish to a highly satisfactory extent. I have many friends and some influence, at least in academic circles. My Honorary Doctorate at the University of Pisa provides me with a certain status and my master's bequest ensures that I am able richly to endow the arts which have begun again to flourish on Tuscan soil. I also enjoy some small political influence. My mastery of Italian dialects, my fluency in French, Geman and English and my stubborn reputation for diplomacy (based as you will hear, on the exploits of a fifteen-year-old boy) make me, from time to time, an invaluable presence at the interminable treaties, undertakings and agreements by which the State of Tuscany is passed between the Empires of Europe. Indeed it was two years ago on my return from the town of Aachen that this present labour was first pressed upon me.

I had arrived in Florence in the late morning and gone straight to my

4

rooms in the Via Calimara. Here I slept for three hours and, having been awakened by my servant, Maximilian, I left the house to visit my library in the Palazzo Medici-Riccardi. The early evening was clear and fine and, declining the services of a chair, I made my way along the Via Roma and turned into the Piazza San Giovanni. The evening sun, slanting across the square, lit the bronze doors of the Baptistery, the greatest work, as you will know, of Lorenzo Ghiberti. I had stopped, partly to admire them and partly to identify, for the thousandth time, the jocular self-image of the sculptor, mischievously placed among the Evangelists and wearing a hat of absurd gaiety, when I heard my name, or rather nickname, called from the direction of the Duomo steps. My first instinct was one of annoyance. I was, after all, seventy-four years of age and few (in Florence or anywhere else) now use my sobriquet. My annoyance became no less when I saw coming towards me, hands raised to forehead in mock adulation, the skittering figure of Tomaso Albinoni, the oldest musical bore in Italy. I had first met him in Rome at the turn of the century when he had been regarded, at the age of twenty-nine, as the successor to Corelli as Italy's Greatest Composer. Since that date, the birth, life, works and death of Pergolesi had eclipsed Tomaso as surely as a storm lantern placed before a candle. The passing of Pergolesi had left him bitter. A sense, no doubt, that his rival had disappeared into the unassailable fortress of immortality. We had discovered at our first meeting, however, that we shared a birthsign – Capricorn, the Goat – a fact which, for some reason, had always caused him to treat me with enthusiastic affection, wholly unrequited.

'Boti,' he called quite unnecessarily as he made his way across the front of the Baptistery door. *'Caro mio.'* He had now unlocked his hands from his forehead and spread them in an oratorical gesture intended to culminate, no doubt, in some form of violent embrace.

Now, my ten years living in England during what has come to be known as the Nine Years' War, as a guest of the Bishop of Salisbury, have left me with an aversion to public clasping. In addition it should be remembered that both Albinoni and I were over seventy years of age and any form of sudden impact carried with it a substantial risk of our both falling over. The prospect of Italy's greatest lexicographer being knocked over by even one of her lesser known composers in the shadow of the Duomo was alarming, and, feigning preoccupation, I turned and made off towards the Via Pecori. I was too late. As I had been in rooted contemplation of great art I made but a slow start. He had the benefit of full momentum and before I had travelled twenty paces I felt both

5

hands on my shoulders and was all but thrown head first onto the cobbles.

'Boti,' he repeated, wheezing heavily, 'you are becoming deaf as a statue.' I turned and reassembled myself. 'Tomaso!' I said without enthusiasm, 'How very good to see you. What a surprise to find you in Florence.'

'Yes, yes, I arrived from Rome yesterday.' He still held tightly to one of my shoulders. 'As a matter of fact, my dear old friend, I have come to see *you*. I tried to find you at the Via Calimara but your fellow, Maximilian, said you were at Arles.'

'Not Arles,' I corrected him, 'Aachen. There has been a Treaty. They wanted me to tell them what it meant.' (Politics, you see, has never been his forte.) I looked at him closely. 'What exactly did you want to see *me* about?'

'Opera.'

'Opera?'

'Yes, Opera – overtures, arias – Opera.'

I looked at him – blankly, I suspect. 'My dear Tomaso,' I said, 'one of the many things which I cannot do is sing.'

'Not sing, *write*. I say, is there any chance of us going somewhere to talk about this?' A group of Austrian soldiers had come into the Piazza and were examining the Ghiberti bronze with the unmistakable jeering cacophony which accompanies, world-wide, the soldier's appreciation of wine, women and fine art.

'Where are you staying?' I asked, optimistically.

'Oh,' he said, 'I've taken some rooms in the Via Spanoni. You can see the Arno. It stinks to high heaven.'

'Very well,' I said with some evident resignation, 'come to the Via Calimara.'

We walked back in silence. Save where the narrow street opened into the Piazza della Republica, the sun illuminated only the red-tiled roofs and upper balconies facing east. At ground-level the gloom deepened.

When we arrived at my rooms the lights were already burning and I sent Maximilian for wine and bread and olives.

'Well?' I said when we were settled by the window. 'What do you mean "write"? You must know that I wouldn't recognise music if I saw it?'

'Not the music, the story.'

'What story?'

'What do you think? Magliabechi, the books, the Bombonis, the

6

arrests, France, Marguérite-Louise, you and Bono – all of it!'

'I'm sorry, Tomaso,' I said, 'I still do not understand. The people you mention are, were, real. The events *actually* happened. There is no ... no *Dramatic Convention*.' I paused but he continued to look at me from the other side of the lamp. Rapidly exhausting my knowledge of operatic matters, I continued, 'There is no "Grand Theme", no "Divine Rules".'

He regarded me with an indulgent, irritating smirk. 'I see,' he said, 'to you an Opera can only concern Gods? Man *learning* about himself through the activities and weaknesses of Gods?'

'Yes.'

'To *you* it must always be Olympian, didactic?'

'Yes, yes.'

'But, my friend, my dear Boti,' he had risen from his chair, refilled his glass and now came and stood directly in front of me. 'Don't you see that Opera *must* move with the spirit of the age? Outside the '*Conventions*' of the stage, man no longer *fears* God, no longer cowers in ignorance before mere *phenomena* that are now totally explicable through Science. Man *proves* God through his Reason. Man perceives his own imperfection and that *very* imperfection presupposes the existence of a Perfect Being, God, The Creator.'

'Of course,' I said, somewhat irritated by this lecture on philosophy, 'the Cartesian theory, but what ...'

'But what has it got to do with Opera? My dear Boti, I will tell you. I feel as though I have known this all my life but only now do I understand. Opera is the *mirror*. Look, here is man, rooted to the stage, a pigmy in the vast auditorium, bound by his own imperfections, lying, cheating, stealing, shitting, belching, fornicating man. And *here*,' his arms encircling the air, above his head, scattering wine unnoticed on his wig, 'is the Music, the Sublimity of God. The players do not *imitate* Gods. They *prove* them by their own travesties, their own bungling imperfections, their own intolerable conceits.' He took a large draught of wine, captured an olive and, after a contemplative chewing, spat the stone into the street. 'I tell you, Boti, in a hundred years we will have Operas about thieves and fornicators, slaves and kings, whores and boozers, pimps and adulterers. Every form of human vice and misdemeanour, from flogging to flatulence, will be performed before our eyes and above it' – more waving, more wine on wig – 'and above it ... this Sublimity of Sound.' He drained his glass, belched slightly and continued. 'And what is more, do you know what we shall have? We shall have *women* to sing on stage. Yes we will! We will have *real* sluts

7

and slaves. No more castrati. No more mutilated, fake sopranos. No more imitation tits. We will have real bosoms.' So saying he cupped both hands, the one still holding the empty wine glass some six inches before his shrunken chest, and gazed at me with wild enthusiasm. 'Well, what do you think?'

Frankly, I was appalled. I had heard several times that he had become peculiar, but to hear one of Italy's leading musicians reducing art to the level of bar-room smut was, quite honestly, distressing. Worse was to come. No doubt mistaking my silence for admiration or, at least, approbation, he adopted a kind of squeaking falsetto and, to a sharp arpeggio, began to caper towards the wine jug.

'Tum tum titty, tum tum tum titty, tum tum titty titty tum tum.'

In order to put a stop to it, rather than out of interest, I said, 'Yes, yes, all very interesting but I don't see what it has got to do with *me*.'

He turned abruptly, jug in one hand, glass in the other. 'But your story, don't you see, has *everything* I need. The end of the old world, the power of Princes, the decay of a great civilisation, the attack on learning, conspiracies, whores, love, torture, death ... I'm sorry, Boti,' he broke off seeing the wince of pain which crossed my face. 'I'm sorry, I know the Bargello was a hell on earth.'

'It was not the Bargello,' I said, 'it was the "whores" that hurt. But go on.'

'Then there is the flight across Europe, the Sun King, the peccadilloes which changed history, the power of friendship and loyalty, betrayal, tragedy, triumph – and done with a dwarf!'

Despite the feelings that were moving within me I could not forbear to smile. 'And who will you find in your *Commedia* who could impersonate Bono?' I asked. 'Where will you find so great a voice from so small a frame?'

As he poured my wine he reflected, apparently seriously, upon the problem. 'I have never encountered a dwarf in Opera,' he said, 'perhaps we could lower a part of the staging...'

'I will not have him ridiculed,' I said with some heat.

'Of course not, that is not my purpose, believe me. My purpose is to immortalise, not denigrate.'

Despite myself, my reservations and my hostility and, yes, the peculiar blend of pleasure and pain which accompanied this memory, I had become excited. Still I demurred.

'But it will never be believed. The world has changed. The libraries groan with books. Galileo is in print in thirty languages. The Jesuit

Inquisition has gone. The Medicis are a memory. No one burns in Europe. The Jewish quarter has gone. Commerce and trade are the new weapons of mankind. The new worlds have opened. Florence is now a still pond at the end of a tributary.'

His voice, now slightly blurred with liquor, came from the other side of the light. 'Yes, but *your* story is not about Florence. It is about the corruption of power, the mutilation of truth. It is as timeless as the imagination. But much more than that it must be, *deserves* to be, *recorded*. Do you think history will do you justice? Do you think otherwise you will be even mentioned in the Tuscan tale except as a tedious wordsmith in a one-line footnote?'

Much later I watched him leave from my window. I had sent Maximilian with him although the city was safer now having been effectively subdued by the recent plague and the Austrian soldiers (who were generally of good order and discipline). I listened to his footsteps turn towards the Via della Condotta which leads to the Bargello and, despite the warmth of that summer evening, a tremor ran through me. It was so long ago. How long? Sixty years? It was, of course, partly the wine, partly the dark, soft Florentine air which carries still its own melancholy in the early night, but tears started from my old eyes. As though coincident with the blurring of my sight, images as sharp as splinters assembled in my brain and with them came the sounds of memory clear as a boy's song.

I had of course agreed to provide him with something. Precisely what I had not said. A background. A synopsis. 'The best my poor recollection would do.' Well, we shall see. As I turned away from the window, nostalgia still lingering like a spell, I fancied I saw a figure in the gloom beyond the light, a crooked form, the head barely protruding in silhouette above a mountainous shoulder, and I felt those eyes upon me which I had closed so many years ago.

'Master?' I said, but my movement into the room revealed the shadow to be my own, cast from the light which hung at the corner of the Via del Lamberti to prevent the congregation of tarts.

'Master,' said Maximilian as he entered the room, 'I have seen him home.' A quiet lad, efficient and unassuming. I placed him well in Florence before I left. 'Will you need anything else? Some bread, more wine?'

'No. Yes, yes, some more wine, and bring me a pen and paper if you would for my *cubiculo*.'

Predictably I wrote nothing. Words evaded sensation like live mussels slipping from a spear. The drink, of course, did not help. I finished the jug, fell asleep in my chair and awoke in the morning chill, head thick, body stiff and saliva coating my chin. I had dreamt, of course, of Catarina and, for the first time for many years, of Bono.

That morning I inspected the library, which was in satisfactory order. In the afternoon I obtained a coach and drove to the village of my childhood, high in the Tuscan hills. In the last twenty years I had passed it many times but had never stopped. I spoke to the new mayor, a pig-faced fellow called Bentoni who, I am sure, obtained an exorbitant commission from the renting of my villa.

In the first two days I acquired a housekeeper, the aforesaid sluttish Maria (another acquisition — I suspect well-used — from the mayor), and sufficient furniture to satisfy comfort and vanity. I stocked the cellar, gave orders for the maintenance of my diet, appointed a gardener with an assistant who could also, if necessary, drive a coach. I left the library in the capable hands of my own apprentice Albert (himself nearly fifty years of age), paid Maximilian a handsome sum, made a valedictory visit to Cordelia Mazzarone, who had, for the past twenty years, admirably satisfied my declining libido, and was gratified to observe signs of regret on her round, slightly pretty and thoroughly commercial face.

I assembled such belongings as befits a country gentleman, purchased new boots and shoes to negotiate the pathways of the rough Tuscan hills, armed myself with pens, ink and an absurdly optimistic quantity of paper and returned to my villa. Here I fretted over the arrangement of the pictures, seduced Maria, irritated the gardeners, bathed more often than was necessary, digested a gluttonous quantity of olives, tottered dangerously up and down the paths of the surrounding olive groves and then finally, one day, applied myself to the *tabula rasa*. It will all cost a great deal of time and money but I don't care. I am seventy-five years of age and still, remarkably, as healthy as I have been all my life. I have outlived all my acquaintances (except Tomaso Albinoni) and there is only one distant cousin to inherit my money, a fat, self-satisfied butcher in Fiesole. I have, of course, left everything to the library, which will disappoint my cousin, and serve him right.

Chapter Two

I was born in the village of San Casciano on the dusty red road on the way to Florence, beyond Poggio Imperiale where the Tuscan hills fold like linen and the poplars stand in permanent exclamation among the grey olives and ochre roofs. A small town it was and is, with little to distinguish it from a thousand Tuscan towns save for its position on the road which led ultimately to Rome. For this reason we enjoyed an unusual prominence and notoriety. Many pilgrims, messengers, Legates, Cardinals, traders, merchants and a seemingly interminable quantity of Englishmen required feeding, wining and watering, having completed the half-day's journey from Florence and before setting out for accommodation at Siena. As a result of this continuous trade the village developed a considerable reputation for the quality of its pasta, the honest fortitude of its wine and the genial nature of its hospitality. The well-known expression, 'as generous as San Casciano', relates directly to this reputation and owes nothing whatsoever to the Saint of the same name, a surly and unpleasant hermit whose canonisation rested solely upon his reported ability, through meditation, to develop holes in his head.

As a result of its position the village had also witnessed the passing of armies of various sizes, complexions and aspirations. Southwards came Germans, Austrians, French, even Swedes, to fight the Turks. Northwards in their turn came the Vatican mercenaries, the crossbow men of God, sent to meddle in the Holy Wars of Succession. Generally they simply passed straight through as Florence had long ceased to be in the front line of any conflict of the slightest importance. On two occasions since the fifteenth century the village had been occupied and fortified by the Sienese or rather their Genoese mercenaries, who behaved, so it was said, with extraordinary punctiliousness, impregnating only by and large by consent and extracting little more than

11

prudent taxation from the local tradesmen, themselves already well bloated by the profits of commerce and geographical opportunity. One full-blooded rape, sufficiently rare to be recorded and pass into local anecdote, occurred in the field directly above our stables. The offender, a Sienese bowman, paid for his hot emission with the loss of his right hand, publicly hewn from him by his own captain in the village square and now said to be pickled in brine in the crypt of the village church, a monument to the wisdom of continence and sexual propriety.

The real irritation was caused by the Englishmen. Their fascination with the customs and habits of my country seemed quite unquenchable. I have a weakness for the English. My years in their country as a guest of Bishop Burnet in the pleasant town of Salisbury convinced me that they are a gentle and eccentric people, without fine art, recklessly in love with their own language. For the most part, however, they travel only for the purpose of self-gratification and producing interminable diaries preoccupied by such matters as the 'excessive' quantities of snuff taken by Italian women.

My childhood, therefore, while rural, was not entirely devoid of cosmopolitan flavour. My christened name was Frederico Szorzi Credi and, thus, during my early youth I was universally known as Fredo.

The climactic events of my life to which Albinoni had referred, my apprenticeship to the great Magliabechi, the savage oppressions of Cosimo III, the deadly, doomed conspiracies to protect the libraries, the concealment of the works of Galileo and the final desperate petition to the King of France all occurred, as you will learn, at about my fifteenth year. But as no web can be created from its centre I must begin by securing my narrative to the branches from which it may be spun; my father, my mother, my master, my mentors and the family Bomboni.

My father, Gallupe Credi, the son of a Florentine dye merchant, had early pretensions to scholarship and received something of a formal education at the Borrenzo Institute in Florence. He had commenced his studies at the University at Pisa when, for reasons even now impenetrable, the Grand Duke of Tuscany, Ferdinando de Medici, embarked on a war with the Pope's relatives, the Barbarini. My father, at that time barely nineteen years of age, was swift to enlist in the Tuscan militia and found himself, virtually untrained, enrolled in a company of fellow students and in the thick of the battle of Mongiorno. Unlike many such battles of the day which involved much posturing, flag-waving, manoeuvring and frequent stoppages for siesta, this was a real contest which left several hundred dead and the Florentines totally victorious.

Without dwelling on the matter indecently it is right to record that my father distinguished himself mightily. His own corps of budding scientists was, as circumstance dictated, kept well to the rear, allowing the real fighting to be undertaken by the mercenary levies. The Barbarini, however, showing a fine disregard for the principles of modern warfare, infiltrated a large column of their own hired thugs in a pincer movement obscured by a line of hills intended to protect the Florentine flank. The sudden onslaught of this heavy brigade of bullies, at least two hundred strong, could well have carried the day had it not been for the magnificent resistance displayed by my father and his fellow scholars. Accounts of the engagement vary but it is quite clear that it was my father who struck the first blow which quite severed the head of the leading mercenary and sent it bowling back amongst the feet of his followers. As my father so frequently remarked thereafter, there is nothing so lowering to morale when engaged in a game of *pallone* as the prospect of the ball being struck through the legs of your own goalkeeper. How infinitely worse it must be when the object is the head of your own captain with which you had recently been discussing, say, the movement of the galaxies or the exorbitant price of brandy. Remarkably, this single blow proved decisive, causing the Genoese to turn and flee as abruptly as they had arrived. My father's company made hot pursuit, which was an error. Perceiving themselves to be followed and believing they were in danger of being overtaken, a small party of the more resolute soldiers turned and provided some stern resistance in order to allow the escape of their own men. The Florentines, who possessed the enthusiasm of novices and, more important, had considerable advantage in numbers, made short work of the fray, killing five before the remainder surrendered. My father, however, received a sword thrust through the right leg which he was lucky to survive.

The wound left him lame but, as a result of his own contribution, he became for a short while a Hero of the City. He was received by the Grand Duke Ferdinando himself and was awarded a life pension which, notwithstanding the corruption of subsequent governments, was paid until his premature and violent death.

Thus rendered both independent and disabled before his twentieth year, my father returned to Pisa where he enjoyed an academic life until the age of thirty-three, studying astronomy and botany and enjoying the soft intellectual twilight of Florentine thought. In 1658 he left for Florence where, three years later in the Medici library at San Lorenzo, he met my mother.

Shortly after she was murdered, distracted by his remorse and guilt, my father destroyed all vestiges of my mother's life. However, following his own death, I discovered among his academic papers drafts of letters written to her, although whether they ever reached her eyes in any form or whether, indeed, they represented the truth of their relationship I would never know. From these drafts I was able, painfully, to assemble the details of their first meeting, an event with which they remained apparently fascinated, perceiving it as the moment when the vagaries of coincidence were fatefully transported into the certainty of bliss.

My mother was sixteen, a girl of striking beauty, the last living daughter of an elderly Levite whose family had survived, and fled, the persecutions and slaughter in Milan. For fifty years her father had lived in the Jewish quarter of Florence where his race enjoyed an uneasy, watchful and ill-omened toleration.

Even during the benign reign of Ferdinando, however, the great library of the Medici (which had for a century lent its books gratis to the people) was closed to the Jews on pain of imprisonment. This circumstance led to the hazardous employment of my mother. From the age of twelve she regularly borrowed manuscripts from the library supposedly on behalf of a Florentine gentleman but in reality for the use of her own father whose academic zeal dictated, even then, an ominous disregard for the risks she ran. The danger was rendered the more acute by my grandfather's near-blindness. This forced him to read at a snail's pace which itself entailed the late return of books and consequent enquiry and fines. Indeed it was a dispute between my mother and a librarian as to the amount of such a penalty which first brought her to my father's attention as he sat working in his *cubiculo*. At first exasperated by the interruption he was swiftly intrigued by the girl whose extended borrowing of *The Theory of Atoms* by Democritus seemed so innappropriate to her age or station. Pretending a scholastic impatience, he strode to the desk, paid the fine himself and thus contrived an introduction so essential to my own being.

Thereafter it is clear that they met every day and my father was swiftly acquainted with the details of my mother's life, her paternity and her race. It is a measure of his infatuation that my father, a 'Hero of Florence', took upon himself the supply of books to Isaac the Jew and, on one recorded occasion, spent a day reading to the old infidel the works of the Englishman Sir Robert Boyle by whom the theories of Democritus, the touchstones of centuries, were utterly destroyed.

My parents were married on the 15th of May, 1662, at the modern Church of Santa Maria Nuova at Cortona. They stood at the portico and two hundred miles of Tuscany stretched out beneath them. As my mother looked at this grey-green fecundity she would have known, even then, that she carried my first sister whose life extended for barely six weeks during the great plague of 1663.

For three months they had courted, my father abandoning his studies and my mother her family and, ultimately, her religion. Old Isaac, my maternal grandfather (who was to die in such terrible circumstances) I never saw. In my youth his house was barred to us by the intolerance he purported so violently to condemn.

Two months after their first meeting my father had sought permission to marry my mother. He went as a supplicant, prepared to forgo anything but his religion. It was precisely not enough. 'Will you become a Jew?' my grandfather said, cold as stone.

'No.'

'So then you will not have my blessing.'

My father had tried to move him. He would, he said, be married according to Jewish law. Equally, married in a Christian church, he would not deny her her Jewish faith. He was even prepared to live out of marriage. He was thirty-six years of age, a dusty but nonetheless perfectly respectable hero of Florence, a man with an income, scholarship, expectations.

'You do not understand,' said the patriarch. 'The Jews are spread gossamer-thin across the civilised world. We have nowhere but our collective birthright to call a country. We are prey to any form of bigotry, xenophobia or political expediency. Our children have died in their hundreds to conceal the inadequacy of Princes and divert the "attentions" of people from starvation and plague. And yet along our gossamer web travels the culture and the genius of a people. Even the works of your Robert Boyle (who hates the Jews by the way – did you know?) travel along these threads.

'Often great holes are torn in this weft of people. In whole villages, towns, cities, districts, countries and continents Jews are slaughtered and chained, raped and broken, their infant children hoisted on spikes or baited to their deaths. And what happens when our web is broken? Does it fall from the tree, shrivel away to its points of adhesion? No, the tissue heals around the tear, reforms in circular threads and with the patience of the millennia is darned piece by piece until the part is sound and itself supports once more the tension of the whole. And so you will

15

understand, Signore Credi, with your knowledge of atoms that it is not the web that creates the strength but each and every individual thread and sinew. *We* are those sinews and once they are corrupted we are nothing. Here in Florence it is starting again. You do not believe me, Signore Credi? Confiscations, the baiting, the beatings, the lash, the rack, we feel them in the air like the resonance of marching men. Why should you feel it? It would take your children generations to develop an instinct that we are born with. If my child wishes to go she may go but if she goes she goes for ever.'

And, thus, she went.

My father had already moved into a comfortable house in the Via della Vigna Nuova close to the Palazzo Strozzi. My mother had married under the assumed name of Ballarini and although the height of her cheek-bones, the thickness and blackness of her hair may have betrayed her race in her own quarter of Florence, the Roman angularity of her nose and, above all, her height (my father topped her by barely a hand's breadth) ensured her immediate acceptance as a Christian wife.

About this time my father had begun to tire of academic research. Whilst possessed of an efficient and enquiring brain he lacked the intuition, the brilliance or the financial necessity to make the journey to the borders of scientific discovery and, despite his disability and his increasing age, he yearned for action. It was in order to satisfy this instinct that he purchased the villa at San Casciano where he spent the heat of the Tuscan summers riding the hills, entertaining rarely and, on occasion, hunting wild boar with the neighbouring *rustici*, one of whom, a man whom he instinctively detested, was the local butcher, Bomboni.

From time to time, during the summer, my father would visit the city to obtain such supplies and *utilensi* as could not be found in the village and to acquaint himself with the increasingly unhappy news.

On one of these occasions, my mother later told me, he returned in a state of some excitement and informed her that he believed he had found a commission ideally suited for his abilities, energy and aspirations and an employer of 'singular appearance'.

'Standing at full height,' he told my mother, 'he would barely reach the crook of your extended arm. He is hideously bent and carries a burden upon his back so great that you expect, at any time, that it will become detached and fall at his feet. It afflicts only one side of his back and the other shoulder slopes away causing the right arm to appear substantially longer than the left. However I do not think that this hump can be of any great weight since his legs, which must ultimately support

16

it, are as thin as rails. From this his leggings droop like the festoons of a May carnival. As to his face, it is, if anything, less appetising than the rest of his appearance. Although both eyes are reasonably evenly set they stand close alongside a vast beak of a nose, the tip of which protrudes below the level of his mouth, somewhat impeding his diction. He wears no wig and his hair is sufficiently sparse to draw attention to the individual tufts which erupt from his pate. His ears are so large and fleshy as to have independent motion and thus, when he moves forward, they resemble the paddles from which he achieves propulsion. His speech is occasionally excitable and then he emits a fine spray of saliva upon the many who attend his words. I think that he is one of the cleverest men I have ever met.'

It was my mother, of course, who recounted this description to me and I doubt the veracity of her recollection. I doubt whether my father, on a first brief acquaintanceship, could have assembled a description of such perfect accuracy.

The historic meeting (from my point of view) between my father and my future master began in the doorway of a goldsmith's premises on the Ponte Vecchio. In my childhood it was recounted so often that I am now able to relate with confident veracity events which occurred many months before my own mewling appearance upon the Tuscan stage. My father, who had entered the shop to inspect a necklace he had reserved for my mother, encountered the hunched figure stepping out, heavily over-burdened with an enormous pile of manuscripts. As they collided in the doorway the papers were scattered about the footpath and, had it not been for swift retrieval by both men, would have been pulped by the passing crowds of Florentines who, contrary to their reputation, when confronted with the printed word like little better than to stamp on it.

The danger to the documents thus had both of them instantly on their knees and, surrounded by the press of commerce, gathering together the damaged pages upon which my father could see lines of Aramaic script and astronomical drawings. When all that could be had been collected both men stood in the cool of the shop entrance attempting some re-arrangement of the pile and exchanging appropriate apologies.

'How very clumsy of me,' said my father, 'I fear I did not see you below the glass of the doorway,' and then he paused, embarrassed, realising the implication of his words.

The crooked face looked up at him and smiled. 'Do not apologise, Signore Credi, Professore, it is I who am at fault. You did not expect to

17

see me but I might very well have expected to see you. I have often considered wearing some form of early-warning device such as a very large hat, possibly with a bell on the top or perhaps a reflecting bauble.'

'I think,' said my father, 'the dunce's cap should rather be on my head. But tell me, Signore, how do you know my name?'

'We have been to the same meetings, Professore, in the Pitti Palace. You do not remember me because on both occasions I arrived early and left late and was sitting amongst those listening to you in respectful silence.'

'Then you are a member of the Cimento!' said my father, delighted.

'Indeed I am – "*Provando e Riprovando*".'

Having thus established their joint membership of the great Society, whose password was 'Prove and Prove Again', my father insisted that he carried a part of the manuscripts to the hunchback's house, whereupon the latter promised wine and olives and the prospect of meeting an 'exciting young doctor' himself about to leave for the University of Pisa. So, both clutching their tattered bundles, my father turning and stooping, the other twisted by nature, each dragging a useless leg, they descended from the Ponte Vecchio like a pair of locked crabs and made their way across the Piazza della Signoria towards the great block of the Bargello. It was very hot and the air, now visibly rising from the cobbles, wreathed and shimmered as though curling from a spit. The sewer which ran along the Via del Proconsolo had dammed and fractured and, a hundred paces short of the Piazza del Duomo, the effluent rose from the street, spreading and puddling between the uneven flags. Both men, wearing unfashionable luccos, were forced to lift their hems as they struggled towards the Via del Corso.

'I fear the city disintegrates before our eyes,' said my future master. 'when you proceed at my level you become preoccupied with the affairs of the gutter. That sewer has been broken for two weeks and no sign of mending. We live in a wonderful city, do we not, above and around us the marvels of Michelangelo and Brunelleschi and beneath us the rising shit?'

'I will write to the Capomaestro,' said my father.

'Little good will it do you. The mending of drains has now been declared a monopoly and sold off. It was bought by the Castanelli brothers who, as you may know, already run the leather market. In some ways it was an appropriate choice but it will not, I fear, tend to the municipal good. Still, at least it provides amenity for some,' and he gestured towards three small boys, near naked in the heat, one bearing, on his legs, the mark of the recent plague, who laughed and splashed in the running stream.

They continued along the Via del Corso some two or three hundred paces when my father's companion stopped before a carved, polished doorway let into the white rendered wall of a villa extending four storeys above the street.

This area of Florence had once been associated with lawyers, pressing towards the Bargello like beasts to a trough. However its position so close to the centre of the city and, thus, to the parts thought most contagious in the recent plagues had rendered it unfashionable in professional circles and it now bore the unmistakable sign of neglect and decay which follows upon the gentry, in any age, as they stampede towards the safety of the countryside. A mixture of abandoned and broken *utilensi* littered the cobbles while ill-defined vegetable matter, compressed between the stones, exuded putrefaction in the raw heat of the afternoon.

'I bought this from a panicking Attorney,' said my future master, banging sharply on the door with the iron handle. 'He took one look at me and assumed that I was the very source of the pestilence itself. I remember that he opened the door and backed away sharply with one hand covering his mouth and nostrils and the other, interestingly enough, clasped over his genitals. Scientific ignorance may, I suppose, be excused in the legal profession but to assume that bubonic plague attacks the phallic member *first* displays a fine disorder of the intellect. Where *is* this fellow?'

As he spoke a bolt was withdrawn and the door swung back revealing a man of gigantic size, fully a head taller than my father (himself one of the tallest men in Florence). Although the servant wore the Italian lucco, the form which now confronted them had not resulted from any European parentage. From the face, itself brown to the point of pitch, black eyes stared unblinkingly along a monstrously curved and dilated nose.

'Thank you, Otto,' said the hunchback, proffering his own pile of papers which the giant received in hands strangely cupped as though in the performance of some ursine obeisance.

As they entered the house my father was also relieved of his burden and his host said, 'Otto is a mixture of Turk and Moor but he is no longer an infidel, are you, Otto? He is now a converted Christian to the point of zealotry and regularly terrifies the congregation at San Martino. He has had an interesting life. He was born and bred a pirate and was captured by a Florentine galley five years ago. I found him at the quayside in Leghorn. He had been nailed to a post ready to be flayed and boiled. They still do it, you know, to make *mumia*. I paid two hundred florins for him although they pointed out, honestly enough, that he was already useless for sodomy. He is, however, very strong and when these twisted bones give me trouble he is of great assistance to me even though he cannot properly open his hands for the ligaments were quite severed by the nails. Some wine, please, Otto, and bread and cheese and olives.'

They had entered into the hallway which, years later, I was to know so well. The walls were painted an unfashionable and unrelieved white. The first flight of the sparsely carved oak staircase, some six feet across, extended down to the centre of the hall which had a floor of rough-cut marble partially covered by antique Florentine rugs dyed in the red ochre to which the city had owed its commercial life, now imitated out of existence. At the head of this first flight the staircase parted, turned up the walls and joined the balcony above their heads from which the first-floor rooms gave in each direction.

The centre of the house formed an unlit well with four similar rectangular balustrades at each floor level, allowing those at the very bottom of the staircase to look at the central dome of the building upon which was a coating of *pietra dura* now so faded as to provide nothing more than a palette of colour like banks of cloud in which the imagination drew its own image.

'A most beautiful house,' said my father.

'Yes, it has become, I fear, a necessary indulgence.'

As they spoke they entered the door to the left of the staircase whereupon my father exclaimed with delight. Stretching before him was a room nearly twenty paces in length, its ceiling supported by pillars of marble and its walls, save for a portion at the extreme right hand, lined with bookcases of red cedar. The floor was of a similar wood, partially covered, again by Florentine rugs whose dye was faintly mirrored in the opaque whiteness of the ceiling. Light was provided by three unshuttered and open windows through which the sound of the street could be heard. Advancing into the room it became clear to my father that, notwithstanding its vast proportions, it was a corridor. At the far right end it gave onto a further area, a little less than half the size of the first, at the extremity of which a great window overlooked a commercially defunct canal which flowed eventually into the Arno. To the right of this window a room similar in proportion to the first ran along the back of the house, its bookcases pausing only to accommodate windows of a smaller size through which the light fell on the red wood and bindings and revealed, in its rays, the fine dancing of dust. At the end of this chamber an open archway gave onto yet another identical room through which it was possible again to make three right-hand turns before arriving back at the hallway on the far side of the staircase and beneath the balustrades. My father, having completed this circumnavigation, paused and smiled at his new acquaintance.

'Signore Magliabechi, I have not seen the like outside Pisa. Indeed I do not think I have seen the like in the University itself. What is the size of this library?'

'I believe, now, we have an excess of twenty-five thousand volumes.'

'It is the work of a lifetime.'

'It is the work of many lifetimes, Professore. Here comes our wine.'

Otto's enormous figure had appeared, from a door apparently concealed below the staircase, carrying a pitcher, two glasses and a tray of olives.

'We will have it by the water, Otto,' said my future master and, continuing to move in a clockwise direction, they arrived again at the window overlooking the canal. Here the servant placed the tray on a small oak table, set two chairs in the light of the window and withdrew with neither expression nor sound.

The hunchback filled both glasses and pushed the plate of olives towards my father saying, 'He has forgotten the bowl of cheese. If you are hungry I will call him.' As my father shook his head he continued, 'Well, Professore, you wish to ask me about my library. How did it start? I will tell you. My father, a rather dull professional man, had a substantial collection of books, part inherited and part acquired as an unwanted dowry from a poor wife. When I arrived in the world and he observed this absurd *grottesco gobbo* he decided that I could expect little from life that could not be gleaned from books. He also found me difficult to talk to. He prided himself on being a Renaissance or rather *post*-Renaissance man with a strong aesthetic sense. Having a son who resembled, in sculpting terms, a jumble of discarded limbs and torsos, offended his susceptibilities. Whenever I wished to speak to him therefore, he gave me a book. My mother died attempting to have a second child, and no doubt fearing that he would father yet another hobgoblin, he contented himself with a number of expensive whores, providing me the while with an ever-increasing quantity of books. On one occasion I asked him a childish question concerning the value of gold. His

21

response, true to character, was to provide me with *De Mineralibus* by Albertus Magnus. I was fascinated. I read it all, several times, and every other work I could find on the subject. Metals absorbed me; their strength and properties, their atomic propositions, the elemental changes through which they could be made to pass, the lustre of gold, the moulding of bronze, the strength and fatal weaknesses of iron, all delighted me. I was entirely self taught and, when the time came apprenticed myself with very considerable difficulty to the best goldsmith in Florence. Since then I have prospered mightily.' He rose, awkwardly, refilled the wine and resumed his seat by the window. 'As our great city has declined into its present corruption, its produce unwanted and its coinage debased, men have turned, as they always will, to the security of metal, a commodity about which I knew more than any man in Italy. So I am very rich and, since my money cannot buy me a straight back or proper limbs or a soldier's face, I spend it on this, the accumulation of ephemeral knowledge.'

'How do you ...?'

'How do I collect? With my obvious and profound disabilities? I employ those with straight backs. I employ those who travel. The manuscript which you so helpfully carried today has recently arrived from the Indian city of Jaipur. I cannot read the script but the illustrations indicate a view of the heavens not markedly dissimilar from our own. I have, by the way, all seventy-two works of Democritus and,' he said smiling, 'the less weighty contributions of Sir Robert Boyle which, I think, you sometimes read to others.'

At my father's startled look he continued, 'I am very sorry, Professore, I should have mentioned to you my knowledge of your father-in-law and, what should I say ... the *identity* of your wife. Do not be alarmed. It is not an open secret but Isaac and his people form a fertile source of manuscripts. It is, indeed, widely believed that I am myself a Jew. It is untrue but a crooked back results in all forms of reputation. Sit down, Professore, please, unless you are rising to pass me an olive.'

My father's disquiet was apparent, 'I had no idea that he would ...'

'He hasn't. He has told *me* because I am his friend. But, Signore Credi,' his voice had now lost all hint of jocularity, 'you must take care, for yourself, for your wife or any children that you may have. Tuscany is about to become a dangerous place for us all, perhaps for you in particular.'

'But what do we have to fear, the Turks ...'

'The danger is not from the Ottoman Empire. The danger is here, in Florence, in the Pitti Palace.'

'I have always found the Grand Duke a most reasonable man. You've seen him at the Cimento. He is its guiding light ...'

'It is not *this* Grand Duke. Weak though he may be and labile, he has a patrician instinct to serve. He grieves for the Renaissance. He can scarce breathe twenty words without reference to his ancestor the great Lorenzo. He sits in the Cimento *willing* a Michelangelo to appear so he can leap upon his back and be borne above the mortality of Princes. No, it is not the poor father in whom the danger lies, it is the wife and son.'

'But where lies the *danger*?'

'Have you met the Grand Duchess, Vittoria della Rovere?'

'No.'

'She is, I fear, an odious woman, bigoted and cruel. Ferdinando neglects her which makes her worse. Whilst her husband plays with his scientific toys and societies she has become obsessed with what she perceives as the weakness of his government. This she blames on the influence of feeble intellectuals, decadent artists and, of course, the Jews. She is encouraged by the Jesuits who are now in complete control of the Inquisition and who long to root out the heresies they believe to be rife in the city. The son and heir, fat Cosimo, is dominated by this dreadful mother, despises his father and longs for power. Worse still, apparently unnoticed by the Grand Duke, his wife has established considerable influence and power among the Medici guards and the Salti who control the Bargello. As time passes I fear that nothing but the Grand Duke's fragile health stands between us and a very dark age which is coming.'

For a while both men fell silent before the librarian smiled and continued, 'But, Signore Credi, I did not bring you here to talk of these things. Your glass is empty and I have given you but a handful of olives. I will go and find my Turk and see that you are fed. Then, please, tell me your views on Sir Robert Boyle. I find his science difficult and his views appal me.'

The air cooled, dusk fell and the lamp between them was lit. Bread and cheese were placed upon the table. They talked of science and phenomena and sensations and the relative merits of lenses and whether the heart by *itself* regulating the supply of blood to the brain could so control the emotions. Darkness had nearly fallen across the canal and my father's view of scientific phenomena was becoming coloured both by the quantity of wine ar.d concern lest my mother should become anxious at his continued absence, when they were interrupted by a loud beating on the street door and muffled shouting in which the words 'Turk' and 'Arsehole' could clearly be discerned.

'Ah,' said Magliabechi rising rapidly, 'the good doctor. I must admit him before Otto gets there. They have a ... strange relationship.'

My father perceived this as the moment to leave and rose himself but was waved back into his seat.

'I think you know Lorenzo Bellini but, in any event, he will want to see you.'

From the noises in the hallway it became clear that the hunchback had failed to reach the door before his manservant and the 'strange relationship' was, as the English say, 'in full swing'. Plainly it was, in part, a physical matter involving the sound of heavy buffeting and half-serious admonition.

The noise was such, even at that distance, that my father did not at first notice the urgent knocking from nearby in his corner of the library. The urgency and volume increased and the irregularity of the tapping indicated that it was plainly a human signal. Instinctively unable to resist so peremptory a demand my father rose and carefully examined his surroundings. Despite the effects of the wine he was able to discover that the sound proceeded from behind a painted screen set across the corner of the room. Since the noise in the hall showed no signs of abating my father approached the screen and, drawing the end panel aside, investigated the area it had concealed. Nothing was there save a doorway set into the corner of the wall which, one might have imagined, opened onto the side of the house. The door itself, however, was plainly an internal door ill-designed to withstand even the comparatively mild Tuscan climate and, indeed, was inset with a 'window' of finely carved wood filigree. From this it was clear that a light burned on the further side of the door and the pattern of the woodcarving was thrown minutely onto the back of the screen itself. Uncertain what to do but moved to action by the continued urgency of the knocking my father adopted a tone of professorial authority and said, 'Who's there?' Immediately he spoke the knocking ceased and, after a pause, a slight shuffling could be heard on the other side of the door. My father's eyes had now accustomed to the comparative gloom behind the screen and he perceived a slender key protruding from a lock at the approximate height of the filigree window. No sooner had he made this discovery than from the other side of the door came a most startling crash as if

24

immense weight had fallen upon a wooden surface. As this occurred, the light, visible through the wooden window, waved wildly from side to side. At the same time my father heard a distorted grunt or yelp of pain, whether human or not it was impossible to discern. It was followed, however, by an unmistakable oath, renewed scuttling and then silence. My father, believing that some serious accident had occurred, hesitated no longer and, turning the key, strode into the room beyond the door. He found himself in a small scriptorium, barely four full paces square, the walls lined with books and manuscripts in no particular order and, in the centre of the room, two desks. At the one was drawn up a wooden chair, padded and plainly well used, incorporating a high wooden back upon which a series of pillows had been arranged in a more or less permanent configuration. A glance was sufficient to tell that it regularly accommodated a deformed shoulder.

Upon the desk a series of manuscripts lay open including, my father noticed immediately, a tract headed 'New Experiments Physico-Mechanical Touching the Spring of Air and Its Effects' by Robert Boyle. The other desk was drawn up close in a manner favoured by professional partners. On it lay a miscellaneous quantity of documents, some illuminated, and a quill pen which had been cut to quite extraordinary fineness. Of newly written work there was no sign. However, the ink on the pen shone in the light and a small pool of the fluid, still convex in shape, had formed beneath the discarded point. The cause of the crash was likewise apparent. Set at right angles to the desk was a decorated *cassone* upon which had been placed a portable bookcase containing three shelves approximately the length of a man's arm. This bookcase had been partly dislodged and had fallen backwards against the far wall of the room. The books had thus been propelled through its open back onto the floor where they now lay in a crenellated heap from which the dust continued lazily to rise into the yellow beam of the lamp.

Of life, human or otherwise, there was no sign.

The most cursory inspection revealed that the room contained no window. Ventilation was obtained by means of an aperture set in the far wall barely a foot square and some nine feet high. Although the room was lined with bookcases the volumes they actually contained were sufficiently sparse in number to reveal the solid walls behind them in gaps irregular enough to preclude the possibility of any concealed exit.

Fascinated and a little alarmed, my father began to search the room, peering into the wells of the two desks, and finally approached the pile of books which, themselves, stood only two feet from the floor. While he was excavating this heap (and, indeed, having ascertained that it concealed nothing) a noise from the doorway drew my father's attention to the hunched figure of his host and, beyond him, the familiar face of Lorenzo Bellini.

'Well, well, Lorenzo,' said my future master, 'what are we going to do with our Professore? First he invades my inner sanctum, assaults my bookcase and is now apprehended sifting through the wreckage, no doubt in search of the works of some English naturalist. What are we going to do with him?'

'Oh, bugger him with a sharp quill,' said the great anatomist, 'or serve him up to that bloody Turk for dinner.'

'You're a violent young man, Lorenzo. Next time I'll let Otto finish you off. Now, be quiet and help us reassemble this mess.'

As they collected the books together my father, who had remained silent, embarrassed and somewhat angry, said, 'How does he leave the room?'

'Who?'

'Whoever was working here and banged on the door when Lorenzo came.'

'But there was no one here, you can see, no exit, no window...'

'So I see,' said my father dryly, 'but you know, do you not, that I did not dislodge your bookcase. I did not put on the light, I did not,' and he picked up the quill from the desk, 'conjure up the ink to fill this.' And he drew the tip of the quill across his outstretched palm leaving a smear of graphite on the skin. 'There is no doubt that there was somebody here.' Looking at them both my father was aware for the first time that Bellini's clothes were in disarray and that he possesed, already, a thick and swelling lip. 'Nor did I imagine the hammering on the door.'

'You are sure of this?'

'I entertain no doubt of it at all.'

'*Provando e Riprovando!*' said Bellini cheerfully and added, 'Perhaps it was a rat that came through the ventilator. There must be hundreds of them in the canals.'

'No rat could have dislodged that bookcase.'

'Or a child, a small child could squeeze through that thing. This area now crawls with urchins who would take the shirt from your back...'

'*And* start noting Boyle's treatise at the same time? *And* hammer on the inside door? Besides, I heard his voice and it was no child. It was deep and...'

'Yes?'

'And ... coarse as in a foreign tongue.'

'I see,' said Bellini, replacing the last book. 'Not the *bella lingua* — now come on, Gallupe, how much wine has this camel given you to drink?'

'Extraordinary,' said Magliabechi, 'Italy's leading anatomist cannot tell the difference between one hump and two.'

'Lorenzo, I did *not* imagine this.'

'Then it is a great mystery. We scientists perhaps should not always require proof of these things. What an interesting start to the night. I have given that black ape a thorough drubbing, bearded the ghost of the scriptorium and now Antonio is going to give me some of this wine which has such magical effects. Or is it the olives, do you think?'

In the face of such obvious disbelief or deception my father resigned himself to ignorance but, as they were returning into the library, he stopped and turned. 'The chair,' he said, 'look at the chair. It's a child's music chair. It has been raised to its highest rung!'

'My dear Gallupe, you must not give way to fantasies. *I* use both desks. When my poor back tires of these cushions I perch like a bird on the other side. But it was not me who you heard. I was watching this clown and Otto re-enact the battle of Lepanto. In this version, however, the Christians were less successful than formerly.'

Indeed, it was becoming clear that not only was Bellini's lower lip grossly swollen but his right eye was also closing and the surrounding skin turning the colour of vermilion.

'Not at all,' cried Lorenzo, 'Certainly I took the odd blow but there can be no doubt who sustained the greater damage.'

At this point Otto re-entered the room apparently unmarked, bearing a further board with black bread and a tray of tortellini.

'See,' cried Lorenzo, 'now I will finish him!'

As the servant lowered the tray onto the table Bellini sprang forward, appearing (as my father later recounted) as though he were about to hurl the servant and himself through the open window. The giant Turk, without moving his feet, swung back his left hand, catching the oncoming doctor a devastating blow in the solar plexus, dropping him upon the Florentine rug like a woolsack falling from a cart.

'Thank you, Otto,' said the hunchback, 'I think that will be all for tonight, unless our physician here needs you to carry him to the *ospedale*.'

From the floor the crumpled figure could be heard saying, with considerable difficulty, 'Press home the attack! Charge! ... I think I am going to vomit.'

'No, you're not, Lorenzo, even I know that the expellation of vomit requires the inhalation of oxygen. I am surprised to hear you make such an elementary error. I don't think he will be needing you, Otto, good night.'

When the servant, as expressionless as ever, had left the room, they both helped Bellini into a chair and provided him with a glass of wine which, after a pause, he poured with difficulty into one side of his mouth.

'You are a child, Lorenzo. You are very lucky indeed that he takes it in such good part. One day he will lose his temper and Italy will lose one of its finest brains. I think you two know each other well?'

'Yes, indeed,' said my father, abandoning all hope of explanation and smiling down on the battered face. 'Where *have* you been, Lorenzo, we have missed you at the Cimento.'

'I've been to Pisa to find some bodies. Did you know they had let me loose with a knife again? Only on dead bodies, mark you, well nearly dead anyway.'

My father looked at him fondly, 'How do they cope with you at that university?'

'Oh, they make you a *professore*. Anything that they see which is out of control they get hold of it and make it a *professore*. They made *me* a *professore* at twenty. Only in theoretical medicine, mark you. They hid all the knives. And now I have become quiet and responsible they have given me Anatomy and returned my choppers. By the way, Antonio, did you know they've named a duct after me? Not just here but everywhere. Even in England it's called the "Bellini Duct". We've all got one. Isn't it wonderful? Even in your mouldy old body there's a "Bellini Duct". I shall be immortalised in the digestive tract. More than can be said for you, Gallupe, and you must be over *forty*!'

'Forty-two ...'

'Forty-two! Well, it's all over for you. I suppose you might just pick up some remote star barely visible to the human eye, the "Gallupe Star", or even, I suppose, the "Gallupe Galaxy", providing it's far enough away. But nothing like a renal duct!'

'Lorenzo,' said their host, levering more wine into his glass, 'will you stop talking about yourself and tell us about Pisa. How is the university?'

'As usual; no money, no proper research. The students are poor and become poorer. The good ones can no longer come, and instead we have the impenetrable children of shopkeepers. The best teachers are going to Rome, Bologna, even Vienna!'

The one visible eye, previously full of mocking laughter, was now bright with indignation. 'The money spent on festivals! How many last year? Fourteen? Fifteen? One for the beginning of May, one for the end of May, one for the beginning of summer, one for the harvest, one for no harvest, one for the wine, one for the autumn leaves, one for the olive-pressing. All Pagan. What about one for the telescopes, one for the microscopes, one for Bellini's Duct? But I will tell you why I don't come to the Cimento, Gallupe. I can't stand that fool Redi. He thinks that by flattering the Grand Duke he will recreate the Renaissance.'

My father and my master exchanged glances.

'In order to render experiments comprehensible to his wooden-skulled patron he indulges in a series of conjuring tricks. Do you know, last month he persuaded a man to eat a snake in order to *disprove* Gallienus's theory that a diet of vipers made you *thirsty*. It disproved it all right. The poor fellow was in bed for a week unable to drink a thing. No doubt suffering from a gross inflammation of Bellini's Duct. The rest of them are as bad. The last time I was there Borelli and Viviani spent *four hours* arguing over their wine about the "movement and stability of the earth". It ended with them both falling from the table no doubt as a result of some instability in the stratosphere.

'The other reason why I do not attend is that I cannot *bear* the Grand Duke. There is nothing so irritating to a doctor as a dying man. And he *is* dying. He has hydropsy and a tendency towards apoplexy. Oh, he'd last for a few years if it wasn't for the treatment he receives. You should *see* what they do to him, largely at the instigation of his fat wife and her Jesuit friends. The last time I was called in they'd bled a litre of blood from him, chopped an ounce out of his bladder, forced *polvere capitale* down his nose, applied cauterising irons to his forehead and disembowelled four pigeons in order to scatter the hot entrails on the sizzling flesh. Praise be for two centuries of medical science! They brought me to him in *that* condition and asked what I could *do for him*. When I said "Not a thing" that odious Cosimo (now incidentally nearly as fat as his mother) smirked at me and said something about God mastering science! I ask you! What *is* going to happen to this country?'

Throughout this dissertation my father and his host had been watching each other and now Magliabechi said, 'You bring us again to our first conversation, Lorenzo. What *is* to happen to this country?'

'Oh, the return of the Inquisition,' said Lorenzo, cheerfully, '*Auto-da-fé*, hot pincers, the rack, all the usual intellectual arguments.'

'Do you think that is possible?'

'I think it is inevitable – and so does Antonio, who knows far more about politics than I do – my knowledge has its frontiers in men's guts not in their brains.'

For a while all three were silent and the sounds of the city came faintly through the open casement, mixed with the lapping of the canal and a gossamer breeze which wracked the shutters back and forth within their brackets. A curious magnetism held my father to this small circle of light.

Bellini spoke first.

'So, Gallupe, how do you think you will fare under the torture? Will you deny your Galaxy, obliterate a million stars like Galileo? They only had to *show* him the hot irons and he had turned the universe on its head – and I dare say would have flattened the world if they'd asked him.'

'Would it matter if I did?' my father replied. 'The Galaxy would remain. A million stars would continue to revolve around a million suns and I would have kept my arms in their sockets. But what of you and your famous duct. It might take mankind a generation to rediscover that small crevice once you had denied its existence.'

'The Grand Inquisitors are not interested in kidneys, besides...'

'The Inquisition,' Magliabechi interrupted, 'are interested in everything – even Veronese's parrot.'

'Veronese's parrot?'

'You have not heard the story? It is interesting enough. When the great artist painted the "Last Supper" he was unable to resist the inclusion of a parrot sitting, if my memory serves me correctly, on a perch immediately behind Matthew the publican. Also for good measure he included a butler with a bleeding nose, two German halberdiers and a scratching dog. None of these eccentricities had the slightest effect on the Central Figure and the painting has a remarkable serenity and power. The Inquisition, however, became obsessed with the parrot and Veronese was summoned before the Grand Tribunal.'

At this moment a thin scratching noise could be heard from beyond the window. Interrupting his story, the hunchback crossed to the casement and looked down towards the canal below and the towpath which ran between its bank and the edge of the house. 'Nothing,' he said after a moment, 'or perhaps your giant rat, Lorenzo.'

'Well?' said my father when his host had returned to his seat and refilled the glasses. 'What happened to Veronese?'

'Oh yes, well, they interrogated him closely about the parrot, no doubt sensing the existence of some heresy. When asked why he had seen fit to include it he said, "Artists do strange things like other madmen!" When asked why the butler had a bleeding nose he replied that he had "perchance come by some accident" but staunchly denied any responsibility for what might have happened outside the limits of his canvas. It all provided the Inquisitors with a serious and testing problem. Whilst the infringement might in itself appear trivial, if allowed where would it all end? The dreadful prospect of Last Suppers littered with obscure beasts could not be ruled out. Finally they compromised and ordered the removal of the blood, parrot and halberdiers, retaining the dog.'

'Did he remove them from the painting?'

'Certainly not, he simply renamed the painting. It is now clearly labelled "Dinner at the House of Levi" and may be seen hanging in Verona.'

'A brave and lucky man.'

'Yes, and perhaps, as he said, a little mad.'

My father rose unsteadily from his chair. 'Signore Magliabechi, Antonio, I must go. I have a wife who, when faced with my prolonged absence, is more terrible than all the Inquisitors of Spain.'

Lorenzo sat, still contemplating Magliabechi's story.

'I'm buggered if I'd let them re-name my guts – "Boyle's Belly" or some such rubbish.'

'Not a likely prospect, but please stay, Lorenzo. I have a short matter to discuss concerning one of your patients, and we must let Gallupe go.'

As they walked to the street door my future master took my father by the arm and said, 'When I last heard you at the Cimento, Gallupe, you were talking about the communication of scientific discovery. You were lamenting the duplication of work which takes place in the great centres of learning.'

'It is *true*,' said my father with some emphasis. 'My own work, as it transpired, had been duplicated in Bologna and some of *that* work we now learn had been undertaken, though with considerable error, at the University of Oxford. In England they are proposing to build a new observatory at a town called Greenwich. The works that we have done at Pisa on refractory lenses would be of infinite value. I have written to the architect involved but, of course, no sensible dialogue can ensue...'

'Yes, that is what you were saying. Now I also know that your work

31

in Pisa has been concluded for the present. No, it is an open secret that the endowments have not been continued. Consider, for a moment, my own position. I am a wealthy man but not wealthy enough to endow a University. Besides, my service, such as it is, lies in the augmentation of my library which, one day, will belong to the people of Florence. But I cannot travel. This ... thing on my back and the multitude of associated problems preclude anything but the shortest journeys. Of course I have my sources and methods, with some of which you are now acquainted. However, to use the metaphor Isaac favours so much, I am as strong only as the strands of my web. I am in need of a traveller. A man who can move across Europe and assess the value of books and manuscripts. He must, of course, be of catholic education and disposition. This age of science has thrown up many quacks and charlatans, he must recognise these and discard their works. It would of course,' he continued, motioning my father to silence, 'mean long periods of absence. I know you are a married man. Soon perhaps you will have children, but I know also that you feel the desire to stretch that considerable brain. I have established many friends and contacts. Your own reputation is unassailable and ... well, perhaps I have said enough. Do not answer now. Talk to Vittoria. It is her decision as well as yours.'

My father often said that the decision was made before he reached the last of the three steps which gave onto the street. On turning to his left he retraced the route they had taken in the afternoon and, when he arrived at the Via del Proconsolo he heard the great bell of the Campanile strike the hour of ten and, upon a sudden instinct, turned right towards the Piazza del Duomo.

The narrow street was dark and, even at that early time, deserted. The broken drain still bubbled at the crossroads and the stench of the effluent, fainter now in the cool of the night, blended with the familiar mud-sweet smell rising from the Arno. As he walked towards the great cathedral his own footsteps echoed in the canyon of the houses and, impossibly, a fine rain began to fall from a clear sky. The Piazza was deserted and he stood watching the perfect cupola appear to chase the distant stars. The building moved him as it had always done, seeming, unlike any other, to lie upon the earth like a perfect form thrown down, at rest. He felt a warmth grow inside him, partly the wine no doubt, and, again, he felt the touch, not of the building, but of its architect surely watching it with ethereal complacency. After a short while he turned, walked the length of the aisle and came to the Baptistery whose bronze doors, now gilded over with damp, shone in the white light which illuminated the compartments and reliefs like facets of polished stone. As he stood before the north door a hand fell on his shoulder and the voice of Lorenzo Bellini said, 'Ghiberti cast those when he was twenty-five years old. That's him there, wearing the fancy hat immediately below John the Baptist. No one will ever create a finer work in bronze. Sad in a way to witness something so definitive.'

'He was even younger than you, Lorenzo.'

'Even younger than me. What unbearable precocity. Are you going to collect books for our crooked bibliophile?'

'He told you then?'

'Yes, he was quite excited about it. It is his child. Apart of course from that ghastly Turk, that library is his *only* child. When it does not grow and expand he frets like a mother with a retarded infant. You are to be its wet nurse.'

My father smiled, 'I had not seen it in that light but yes, of course I will accept.'

'You have no children?'

'No. We have had two daughters but neither survived three months. It is the will of God.'

'Perhaps. Perhaps not,' and, with a sudden change of mood, 'Forgive me, for how long did your wife have the contractions?'

'In both cases more than twenty-four hours.'

'When your wife comes again to labour, please send for me. In Florence I lodge in the third house of the Via del Giglio. In Pisa I have lodgings at the University. If I can attend in time I will. I have some small knowledge beyond the digestive tracts. No, no, it would be my pleasure. They seldom let me loose on live bodies. And now, Professore, I must leave you again. I have another anatomy to inspect, entirely theoretical, of course,' and, smiling broadly, he turned and disappeared into the darkness of the Via de Pecori, his footsteps seeming to increase in speed as they died away into the Tuscan night.

Chapter Three

So it came about that my entry into the world was attended by Italy's greatest physician. At the time he expressed the view that I was likely to be a 'difficult bugger', the truth of which you may observe. My mother was overjoyed and I, far from succumbing within the first day, consumed sufficient of my mother's milk to account for both myself and my poor dead sisters, signs of an appetite which remains with me now in my seventy-fifth year. My father had recently returned from his second journey at the service of Signore Magliabechi, bearing with him, I am informed, a collection of modern works so diverse in character and mutually hostile in content that they would have strangled each other to death in the saddlebag had they the means to do so. *Tartuffe* and *Phèdre* rubbing spines uncomfortably with *Paradise Lost*; the *Pensées* of Pascal (in manuscript) uneasily wedged against the *Fables* of La Fontaine whilst the *Essay Concerning Toleration* sat uncomfortably on Locke's *Thoughts Concerning Education* (revealing the foul practices of an English school called Westminster).

On the same day as my entry into the world, May 27, 1670, the Grand Duke Ferdinando departed as a result of an apoplexy and a year's sustained torture at the hands of his medical advisors. For half a century he had reigned over the declining state of Tuscany. He was the last of the Patrician Princes. At precisely one o'clock in the morning he was succeeded by Cosimo III and the persecutions began.

During my early years we lived, almost exclusively, in San Casciano. I grew up with olive groves and the poplars against the hard blue sky. Now that I have returned I realise that it is the place of which I have always dreamed, the image lost in the morning light but the sensation thick in the brain like a Tuscan honey. I even endured easily the bitter cold of the hills in winter, sitting with my mother in the tallow vapour, eyes and nose running red, inhaling the salts of camphor. Or we would walk the frozen ponds and pity the world from the warmth of our wool and fur.

In those early years my father was an arrival of horses and a loss of my mother. Initially he would stay for two days and the great table in our room overlooking the valley would be covered with paper and books, bound and unbound, printed and manuscript, and I, not yet table height, and accustomed to using the space beneath as my own house and fortress would see them hanging like festoons about the edge. Listening cross-legged beneath the boards to my father's voice and my mother's silver laughter, I developed a dislike of literature as profound as is possible in one unable to read a single word. I sulked, and listened. Here it was where I first heard of the Parisian *demi-monde*, first learnt of Racine and Molière, Boileau and La Fontaine.

My father talked of 'soirées' in the Rue Saint-Honoré. 'Fifty actresses, not sluts you understand, at least not all of them.' And he laughed and I could see his legs stretch out under the table close to my bare knees and my mother laughed too and slapped his hand and said, 'Now, Gallupe, I hope you behaved like an Italian gentleman and a Professore.' And he said, 'I am there only for the benefit of my master.' And she said, half-serious, 'I will not have you turning into a Frenchman, Gallupe.'

And he said, 'But I have spent most of my time in England.' And he talked of the cold and the rain and of a blind poet who had died several days before he left but whom he remembered as the 'gentlest and most amusing man'. And then he read some of his poetry, a language all thick and heavy like the oak table leg, his voice assuming a mock solemnity which made me, even then, cringe with embarrassment. She suddenly said, 'Where is Fredo?', and I stretched out swiftly on the floor and heard my father's voice say, 'Look, oh look, he's asleep under the table.' And he took me to my room, my eyes mock-bleary, and held me with a kind of half-hearted manly cosseting, whilst I loathed the sweat and wine smell and the great eyebrows and the rough chin and I smiled a boy's smile while my bones creaked and my head span.

Later, when she put me to bed and I tried to look stern and unforgiving, she would say, knowing as always, 'You must be kind to Papa. He wants to please you so much. But when he has been away for a long time he finds you have grown a little upwards and a little away. Tomorrow he is going to see Signore Magliabechi and then, when he comes back, he will be here for a long time and he has a present for you!'

It was another horrible book. This one illuminated and illustrated with pictures of foxes and beasts and wolves and donkeys. I still have it today.

I was not a soldier's son, you see. My father's long absences and repeated returns constantly reawakened my jealousy and, by so doing, gave it life long after those boy's feelings have normally been displaced by the hardening of the soul.

Also, I knew he mounted her. At the age of seven I had watched with horror as he pinned and rode her, convex-backed, his great face thrust up like a dog at the moon.

Also, I was fat. Incomprehensibly so. My parents' bodies were as hard as statues. In the hot summer when my mother wore the cotton *lucco* her body appeared always in tension like a string beneath a bow. Mine fell about me. My first considered response to myself was one of distaste. Fortunately, however, I had inherited a little of my father's looks. My hair was, and indeed is, tight-curled. My eyes are as black as my mother's, set well apart, and my nose (too short to reveal my semitic origins) evenly bisects my face above a not ungenerous mouth. I have a tendency towards jowl and a lack of facial hair which has generally enabled me to pass as a younger man and even, on one occasion, as you shall hear, as a woman.

My early aversion to men was not universal. I had, in particular, the deepest affection for my volunteered midwife, Lorenzo Bellini. Having presided over my successful birth and even more successful survival it was natural that he should become my godfather. By taking a tortuous, but not wholly eccentric, route San Casciano can be found between Pisa and Florence and he became a regular visitor to our house in the course of his journeys to and from the University. More often than not these visits occurred during my father's absences. Lorenzo was much closer to my mother's age and, curiously, this very fact eradicated any feelings of rivalry. Believing, on the basis of my limited experience, that the horrors of sensuality were awakened only between those of vastly differing age I regarded Bellini as my mother's brother or childhood friend. And so indeed did he behave. The odious pawing and kissing practised by my father was entirely absent from their relationship. Instead they maintained a very proper distance, scarcely pausing on his arrival and departure to touch cheek against cheek in a gesture as antiseptic as a surgeon's mask. It is true, they would look at each other, across the table, for what appeared to me to be a quite unnecessary interval of time and on one occasion, when I was perhaps in my tenth year, I heard them talking late, late into the night with an intensity I could not comprehend. Their relationship, when my father was at home, changed markedly. Bellini appeared almost indifferent to her presence and she displayed something very close to hostility. So marked did it become that I recollect my father saying, as we stood on our terrace and watched Lorenzo disappear along the dusty Florence road, 'Vittoria, *cara mia*, you must bear with Lorenzo. I know he can be a perfect fool at times but he has a heart as big as Italy.' She said she *would* make an effort and we all returned his wave as he reached the bend in the road and disappeared into the darkness of the trees.

In my father's absence Lorenzo was a whirlwind of manic wit and amazing revelation. At first he brought me toys from Florence and Pisa but, sensing a rather priggish disregard for the ephemeral, he revealed to me, increasingly, the remarkable tools of his trade.

'Now,' he would say, showing me a wooden and metal device incorporating screws and callipers and, at the extremity, pincers like a beetle's horns, 'that's for fishing out stones.'

'Stones, where from?'

'From deep inside the body, down there.'

'I haven't got any stones down there.'

'No, but some people do and very painful they are too.'

'How do you get them out?'

'Well, first you catch your patient. Then you slice him open, get hold of this and,' he approached the table, arm recoiled like a matador's before the final *coup de grâce*, 'and then, aaah!, and one stone.'

And there it was, by some delicious sleight-of-hand, the perfect gallstone placed upon the table.

'Is that one of them?'

'It certainly is. I took that from a professor of mathematics only last week. He's quite dead now, of course, poor fellow, but we've got the stone and that's the important thing.'

It went on and on. A magical succession of gallstones, fingers, toes and even eye-balls staring from a murky ether were produced from his saddle-boxes to squeamish delight. Infinitely more rewarding, as you may imagine, than *Paradise Lost*.

So I had the best of it all. A rustic life saved from idiocy by the visitation of science. But two clouds grew in my Tuscan sky. The Bombonis and the news from Florence.

The Bombonis were famous — at least in San Casciano. The father, Alessandro Bomboni, was the local butcher and the town bully. I do not hold with the notion that a life-time spent hacking and sawing at flesh and bone necessarily brutalises the man. Indeed all the butchers with whom I have dealt after Bomboni (and there have been many, of all nationalities) have been gentle, God-fearing men. Mean, grasping and dishonest, certainly, but brutal I have not found them to be.

Alessandro Bomboni, however, conformed to the archetype. Not a tall man (my father topped him by a full head), he was as wide as a cart and, from the rear, his shape from shoulders to buttocks appeared to be a perfect rectangle. Below this superstructure were two alarmingly small legs as thick as young oak trees but bent like a blacksmith's pincers. These exceptionally stunted limbs rendered it necessary for him to scurry or trot to keep an equal pace even with those whose height was in total somewhat less than his own. All this gave the impression of an unstoppable propulsion (although his reputation, in itself, would have ensured his unimpeded progress through any crowd in the vicinity of our town). Not apparent from the rear was his enormous girth, under-slung and supported by an ancient leather belt whose cracks and crevices compacted with the dried blood of slaughtered beasts. Hair sprouted from the top of his jerkin and surrounded his bull-neck in a kind of ruff. He was almost entirely bald, a fact which he sought to conceal by pasting strands of hair across the shining flesh. His choleric face had an unmistakably porcine aspect although, to be fair, it was the tiny eyes, small pursed mouth and angry demeanour which resembled the pig rather than any other facial contours, which were, for the most part, unremarkable.

The Bomboni house, shop and yard stood at the end of the village, some twenty paces back from the road and partly masked by four poplar trees and a wheel-less cart propped upon two pyramids of rock which, together with the missing shutters and absence of recent paint, gave the whole edifice an air of neglect and dilapidation. Signora Bomboni was notable for her bones. These protruded through her tightened skin at every conceivable extremity, giving her the appearance of some makeshift tent, a child's hide-away perhaps, within which animation was barely visible. She had been, so it was said, a girl of considerable attraction, coquettish to the point of scandal. Fatally attracted to Bomboni, the village tough, she had married him when carrying their first child who was christened Giovanni but who was universally know as 'Pasto'.

Unlike his father, Pasto Bomboni was well-favoured. He had a tend-ency towards fat but, no doubt due to his mother's inheritance, his legs were of pefectly normal size which elevated him, at the age of twelve, or thereabouts, above the balding head of his own father. Despite an impression of fleshy consumption his face was by no means ill-formed and found favour with many of the village girls. My mother had always remarked upon his 'small wet mouth' but this defect did not appear to cause any difficulty in his sexual pursuits. He was six years my senior. His younger brother, Filippo, some three years older than me, might have been cast from his father's mould and was, by all accounts, the favourite child, which was no great claim considering the treatment which was accorded to the daughter, Nicola, my direct contemporary. This unfortunate child, plain in looks and apparently deficient in intellect, was the ultimate butt of the family humour. Mercilessly teased and bullied from the cradle, she lived a life of miserable servitude. Conscripted to every drudgery and denied comfort or companionship of any kind it was widely said in the town that her base stupidity saved her from the true agonies of her humiliation. For myself, I doubt it, having observed throughout my life that imbecility is not infrequently the mask of persistent despair.

As I have said, this unappealing ménage was famous throughout San Casciano and indeed the wider region. The house itself was surrounded by a never-ending cacophony of noise. In the morning the male Bombonis set about the business of slaughter which, it was said, they carried out with considerable relish. Thus, until midday, the sound of plaintive lowing and whimpering mixed with much shouting and exhortation emanated from the yard. At midday Alessandro Bomboni would trot down to the smallest of the village inns, owned and managed by a Franco-Italian by the name of Louis Bonelli. There he would consume considerable quantities of Barolo in the company of a number of cronies, the most sycophantic of whom were two brothers known simply and universally as Tozzo and Metso. In their company Alessandro would reduce himself to a state of tottering inebriation whilst indulging in an increasingly noisy political harangue at peasantry and tax-collectors alike. 'If it were not for the industry and commonsense of shopkeepers,' he would bawl at his captive audience, 'the state of Tuscany would, long ago, have dissolved into chaos.' In the early evening, fired with self-righteous anger, he would weave down the rocky path from Bonelli's, scattering the population before him. Once safely at home he would begin the physical attack on his family. Some said that the beatings were quite indiscriminate. Others that he appeared to follow a systematic policy. Whichever theory was true, the sounds which echoed across the valley never varied. Screams and blows, occasionally punctuated by gunfire, continued often into the early hours of the morning and, even then, occasionally erupted throughout the night before the morning slaughtering began.

Despite his lamentations as to the unrewarded status of butchers and shopkeepers Bomboni professed himself a strong supporter of the Medici family and Vittoria della Rovere in particular whom he saw as a 'woman of her time'.

Other contradictions were apparent. His persistent attempts seriously to injure and wound his family were matched only by the enormity of his indignation if he perceived them to be in danger of injury from anyone else, whatever the merits of the case. On one occasion, shortly after my tenth birthday, he became obsessed with the idea that one of the local olive-growers had been 'making up' to his daughter. The man in question was a poor fellow, past sixty with a desperate squint and a compulsive habit of scratching his inner thigh. These disabilities had, of course, given rise to the dark rural suspicion that he was a man of unrequited sexual vigour but, even were this the case, it is doubtful whether he would have spared a glance for Nicola, the wretched, unanimated drudge already bent-backed under the weight of the Bomboni yoke.

Nonetheless, once this idea of molestation had been fixed into the drunken brain, no doubt by Tozzo or Metso, Bomboni lost no time in defending his daughter's virtue. He began by giving her a public hiding by the poplar trees in front of the shop. He then armed himself with a cudgel and made his way through the town, the people disappearing before him like leaves in a gale. Finding the suspected paedophile picking olives in the afternoon sunshine he struck him several times, fracturing his skull and breaking both fore-arms. Indeed he would certainly have killed the poor man had he not taken a step backwards the better to attack the prone figure, caught his foot in an olive root and rendered himself unconscious by striking his head against one of the white boundary stones.

The story had a strange, but not unhappy ending. Perceiving that Bomboni was unconscious a number of townspeople, who had followed him, rescued his victim and took him to our house where, by chance, Lorenzo was staying. He was able to splint both arms whilst the man was unconscious, thereby saving him the considerable pain which is involved in such a process. When he recovered his wits and opened his eyes it became immediately apparent that the blow to the head had quite rectified the squint. The news of this miracle spread like fire throughout San Casciano accompanied by the rumour, mischievously started, that Alessandro Bomboni was possessed of miraculous powers of healing and was certain to be a candidate for canonisation. It was subsequently gleefully reported that Bomboni, who could now be seen sporting a substantial handkerchief around his bald head, had taken the rumour seriously and spent the afternoon addressing Tozzo and Metso in Bonelli's bar with something that bore an uncomfortable resemblance to the Sermon on the Mount.

The universal enjoyment of this joke was mixed with some alarm, felt particularly by those with various physical infirmities, that he might take it upon himself to carry out further miracle cures by the same means. Their concern was ill-founded for Bomboni, having waited several weeks for the arrival of the Papal legate, tired of his messianic role and reverted to type.

It was not quite the end of the matter for, several months later, a Vatican messenger did, indeed, stay at the village on his way to Siena. The prime mischief-maker of the village, an agreeable and good-natured fellow called Pepone, arranged for a message to be carried to the Bomboni household to the effect that the Papal envoy was staying in the main square and wished to see a certain Alessandro the Healer together with his Divine Instrument. Within minutes Bomboni could be seen scurrying down the main street towards the Albergo Niccolo unseasonally clad in a borrowed *lucco* and carrying his cudgel.

On that particular evening the Papal legate was not the only luminary staying at the Albergo Niccolo. Also in residence was the famous Englishman, John Finch, whose remarkable career had included his appointment as Professor of Anatomy at Pisa University in the year before my birth.

In any event, this great man, who was visiting Florence for the last time (and, as it transpired, in the last year of his life), had heard that Lorenzo Bellini was staying in San Casciano. Wishing to meet the Professore upon whom his own mantle had been thrown at so early an age, he had taken a coach to the town, booked into the Albergo and sent word for Lorenzo to join him. Lorenzo, overjoyed at the prospect of meeting his predecessor, had practically run to the inn, pausing only to take hold of me (for my own edification) and, on the way through the town, had breathlessly informed me of the virtues of the intellectual giant we were about to meet. Thus it came about that I was sitting at a corner table overburdened with scholarship watching the nearby Papal legate delicately picking his way through a smoked quail when Bomboni arrived with his cudgel.

41

It took him barely a moment to apprehend the whereabouts of the Holy personage and, having done so, he trotted across the room, lifting the hem of the *lucco*, his pig-like features aglow with potential sanctification. The legate had just finished gnawing at the second tiny wing of the quail and was carefully picking his teeth with the end of a paring knife when Bomboni appeared before him. In his haste the butcher had clearly not prepared any formal means of address. He thus stood for a moment beaming down upon the Roman dignitary who, in turn, regarded him with patent distaste.

'Well, your uh Magnificence,' he bawled suddenly, 'here it is!' So saying, he whipped out the cudgel from the folds of the *lucco* and brandished it above the table.

Now Papal legates, particularly those who are entrusted with lengthy journeys across the face of warring Europe carrying the Vatican's secrets on their person, are not the pompous pederasts which Rumour brands them. For the most part they are retired soldiers and substantial athletes in their own right. This one was no exception and, perceiving himself to be under attack from a misshapen madman, leapt backwards from his seat, his left hand upending the table towards Bomboni whilst the right hand, carrying the paring knife, was thrust forward in the classic defensive stance of the street fighter.

' 'Ere!' said the would-be seraph, wildly brushing quail bones from the front of his *lucco*, ''Ang on! It's me, Bomboni the Butcher, I've come about the miracle.'

Not surprisingly this did nothing to reassure the Papal legate who, maintaining a tense crouch, backed warily towards the kitchen doorway.

'No, come on, come on,' said the butcher, advancing steadily, 'this is it. This is what I done it with.' And so saying he raised the Holy cudgel into the air in an act of demonstration promptly, and excusably, misunderstood by the Papal emissary. Moving at a speed remarkable for one wearing a full surplice and taking advantage of Bomboni's upraised arm, the Papal legate feinted swiftly to the left and, using Bomboni's instinctive movement, kicked him smartly and with great force between the legs. The butcher uttered a short of whinnying croak and collapsed forward onto the floor clutching the front of his *lucco*. Still moving at blistering speed the legate was upon him, jamming one knee into the butcher's chest and inserting the point of the paring knife into the folds of flesh now heaving and quivering beneath Bomboni's chin. He reached for the fallen cudgel, picked it up and flicked the sacred object across the room a full twenty paces beyond the reach of his adversary.

'Now,' he hissed into the butcher's ear, 'who are you and who sent you?' Then, receiving no reply but a kind of wide-eyed gurgle, he added, 'Speak quickly, my friend, and do not be deceived by these Holy vestments. You will not be the first heretic that I have sent to hellfire.'

In view of what I had suffered at the hands of his son and what was to take place barely three years later, it is difficult to imagine that I ever had sympathy for Alessandro Bomboni but I think I came close to it that evening.

In a voice scarcely audible despite the profound silence that had fallen upon the room he said, 'I'm Alessandro Bomboni, the Butcher. It was me what done the squint miracle.'

A look of concern passed across the face of the Papal legate. Such men were, of course, possessed of an infinite number of secret signs, passwords, codes of recognition, and it was clear that, for a moment, he doubted whether there was, perhaps, some secret code which had been omitted from his training.

'Squint miracle?' he demanded in emphatic tones of interrogation. 'What is a squint miracle?'

'I 'it 'im on the 'ead. It was an accident really.'

At this point, no doubt to the disappointment of many of the local people who had crowded into the end of the room, Lorenzo Bellini intervened.

'Father,' he said, leaving his chair and moving to the centre of the room where he squatted above the fallen figure, 'Father, this is indeed the local butcher. His name is Bomboni. He was involved in a … an incident during which a poor fellow was struck on the head and so was cured of a long-standing strabismus. It is not uncommon. The traumatic effect of the blow releases the sphincter muscle either directly or by affecting that part of the brain which has held it in paralysis. That is what he was trying to tell you. He believes it to be a miracle, and in a way it is. I assure you that he poses no danger except to himself.'

The legate continued to eye Bellini with some suspicion.

'No heresy?' he asked with a faint note of disappointment.

'No heresy at all of which I am aware. I think you would find him much too stupid to be a heretic.'

The legate looked sharply at Lorenzo and then smiled. 'I see. Well, well, well, Signore Butcher. You are very unlucky. I can tell you that it

43

is much easier to achieve canonisation after one is dead. And, just think, if I had slit your gizzard you may have dined with the angels.'

This small witticism had the effect of breaking a spell and the whole room, which by this time held some fifty to sixty people, erupted in noisy laughter.

The legate regained his feet, handed the knife to Lorenzo and offered a hand to the prostrate figure. Bomboni lay unmoving, his eyes tight shut. Suddenly he stood up in a movement so swift that it silenced the noise in an instant. He stood with both fists tightly knotted, his ugly face contorted with malice and rage. Then, looking directly at Bellini, he said through clenched teeth, 'I will have you all for this.' He turned and crashed to the door, parting the onlookers as he went, and disappeared into the early evening air.

The cudgel could not be found but it reappeared a week later artfully placed among the Holy relics in the village church. Pepone was suspected.

The Papal legate was, indeed, a former soldier and before his service had studied mathematics at Bologna University. After a while I left the three men happy over wine and olives and made my way home under the great wide star-sprayed Tuscan sky.

The notoriety of the Bomboni brothers, Pasto and Filippo, was, if anything, greater than that of their father. Pasto, in particular, had developed by the age of eleven a quite legendary reputation for cruelty. Stories and rumour mixed and spread like water falling from the hand. 'Pasto Bomboni nailed his sister's dog to the door' ... 'Pasto Bomboni has nailed his sister to the door' ... 'Pasto Bomboni has set light to one of his hens' ... 'Pasto Bomboni held Giuseppe Mancini's head under the water till he nearly *died*.'

For the last of these I can personally vouch. I was there. In my very early years Giuseppe Mancini was my only friend. This was not surprising since he was the only small boy whom I was allowed to meet with any regularity. His mother lived a little further down the hill towards the centre of the village in a villa not dissimilar to our own. A timid woman of some intelligence she was the widow of a galley captain lost with his ship when the child was but five years old.

My father's repeated absences conferred upon my mother a kind of honorary widowhood and it was therefore natural having two boys of identical age that much of their time should be spent together. I sensed that Giuseppe's mother, Anita Mancini, disliked or disapproved of

Loenzo Bellini and was rarely at the house when he stayed. Otherwise, however, we saw much of her so Giuseppe and I, perforce, became friends. I have already mentioned my own unprepossessing physical characteristics. However, compared to Giuseppe Mancini I was a veritable Achilles. It was, I suspect, his diminutive size and stooping frame which provoked his mother so frequently to extol the physical virtues of her former husband. (He was, apparently, a lion of a man, tawny and huge to the point of embarrassment.) Giuseppe's physical imperfections, however, did not stop with his stature. He possessed a wizened musteline face and, when he cried, which was frequent, his eyes became pink, and the resemblance to a frightened ferret was quite wonderful. Possessed of little he guarded that which he had with fanatical guile. All his playthings were numbered and reserved strictly for his own use. Any attempt to examine them, however perfunctory, led to prolonged screaming and the summoning of his anxious mother. She would explain carefully that the particular cart or top was his (Giuseppe's) *'very special'* cart or top given to him by his father, whereupon both of them would cry and I would be left full of sickening guilt and embarrassment, staring fixedly over the Tuscan landscape. When she had left Giuseppe would carefully reassemble his toys in their appointed slots and retire to a chair looking hurt and sad.

Man and boy I have always been of a kindly and gentle disposition but I confess the temptation to batter him senseless was at times almost irresistible.

Our common bond was a mutual terror of the Bombonis and their acolytes. Our contact with them in those early years was mercifully small. On specified days of the week we would both be taken by our mothers into the centre of the town in order that provisions and wine might be obtained and our mothers could avail themselves of what little passed for society and from time to time obtain news from Florence which was, even then, uniformly depressing and bad.

Close to the centre of the town there was a small grass area adjacent to the river, which followed the main road down from the hills and, in the town, parted company from it only to the extent of this open space. This is where we were deposited with severe admonitions against entering the water notwithstanding our vigorous protestations against being abandoned in such a place. Timid though we were, however, some atavistic sense of honour prevented us from revealing the true reason for our apprehension, namely the proximity of the brothers Bomboni. Our problems were rendered the more acute by the custom then fashionable in Italy of dressing male children as girls until the age of eight. Thus deserted and sitting uncomfortably in our dresses, our carefully ringleted hair falling upon embroidered jerkins, we were, as the English vernacular has it, 'sitting ducks'. During the summer the river bank a little further off was the favourite haunt of the Bombonis and their numerous cronies. At first our visits to this spot excited little more than vulgar jeering and obscene gestures, particularly from Pasto, then aged thirteen and already developing a fine repertoire of violent sexual abuse.

'Come on, girls, show us your cunts!' he would scream down the river bank to the wild enjoyment of his friends.

As time wore on the attacks assumed a more physical nature. Great clods of mud, sometimes concealing small boulders, came flying from the river bank. These were mixed with other missiles of increasing unpleasantness; dead fish, water snails, live eels and, on one occasion, a live terrapin all formed part of this aerial warfare. Needless to say some, at least, of these missiles found their mark. At first our mothers blamed us for the damage to our clothes, forcing me to endure the double indignity of public admonition witnessed from afar by the sniggering Bombonis. Still we said nothing. Then came the day of Giuseppe's ducking.

It was a humid September day, cloudy with a threat of rain. Anita and my mother deposited us in the usual place, leaving us with fond smiles and exhortations against the throwing of mud. As they disappeared through the town square I heard the familiar jeering of Pasto Bomboni begin from the river bank.

'Ciao, girlies! Who's got nice white titties then?' And a large lump of mud concealing a jagged rock sailed over a nearby bush and struck Giuseppe. Whether through some inherited maritime heroism or as an act of childish frustration he rounded on the missile, picked it up and, exerting all his puny strength, attempted to throw it back. His aim was poor, the projection weak and the rock fell far short of Pasto Bomboni, who could be seen grinning evilly by the riverside. Unknown to us, however, Filippo Bomboni together with a number of his cronies had crept close to the grass bank and were concealed immediately below its lip as it gave onto the river's edge. The rock, it transpired, landed full square on Filippo Bomboni's head.

Although barely three years older than his brother, Pasto immediately adopted the parental, protective role to which I have already referred, investing it with a similar degree of self-righteousness.

'You little fucker,' he shouted as he bounded across from the hedge and proceeded to examine, with exaggerated care, the tiny cut which had opened above Filippo's eye.

'He's fucking cut me,' said Filippo quite unnecessarily.

'He fucking has, look, there's fucking blood.'

During this display of sibling tenderness and anxiety Giuseppe and I remained paralysed with terror as though our continued immobility might render us proof against the dire retaliation which was now inevitable. With the arrival of further Bombini supporters, however, I regained my senses and, grasping Giuseppe's skirt, turned and made for the road.

I had travelled five paces before I was gripped from behind and hurled forward onto the ground where I lay, winded, listening to the sobbing of Giuseppe barely an arm's length behind me.

'You know what,' said the voice of Pasto Bomboni, 'you fucking stink. It's time you had a fucking bath.' This proposal, not immediately directed towards me, was met with universal jeering approval. I was hauled to my feet with my arms forced behind me by a fat, unpleasant youth whom I recognized as Michele Bonelli, son of the innkeeper and inseparable from the Bomboni family. In front of me Giuseppe had been bodily lifted by both Bombonis and carried to the water's edge. There Pasto entered the stream, carrying Giuseppe by the shoulders and neck. Behind him the boy's feet were upended by Filippo who remained standing on the bank. Thus suspended, Giuseppe began to scream, a sound which abruptly ceased as his head was thrust beneath the surface.

'How long shall we give the little fucker?' said Pasto, looking at me.

Unable to utter a word I watched in horror as the rose-embroidered jerkin ballooned away from the water and Giuseppe's flailing hands beat wildly against the surface. It was Filippo, eventually, who said, 'All right, that's enough!'

'No, look at him, he's still kicking.'

Giuseppe's legs, bare now from the linen skirt, had begun to move suddenly in spasm. It was this that released my tongue.

'He's drowning! He's drowning!' I screamed, and then, 'Help! Help!'

Even then, for all my youth and in the extremity of panic and terror, I realised that something quite strange had happened to Pasto Bomboni. His small mouth had turned downwards in a tight inverted bow. His eyes became dull and glazed as one suddenly drunk into stupor. His right arm, which pinned Giuseppe's neck, also began to pump downwards into the water as though in rhythm with the spasm of the legs. I was not alone in noticing this change. The bully who held my arms now himself shouted, 'Hey, Pasto, that's enough, let him up.'

I looked desperately to my left across the road towards the town square and the market stalls which stood on the far side. Within earshot nothing stirred. The sun which had broken the morning cloud was now at its hottest and had drawn the townspeople towards the awnings which surrounded the market lanes. Upon an impulse I shouted directly at Filippo Bomboni, 'He's killing him! Look! Look! He's killing him!'

Filippo had clearly recognised something happening to his brother. He himself now began to panic and screamed back to me, suddenly a ten-year-old boy, 'He won't stop! I can't stop him!' He dropped Giuseppe's legs into the water and, for a moment, I thought he was about to run. He only turned, however, to the river bank and, seizing what may have been a branch or some fashioned object now worn smooth as flotsam, took two paces back into the water and struck his brother a dreadful blow on the side of the head. The latter, who had plainly entered some form of trance, neither saw nor anticipated the violence of the impact which knocked him clear off-balance, his body all but disappearing into the water.

Giuseppe's body, now released, remained face down in the stream, the air-filled jerkin with its embroidered roses giving the still form a curiously festive appearance. Suddenly released myself, I ran to the edge of the water, passing, as I did so, Filippo Bomboni himself running at full speed towards the road. Taking hold of Giuseppe's legs which had fallen clear of the water's edge, I pulled as hard as I might and, aided no doubt by the frailty of the body and the buoyancy of the clothes, succeeded in dragging him entirely onto dry land. Scarcely had I done so when I felt a hand on my shoulder and, looking up, I saw the wild face of Pasto Bomboni, his hair plastered about his eyes and blood running from a vivid gash on the left-hand side of his forehead.

'You little bastard,' he shouted, 'did you do this?'

My recollection of this scene, now over sixty years ago, is as clear as the morning air. I remember feeling a curious stillness, no fear or any other emotion for that matter, simply an isolation as though I was seated in a plain white room devoid of sound. As you will hear it has come upon me from time to time and has always served me well.

'He is dead!' I said in a voice as flat as stone. 'You killed him. I saw it.' And then, with an instinct for survival as sure as breath, I added, 'Filippo tried to stop you.'

The conflict in his eyes could be read like a book. 'Filippo ... ?'

Suddenly turning on the inert shape of Giuseppe he took the child by the shoulders and rolled him onto his back. The boy's face, I remember clearly, was blue as ice and a trickle of water ran from his half-open mouth. Leaving him immediately, Pasto grabbed hold of the front of my own jerkin and pulled me to him. His face barely a hand's width from mine, he said, 'You breathe a fucking word about this and you'll fucking go too.' Pushing me away he turned and ran across the road and disappeared between the houses on the right of the Piazza.

Too exhausted to move and too terrified to touch Giuseppe's body I sat on the grass, a shrunken child, and cried. So was I found by my mother and Anita Mancini as they returned laden with the produce of summer.

I was told by Lorenzo much later that Giuseppe's life had probably been saved by two things. First, the instinct of his mother to gather him in her arms, his chin falling suddenly over her shoulder which had dislodged the tongue from his throat, causing him to vent a quantity of water and vomit which I recollect pouring down her back. Second, he speculated upon the effect of the jerkin which, he said, had plainly trapped a quantity of air not only behind Giuseppe's head but, possibly, in bubbles below the surface of the water. In all events he lived. But he did not recover. The effect on his timid disposition was to drive him into silence as though entering a void, proof against the elements of uncertainty and fear.

His mother had allowed herself for some time to be courted, without enthusiasm, by an elderly snuff-maker from the nearby town of Poggibonsi. Now, ostensibly for the benefit of her son, she ceased to resist his advances and was married to him, a year later. It was generally assumed that Giuseppe, as soon as age permitted, would take orders and enter a monastery, thereby embracing in the most physical terms the vacuum into which his spirit had already fled.

Despite the dreadful warning of Pasto Bomboni I revealed, of course, the nature of the crime and the identity of its perpetrators. On the following day, Giuseppe having been lodged safely in the Carmelite hospital some ten miles distant in the direction of Siena, my mother and Anita Mancini made their representations at the Prefecture. According to the most recent intelligence my father was still in Amsterdam and Lorenzo Bellini, to whom my mother had immediately sent word, had left Pisa for a short visit to Bologna.

The Prefect at San Casciano, a direct Court appointee and a weak, kindly man, deemed unfit for the robust work of tax-collection, listened with sympathy to the account given by the two women and, also, to the unembellished story which I was able to provide.

No meat-eater, the Prefect had little time for the Bombonis and promised a full investigation of the complaint. Immediately thereafter Alessandro Bomboni together with his two sons were summoned to the Prefecture to answer the depositions sworn by myself, my mother and Anita. Further witnesses were summoned whose identities were rapidly circulated in the town. Some of these were children barely older than myself, known by me to be close confederates of the butcher's family. Even at my early age I felt some apprehension of injustice. Whilst most of those summoned could by inclination indeed have played an active part in the attack, none, to my knowledge, were in the vicinity when it actually occurred. A week later my mother and Anita Mancini were again asked to attend at the Prefect's office. Whilst not expressly required I was taken to this appointment, should further testimony be necessary.

The Prefect raised no objection to my presence, indeed his nervousness was such that he seemed hardly to notice.

When my mother and Anita were seated he smiled hesitantly over his glasses and began, 'Well, well, Signoras, it appears, I am afraid, that there are two sides to every question.'

'Two sides!' said my mother. 'But the child was nearly drowned...'

'Oh, yes, yes, there can be no doubt about that. I have a report from the Mother Superior. A most lucky escape, certainly. However a number of witnesses, rather older than your own son, have put a rather different complexion on the events.'

'What have they said?' asked Anita, her voice as tight as a bowstring.

'Well,' said the official, nervously sifting a number of papers before him, 'well, if you put aside the accounts of the earlier matters...'

'Earlier matters?'

say, ignoring that what appears to have happened is that your two sons had begun the proceedings, as it were, by endeavouring to push Pietro Gastone into the water.'

I received this news with disbelief and the first sickening realisation of the power contained in calculated, total mendacity. Pietro Gastone was an unfortunate, stunted child, lame at birth. Thereafter both he and his mother had swiftly contracted the plague from which she perished. He had been left nearly blind in one eye and of permanent sickly disposition.

The father, also called Pietro Gastone, had worked on the land of the Marzetti family until the depredations of the same plague destroyed the market in flour. Losing all hope of employment he had been brought close to beggary obtaining only ill-paid casual work at the mill or Bomboni's knacker's yard. The child, lame and ill, was a pathetic creature but devious and cunning as a sewer rat. He had, indeed, been one of those summoned to the Prefecture.

I blurted out, 'Pietro Gastone was never there!'

The Prefect raised an eyebrow in the direction of my mother who shook her head as he continued, 'Several witnesses say that the Bomboni brothers intervened only in order to help Gastone. It was in the ensuing struggle that Giuseppe, unfortunately, was pushed below the water.'

'But that is quite untrue,' said Anita, now shaking with rage.

'Possibly, possibly,' said the official unhappily, 'but I must go by the evidence that is available. On the one hand I have the evidence only of your son,' indicating my mother, 'barely aged eight, whilst on the other I have no fewer than,' he unnecessarily consulted a list before him, '*seven* witnesses who will say the contrary. This is a most serious allegation and would have to be referred to the Bargello. This I can only do if I consider that there is adequate proof. On the basis of the present evidence I simply cannot say that this is the case.'

My mother broke the silence with a voice already weary with resignation, 'Well then, there is nothing more that we can do?'

'Nothing at all, I am afraid. I really am very sorry.'

Two weeks later my father returned. My mother's joy was tempered by her news and I was swiftly summoned to repeat my account. My father listened, his face closed and tense. At the end of my story he said, 'You have done well, Fredo. A clear account honestly given and one which does you credit.'

'But,' I said, 'it's not fair! He knew they were lying. I know he did!'

'Oh yes, Fredo, he knew. But it is not a question of right and wrong. It is the strength of the case.'

'But he knows that he has taken the wrong decision!'

'In his heart he knows, but he must apply a rational approach. So many witnesses. Such strong evidence is difficult to refute.'

I asked him a direct question, 'Will they go to hell?'

'Who?'

'Pasto Bomboni most of all, will he go to hell?'

'From what you have told me, he is already there.'

This, as you will hear, was not the end of my childhood dealings with the Bombonis but, in announcing to them that he intended to take no further action, the Prefect told them in the strongest terms that no further acts of brutality would be countenanced in San Casciano. He also hinted that, *should* any further skulduggery occur, the niceties of proof and legal processes might well be suspended just long enough to ensure their committal to the galleys at Leghorn. This warning had some immediate effect. Even when in the village I remained unmolested and as the months went by I believed myself to be safe from the retribution that had been threatened. Also, coincident with my father's return, came a further factor which added to my security and well-being: the arrival of Patrick Morahan.

Chapter Four

He was a mighty fellow, red-haired, bearded, with a girth substantially greater than that of Alessandro Bomboni himself. He also topped my father by a full hand's breadth and, when fully dressed in the habit and cowl of a Benedictine monk, he assumed truly mammoth proportions. A devout man, he rose always at five in the morning and could be found sitting in a number of chosen spots high on the Tuscan hills, muttering in his native tongue or his execrable Latin the incantations of his faith. Looking back over a long life he was the finest teacher and the most dedicated (if not the most successful) fornicator I have ever met. His life history, haphazard and devoid of chronology, was gleaned by me in the course of the next six years during which time he lived in the tiny lodge in the grounds of our villa and founded and built the best boarding school in Tuscany. Part of this early life I now relate, giving to it such coherence as memory and adulation may allow.

He was, so he maintained, the bastard son of the Provost of Trinity College, Dublin. Despite his illegitimacy his parentage ensured him a place at one of the schools which sprung up around that great University and, by the age of seventeen, when he was formally admitted to the College, he had a sound mastery of Latin, a colloquial knowledge of Italian and a broad education in mathematics, astronomy and, so he maintained, the great flaxen-haired, green-eyed girls to be found in Dublin, like autumn leaves. Despite his evident proclivities he had set his mind upon Holy Orders and having an instinctive didactic gift had already been accepted by the Benedictines. He was in his second year at the University when Oliver Cromwell's forces landed at Dublin. By this time, in addition to his 'beloved mother' (whose name never failed to bring tears to his eyes), his family numbered a step-father (married shortly after his birth) and two step-sisters aged ten and twelve years. Following Cromwell's landing they fled, together with a great host of

Catholic families, to the fortified city of Drogheda. Once inside the town he was immediately conscripted into the militia and, having been provided with a sabre (with which he was in any event proficient) and an ancient carbine with five rounds, he found himself stationed upon the castellated walls watching the approach of the English Army.

When he arrived the town was under full preparation for siege. In other words all was chaos and disorder. Attempts to billet the multitude of families, priests, monks and friars who had invaded the city had collapsed in the face of crass inefficiency, the demands of the military and the sullen reluctance of most of the townspeople to provide accommodation. Many of them were, in any event, wholly opposed to the concept of the siege, fully cognizant of its dangers and ready to espouse any form of Parliamentary Protestantism, while pointing the Model Army in the direction of Wexford.

Such a state of affairs was, of course, a recipe for swift and cataclysmic disaster. And so it proved. Many accounts exist of the sack and pillage of Drogheda by the English Army and of the wholesale massacre which followed. In all of them, however, one event occurs with sufficient consistency to be beyond historical doubt. The last desperate and courageous resistance to the Parliamentary soldiers was offered by an ill-assorted group of priests and royalists trapped and surrounded in the spire of St Peter's church at the north end of the town. After several unsuccessful and costly attempts to storm the building, the decision was taken to fire the church and, in the ensuing conflagration, all the defenders perished, defiant martyrs to a lost cause. All save one. Anecdotal evidence is united in the description of an enormous red-haired man, himself blazing like an angel of fire, leaping from the highest turret, sixty feet above the ground, and escaping unhurt save for the partial severance of one hand on the point of an upturned pike. According to those appointed (or self-appointed) official chroniclers of the time, this feat so moved Cromwell that he ordered the man to be spared and condemned to slavery, muttering as he did so Milton's words: 'Now thou art gone and never must return.'

Patrick's account, let it be said, differed substantially from the 'official' versions. He had, so he maintained, fallen directly on top of the Lord Protector and owed his subsequent survival to the clemency (and silent approval) of the surrounding soldiers. Whatever may be correct, certain it is that he spent seven years a slave on the island of Barbados before escaping aboard a galley bound for Venice. From there he travelled to Siena and entered the Benedictine monastery, where after a difficult and, by all accounts, turbulent postulancy he was finally ordained at the age of thirty-five. Thereafter he travelled Europe, founding schools, teaching with the manic vigour of the inspired, whilst living permanently on the verge of excommunication as a result of his penchant for humanism, the natural sciences, teaching in the vernacular, strong wine and large women.

My father had met Patrick in Amsterdam, where he had immediately engaged him as my tutor. They had not travelled to Italy together. Patrick was to face yet a further disciplinary hearing by his Order and my father had arranged to meet him in Florence both to simplify the journey to San Casciano and, also, to present the remarkable Irish Benedictine to Antonio Magliabechi whose enthusiasms as a collector were not confined to bibliography. Thus they arrived at our home together, having spent the night at the Via del Corso, and, after the necessary introductions, Patrick was a silent witness to my mother's account of Giuseppe Mancini, the Bombonis and the impotence of the Prefecture. My father's reaction, as I have recounted, was measured, resigned, magisterial. There was, regrettably, nothing that could be done. However, although I was barely eight years old, I sensed a different mood in the tall, unspeaking red friar with the strangely disfigured hand. When I added my own account of the attack and the behaviour of Pasto Bomboni I watched his eyes glow like coals.

So fierce was this mute anger that I found the courage, shortly thereafter in one of our early lessons, to seek his favour and complicity by remarking that 'I hate the Bombonis more than poison'.

'Why do you say such a thing, child?' he said with such sternness that I quite lost my composure and stammered, 'Why, because of the awful things they do.'

'Precisely, you do not hate *them*, you hate what is *in* them. Particularly, Pasto Bomboni. There is a boy who needs all our love.'

'Love?'

'Yes, love and compassion, too, and mercy. That poor boy has the devil in him. As for Filippo, from what you say he is far from lost. You must pray for them both, Fredo.'

'I do pray ... that they go away for good!' said I, with a certain spirited (and truthful) irreverence.

'Fredo,' he said, smiling, his great red face falling into creases as though stirred with a fork, 'you don't hope they will go away, you hope what is *in* them will go away.'

'Mama says that they are like that because Alessandro beats them.'

'Then I am afraid I do not agree. Every man has the power to resist evil. If you are *very* cruel to him you may weaken his resistance to the devil but that is all.' Then after a pause he said, 'Have you tried forgiving him?'

'He hasn't done anything to me.'

'Oh yes, he has. He has put you in fear and that is the worst thing anyone can do. Inflicting pain is nothing beside that.'

I think I indicated that I did not necessarily accept this as a premise but, nonetheless, he continued, 'If you try forgiving him, *really* forgiving him, you will be surprised how much better you will feel.'

I tried and didn't, but I did not say so, but then I was only eight.

My father's lack of anger at the Bombonis and the local Prefect could be accounted for, in part, by the dismal and frightening news from Florence. Baiting of the Jews, which had increased markedly on Cosimo's succession, had now lessened but only, it transpired, because of a greater crisis.

The harvest had been poor largely due to the amount of land which now lay fallow and uninhabited. Rumours of the impending sale of the flour monopoly and the reduction in the central ration had provoked near riots outside the Pitti Palace. For some years the Grand Duke, or more accurately his mother, had relied entirely upon the intelligence provided by the Inquisition which had, through accident of design, concealed the growing risk of disturbance. Alarmed by this unexpected show of resentment and force, Cosimo ordered that swift concessions be made which, in part, pacified the mob but infuriated the merchants, dealers and would-be monopolists upon whom the Grand Duke and his government relied for their financial support.

To redress the balance, the purported ringleaders of the insurrection were identified and arrested. Two, it was said, had died on the rack whilst four were publicly executed at the precise spot in the Piazze della Signoria where Savonarola had been burnt to death. At the same time proclamations were issued which blamed the escalating prices on the money dealings and machinations of the Jews.

Also at this time Antonio Magliabechi became Chief Librarian to the Grand Duke. My mother had, initially, expressed horror at this news but my father had said, 'He was persuaded to take the appointment by Cosimo's mad wife before she returned to France. When he told me he had accepted the post he said, "I want to know what's happening. If I know what's happening then my friends will know and they will stay alive." A strange thing to say but I think I understand what he meant.'

More sinister news was to follow. A series of edicts 'regulated' the movement of documents and manuscripts and, worst of all, shortly after my ninth birthday, unbelievably, my father brought the news that Lorenzo Bellini had been arrested.

'Lorenzo!' cried my mother. 'Lorenzo! Arrested!'

'Yes, yes. But don't worry, he has been released. I did not have time to see him before I left but I had word that he was safe and with Antonio Magliabechi.'

'Why didn't you go to him? Has he been ... hurt?'

'I was told by Antonio to stay away from the house. I think he is anxious to keep my visits to a minimum lest they are associated with the regular supply of manuscripts. As to Lorenzo's condition, as far as I can tell he was unharmed.'

This indeed proved to be the case. Four days later Lorenzo arrived in rude good health. He had even brought for me a device intended to demonstrate the transfer of force and momentum. It consisted of a small frame in which hung a number of brass balls. The cords which held them were secured at regular intervals in such a way that, when at rest, the brass spheres barely touched each other. When one of them, at either extremity, was raised and allowed to fall against its neighbour the ball at the *other* end was propelled outwards with similar force. When that, in turn, returned to strike its own neighbour the original sphere was again thrown backwards. Variations were possible as when two balls were raised and allowed to fall, whereupon *two* balls (and no more) were propelled outwards at the other. Likewise with three.

Grasping this new delight I disappeared into a corner of the room, close to the fireplace, and behind the cover of a wooden settle where I contrived, after a short while, to remain silent and hear the account which Lorenzo gave of his recent incarceration.

In addition to my mother and father, Patrick Morahan was also present in the room since he had rapidly become a trusted confidant and, indeed, from the warmth of their greeting it was apparent that both he and Lorenzo Bellini held each other's reputation in some considerable esteem.

Having been provided with wine and bread and cheese and a bowl of figs which I had myself picked upon his arrival, Lorenzo began his story.

'I had been staying for two days at the house of Vincenzo Viviani. I had to see him concerning a paper he had presented to the Cimento and which I had been asked to acquire for the University. As you know,

Gallupe, the old man was Galileo's pupil. He was *with* Galileo when he was arrested and thereafter remained with him until his death. Indeed so great was the trust between them that it was to Vincenzo that Galileo entrusted his manuscripts.' From my position behind the settle I heard my father give a loud exclamation of surprise. Lorenzo's voice continued. 'Precisely. The whereabouts of the original manuscripts has been a celebrated mystery. I appreciate that there are *some* originals at Pisa and also some others (or at least very early copies) at Bologna. But the majority of the original manuscripts have been in poor Vincenzo's attic. *I* did not know this until I went to see him, as I said, a week ago. It was then that he blurted it all out. Now, Gallupe, you know Vincenzo and you know that, despite being as stubborn as a mule when arguing about some totally ephemeral and useless academic point, he is about as robust as a whore's virtue. It transpires that his old master, having been given a guided tour of the hot pincers, hot coals, thumbscrews, bollock-crushers and body-presses somewhat lost his confidence in the onset of the Age of Reason and Enlightenment. Even when he was in Florence and supposedly under the protection of the Medicis he was wise enough to appreciate that the so-called New Age rather than being the dawn of civilisation might well be a circle of candle-light in the middle of a dark night. As he grew older he became increasingly concerned about his original work. Oh, I know that there were copies taken almost as he created the originals but he believed, probably rightly, that his own genius was sufficiently unique and unrepeatable that any attempt to discredit his conclusions would be likely to succeed if the *original* manuscripts could not be produced. Also, of course, if one copy is discredited as a fake then all copies are discredited as fakes.

'In any event the great scientist ordained, shortly before his death, that, until such time as science rendered his current research valueless it was to be placed in secret safe-keeping. Whether he had quite lost his wits or whether Vincenzo was the only available pupil is unclear but, whichever is the case, Vincenzo was selected. He thus became the custodian of the secrets of the Heavens and the boundless intellectual wonders of the Universe and has been shitting himself with anxiety ever since. Not only, of course, was he entrusted with their safe-keeping but he was also the sole judge of the point at which they could be safely disclosed. He was, as you can imagine, desperate for a collaborator. But who? He hated everybody in the Cimento except you, Gallupe. He was about to confide in you when you began to travel for Antonio Magliabechi. He had just decided to confide in Antonio when he learnt of Antonio's appointment as librarian to the Grand Duke and he therefore became a doubtful sympathiser.

'His worries reached the point of agony with the rumours now circulating in Florence that all scientific works are to be registered. Unable to bear it alone any further he finally told *me* when I went to collect this unimportant little paper for Pisa. At first, of course, I thought he was joking, unprecedented though that would have been. When I realised that he was serious I asked, at once, if I could see the evidence since it transpired that he has been literally paralysed with fear and has not touched the bundles for nearly forty years! Some, of course, are bound and he is fortunate that the others were all linen-wrapped and the attic, perchance, has proved a perfect storage. I hope you don't mind if I break off, I must just have one of those figs.'

Despite the interposition of the oak settle I could sense my father's excitement as I heard Bellini raise his glass and murmur in appreciation at my offerings. Shortly he continued.

'Well, Gallupe, I may be just a humble explorer of men's guts but, as I opened those drawings and calculations, I had a quite *extraordinary* feeling of elation. *His* work, his errors, calculations, measurements, diagrams, jottings and drawings; at once the greatest truths and the greatest heresies of the age. We sat up most of the night. Much, of course, was in disorder. Some documents were damaged by the folding but otherwise there was little of concern. I established immediately that *you* should be the one to consider them. No, no, Gallupe that must be right in all the circumstances. I have also convinced him of Antonio's bona fides despite his appointment by the Grand Duke. Although, to a certain extent, he was like a beast unburdened, he remained desperately concerned about disclosure and, in particular, the dangers in Florence now that the Inquisition is so strong. It was perhaps because of his infectious trepidation that I was prepared for what happened the following day.

'Vincenzo had gone to bed and left me with the documents spread, literally, all over his study. I confess that I fell asleep at the table and was awakened in the early hours of the morning by a monstrous hammering on the door. His study is on the first floor of the building and, standing well back from the casement, I could just make out the helmet tops of a number of Salti from the Bargello prison. I had no time to touch the documents. They were on the verge of breaking the door in when I opened it with a welcoming smile. There were five of them. A captain and four bullies all replete with cudgel, rope and sword.

'Acting on a pure impulse I said, "Good morning, Captain, I trust you are looking for Bellini."

'Well, he was a little taken aback by this and it was the corporal immediately behind him who said, "Yea, where is he?"

'I confess that I *also* was surprised but my first thoughts, the product of a guilty conscience perhaps, were for the manuscripts spread out in the study above me so I said, "You mean the famous Bellini?"

'"Yea, so they say," said the captain, now eyeing me suspiciously.

'"Right," says I, affecting a conspiratorial air, "and I suspect, Captain, that you are not so much interested in him as in what he has *done*?" At which the fool nodded vigorously having, I suspect, no other orders but to effect an arrest.

'"Then I will tell you where to go immediately," says I, "You know the Uffizi, the Grand Duke's art gallery?" They all nodded like puppets. "As you know it is open some mornings to the public. If you go to the third room on the first floor, immediately inside the doorway on the left you will find what you seek." The meticulous detail contained in the directions had entirely the desired effect and the fellow set off to the Uffizi. Unfortunately, before he goes he has a brainwave.' Bellini's voice now lapsed into a stage imitation of the Salti captain: '"Right, you, Luigi, go round and guard the back of the house. You, Franco, stay here by the front door. Don't allow anyone out or in. If this Bellini turns up grab hold of him. Come on."

'They set off down the street at a fine pace so I smiled politely at Franco and withdrew into the house. Flight, of course, was useless and, even had it not been for the two thugs front and back, I would have chosen to remain. I had all the time I needed and engaged myself packing up the manuscripts, waking Vincenzo who virtually succumbed with terror, and replacing the books and linen packages in the attic space. I then directed Vincenzo to go back to bed, poured myself a glass of Orvieto and sat down to await the return of the captain. Sure enough within the hour there is another furious pounding on the door which I hastened to open. They are all there again, except Luigi, the captain scarlet in the face partly through rage and partly through his exertions in the morning sun. His lack of breath enabled me to get in the first word.

'"Well, Captain, is it not a most fascinating work?"

'"What? Now look here. It's not open and when we *did* get in there's nothing there."

'"You looked where I told you to?"

'"There's just bleeding pictures..."'

'"...of an old geezer standing on a backgammon board with arrows in 'im," said the corporal helpfully and inaccurately.'

'"Ah, yes. 'La Pélérinage de l'âme'. It is an allegorical work, of course. Interesting but obscure, based, I gather, upon a text by Guillaume de Guilleville. The work is intended to convey a sense of tranquillity, peace and..."'

'"But where's this fucking Bellini?"'

'"But that *is*..."'

'"I think you're fucking Bellini."'

'"Certainly I am *a* Bellini but not *the* famous Bellini. I can't think why you would want to see me, or anything that I have done. I am a doctor. A humble sawbones, an explorer of guts."'

'"Right!" said the captain with the air of one who has wrestled successfully with a substantial problem. "Get 'old of 'im."'

'Well, the next part was really very unpleasant. I was bundled into the house past Vincenzo who had, to his great credit, emerged like Lazarus from the tomb. I was forced to wait while they carried out a perfunctory search presumably in order to ascertain that there were no further Bellinis in the house, allegorical or not, and then I was marched down to the Bargello. I will not pretend that I was not very frightened. The effect, however, was most curious. I became quite light-headed, detached. I also developed a clarity and sharpness of sensation that was almost painful. I have never been arrested before and I suppose I contemplated the world as though I was seeing it for the last time. The morning shadows falling across the Piazza della Signoria, the accumulating warmth of the sun through which I could hear the icy coldness of the fountains as though all my senses were acting in harmony. I could *feel* the "David" as we passed him, the blind alabaster eyes, the tension of the sinews, even the crust of pigeon shit were sharp and clear as birdsong.

'"You're a cunt, you are, sending us off like that," said the corporal, "bet you thought it was funny. You'll be laughing all right by this evening, I tell you."'

'He was a big boy, not fat but thick. I spoke to the captain.

'"Do you get pain in your back, Captain, on the right-hand side low down by the belt?"'

'"How do you know?" he said, suddenly very suspicious.'

'"The blood vessels round the nose. Pepitchiae we call them. It's a warning that there's something wrong with your liver."'

61

'"There'll be something wrong with your fucking liver if you don't shut up," said the corporal from behind me.

'"Shut up, Petroni," said the captain, eyeing me with anxiety. "What's the matter with my fucking liver?"

'"Difficult to say. Don't normally give diagnoses on the move. Come and see me about it later. You know where to find me."

'We walked on in silence past the side of the Palazzo Vecchio. When we came to the Piazza San Firenze and I saw the great pile of the Bargello crushing down like an anvil on the one side and the tower of the Badia, thin as a pencil, rising beside it, both stone-set against the unmarked blue sky, I very nearly wept. We entered the Bargello through a small wicket which gives onto the Via del Proconsolo leaving three of our escort in the street behind. The door was closed and locked behind us.

'My first feeling was one of surprise. This is no dungeon, I thought, for we had entered directly into a room of considerable size and imposing height. The walls were, for the most part, panelled and where they were not they were hung with fine tapestry. On the polished wood pictures were set, some of outstanding beauty, and in the corner of the room a Cellini bronze which I had seen (or possibly I had seen a copy) on one of my visits to the Pitti Palace. My diminished escort now turned immediately to the left and we marched through a series of rooms, no less imposing, until we turned right and emerged into a courtyard containing a fountain playing in the middle of a garden as green as any I have seen in Italy. Surrounding the garden was a colonnade of perfect Gothic proportions within which white marble sculpture gleamed, luminous in the silent gloom.

'On the far side of the courtyard a stone staircase rose to the first-floor level and, having negotiated two sides of the colonnade, we arrived at its foot and climbed towards the oak doorway set some twenty feet above the ground. Entering this door we came into a magnificent vaulted hall empty save for a table of polished oak and, at each end, monumental sculptures which I recognised immediately as the works of Donatello. We walked the length of this hall echoing like an army and stopped before a brass-studded door on one side of which, mounted on a shelf, was a bust of a woman and child both smiling hugely as though at some maternal teasing. My captain knocked upon the door and, hearing a short command from within, opened the latch and he and I, alone, entered.

'Two men were in the room. One, plainly a scribe, was seated at the end of a cheap undecorated table which was set below a candelabra. This was unlit in deference to the morning sun which streamed through the open windows. By my calculations we were, once more, in the south side of the building and through the high mullion I thought I could see the extreme top of San Filippo Neri. The other man, who turned from this very window as we entered, was wearing a simple *lucco* and carrying a book which he had clearly been offering to the light to assist his weak eyes that now blinked at us through iron-rimmed spectacles. An angular, pointed nose and chin together with a nervous deftness of movement gave him a bird-like quality unaffected when he spoke in a high piping Italian with an unmistakable Roman accent.

"'Ah, Signore Dottore," he said, waving the captain from the room. "I have just heard from my colleagues at the Uffizi. It seems you have been leading that oaf a merry dance."

"'I only . . .'"

"'I know what you did, Dottore. Most amusing. You must understand that the Salti are not chosen for their sense of humour or for their knowledge of fine art. In fact one might say that a sense of humour, however vestigial, and a knowledge of fine art, however rudimentary, would be disqualifying factors in their selection. They are occasionally called upon to carry out tasks which any sensitivity would render almost impossible. We aim to attract the kind of a man who would as soon piss on the Pietà as in an earthenware bowl. Sad to report we have very little difficulty in recruitment. I, on the other hand, have always admired the 'Pélérinage de l'âme'. I appreciate that there are members of my Society who regard allegorical works as a heresy but I have never subscribed to that view. Reality can be so painful, can it not, Dottore?"

"'I have often observed it to be so. May I ask which Society?'"

"'Do you have to, Dottore? Very well, I am Andrea Cortese. A member of the Society of Jesus, if you will, a Jesuit. As you know we do not always wear our habits. This Florentine custom is so much more comfortable particularly in this infernal heat."

"'Why have I been arrested?'"

"'Arrested! My dear Dottore, you have not been arrested. You have been kind enough to come here in order to tend the sick.'"

"'I am free to go?'"

"'Of course. I should warn you, however, that, unescorted, it is easy to lose one's way in the Bargello. An irritating old building, full of crevices like the mind of a Turk. One can wander about it literally for days. No, Dottore, we do not arrest the greatest medical genius in Italy even," he added smiling, "if we had the power to do so. And then, even *if* we had the power *and* wished to do so, why should we do so — you have committed no heresy? Have you?"

'"Not that I am aware of. Nowadays it is so difficult to know." This appeared to amuse him enormously and he said, "So it is. The Almighty should really have built an alarm bell into us all like the great Vacca that they rang in the Republic. Every time we sinned or erred it would sound inside our heads, boom! boom! Then we would know and everyone around us would know. And, just think, what a cacophony there would be in Florence. But sit down, Dottore, let us enjoy our little talk."

'And he motioned me into the chair opposite the table and indicated to the scribe who immediately took up his quill.

'"Ah," I said, "of course, the Inquisition. All is recorded."

'"You would not disapprove of that, Dottore? Certainty is essential, is it not? *Provando e Riprovando!* But now, let us begin."

'He sat down on the opposite side of the table and opened the volume which he had been carrying. I realised with something of a shock that it *all* concerned me.

'"A very impressive document, Dottore. Born 1643, a year after the death of Galileo. A misfortune that two such great luminaries should not inhabit the earth at the same time." (I was beginning to become angry.) "Entered University at the age of fourteen. Professor of Theoretical Medicine at the age of twenty-one."

'"Twenty."

'"Dear, dear." Leaning across he removed the quill from his scribe and, holding it remarkably as a painter would use the smallest brush for detail, head back and lips pursed, he made the tiniest alteration on the manuscript. Returning the pen he continued, "Twenty. Awarded the Chair of Anatomy at the age of twenty-six. Extensive travel including dissertations delivered to the Acadèmie Française amd the Royal Society in London. This in addition of course to regular lengthy visits to the Universities of Bologna and Padua. Over and above these academic achievements there is also evidence, I think you will agree, of a certain pugnacity. Including a physical attack upon a botanist in Vienna."

'I was tempted, of course, to interrupt him, to expostulate, even to correct him (it was not a botanist, it was an etymologist). There is, however, a certain fascination in listening to your own life so meticulously dissected even when one is in the greatest peril. What was to come was even more frightening.

'"And, Dottore, your achievements do not end there. Your output on, shall we say, philosophical, political and religious matters is no less prodigious. Recently you have published a Refutation of the Englishman Hobbes in defence of Monsieur Descartes. Also a recent correspondence with the Englishman John Locke (living now, I understand, in Paris), pointing out, unless I am mistaken, that theories relating to sensation and material phenomena pay insufficient attention to the advances of medical science particularly in relation to digestion." (Another colossal inaccuracy, but I digress.) "Further correspondence with the Englishman Robert Boyle (a remarkable man, don't you think, who can attack the Jews and alienate the Jesuits at the same time). I have also read with interest your dissertation on Occasionalism and in particular your criticism of the incomprehensible Dutchman Geulincx (where you doubt whether changes in the nervous system are necessarily followed by a mental change, commenting, somewhat scornfully, that our capacity for love cannot be conditioned by the movements of the bowel). You put forward the interesting hypothesis that the human capacity for love is a reservoir which can produce only as much as is placed in it. There are, of course, numerous other works and dissertations of a medical nature which I would not presume to mention. I understand, in addition, that you have been no stranger to the Royal Court. During your membership of the Cimento your personal friendship with the Grand Duke Ferdinando allowed you, among other things, privileged access to his gallery at the Uffizi which enabled you, no doubt, to play that interesting game with the Salti."

'At this point, Gallupe, as you may imagine I felt very conflicting emotions. On the one hand I was angry to the point of violence. On the other was a horrified fascination that so much information (albeit *academically* inaccurate) should have been *collected* in this way. Even worse was to come.

'"Your busy academic life, Dottore, has not prevented you acquiring a considerable number of friends. Many of them men of considerable distinction. You lodge, do you not, with Vincenzo Viviani, an apprentice of Galileo's? Nor should I forget the closeness of your friendship with our own crook-backed librarian and his messenger boys."

'By now I had taken enough. All my fear had dissolved into a blind anger directed towards this pompous smug self-satisfied little bastard and I shouted at him, an error as it transpired, "Why the hell do you know all this?"

'As I said it, his whole manner, no, his whole physical character, changed. Before he had *twittered* at me, looking down at his script; now his spectacles flashed up at me and behind them the eyes appeared to inhabit the whole of his face. His voice became jagged as glass.

'"Why? Why? You ask *me* that, Signore Bellini? Do you know who we are? *Why* we are? Of course you do. We exist in order to deal with people like you.'

'"People like me?"

'"Yes, people like you, the egghead brigade, whatever you call yourselves, Cartesians, Ontologists, Occasionalists, Jansenists and even the fucking Pantheists."

'For some reason I found the vulgarism delivered by this punctilious bespectacled priest strangely shocking. As though I had been struck. But I did my best.

'"The Cartesian theory," I said, "seeks only to prove the existence of God."

'"Oh, really! How remarkably useful for the Almighty that may prove to be. 'In seven days I perform my creation. I hand it, together with the glories of the Universe to Mankind which I fashion in my own image. I suspend the stars in the great cover of the skies and to this gigantic work I add the capacity to marvel. And for what end, what is the purpose of my Creation? Ah, so that some fucking Dutchman with an incomprehensible name can prove that I exist.'"

'"There is no harm . . ."

'"No harm!"' He had risen from his desk and was now standing before me blazing like a bonfire. 'Has it never *once* occurred to you, Signore Bellini, that that which can be proved ceases to be the object of wonder. Where there is no wonder there is no fear. Where there is no fear there is no discipline and where there is no discipline there is chaos. God is not threatened by the pagan. The pagan may be taught, converted, persuaded, if necessary burnt. God is threatened by those whose scholarly ambition is to prove that He exists. Do not tell me, Dottore, they are doing it for the benefit of God. They are doing it for the benefit of their own fucking vanity. If you look out of that window over there you can see directly into the Piazza San Firenze. It is full of people; it is morning; they are buying bread and olives and wine; some are makers of cloth; others make shoes, bags, bricks and mortar, repair houses, fashion shutters, wait at table, sell their bodies, piss against the wall and defecate in the gutter whilst others beg and die close to the open sewers in the street. What do any of them know of your 'phenomena', 'sensations', 'empirical method', 'subjective idealism', 'progressive syn-

66

thesis'? As the turds fall into the gutter what does the defecator know of your renal duct? As the beggar dies over his bowl what thought does he give to the 'causal action between finite existence'? But do you know what *they* all have? *They* all have faith. Faith that they are part of the Divine Scheme, faith that pain is penance and that in God's justice their pain will be rewarded. That is *their* syllogism."

"'Their pain is human poverty."

"'You would take away their faith too? In addition to the misery of want you would visit upon them the anarchy and lawlessness of a world that has ceased to *fear* God?"

"'My own knowledge, great as you say, has never caused me to cease to wonder."

"'Perhaps not but what have you learnt? Can you tell me, for instance, in which part of the body resides the human soul?"

'At this moment, I confess, I lost control of my temper. "Yes," I said.

'It stopped him. He blinked at me, wildly, suddenly unsure.

"'You *know*? You can *prove* it?'

"'All my research into theoretical medicine and the practical study of anatomy has led me to the inescapable conclusion that the soul resides in the male member."

(I, sitting behind my oak settle, forgotten, heard Patrick snort with laughter.)

'He looked at me as though I had bitten his arm and said, "You ... you seek to jest with *me*?"

"'It is no jest. Consider the evidence yourself. It is the only part of the human anatomy which moves apparently of its own volition and without cognitive intention. It provides the consummation of physical love, the preservation of the species, and is supposedly dormant in priests. Can there be any more compelling argument than that to suggest that it is the seat of the soul? Women, of course, we know do not have them."

'He looked at me, his face set like a rock, and then he turned to the scribe. "Erase that!"

"'From where?" said the scribe, patently a dull-witted fellow.

"'From 'the male member', you bloody fool, and replace the entire passage with 'liver'".

'He turned back to me and said, "You are unwise to jest with me, Signore Bellini. Let me tell you now that we will search you out. You and all your friends. We *may* not burn you like the Dominicans but we will burn your works. Wherever government seeks order and discipline and to rule by Divine providence we will burn your works and, by the time we are done, you will all swear that they had *never ever been*. Captain!"

'There was clearly no more to say and I was, frankly, shaken.

'"Take him to see Collangi. Mark well what you see, Dottore, mark it well and spread the word."

'I left the room with as much confidence and dignity as I was able to summon and we retraced our steps, past the smiling mother and child, across the hall and into the intense midday heat of the courtyard. As we descended the stone steps the Captain stopped and turned to me.

'"About these apaches."

'"I'm sorry, Captain..."

'"The apaches." And he jerked a thumb in the direction of his own snout. 'The ones that are 'urting me back. Gets me terrible it does down the right-'and side. Standing up, sitting down, sometimes I can't keep me food down at all."

'"Ah, the pepetchiae. They are only the..."

'"Yeah, 'ow do I get rid of 'em?"

'"Do you drink three bottles of wine a day?"

'"'ow do you know?" he said, quite startled.

'"I employ my eyes, your eyes, your nose, my nose and your breath. Am I right?"

'"Yeah, well, give or take..."

'"You also worry too much in this heat, and you are too fat. What is that?" (I indicated a folded paper which he was holding in his right hand.)

'"It's a warrant, nothing to do with you."

'"Right, give it to me." I removed my sketching crayon from my pocket and taking the warrant (and most of my courage) in the other hand I scribbled on it.

'"'Ere! Give that..."

'I handed it back to him immediately and said, "Take that to any decent apothecary. Ask him to give you what is written on the paper. He will refuse at first and you will have to mention my name. He will charge you a small sum. Take a spoonful every night and every morning. Drink not more than two bottles of wine a day. Twice a day you must walk from the Bargello to the Piazza del Duomo where you must walk twice round the cathedral on the *inside*. When you are beneath it look up into the cupola. Reflect that it was built two and a half centuries ago by Brunelleschi and reflect that whilst it is the most sublime construction in the world it is less of a miracle than the chicken's egg. Then go into the first chapel on the right where you will find a statue. Stand and look at it, perfectly still, for at least three minutes every day. Do not move and inspect it until you can feel the very texture of the stone."

'"What's all this gonna do?"

'"After a week you will feel infinitely worse particularly when standing in the chapel where you will be cold and bored. After two weeks you will feel better and after two months you will be a new man. If you fail to do any of these things it will not work."

'"What's this stuff?' he asked suspiciously, pointing at the disfigured warrant.

'"If I told you the name you would be no wiser. Do not worry yourself. It is not poison."

'"Oh no," he said, smiling, "I'm not worried about that."

'I looked at him in a new light. "You are a very trusting man to take what a stranger directs you."

'"Yeah, yeah. You could say that — but I'll give the wife some first anyway."

'We proceeded in silence down the steps and across the courtyard, keeping well into the shadow of the colonnade where the intense heat fell only in inverted arches upon the stones. We did not return the way we had come but took the third side of the square and arrived before another studded door for which the Captain had a key. As we entered I realised at once that we were in a very different part of this strange building. We were in a short undecorated stone passageway lit by great yellow candles, their ends jammed onto spiked hooks set into the wall. Accumulations of wax like prophets' beards clung to the stone on either side. Ten paces before us steps led steeply downwards.

'"Ah," said I, attempting to prolong a new-found familiarity, "the dungeons."

'He simply grunted and we descended no more than a normal cellar's length until we came to a further door which the Captain, again, opened. He went in first and I heard the sound of other men moving beyond the door as I entered that awful place.

'We were in a cellar, constructed, I suspect, originally for wine, its roof vaulted and suspended on pillars cut square to accommodate casks or barrels against them. There was no wine here. This chamber extended some thirty paces in each direction. To the left some natural light and ventilation proceeded from a series of grilles. These were set into the wall over the ends of shafts, which by my calculation, would extend to the east side of the colonnade. On the right hand were a series of doors, a dozen or so, set into the wall. An open passageway also entered on that side and along its length could be seen further candles reflecting on yet another series of doors. Unmistakably cells. In the chamber itself there was little furniture but what there was made my flesh freeze. I had never before seen the rack although, I must say, my imaginings contained a great deal of accurate detail. Two of these dreadful machines were set side by side. Flat beds of pain with spoked wheels rising at either end. I noticed with a sense of strange revulsion that one of the wheels had been inlaid with a crude decoration of some white shell or stone. Even then, I reflected on the mind of a man who could adorn such handiwork.

'Two men stood by the machines and, as we drew closer, I noticed with ill-concealed relief that no body was stretched upon either. I recognised one of the men as being a member of the party which had carried out my arrest and he, for his part, recognised me.

'"'Im again," he said, "cheeky sod."

'"Watch your fucking mouth," said the Captain. "This man's a fucking doctor. 'E's come to see Collangi."

'"That Jew bastard. 'E don't need a doctor, 'e needs a Rabbi."

'"Where is he?" said the Captain.

'"Down there, number ten."

'We crossed the chamber and my eyes, sharp and observant with terror, picked up more dreadful instruments of that trade which I need not describe to you. We entered the passageway and stopped at a door some twenty paces from the chamber. No key was required since it was secured by a bolt and falling latch. Shooting this aside the captain entered the cell and I followed. Inside, it was dark but, from the candle which burned at the far side of the passage, I could make out a human form on a crude cloth mattress to the right of the door.

'"All right, Collangi," said the Captain. "Someone to see you."

'From the moment I looked at him it was clear that there was little life in the man. His breathing was shallow and, mercifully for him, he was unconscious. I will not dwell on it in detail. Both arms had been torn from their sockets and his face was badly burnt. Since there was no prospect of his regaining consciousness there was little that I could do even to relieve the pain.

'I felt exactly as I had done when we crossed the Piazza della Signoria. Acutely aware of my surroundings, the smell, the weft of the mattress cover, the drip of a tap, a protruding cornerstone shining and damp, a hand's-breadth from the burnt face. I stood up and said, "Your friend is right. There is nothing that I can do."

'The Captain's eyes did not leave mine and he said, "They went too far. Stupid bastards. Hate Jews, you see.'

'"What had he done?"

'"Who knows. Pimping, living in a Christian house, smuggling books, trading in metal. Who knows?"

'We both looked down at the body on the floor and then he said, "Well, that's it then. Shouldn't have wasted time talking about my back." And, remarkably, I felt moved to say, "It would have made no difference. He was dead the minute they finished with him."

'We returned to the chamber leaving, I noticed, the door unbolted. When we were there the Captain said, "Well, you've fucked it up this time, Franco. He's near dead as mutton."

'"So fucking what. One less Jew bastard."

'Moving swiftly across the room the captain reached Franco and struck him a fearsome blow in the belly. As he collapsed to the floor the captain followed him down, speaking the while. "You will kill the bastards when you are told to kill the bastards and not before, do you fucking understand? It is a matter of fucking principle..." and, removing a small paring knife from his belt, he grasped the fallen man's left ear and slit the lobe from top to bottom. "Every time you look at your ugly face, Franco, I want you to remember the value of good order and discipline."

'We climbed the steps in silence, skirted the colonnade, re-entered the tapestry-hung rooms and arrived at the small gate to the Via del Proconsolo. Before he opened it he said, "Good order. They don't understand it's for their own fucking benefit." As I walked into the street he said, "Dottore, what's the statue?"

'I returned at once to Vincenzo's house and checked that all was well. No search had been made. I then went to the Via del Corso but Antonio was at the Riccardi Palace. When I found him and told him what had happened he told me to return to Pisa ... and to come here first. That was to tell you, Vittoria, that he has seen Isaac and that he is safe and well.'

My mother muttered some thanksgiving and then there was silence in the room, now evening-grey and cool. Patrick said, "My God, they're worse than bloody Cromwell."

I heard my father say, 'What is going to happen?'

'God knows, Florence has become a desperate place. In addition to the poor who have always been there, many, dispossessed from the land, have gone to the city. There is a permanent danger of plague. Save for festivals the Medicis provide no money. Medicine is in short supply. Crime is everywhere. *Some* crime is that of desperate men, some not. The executioner makes no distinction. Six died on the block last week, in public. Many more were flogged. Hemmed about by Jesuits and imprisoned in her own bigotry Vittoria della Rovere does not see what is happening in Tuscany and does not care. Antonio Magliabechi is, of course, now close to the Court. He thinks they will increase the persecution of the Jews. He, himself, is a target. The Jesuits suspect him of sympathising with the Jews and spreading heresy. He fears for his library. The Medici library is already the subject of control.'

My father said, 'What of Cosimo?'

'He is to concentrate on "foreign affairs" while his mother controls Tuscany. In reality he is trying desperately to marry off his appalling children. Notwithstanding his own disastrous marriage he seeks as much for them. Knowing the state of Florence, France and Spain treat him with contempt, besides they have their own Jesuits and heresies to contend with. Unable to obtain influence through government Cosimo now seeks it through the marriage bed. He has precious little ammunition with which to do it. He grows morbid, cruel, and turns to his mother and she turns to the Jesuits.'

Again the silence was broken by Patrick. 'Well,' he said in his dreadful Italian accent, 'I thought Ireland and Barbados were in a bloody mess but they are Athens compared to this! Who gave them all the information about *you*?'

'Much of it, of course, is widely known. Details of my *correspondence*, however, could be obtained only from a limited number of sources.'

'*Very* limited indeed, I should think,' said my father. 'Even *I* did not know of your communication with Locke. *Who* then could have assembled all this information?'

'I have little doubt that Redi is behind it.'

'Francesco Redi?'

'Of course.'

'But he is a fellow academic, an entomologist.'

'*Was* an entomologist. He has not worried a bug for these last five years. He has turned himself into a physician. You will remember, Gallupe, that he attended upon the old Grand Duke. There is nothing better calculated to enhance a medical reputation than killing your patients, particularly if they happen to be the ruling monarch. Since that débâcle he has gone from strength to strength. His method is perfectly simple. He informs all his patients that they are about to die. (It's an adaptation of a lawyer's trick really.) Some of them, of course, *do* die, thereby confirming the accuracy of the diagnosis. Many survive, in the way that perfectly healthy people will. These "cures" are then regarded as miraculous. It is essential, of course, that the treatment should be extremely painful. Copious bleeding can be guaranteed to make the patient *feel* dreadful, weak and debilitated. Insisting that he is woken regularly throughout the night has a similar effect. The administration of numerous enemas and hot irons also adds general weight to the prognosis of an early and horrible death. At this point our converted dissector of earwigs announces that there is "a last desperate measure that may be tried". The poor patient is then placed through some further awful agony which he survives and, God be praised, then recovers. Praise all round. Plaudits for the doctor and, of course, the patient whose stoical endurance of the torments he has suffered is widely recognised as a strong contributing factor to his well-being. Prudence, of course, dictates that he should be subject to *long-term* observation to safeguard his continuing health and happiness. Meanwhile thousands more flock in to be bled, buggered, scorched and boiled in return for the payment of a substantial fee. Ever since his birth Cosimo has had a morbid preoccupation with his horrible little body. At first my own services were sought and I informed his mother that there was nothing wrong with him that a diet of figs and fresh air would not cure. Mere flatulence is, of course, not a *noble* complaint and my diagnosis was therefore ignored. Redi has invented all manner of maladies which ensure his continued presence at the Pitti Palace together with his little team of sychophants. You know it really is *amazing* how many tyrants suffered from hypochondria. One day I really must write ...'

'But why should Redi have provided this information about you?'

'Oh, yes. I digress. I know he is a charlatan, albeit a very clever and gifted one, and he knows that I know. I make no secret of my knowledge or my view, which earns me his enmity and distrust. The information could well have been obtained at the Cimento or from any number of academics within that circle. No one else is as close to the Court except, of course, for Antonio Magliabechi whose contrivance is, of course, unthinkable.'

The long gloomy silence which followed this catalogue was finally broken by me, still crouched behind the wooden settle. My childish years precluded, of course, a full appreciation of what I had heard. That it concerned cruelty, fraud and deceit was very clear but I do not recollect the rising bile which I feel, even now, at the works of the Bargello. My attention, frankly, had wandered. Unable to resist tinkering with my new machine I had raised two of the metal balls which now slipped from my fingers and the room was suddenly filled with the repeated clack-clack of perfectly transferred momentum.

'What on earth is that?' said my father, and Lorenzo said, 'If I am not much mistaken young Fredo is behind that seat.' Seconds later my mother's face, large as the moon, appeared over the wooden back and she said, 'Fredo, how long have you been sitting there?'

Lying was plainly useless and, in any event, I remember feeling somewhat aggrieved that my long absence should have been so unremarked.

'Since Lorenzo told his story,' I said defensively.

'Come out, Fredo,' called my father, and I emerged clutching the wooden frame which now jangled in unhappy discord.

All three men were plainly worried. 'Did you hear *everything* that Lorenzo said?' my father asked.

'Yes, most of it.'

'Fredo,' said Lorenzo, 'it is very important that you do not repeat what I have said. Do you understand?'

I nodded my head vehemently, excited by the prospect of conspiracy with the heroes of my small world.

'Very well,' said my father. 'I know we can all trust you, Fredo. But now it is time you went to bed.'

Thus was I banished from the magic circle in possession of my first State Secret. Having consumed a bowl of soup and bread I lay awake a long time listening to the hum of voices.

When I slept I dreamt of the Bomboni brothers in the cellars of the Bargello. Between them they held a human figure recognisable, alternately, as Patrick and the Town Prefect. As I watched, Pasto Bomboni plunged the Prefect's head into a bowl of steaming water, crying, 'That's the final cure. You'll be all right now, don't worry.' I ran towards them, myself shouting, 'No, it's not – give him figs.' A hand held me back grasping my arms behind me as they had been held by the river. I twisted my head and saw not Bomboni's bully but an extraordinarily ugly head, bald save for tufting patches of hair and sharp small eyes set alongside a long curving nose falling, at its tip, below the level of the mouth. 'Let me go, let me go,' I cried, but my captor held me still and said in a voice strained but not unkind, 'No, Fredo, you cannot stop them. You must write a letter, to England, telling them about Giuseppe.'

And I said, 'He will be dead by the time the reply comes.' 'Not so,' said the face, 'with modern medicines, a man can live a long, long time.' Then the scene changed.

I had never been there but the room was as familiar as a mother's caution. Books lined the walls stacked on shelves of red cedar. A light burned on a table close to a corner from which an irregular, urgent tapping could be heard. Across the corner was a wooden screen. Unwilling to move but unable to restrain myself I approached and pulled aside one of its panels. Behind it, set in the wall and forming a break in the bookcases, was a door with a filigree window. Through the window a light shone, forming an ornamental reflection on the reverse side of the screen. I wished to call out, to announce my presence, but I remained unavoidably mute, the sounds caught and constricted at the back of my throat. As I watched the door it began, as I knew it would, to swing inwards and the trickle of light became a stream which spread across the floor and halfway up the black obstruction of the screen. At first the light was unrestricted and clear but, with the door now fully open, a shadow began to emerge, indicating the approach of a human figure; the head and shoulders growing in the light and finally touching the foot of the screen where my eyes were held as though locked in a vice. Finally when the shadow ceased to move I knew that the figure was standing, feet away, in the doorway itself and, with immense difficulty, as one suffering from some dreadful disability of the neck, I turned my head towards the lighted room.

Suddenly the constriction in my throat was removed and I screamed and screamed and screamed.

'Wake up, Fredo! Wake up! Fredo! Fredo! Stop.'

I clasped my mother as she hauled me from the receding images and she held my head and ran her fingers through my hair and said, 'It was a dream, Fredo, only a dream. See, we are all here. I am here and Papa and Lorenzo and Patrick. No one can hurt you now.'

Chapter Five

Despite the one incident, a year later, and the gathering gloom from Florence, the next four years of my life, culminating in my father's attack on Pasto Bomboni, were among the happiest that I can remember. As his reputation suggested, Patrick was a gifted teacher. It is because of him that my present aversion to the written word has taken sixty years to develop. He was better in the morning before a substantial quantity of Tuscan wine rendered him garrulous but since we started our lessons before six and concluded our morning's work by midday the post-prandial babbling did little to hinder the serene progress of my education.

My father had decreed a catholic mixture of studies and whilst some of my scientific coaching may have lacked strict accuracy of definition it was pursued with a reckless enthusiasm infectious even to the most recalcitrant mind. However, unlike my father, I was no scientist. This fault lay not with Patrick but with my own inclinations. I do not hesitate to say that I was (and indeed I am) a gifted linguist. Patrick himself was fluent in French, German and Italian, when due allowance was made for his Irish vowels which rose like monsters in the smooth waves of the *bella lingua*. Occasionally, when he was excited (or a little drunk), snatches of his mother-tongue would intercede, dropping expletives well learnt, apparently, on the island of Barbados.

We developed the habit of changing our language by the hour. Thus from six to seven we would speak Italian. From seven to eight Latin, from eight to nine French, from nine to ten German, from ten to eleven English, whereupon we would relapse once more into Italian, a language more suited to the midday Tuscan sun. At twelve my mother brought wine and olives and, shortly thereafter, more wine, bread, cheese and sausage. Whilst eating, to impress my mother, we would occasionally converse in our own special tongue. This was a mixture of all the words which we most enjoyed; great round French words, sharp splinters from

Germany, didactic arpeggios from Italian wrapped with the long sinewy fingers of Anglo-Saxon (Gaelic form).

Patrick was also an athlete. Despite the absence of a number of left digits and his large girth he could walk effortlessly on his hands, recite Livy standing on his head and, tucking up his Benedictine habit, could run at blistering pace the full circumference of our land in the traces of the dog cart to which I hung, transported with delight.

On my tenth birthday he pronounced me fluent in all the living tongues which we had studied. He confessed to my father that my aptitude for the natural sciences was unlikely to provide me with a living and that an academic or religious life seemed inevitable. Such a future was also dictated by my own physical limitations. Despite serious attempts to emulate the physical rigours of my tutor I remained obstinately stout and ill-coordinated. Even at that early age, however, I began to observe that women were not altogether displeased by this rotundity. I had, you see, the kind of body which, at whatever age, invited being picked up. Literally, of course, this was most unlikely since I became, in my early years, very heavy as though containing matter of great density. I was to learn, much later however, that these urgings towards elevation could well be converted into other instinctive forms of behaviour.

My father was home for my tenth birthday which we celebrated on the terrace together with two local families whose identities I have long since forgotten. After they had left, however, Patrick, who had drunk a little wine, informed my father of his intentions.

'A school!' said my father. 'What here? In San Casciano?'

'Why not? It seems to contain the necessary quantity of ignorance, prejudice and idleness. Even the so-called gentry have minds as thick as a Hindu's porridge.'

'Oh, I do not dispute that there is a *need*. What concerns me is whether there is a *demand*. Those who continue to have wealth regard schools with contempt and, as for the poor, given the present state of Tuscany they are preoccupied with their bellies not their brains. Furthermore, Patrick,' my father added gently, 'you cannot have forgotten that you have been forbiden to teach by your own Order.'

'By one bloody Abbot!'

'No, by *the* bloody Abbot.'

'All right. But he's wrong. *You* know he's wrong. We must be able to teach the vernacular. What good is it to the local butcher to be able to recite the speeches of Cicero while he's sawing his bones and chopping his kidneys?'

'As a matter of fact,' said my father, 'I would give quite a lot to see our butcher reciting Cicero whatever he was doing. But of course you are right and many know you are right but that will not save you from excommunication, or worse, if you are caught. Furthermore, my dear friend, you must be aware that you have not been proscribed as a teacher simply bcause of your modern methods.'

'That was the only charge.'

'Of course, but the *real* reason, as you well know, was your pesistent and flagrant fornication.'

'They had no proof...'

'Nor did they need any. Your methods of teaching provided quite enough with which to have you indicted and sentenced. Teaching in the vernacular they *may* have overlooked. Teaching humanistic work they might have overlooked. Fornication they might have overlooked. But teaching humanism in the vernacular whilst screwing your pupils' mothers was too much even for *your* Order. You are indeed very lucky that you are still wearing a habit.'

From my position beside the window of the upstairs room I could not see Patrick's face but I could tell from my father's tone of voice that he was laughing and I assumed that all would be well.

The prospect of Patrick starting a school, even in the near vicinity, filled me with horror. I had enjoyed his undivided attention and the prospect of sharing his genius with the village children, the majority of whom I regarded as little better than savages, was too dreadful to contemplate.

I was determined, however, to ensure that the whole idea was abandoned and, for the next three months, during one of my father's absences, worked with such conspicuous energy and produced work of such prodigious volume that I reduced both of us to a state of near-exhaustion. Little did I know that this stratagem designed clearly to illustrate the inexpediency of further pupils was in fact to have precisely the opposite effect.

On my father's return I was anxious to hear the report of my progress which Patrick invariably gave (supposedly in confidence) during the first convenient evening when he and my father sat on the terrace, a bottle of Tuscan wine between them, contemplating the eternal verities and my academic attainments.

'Frankly, I am very concerned about him,' said Patrick in answer to my father's question. (Neither, of course, was aware of my presence behind the open window above their heads.)

'Really?' said my father with some alarm at this unexpected and unprecedented reply. 'Why is that?'

'Putting it bluntly, Gallupe, he has become the most dreadful swot. I can't stop him working. He's been translating the tragedies of Seneca as though they were nursery rhymes. He positively *devours* Tacitus and has developed what I regard as an unhealthy predilection for *Paradise Lost*. I simply can't keep up with him. He solves algebraic problems almost as fast as I can set them and then demands more. He's running me to tatters. I've tried every form of physical diversion from long walks to handstands but he simply regards me with a kind of good-natured indulgence, waits till I've finished fooling around and then embarks on a further headlong rush into Academia. I can't remember the last time I had more than a single glass of wine and the requirement for a clear head makes visits to the town impossible.'

All this, of course, was delivered in a mock-serious tone of joviality, but then he said, 'Seriously though, Gallupe, I am worried about him. I am very concerned that he will become dull. He has no friends and, for all his knowledge of the world, might just as well have entered a cloister at the age of eleven. What he requires, my friend, is *schooling*.'

'What you mean, Patrick, is *your* schooling.'

'Of course, Gallupe, that is what I mean and I do not suggest that it would not be of benefit to us *both*. I am certain that it can be done. Some small artifice may be necessary. You, for instance, would be the formal Principal of such an establishment. I could assume some menial role sufficiently far from the curriculum to pose no threat to the infant brain.'

A long silence followed these observations, filled, for my part, with a growing trepidation. I heard the sound of pouring wine, imagined the ruminative chewing of olives.

'Well,' said my father at length, 'I suppose it does have very considerable advantages. And it would be of great benefit to the town.'

By now I had reached a pitch of unease and frustration. I could, indeed, barely restrain myself from shouting, 'What about the vernacular fornication?' but my father was already there.

'Perhaps, on reflection, you are also right about your own risk. Even in the last two years teaching in the vernacular has increased — in Germany, indeed, I observe it everywhere I go. Also,' he added with a trace of mirth, 'your own libidinous activities must have been curtailed by these sudden academic demands.' Then he added with a tone of finality, 'Very well, Patrick, let us see what our young Aristotle does in the next few weeks and investigate, in the meantime, suitable premises in the town. I have no reason to travel for the next two months so we may build this Institute together!'

So it came about that San Casciano got its school; due in no small measure to my own exertions. Of course, at that late stage, I attempted to sabotage the whole business by an unprecedented display of idleness, physical exercise and buffoonery accompanied by a loudly expressed contempt for the Ancients and all their works. I discovered new ways of murdering Suetonius, produced geometry pages like spaghetti and used *Paradise Lost* as a goal-post for my own private *pallone*. None of it did any good since it was regarded simply as further evidence of mental instability caused by my monastic existence. Finally I gave in and accepted, with as much grace as I could muster, my role as a Roger Bacon and prepared to convey enlightenment to the mob.

(And, indeed, as you will hear, that is what I did. The attainments of our early pupils were so low and the pace of learning so testudinal that my role became, increasingly, magisterial. As a teacher I had been well taught and, though barely eleven years of age, I understood the priceless benefits of enthusiasm and the prime necessity of patience. Thus, during the day, I taught with my teacher and, in the cool of the evening, continued my own studies in an atmosphere as close to arcadian and academic bliss as I have experienced in my life. All this, however, was a long time coming.)

The school building which had been purchased by my father for a tiny sum (dictated by the parlous state of the local economy) was a formidable stone edifice under a red-tiled roof which admitted insufficient water, even on the worst days, to interfere with the lessons below. It had formerly been used as a storehouse for grain and that peculiarly fecund smell even now forces my recollection to those rows of vacant faces. Surrounding the building was an area of packed earth, eminently suitable for recreation, onto which our charges were released, for ten minutes, after three hours' toil, at ten o'clock in the morning.

The only disadvantage lay in the building's proximity to the Bomboni residence. Thus a generation of local children took their first steps towards elementary literacy to the accompaniment of noisy slaughter and battery. Also, during the first year, the atmosphere was not improved (indeed it was positively poisoned) by the malign presence of Pasto Bomboni. From an early stage in the cleaning and conversion of the building he had a strange fascination with our activities. As the purpose of our work (and indeed its success) became apparent so his hostility increased. Not that we started well. Notwithstanding considerable publicity our first roll-call contained four students including myself all sitting conspicuously at the rear of the newly painted classroom containing a further twenty empty chairs and desks. Two of my fellow novitiates came from families known to my father and who had been persuaded, with some reluctance, to support our fledgling venture.

The fourth, remarkably, was Pietro Gastone, the purblind cripple whose false evidence had effectively protected Pasto Bomboni from the Prefect's inquiry. His presence was plainly regarded by Pasto as a major defection and, at the end of the first day, shortly before noon, he was accosted by Pasto and Filippo as he left the gate of the school building and turned onto the road. The following day he did not appear but, on arrival at seven o'clock, there was a quantity of bones, fresh from the slaughter yard, still streaked with blood and gristle lying at the door of the school.

The unpleasantness caused by this discovery was mitigated by a replacement for Pietro. He did not last long. A shy, retiring lad whose father kept the horses at the Albergo Niccolo he also was seen, at the conclusion of the day, in nervous conversation with Pasto Bomboni and one of his cronies. On the following day we were reduced to three pupils and were obliged, once again, to pick our way through a litter of animal bones.

To my disappointment Patrick appeared to receive these setbacks with a phlegmatic air, bordering on complacency. On the third day he even smiled upon the scowling figure of Pasto Bomboni as we left the school building and walked home. Nevertheless I could feel the anger within him and, on the way, I said, 'What are you going to do about him?'

'That is very simple, Fredo, I shall pray for him.'

'Do you think that will stop him?'

'If God wills, then it will.'

'What do we do if it doesn't?'

'Ah, then, I will probably knock his head from his shoulders.'

The following day our numbers increased by three. These were the sons of the local miller whose enthusiasm for education had strict frontiers which he made immediately apparent as he arrived with his progeny at the door of the school.

'Will they learn Latin?' he said, eyeing Patrick with professional distrust.

'Why, do you want them to be priests?'

'No, I bloody don't.' And he spat onto the dried mud.

'Well, what do you want them to learn?'

'I want them to grind flour. But I can teach them that. Can you teach them enough to sod up the tax collector?'

'Oh yes,' said Patrick, 'I can certainly teach them that.'

'Excellent,' said the miller, 'that's what I wanted to hear. Now,' he said, addressing his waiting kin, 'you fucking *listen* to what he says.'

The miller's party had arrived at the school shortly before eleven, no doubt at the end of the morning's work. By coincidence, as the miller departed, leaving his offspring in our care, he met the squat figure of Alessandro Bomboni on his way to the inn of Louis Bonelli. The two of them fell into conversation and disappeared towards the town.

By midday Pasto Bomboni had once again taken up position by the school gate, intending, no doubt to intimidate any further new recruits. Patrick, I noticed with disappointment, took no real notice and was about to dismiss his small class. It was then that I saw him staring fixedly from the windows. Following his eyes I saw the figure of Alessandro Bomboni trotting rapidly back towards the school. Behind him, in the middle distance, the figure of the miller (perhaps a little the worse for drink) was making more leisurely progress.

'Ah,' said Patrick softly, 'he has learnt the value of scientific discovery.'

As we watched, the trotting figure of Alessandro reached his taller son and a brief argument took place; this Alessandro brought to an end by striking Pasto firmly on the end of the nose with his fist. Whatever the respective difference in height the butcher clearly maintained a substantial advantage in strength and Pasto dropped to the ground as though struck by a cart. Displaying the craft of his trade the butcher briefly bent his back, gathered Pasto upon it and was last seen marching towards the knacker's yard.

The following day no bones or offal could be found on the school premises. Instead our growing numbers were further augmented by the sullen face of Filippo Bomboni nursing a thickened ear and alert, no doubt, for the first mention of fiscal evasion.

As we walked home happy in the midday sun Patrick intoned his favourite plainchant (stopping only to observe that 'Strange agents are employed in the Divine catalyst').

Filippo Bomboni did not last long. His span of concentration was so short as to be worthy of scientific investigation. Patrick's teaching gifts were such that enthusiasm was injected into the driest and least accessible of lessons. However, the minute he began to speak Filippo's eyes clouded over as though fresh milk had been poured into water. He would sit thus in a rigid and uncomfortable trance throughout the morning's work. During the ten o'clock break he would stand sullen and alone bitterly gazing across the road at the knacker's yard whence emerged the cacophony of bangs which accompanied the end of the morning's killing.

Plainly following his father's dictate, whilst he received no benefit he also gave no trouble. After the break he returned to his fixed and immobile posture, preferring the exquisite and unrelieved agony of boredom to the physical abuse which would undoubtedly follow any deviation from the 'Via Erudita' down which he had been thrust. Patrick, to my disappointment, treated him with a kindness and compassion generally reserved for the long-term sick and, whilst not immediately converted, Filippo began to treat his teacher with a kind of wary respect like an ancient mariner in uncharted water believing himself close to the world's edge.

Filippo's agonies were finally brought to an end by the departure of his brother Pasto. This happy and much desired event took place when the latter was nearly eighteen years of age and after a characteristically violent disagreement with his father. It was rumoured that he intended to find his future in some military capacity which engendered a fervent and widespread desire that he should be placed, like Uriah the Hittite, in the very front-line of the first and bloodiest battle which followed his enlistment.

This defection left Alessandro with a shortage of unpaid labour and Filippo's enlightenment and education were thus brought to a sharp end in the interests of commerce and butchery.

'Ah, well,' said Patrick the following day, 'I see we have lost our foremost bibliomaniac.' It was the only joke I ever heard him make at his pupils' expense.

The school now developed at an almost alarming pace. The miller's eldest son, Maximilian, universally known as 'Masto', was an exceptionally able pupil, particularly at mathematics. Whether as a result of this erudition or not, his father did succeed, that year, in outwitting the tax-collector. At least that was the rumour which circulated, no doubt resulting as much from dislike of the miller as from any hard basis of fact. It led, however, to a sudden and quite impossible demand for places at the school. Very soon we had more than thirty pupils of widely differing ages and were forced to reject almost as many more. With such numbers and such ranges of talent, simply *assisting* Patrick was no longer possible and, whilst yet wanting some weeks of my thirteenth birthday, I became a fully fledged teacher with a class of my own, the eldest pupil barely three years my junior. I will not pretend that I did not enjoy the status which this conferred. Indeed I do not think that I have had any employment in which I have found greater satisfaction and happiness. Most of my pupils were eager and ready to learn whilst unruly and undisciplined behaviour simply did not exist within Patrick's scholastic empire.

'As a Benedictine I believe in the most modern teaching methods as practised in the gymnasia of Germany and Holland entailing, as they do, the very minimum of physical correction,' he said, firmly thrashing Alberto Bonelli's buttocks with the draw-cord of his habit. 'But you, Alberto, have caused me to reassess the fine details of this doctrine. What it is that possesses you and causes you to inflict pain on others I can only guess. However, whichever demon it is he, or she, will doubt-less benefit from an immediate knowledge of its consequences.' I confess that this was not the only exception which Patrick made to his educational credo but it was sufficiently rare to be memorable in a scholastic environment famous for the peace, serenity and kindness of its founder.

I remember the occasion well. Alberto Bonelli, an unpleasant, thick-witted lout of a boy and the younger son of Louis Bonelli the innkeeper, had arrived at the school no doubt driven by his father for similar motives to those which had caused Alessandro's conversion.

Shortly after Filippo had been recalled to his butchery Alberto was discovered in the school's ground energetically molesting Nicola Bomboni who was (it will be remembered) the youngest and most unfortunate of the butcher's children. At the time of his apprehension (by Patrick, at my direction) Alberto had pinned the unhappy child's arms behind her neck, thrust her head into a ditch and was in the process of removing her pitifully ragged skirt. Despite Alberto's protestations that it was 'all in fun' this piece of gratuitous brutality had raised Patrick to uncharacteristic wrath, hence the condign punishment.

Nicola's arrival at the school had come as a considerable shock and surprise. Although rarely seen in the village her appearance never failed to engender pity and disgust. Her awful existence in the Bomboni household, if anything, deteriorated over the years as though her pitiful condition was, itself, a provocation and incentive to increased physical abuse. Thinner even than her mother, her small pinched face lacked any expression beyond that of apprehension and her thin, grey disordered hair appeared in texture and condition not dissimilar from the clothes which fell about her rail-like limbs.

Her appearance at school resulted, of course, from her father's dilemma. Hearing of the miller's purported victory over the tax-collector and having, that year, been particularly savagely assessed (as a result, he considered, of his own inability to understand the calculations which were made), he was now plunged into an agony of indecision. His position was not improved by his crony the innkeeper Bonelli, himself an associate of the miller's, who lost no opportunity to extol the necessity of modern education in a commercial world. Returning Filippo to school was out of the question. Even if there was a vacancy, it would deprive the butcher of his only remaining assistant. Also, even Alessandro suspected by now that the intellectual attainments of his younger son were unlikely to form a sound basis from which to attempt a complicated fraud on the Medici taxmen. It was clear to Bomboni that his potentially desperate position required desperate measures and he therefore decided, despite the resistance and incredulity of his wife, to embark upon his daughter's education. At the time of their arrival the school was already full but Patrick, taking one glance at the child standing beside her father's bulbous legs, agreed immediately to her admission and also to the provision of intermediate reports on her progress as Bomboni indicated that she was at school only for a 'trial period'.

Whatever natural ability Nicola may once have possessed it was now wholly submerged by the results of a lifetime of neglect and abasement. Her initial reactions, whilst not so patently obtuse, were as uncomprehending as those displayed by her brother. Patrick immediately discerned the danger that she was in. Failure on her part would result not merely in her return to her previous misery but would represent a loss of her menial labour over the fruitless period of her schooling for which she would undoubtedly be punished.

He therefore embarked on a subterfuge for which he requested God's forgiveness and my participation. After a short while he began to produce for the butcher a series of increasingly radiant reports. Whilst emphasising that Nicola was starting from an extremely low level he repeatedly emphasised that her progress was remarkable and that further advance could be confidently anticipated particularly, he emphasised, in the field of mathematics. A difficulty which was anticipated was the actual production of some form of evidence. Most of our work was, of course, done on slate and it was the habit of our children to carry home the last lesson for inspection. This difficulty was easily circumvented by me. At the end of every day's school Nicola was sent to me for a 'demonstration'. This would involve my delivering a short lesson on primary mathematics whilst sketching out the calculations before her uncomprehending eyes. She was then invited to copy the hieroglyphics onto her own slate which she bore back towards the slaughterhouse.

A combination of these reports and the graphic proof of their accuracy swiftly led to a marked change of attitudes within the Bomboni household. This was, in turn, encouraged by Patrick who indicated in his 'reports' that her intellectual progress was hastened and improved by her physical well-being. Change occurred slowly at first but rapidly gathered momentum, living vindication of Lorenzo's view that the best medicine is the natural resilience of the human body. Within six months the change in Nicola Bomboni was remarkable. Within twelve months no one who had been absent from the village would have recognised the same child. As good fortune would have it, that particular year, 1683, marked the defeat of the Ottoman armies before Vienna. This considerable feat had been achieved, in part, by the exploits of the Tuscan Navy which had denied to the Turks the essential control of the Mediterranean. Such was the joy of the Grand Duke and his mother (who confidently predicted a return of Tuscan power and influence and an early marriage for Cosimo's children), that a year's moratorium was granted on certain taxes. These, perchance, included the bulk of Bomboni's liability, thereby rendering Nicola's mathematical services unnecessary. To Bomboni's mind, however, persistently reduced as it was by inordinate quantities of Barolo, the coincidence of the two events was enough. His behaviour as a father, at least to Nicola, now moved from the acceptable to the doting. Her juvenile figure passed from a skeletal condition to one of positive plumpness. Her face and expression were no longer haggard and haunted though both, unfortunately, began to take on some of the characteristics of her father. Much of this development would have been entirely satisfactory were it not for the fact that it was accompanied by a marked and growing infatuation for me. I was perceived by her, quite rightly, as one of the architects of her sudden unbelievable good fortune.

However, such was my youth and the sheltered nature of my upbringing that I did not, at first, accurately diagnose the meaning of the limpid eyes, moistened mouth, fidgeting buttock and loosened dress which comprised the sexual preamble of the aroused Bomboni. I was therefore somewhat slow to grasp her meaning when she suggested one evening whilst I was fabricating her mathematical genius that I might want to ''ave a look at it'.

'What?' I said, looking up from my simple equation.

'You know, well, do you, eh? Want to 'ave a look at it?'

Since I did not know what she meant I might just as well have said 'no' as 'yes'. As it was, being naturally positive and optimistic, I assayed the affirmative.

I can't say that I enjoyed it but it *was* a revelation and, according to the rural mores of the time, somewhat late in coming. I have often reflected that my first sexual experience, however fleeting and disagreeable, was based upon sustained intellectual mendacity — as, indeed, were so many in my later life.

Chapter Six

It was widely believed that the Benedictines tolerated and connived at Patrick's teaching. Prior to his engagement as my tutor he had been formally forbidden to teach on pain of excommunication. That he continued, however, could scarcely have been concealed from them. San Casciano was a major thoroughfare and our school lay upon the principal road leading to Florence. In addition our continued and growing success ensured a reputation well beyond the narrow confines of the town and this, together with the scarcity of alternatives, ensured a regular flow of applications from the entire region.

It was generally assumed, with justification, that the school was a Benedictine foundation and that the enormous red-faced friar pursued his calling with the blessing of his own Order. This, in turn, provided a dilemma for Patrick's Abbot who, whilst wishing to uphold his own rulings, had no desire to exterminate, or be seen to exterminate, so vigorous a plant. The Abbot of Patrick's House was, in any event, by no means ill-disposed to his erring Brother. Indeed, it is certain that he would never have been party to Patrick's proscription and banning had it not been for outraged representations made by the Dominican Order, (together with threats that the whole matter might be referred to Rome), after an officious visit by a number of their brethren to Patrick's school in Antwerp. Their zealous and noisy protests concerning the teaching of the vernacular had resulted in their summary ejection, one of them at the end of Patrick's boot. Public brawling between monks was not uncommon at the time and generally caused little more than public amusement and, occasionally, an official reprimand. Patrick, however, had placed his foot upon the backside of a particularly vindictive and unpleasant individual who had borne his grudge and news of the heresy the length of Europe to Patrick's own monastery outside Siena. In the event Patrick had eased his Abbot's path by cheerfully admitting the charges and accepting the inevitable consequences.

Of rather more pressing concern was Patrick's widely known relationship with a number of the village matrons, several of whose children were the subject of his daily tutelage. The inhabitants of our part of Tuscany are generally dark, swarthy and squat (Alessandro Bomboni's configuration could be advanced as an archetype). Enormous red-haired Irish monks were not therefore the best choice as partners for a clandestine and adulterous liaison. Patrick, it should be recorded, was also extremely noisy in everything which he did, an essential element of his incorrigible and infectious enthusiasm. Indeed, as I sit here writing these words upon a fine summer's day on my vine-clad terrace, I can see below me the stooping figure of my gardener, Paolo, himself near sixty years of age and the second son of the old village blacksmith, now long since departed from this world. Paolo is a splendid and popular figure towering above his fellow villagers whom he entrances with his bright blue eyes set in a good-natured face surrounded by a thick ruff of red beard. He wonders sometimes, I have no doubt, why I treat him with such fond affection, even extending to spontaneous embrace when only a little the worse for my midday bibulation. I have no doubt that there are others in the vicinity who bear his physical traits, and being alert for signs of their existence forms an interesting diversion during my visits to the town.

So high was Patrick's standing in the locality that even these peccadilloes could have been overlooked were it not for the third problem which lay in the conspicuous success of his enterprise. The waiting list for admission to our small establishment was now impossibly long. The original expenses, which had included the purchase of the premises, their rudimentary conversion and the provision of texts had been met by my father. Generous though he undoubtedly was he simply lacked the funds to provide an extension to our overburdened facilities.

At this point Salvation and Nemesis arrived simultaneously in the person of Giuseppe Mancini's step-father. This gentleman, you will remember, was a wealthy snuff-maker from the nearby town of Poggibonsi. That lacklustre little settlement had a world-wide reputation for the production of this noxious substance and nothing else. It was widely put about that the sound of sneezing from Poggibonsi would be heard in the Vatican. This I know is quite untrue not only because of the geographical limitations but also because virtually no one in the town of Poggibonsi actually takes snuff. To a man (and a woman) they are far too conversant with the ingredients, the mode of production, the ghastly physical effects (not to mention the public nuisance) associated with this filthy habit. It is true, of course, that in the many shops and warehouses engaged in selling the brown powder together with the boxes, handkerchiefs, dribble-dabbers and other ancillary objects, there were numerous people, particularly women, who could be seen ostentatiously sniffing and snuffling like pigs at a trough. They, I can inform you with certainty, were not and are not native inhabitants of Poggibonsi. They are a collection of layabouts, sluts and other riff-raff specially imported from Leghorn by Giuseppe Mancini's step-father and his fellow-manufacturers. It was this crowd of sniffing harlots which prompted John Evelyn's famous observation on the quantity of Italian women apparently addicted to snuff. Many years later whilst at dinner with my friend the Bishop of Salisbury I was able, with some satisfaction, to point out to Mr Evelyn this elementary error – an example I believed of the many slanders and inaccuracies recorded by itinerant Englishmen during their irresistible wanderings on Italian soil. 'Ah well,' he said, smiling across the silver candelabra in an atmosphere of reason, serenity and intellectual debate. 'S'nuff said about that then.' That this idiocy should have been greeted by gales of laughter simply demonstrates the extraordinarily vacuous humour possessed by even the most distinguished Englishmen.

But I digress. Giuseppe Mancini's step-father was an exception to the general rule in Poggibonsi. He inhaled large quantities of his own product and, as a result, presented a most repellent spectacle. The front of his expensive clothes was quite coated and smudged with fine brown powder as though he had spent the day wrestling with the disintegrated bindings of a book. He was unable to conduct the shortest and simplest conversation without regular snortings achieved by pinching the thumb and index finger and thrusting a large quantity of the weed into the far extremity of the nasal cavity. Years of this habit had caused his nose to spread across his face until it now resembled an inverted blunderbuss of the two-bore type now popular in Germany. To this monstrous appendage he would periodically apply an ornately embroidered dribble-dabber causing large gaps in his otherwise voluble discourse.

This gentleman spluttered and dabbed his way, unannounced, into our school shortly after midday in the late spring of 1685 when Patrick and I were packing away our scholastic impedimenta. He had come, he said (sniffle, sniffle, snort, snort, dab, dab), to enquire when it would be possible to enrol his two sons, aged nine and eleven, in our educational establishment (dab, dab,). These were of course his *natural* sons and not the unfortunate Giuseppe Mancini (sniffle, sniffle) whom he had given a home but who was quite struck dumb (snort, snort), following the terrible incident which had ocurred in this very town (dribble, snort, dab).

Yes, said Patrick, he had indeed heard of that dreadful business and, what was more, the other victim was the young gentleman standing before him.

'Well, well' (sniffle, sniffle). 'So it was. Who would have thought ... quite extraordinary ... family like this' (dab, dab) '...considerable reputation. In any event, early start on sons' education clearly desirable ... fine potential though possibly appearing rather dim-witted ... unfortunate characteristic of first dear wife' (snort, snort, dab, dab).

Patrick listened to this with his usual good-natured tolerance and patience and then pointed out to the snuff-maker that there were at present over thirty children waiting to enter the school and the prospects of accommodating his wishes were therefore effectively non-existent. He would however be delighted to place their names upon the...

'Oh, no this will not do at all. Schooling at Poggibonsi lamentable. Attempts to provide private tutors unsuccessful due largely to lack of perseverance in the face of good-humoured boisterous high-spirits' (dab, dab, sniff, sniff). 'Formal education essential, preferably at some distance from Poggibonsi.'

During this discourse Patrick's grin had widened like a beacon but at the end he shook his great red head and told the worried manufacturer that, whilst he would have been delighted to assist in such circumstances (which he could well imagine), he was unable to do so for the simple reason which he had already expressed. After this the poor fellow left, ruefully shaking his head and lamenting the absence of proper educational provision. The following day he was back.

The answer, he announced, was quite simple. Since the school could not take more children the children must have more school. He was in fact quite fired with enthusiasm to the extent that much of the snivelling had now stopped. More space, more books, more teachers, although, *of course*, they would remain under the direction of the present major-domo.

Patrick replied, with a trace of irritation, that all of these things, whilst desirable, required money that was not available. He had no intention, he said, of selling places in his school whatever the difficulty in obtaining funds.

At this point the snuff-maker brimmed over with enthusiasm. Of course, he understood entirely and approved *totally* of Patrick's sentiments. But what he had in mind was a substantial endowment of the *whole* school, the money to be provided by himself and his fellow snuff-makers who had enjoyed unprecedented success in their trade following the defeat of the infidel Turks. (Quite how this military triumph had affected or encouraged the snorters of Europe was never satisfactorily explained, nor did either of us deem it necessary to enquire.) By this means, continued our potential benefactor, *all* of the children on the waiting list could be accommodated and educated on the proceeds of snuff. In addition, he added, he was sure that even the present provision, excellent though it undoubtedly was, could withstand some improvement. Of course, he added, those who put forward the funds would expect, in return, no influence whatsoever in the actual running of the school. In fact they would be grateful to be molested as little as possible after their respective progeny had been safely lodged in the town of San Casciano. Suitable provision could be made for safeguarding the future flow of money by the lodging of a suitable capital sum in the Medici bank, the Vatican bank or any other financial house thought to be suitable.

As luck would have it my father was at home from his travels and Lorenzo Bellini was staying at the house. That night the five of us carefully considered the offer, I now being accredited with sufficient status to express a considered view. All in all no rational objection to the scheme could be found. There was, of course, a certain priggish reluctance to infect the academic grove with clouds of choking tobacco but, as Lorenzo pointed out, the great library of Antonio Magliabechi was based upon the smelting of gold and the Medici family who, until recently, had been history's greatest patrons of learning had long since given up the medical profession in favour of international usury. Arrangements were therefore made for my father to travel to Poggibonsi to meet the benefactors and bring to the scheme his own wider commercial wisdom. When he returned he was a troubled man.

'There is one substantial difficulty,' he told us all that evening. 'Our snuff-makers believe, as indeed does everyone else, that the school is a Benedictine foundation. It would be difficult to assume otherwise given Patrick's somewhat conspicuous presence. Our benefactors therefore expect, and indeed insist, that the funds should be placed through the Benedictine Order. This, of course, involves an element of sanctification and they are thereby keen not only to ensure the education of their offspring in this world but their own untroubled passage into the next. Whether they fear that the gates of Heaven will be closed to their trade

I know not but certain it is that they will not simply part with their money to a secular enterprise.'

At this news there was general resignation since the arrangement proposed by the would-be benefactors would immediately involve Patrick's *public* exposure as a banned teacher. Worse, however, was to come.

'They have, I am afraid,' said my father, 'already contacted the Abbot at Siena and intend to visit him next week. At present the Abbot is ignorant of any details of their proposals but once they have been placed before him he will then *publicly* possess knowledge that his own edicts are being disobeyed. The consequences for Patrick and the school will be disastrous.'

This news caused general consternation. Long and painful discussion followed, at the conclusion of which it was decided, despite Patrick's noisy and vehement objections, that the most important consideration was to protect his position. It was therefore further decided, again in the face of Patrick's disapproval, that, in two days' time, my father was to arrange a further meeting with the snuff-makers and enlighten them as to the true nature of the school's foundation and inform them that, under no circumstances, would, or could, funds be accepted which passed through the Benedictine Abbey. My father was to point out that any revelations made to the Abbot could only be on the basis of some form of vindictiveness which would serve the purposes of no one, least of all the children of the manufacturers themselves. If really necessary, it was decided (again in the face of noisy opposition), that my father should indicate that some preferential consideration might be given to the children in view of their 'educational difficulties'.

'But then the school will get no money!' said Patrick. '*And* we will be forced to take those snivelling little bastards at the top of the list.'

'The only alternative,' said my father, 'is that the school gets its money but loses its founder.'

'And probably none the worse for that,' said Patrick. 'It is now well-founded, in good heart, and there are many gifted teachers in the Benedictines who would be pleased to take on so well-endowed an establishment.'

My father, however, insisted that the matter was closed and, on that unhappy note, we all retired to bed.

The following day Patrick seemed quite resigned to the decision and the morning's first lessons passed without incident. After the morning break, however, he assembled the whole school and announced, without consultation with me, that the onset of spring and the end of winter was a proper time for a short break in our studies. He therefore proposed that the school would be closed for two weeks which would bring us back, refreshed for the joys of scholarship.

When school had ended I asked Patrick why he had taken such a step.

'We all need a break,' he said, 'and besides, if your father is going to talk to the nose-dabbers we need all our concentrations on that matter.' He was not to be drawn further and we returned home for our own personal afternoon tuition. That evening he was unusually quiet and, at his suggestion, we walked back through the village and stood in front of the knacker's yard. The Bomboni household was also uncharacteristically quiet and the spring air of Tuscany was as sweet and scented as honey. The shadows of the poplars fell across the hard backyard and divided the squat stone and red-tiled building, providing a sharp angular contrast to the warm undulations of the roof against the grey hills and pale clear blue of the sky. He stood there a short time looking at the scene and holding his damaged left hand against the rays of the setting sun. We then walked back to supper at which his accustomed joviality gave no hint of his intentions.

The following day he was gone. He carried with him little enough in any event and so, at first, I could not believe the evidence of his parting. I soon discovered, however, the inevitable letter for me together with another addressed to my parents. I still have my own, a short document which I will now relate.

Fredo, *caro mio*,

Have no doubt whatsoever that we will meet again. Almost certainly in this tired old world but, if not, in a fresh young eternity full of scholarship and sensation. Do not regret my passing. Cromwell taught me the benefits of travel, compulsory or otherwise, and it is time that I found new minds to confuse. Be confident that you are a gifted scholar. You are now nearly fourteen and must go next year to Pisa where, God help you, Lorenzo will be a guide and mentor. I have assembled a quantity of your better work (do not search for the rest of it, it has gone for ever) which will ensure your entry. I look forward to hearing that they have made you a professor at an even younger age than Lorenzo which will serve him right.

Remember, forgive your enemies and what appear to be the

misfortunes of fate and you will remain the happy and compassionate fellow that you have become.

God guide you.

Patrick.

Well, of course I wept. We all did. A blind man would have assumed that he was at the wrong end of the village from the cacophony which came from our terrace. My father kept on saying, 'The fool, the bloody, bloody fool.' But Lorenzo said, 'No, he's not, he has done the only thing which he could.' And of course he was right.

The Abbot realised, immediately, what had occurred. My father informed him directly of Patrick's absence and the fact that he had, for some time, been carrying out 'menial tasks' at the school which had been taught by 'Signore Credi'. The account therefore bore some remote semblance of the truth. It reopened on time, staffed by two excellent Benedictines, both of whom shared an abiding faith in the vernacular. During the course of the summer it was closed for substantial rebuilding to take place and, in the autumn of 1684, it reopened with four teachers and swiftly became one of the best free schools in Tuscany. So great was its reputation that, even in the coming horrors of the Inquisition in Florence, it remained relatively undisturbed, partly, perhaps, due to a persistent and lingering rumour that it specialised in methods whereby the tax-collectors would be 'sodded up'.

Chapter Seven

The News from Florence continued to form a major element in my childhood. It preoccupied my mother and her anxieties transferred themselves to me, tuned, if anything, to a higher pitch by ignorance and the imagination. I had, of course, never seen the city although it was possible on the clearest day to discern the glint of the Arno and a tiny patch of darkness cut off by the folding hills. The news brought by both Lorenzo and my father was uniformly bad. Much has become comprehensible only with hindsight but there was no mistaking the general import. Tuscany was an impoverished land. Its size and geographical position precluded the commercial advancement now centred in Northern Europe and moving like fire towards the New World. The seemingly interminable succession of earnest Englishmen continued across Italy and their portentous chronicles amount to a smug litany of lamentation. But the evidence was clear nonetheless. Successive poor harvests and incessant plague reduced the mean to the poor and the poor to misery. In the Pitti Palace Cosimo III ruled his people, Vittoria della Rovere, his mother, ruled him, and the Jesuits ruled her.

To maintain the needs of the city taxation fell upon the surrounding country. Increasingly the land, even within riding distance of San Casciano, became desolate and bare. The peasants moved to the city, the landed nobility took what the peasants left behind. The great city monopolies were sold off as the Grand Duchess turned the Pitti Palace into a corner shop. Within the stories from Florence came new names, new notorieties, the new power élite of Tuscany: the Castanelli brothers, who controlled the leather trade, the Assinari brothers who acquired the salt monopoly, and the del Rosso brothers, Andrea and Lorenzo, in whose hands lay the pricing, selling and distribution of flour.

It was not until I was fourteen years of age, in the summer of 1684, following the departure of Patrick, that the impact of this again reached my small world and then it did so in the most dramatic way. My father, after a journey to the north, set out for Florence with his consignment of paper for Antonio Magliabechi. Bellini, by chance, was at the house travelling back to Pisa. To our surprise, in the early part of the evening when we were sitting in the gathering dusk, we heard my father's voice in the street urgently calling to our groom, Mario, ordering him to conceal the horses with all haste. Moments later he arrived in the room, his saddlebags slung over both shoulders, and we all rose at the sight of him.

'Gallupe, my dear fellow,' cried Bellini, 'what has become of you?'

He was indeed much distressed. His tunic and doublet were torn and his shirt, visible beneath his cloak, was stained with blood. One eye was near-closed and an ugly welt ran along the left-hand side of his face. His limp, now the more marked, took him just to the fireside chair where he collapsed as my mother and Lorenzo reached him. At his bidding I took the saddlebags and placed them in his room whilst Lorenzo obtained wine and my mother, ensuring that the blood did not proceed from any obvious wound, fetched water and bathed his face and hands. He was silent for a while, drinking the wine, then he said to Lorenzo, 'Will you take the books for me? I do not think I can be seen on the road to Florence for some while.'

'What *has* happened?' said my mother, and since I remained unbanished (and indeed unnoticed) I sat behind my father as he told them.

'I had nearly come to Gallaza when I found the road blocked by a great crowd of people. I could not see at first what they were watching but, apart from some shouting at the front, they were completely silent, with faces like stone. In the centre of the crowd, where the shouting came from, I could hear screams and the sounds of beating with a whip or cane. I asked what was happening but no one would speak so I dismounted and left the horses and pushed my way through into the crowd. I knew no one. They were peasants for the most part, whole families, children too. At the front of the crowd there was a group of men, wearing some kind of uniform — I had not seen it before. I recognised one of *them* though, it was the eldest Bomboni boy, Pasto. The one who went to Florence two years ago. He appeared to be in charge. They had some poor fellow on the ground, a peasant quite clearly, although he had no clothes, which were in a pile, with his boots, by his head. A full one half of his face was quite ... quite broken. Yet two of these men held him by the arms and another by the feet while a fourth was lashing his back with a fruit cane. I went up to the Bomboni and asked him what in God's name was happening and he said the man had been making *salt*! And he *laughed* and told me that he had been caught making salt from the brine left over at the end of a barrel of sardines! (As you know, it would barely provide a cupful.) So I told him, of course, to stop. I *shouted* at him to stop and he said, "Don't interfere here, Professore. This is about salt not stars." So I yelled at him, "You've no right to do this to this man." And he said, "Oh no, well, what's this then?" And he thrust a paper at me. Well, of course I didn't read it all but it was quite obvious what it was. It bore the Medici crest and was some kind of authority given to the Assinari brothers and he said, "I'm working for Paolo Assinari, see, now go back to your fucking books." Well, at this point the fellow on the ground made the most awful noise so that even the bully who was laying into him stopped for a moment and looked at Bomboni. He nodded to them to carry on and I ... I just hit him. He wasn't expecting it and I knocked him straight over. Well, then everything happened very quickly. One of the bullies came rushing at me with his fruit cane and gave me this so I hit him back and then, thank God, the crowd joined in. There was a terrible fight. There were more of Bomboni's people, you see, keeping the crowd back. I found myself lying on the man who'd been beaten – this is his blood, I think – then I was pulled off and he was carried back into the crowd. Somebody, a woman, I believe, helped me to the horses and literally threw me on. I just came straight back, keeping off the road as far as possible.'

During the course of this story my father's voice had been steady enough but, as he reached the end and raised his tankard to his lips, his hand and voice began to shake and my mother took him in her arms as one would a child. He was fifty-seven years of age and had, in any event, been troubled lately by his injured leg and his back, strained and compressed, as Lorenzo said, by years of travel. When he had been placed in bed and I had been stood before him and he had sought my hand and smiled and said something that I now forget, my mother and Bellini returned to the table and I, sitting by the cold fireside, was again unheeded.

She said, 'How is it with the Jews in Florence? I want to know the truth, Lorenzo. I think you have been sparing me.'

'No, I have not spared you but the position is very bad. If anything Cosimo has become worse after his mad wife went back to France. He is now totally in the hands of his mother and the Inquisition. But of course it is more complicated. Everywhere the poor become desperate. Many do not stop at extracting salt from their pilchards. Closer to

Florence and in the city itself there is much brigandage, houses are forced, some travellers, even those who are guarded, are taken and robbed on the roads. Cosimo increases his guards and increases the penalties. We now have six public executions a week, the hot pincers are used again in the Bargello and the penalty for any theft, however trivial, is fifty numbered lashes, *cinquanta frustrate ben conte*, whilst strapped to a column in the market. To pay his guards and the Salti from the Bargello, Cosimo requires more money which he extracts from the poor. This is done by taxation and monopolies which he rents to the rich. Thus the circle is made.'

'I know these things, Lorenzo, but what of the Jews?'

'Cosimo and his mother are genuine bigots. They would persecute the Jews *as Jews* but there is no doubt that Cosimo sees them as a way out of the circle. If he can turn the poor against them then he will sustain his own government *and* satisfy the cravings of his Christian soul. So Christians and Jews may no longer live in the same house, may not share a door, window, well, roof, terrace, or any other convenience or mode of communication. Jews are forbidden to visit Christian prostitutes. Women so convicted are stripped and publicly lashed and thrown into the Stinche prison which is, I hear, worse than the Bargello. The edicts that he passes become daily more manic. Jews may not have their children suckled by Christian women nor vice versa.

'The lunacy does not stop, of course, with the Jews. Only hand-picked students may now study at Pisa. As a result of which we have even more zealots and boneheads than we did before. Books, manuscripts and authors are proscribed and forbidden apparently at random. We learnt the other day that the works of Democritus are now banned! As though anyone had touched him for years. I am told that the tragedies of Seneca are also on the banned list! This is, presumably, because he wrote a sketch debunking the deification of the Emperor Claudius. It is unlikely to be because of his *astronomical* works which place the world firmly in the centre of the universe precisely where our Jesuit friends would hope it is. The works of Galileo himself, whilst not yet prohibited, are regularly denounced. There is official 'concern' as to the whereabouts of his original manuscripts. The Grand Duke apparently wishes to have them in the Medici library. How long they would remain there intact is a matter of conjecture. Still, they do not know where they are and I hope they never will!'

My mother looked at him and said, 'Have you seen my father?'

'No, but Antonio sees him and he is unharmed. As you know he is now quite blind and never leaves the house.'

'Does he speak of me?'

'Antonio speaks of you and Gallupe and he listens. But I am afraid that, whenever he is asked, he denies that he has a daughter.'

Again there was silence and then she said, 'What will happen now?'

'What, about Pasto Bomboni and the salt? It is dangerous. Gallupe has been identified. Something will happen. I have no intention of going to Florence or Pisa yet, books or no books, gallstones or no gallstones. The Assinari have become as powerful as any family in Florence and I wish to be here should they decide to visit.

'Do you think they will come for him?' And then, before he could answer, 'Fredo!'

'I have been asleep.'

Having discovered my existence they became almost jovial as though released from some drudgery. My mother's behaviour, indeed, was quite skittish as she came to my bedside and, despite my protestations, removed my lamp and left me to the darkness of my imaginings. Later I heard her crying and the soft voice of Lorenzo Bellini, monotonous as a lullaby, drew me, hypnotic, into sleep.

The following day my father remained in his bed. Lorenzo, for the most part, read on the terrace and my mother meticulously performed the domestic round, seeking, as I realised then, comfort in dull familiarity. I was told I could not walk in the hills and so I sat close to Lorenzo and, partly through genuine curiosity but rather more to excite his interest and admiration, applied my time to one of the manuscripts with which my father had returned and which should, had all gone well, have already found its place in the library in the Via del Corso.

After a while my attention wandered, not unnaturally, to the Bomboni family and, despite the fine autumn sunshine, I felt cold with apprehension. Seeing me staring across the valley Bellini said, 'Now come on, what are you reading, Fredo? Plainly you find it a resistible text.'

I was at an age for blushing and of late a certain formality had come between us, so I smiled and handed him the manuscript.

'Ah, *Hypothesis physica nova* – so your father has been to Brunswick and got himself into bad company. Well, Fredo, what do you think of it?'

I had, of course, read very little and barely understood that but I did my best and said, 'Well, I think the idea that all our movements are made possible by some form of fine elasticity linking us to the centre of the earth very, very ... interesting.'

'Bollocks!' said the great physician. 'It's rubbish and *he* – indicating the manuscript in my hand – 'knows it is. That's why he's dedicated it to the Royal Society *and* the French Academy so that neither will reject it. What you have there, Fredo, is the work of the most dangerous genius in Europe.' (I put it down at once.) 'At the age of twenty he *refused* the Professor's chair of Law at Nuremberg University, preferring to become a statesman and mathematician. Before he was *thirty* he had discovered a mathematical concept called "differential calculus". I don't pretend to understand it but it is, apparently, the greatest mathematical deduction of our century. Whilst carrying out this small venture he has produced a number of essays on the mysteries of physical matter (*that* is one of them), attempted to reinstate Aristotle and cast doubt on the works of Descartes. In addition to this he has attempted to reform the entire Christian Church into a religious unity of Europe (under the leadership of the united German states) in order to wage a Holy war on the Egyptians! In this last venture he has, apparently, obtained the active support of most German princes. In his idle moments he has produced several substantial works defending and promoting the concept of the Holy Trinity, not, one would have thought, an exercise for which differential calculus was essential.'

'An amazing man,' I murmured, conscious of the inadequacy of the response. 'Why do you say he's dangerous?' And then, daringly, 'Wouldn't it be a good idea to have one Church?'

'Certainly, Fredo, as it would be a good idea to have one language, one people, one race, one God, but if any of this is to be achieved by mass warfare against the heathen in general and the Egyptians in particular it would do little for the service of mankind. The problem with Herr Leibniz, Fredo, is his mathematical certainty about all things. There is nothing from the existence of God to the making of gold or the coital thrust that cannot be explained by his ontological method. Descartes proved the existence of God by the starting point, "I doubt therefore I am." Leibniz might have done so by saying, "I'm *certain* I'm right, therefore I am." Now of course none of this matters so long as it's in the hands of mad academics like us. But when you start applying this dreadful rationality to *politics* it becomes very dangerous.

'For so long as Princes claimed to rule by the will of God they were relying on some mysterious unknown, almighty power which was *greater* than them. And, anyway, everybody knows it's codswallop. But when they start governing because they *know they are right*; because they are part of some *predetermined* rational force, then there will be no stopping

101

them. To believe that God is on your side is no more than eccentric optimism. To believe, to *really* believe, that your side has a monopoly of Reason leads to dangerous mania.'

'Don't you believe in Reason, Lorenzo?'

'I don't know what it *means*. If you mean a mathematical certainty, a series of calculations, then I do not need to *believe* in them. They are a fact of life like this table. If you mean can we use that mathematical method to account for our very existence and, more important, that of the Creator, then, no, I do not believe it. Modestly I can say that I am one of the best doctors in Italy, perhaps in the world. I have seen men with sicknesses from which they *cannot* recover. And I have watched as they became whole men. I investigate. Now I can understand *how* they improve but as to *why* they do I know no more than you or that hen crossing the road. I will put it another way, Fredo. Herr Leibniz will continue to look for perfection. Perfection in mathematics, perfection in method, perfection in politics and ultimately, perfection in people. I, as a doctor, know he is on a fool's errand. I who work day by day with this sack of blood and bones know that the divinity of man is in his imperfection, his flaws, his hopeless aspirations, his vainglorious, posturing inadequacies. Try this: "God made man in His own image. God is perfect therefore man is perfect." True or false?'

'The conclusion is untrue.'

'Exactly! If man is part of the Divine Comedy his very existence is based on a false syllogism.'

Whilst I retained all this and dutifully record it I confess that I understood little of it. But I said, 'What about the Devil. Was not man perfect until tempted by the Devil?'

He looked at me keenly and smiled.

'Very well, my little Jesuit. Let us go further. Are we to believe that Heaven is a *rational* place?'

'I . . . suppose so . . .'

'Of course, it would be unfortunate, indeed, would it not, if we spent all this time rationalising an irrational God? But let us go further. Do we agree with Messieurs Descartes, Spinoza and, indeed, Herr Leibniz, that to know all is, ultimately, to understand all by a process of reason?'

'Of course.'

'Very well. Now answer this. Why should God have failed to convince the Devil of God's own omnipotence and the futility of the Devil's works?'

'Convince him?'

'Certainly, we must assume, must we not, that God's behaviour would be rational? Or at least sensible,' he added with a smile.

'Perhaps He *did* try to convince him,' said I, perceiving the trap immediately I had entered it.

'And failed?'

I stared at him helplessly. 'Well, perhaps...'

'Perhaps He didn't try very hard? Unlikely, don't you think. The only *rational* explanation is, is it not, that even at the highest level rationality is powerless in the face of Evil.'

'Perhaps the Devil did not understand...'

'Oh, Fredo, we have already dealt with that and, besides, does any of our experience lead us to think that the Devil is somehow intellectually impaired. Look at his messengers on earth. Some are the cleverest men in the world, they are not all dimwits and bullies like the Bombonis.' He pursed his lips and frowned in annoyance realising that he had reintroduced precisely that subject which his theological discussion had been calculated to avoid. (I learnt, later, that his attack on Leibniz had been mere badinage. They had never met, but a good-natured correspondence had passed between them for many years, subsequently destroyed. I had learnt, as well, that in moments of great anguish and danger, when one is truly, as the English say, 'in the shits', there is no antidote so effective as prolonged theological debate, however inconsequential.)

A cloud now settled upon us and I felt again that cold, clammy apprehension coupled with the desire to run, to hide, to *act*. I said, 'What will happen now?'

'We must wait and see and take some comfort from the fact that we have no choice. Your father had no choice and did precisely what any good man would have done in the circumstances. Now we have no choice but to await the outcome.'

'But the Assinari brothers...'

'Have a reputation to maintain, yes, but do not forget, Fredo, that your father has a reputation too, and many friends.' I took some little comfort from his words and returned to my snail's journey through the Theory of Movement and Matter whilst my mind, like an errant child casting forbidding glances at some atrocious act, returned again and again to the family Bomboni.

Days passed, then weeks, then months, and nothing was heard of the brothers Assinari. The summer days lengthened. The town, unlike the surrounding areas of Tuscany, continued to prosper and serve the peripatetic wanderers of Italy. The weather was very hot and the air, dancing above the street, merely served to emphasise the stillness of the long afternoons. Lorenzo Bellini finally left for Pisa with the assurance that, having carried out the minimum of his duties, he would journey straight to Florence and then bring us word of the state of the city and, in particular, the repercussions, if any, which had followed the incident at Gallaza. With the passing of time apprehension diminished. My father, now fit and well, confined himself largely to the terrace where he read his latest acquisitions, occasionally scribbled and, so it appeared to me, approached his only son with increased familiarity and respect. We discussed his manuscripts and the prospects of my early departure to Pisa following upon my anticipated acceptance on the basis of the portfolio which Bellini had taken in his saddlebag. Upon this work, previously unseen by anyone save myself and Patrick, I had been warmly commended and my future, at least academically, now seemed as secure as could be wished. My mother sometimes joined us in these discussions but, more often, sketched or painted the view from the terrace, thereby capturing, with subtle accuracy, the changes in colour and vegetation which occurred day by day under the remorseless Tuscan sun.

Occasionally we would walk in those very hills; my mother, not yet forty, long-limbed and fit as a Greek athlete, waiting impatiently from time to time as my father limped and I puffed and sweated along the dusty, lizard-strewn tracks.

Notwithstanding the Arcadian tranquillity I was aware of a sense of physical dissatisfaction; a kind of secondary pulse, uncomfortably strong but appearing to provide no observable energy or motion. At first I considered it to be the result of Patrick's absence and the end of my early experiences as a teacher. It did not take me long, of course, to discern the true cause of this physical agitation. As we occasionally passed girls working in the fields who stopped and smiled, generally at my parents, I experienced an uncomfortable quickening of this mysterious internal tempo. Furthermore as I closed my eyes and strained for sleep against the relentless heat of the night the vision of Nicola Bomboni's pudenda, so distasteful to my initial protesting glance, now presented, unaccountably, a more attractive image worthy, indeed, of prolonged contemplation.

It was shortly before September that Lorenzo returned, direct from Florence, bringing a mixture of news. My own place at Pisa was now assured. My portfolio had excited the anticipated response and I was to enrol as a student at the beginning of November.

What of the Assinari? We all sat on the terrace in the late morning regarding Lorenzo with concern. I had before me a glass of Orvieto, suitably watered, to which I had already developed a considerably partiality. Bread and olives were on the table, still cool in the morning shadow of the vines.

'Well,' said Lorenzo, 'as we expected it did cause a very considerable stir. The selling of monopolies is causing great unrest in the city and the Gallaza matter has been widely seen as an inevitable, though early, result of the policy. In many ways it could not have been more dramatic. I think you would be surprised, Gallupe, at the extent to which your reputation is still alive with the people. The hero of Mongiorno has not been forgotten and, even if you had fallen into some obscurity, this incident has done more than enough for you to be re-established as a saviour of Florence. Indeed some of the accounts of the battle which I heard have reached a level of exaggeration which even I could no longer encourage. According to many of the bar-room historians, had you been at Thermopylae the entire Persian Army would have been routed without a single Spartan life being required.

'All this, of course, has provided very considerable difficulties for the enemy. The Assinaris and their bullies are extremely unpopular. Even the bone-headed Duchess in the Pitti Palace is aware of this fact. For their part the Assinaris realised that any direct revenge on you could not go unpunished in the inevitable public outcry which would follow. This did not stop them and their friends making strong representations to Cosimo that you should be clapped into the Bargello and indicted for an assault on an authorised collector of dues. In putting forward this proposition the Assinaris enlisted the support of the Castellanis, the del Rossos and several other grisly so-called merchants who have benefited from the Medicis' latest indulgences. The Inquisitors and Jesuits were also of the view that a salutary lesson was necessary in the interests of good discipline. The defeat of this regiment of bastards owes much to Antonio Magliabechi. He ransacked the Medicis' library and his own and assembled every single word, official and otherwise, which has been written on the battle of Mongiorno; some of it at least as florid as the accounts available at the dockside inns. Using his position as chief librarian, "in order to provide some assistance in this difficult case", he treated the Court, publicly, to an hour-long dissertation on the great victory and your part in particular. I was not there but I have seen the verbatim transcript which he caused to be widely distributed in the city.

He concludes by saying, "On the basis of all this evidence, Grand Duke, you *may* conclude that *if* Signore Credi has erred then he fell into error as a result of precisely those qualities of courage, vigour and, yes, impetuosity which once saved the Tuscan people. In addition *if* there was an error of judgement you might conclude that the pain of the terrible wound which he has carried for so long may well not assist him in reaching that careful and mature assessment of fact which you, Grand Duke, are so able to employ in deciding this difficult and, if I may say so, potentially dangerous matter." Well, that did it. Cosimo, it is rumoured, for once ignored his mother's advice and refused to order your arrest or interrogation. However, some form of face-saving was thought to be necessary. The Assinari are to be compensated in the sum of five hundred crowns for any losses which may have been occasioned by your intervention. In addition Pasto Bomboni, the directly injured party, has been offered a commission in the Salti with the immediate rank of Captain. This effectively gives him the day-to-day running of whole areas in the city and his reputation already exists like a gasp of foul air before the flood.'

'My God,' said my father, rising from his chair, 'I would rather have gone to the Bargello and...'

'No you would not, Gallupe,' said Lorenzo quietly, 'you have much support but the mind of the people is fickle. Once you were safely incarcerated rumours would have been started suggesting that your heroism was a fraud. Signed confessions would have been obtained — oh yes, they would — to that effect. Pasto Bomboni would still have been promoted and you would have simply become one of a large number of public executions, your reputation dying as your head fell from the block. As things are now your reputation is, if anything, enhanced and, for all his promotion, Pasto Bomboni remains a well-known bully, rightly admonished by a popular hero. What occurs in Florence cannot be changed by grand gesture. The poor, of which there are many thousands, are for the moment being fed and, to an extent, pacified by a diet of public festivals and celebrations, like manic laughter issuing from a corpse. Antonio is right. The only remedy is to stay as close as possible to the centre of power and save and salvage what one can.'

When Lorenzo finished there was silence but an unspoken question hung over the terrace, now hot and baking in the midday sun. He took some olives and a little wine and then said, 'I know that you want news of Isaac. I fear that there is none. It is now very unsafe to enter the

Jewish quarter. There are persistent tales of baiting and cruelty and virtually all contact between Christian and Jew is now forbidden. Even Antonio dares not go there often and for me to do so after my visit to the Bargello would be foolhardy and for no purpose. As I have said before, it is generally believed that those who remain at home are safe. Even the Salti have not reached the stage of storming houses to attack the old and blind. And what could we do? Isaac would never consent to leave Florence. As you know he would certainly never consent to come here. He is as conspicuous as Abraham and would not even contemplate any form of subterfuge. Antonio will continue to search for news but it is very difficult. He is under suspicion and there is no shortage of those who wish to discredit him entirely. It is even put about that he is himself a Jew, a rumour which, occasionally, he appears positively to encourage.'

'I must get some food,' said my mother quietly, and left the terrace containing two men and a boy, each, I noticed, with fingers pressed to the forehead in studied contemplation of the flagstones, dull red beside the watered pots of carnations and thyme.

Chapter Eight

I knew, at that moment, that she would go. I think that we all did. Yet when she returned with more olives, wine, cheese, sausage and a plate of tortellini she appeared in good spirits, infectious to the point of gaiety. I must confess that I felt little personal anguish for a grandfather that I had never met and who had apparently shown no concern for my existence let alone my well-being. In fact his continued rejection of my mother instilled in me feelings close to outright hostility. This feeling was, if anything, heightened by the knowledge that my mother intended to make the perilous journey to Florence for no better reason than to ascertain his safety.

No sooner had I divined her intention than I had planned the method by which it might be frustrated. I had decided, immediately, to inform her that should she wish to go to the city she would not do so without my company. She could not, of course, physically prevent me from following her on her journey and this fact, I knew, would render it impossible for her to go. That night I slept secure in the knowledge that I could, if necessary, control events. I had decided to inform my mother of my intentions after the departure of Bellini, to Pisa, on the following day. In the event he did not leave until the early evening, having been persuaded to eat with us at midday and discuss with me the delights to be offered by his University. No sooner had he gone than my mother also disappeared into the village on some domestic errand, leaving my father and me somewhat uncomfortable in each other's company. She did not return until after dark by which time portentous announcements of my own resolve seemed singularly out of place. She showed no signs of immediate decampment and I began to wonder whether my initial convictions had not been ill-founded. I was, I reasoned, at least close to some form of independence but my father's disability and increasing age argued against her undertaking any journey or mission so fraught with danger.

When I woke the following day she was gone. She had asked my father to collect bread from the town and, during his absence, had ordered Mario to harness the small carriage and, dispensing with the services of our coachman, had left on the road for Florence. I will not rehearse the letter which she left. It was, in any event, a very short document stating simply that she would be away for the day and the evening, and instructing me to carry out certain chores including the gathering of figs. The brevity of the communication, clearly intended to allay fears or forebodings, had precisely the reverse effect.

My father, on returning from his errand, was at first intent upon pursuit. However, on reading his own letter, his agitation appeared to subside and I discovered later that my mother had informed him that her intention was only to visit Antonio Magliabechi in order to ascertain, at first hand, the degree of danger to which her father was now subject. This letter, together with my own presence and the risks necessarily attendant on his own arrival in Florence, resulted in his remaining and, with as much equanimity as we could display for the benefit of each other, we prepared to spend the day awaiting my mother's return.

She did not appear before nightfall; even though the return journey to Florence could have been accomplished well within that time. Thereafter I spent a sleepless night, in part upon the terrace in the thick, unyielding heat and in part lying awake staring at the dark furniture, those nightly monuments of childhood, straining for the sound of horses or carriages upon the road. In the early morning I must have slept a little for it was past ten o'clock when I emerged from my room and made my way onto the terrace. My father appeared hardly to recognise me and his acknowledgement was a perfunctory gesture of the hand. His face had become gaunt overnight and his sixty years now sat upon him like ashes on an old fire, its contribution long spent. From the extremity of the terrace it was possible to see the bend in the road to Florence and he sat at this point, red wine untouched before him, staring past the vines and across the stunted olive trees, starting forward with every movement, real or imagined.

That morning the domestic commerce of the house continued unaltered. Carletta, our crone-like maidservant and occasional cook, made her ill-tempered way around the house grumbling at my father's immobility as she fussed and swept beneath his bench. Luigi, the olive-grower, whose squint had been so dramatically cured, arrived to tend the olive trees as he had done, without payment, since that day as an obscure obeisance to fortune. He brought a plate of the best olives onto the terrace, partly for our immediate enjoyment and partly as an excuse to impart the gossip of the town. Obtaining no response from my father he chatted to me about the exorbitance of market prices and the municipal incompetence of the Prefect until, sensing my own pre-occupations, he wandered down the road scratching his thigh and shaking his ancient head. In the absence of any sign from my father I dealt also with Carletta's wages and Mario's enquiries as to the exercise of the two horses which remained in our stalls. Time passed. Unbidden, I poured myself a glass of the new milk which tasted flat and unpalatable after the olives which I had chewed compulsively throughout the morning. At two o'clock, after a meal prepared by Carletta had been brought to the terrace and removed untouched, my father appeared to regain something of his composure. Perhaps he had convinced himself that the absence of any news augured for the best for he at least assumed a confident cordiality.

'How very inconsiderate of your Mama to leave us at the mercy of Carletta,' he said, forcing a smile through his pallor, 'she could have poisoned us both.' I smiled encouragingly in reply and he added, 'If she does not return by this evening I think I will leave for Florence first thing in the morning. You will be all right, Fredo, with Mario and Carletta, will you not?'

I replied energetically in the affirmative although the prospect of being wholly deserted in such circumstances filled me with abject fear.

Unable to offer any words of advice or encouragement but unwilling to remain in this atmosphere of despair, I announced my intention of walking in the hills and set off into the heat of the afternoon, ignoring the stares of those whom I passed stretched in siesta beneath the shadow of the walls and trees.

Unlike my present, grandiose, establishment our house was comparatively close to the bottom of the valley and I walked towards the rising hills on the far side of the river which ran surprisingly high throughout the summer months. Crossing the stone bridge I could see the mill, towards the centre of the town on my right-hand side, and the corpulent figure of its owner moving sacks into the shade of an open shed. Seeing me on the bridge he waved in greeting before resuming his tasks. On the other side of the valley I began to climb the path which grew steeper as the olives gave way to vineyards set on the narrow terraces cut into the thrifty Tuscan soil. Here, in the abundance of greenery, it appeared noticeably cooler than on the valley floor and I continued my ascent towards the ragged lines of poplars which dominated the skyline above the hills, the occasional giant thrusting towards the sky like a green spire of some natural cathedral or church. Deliberately I pushed myself to exhaustion and, equally with purpose, I kept my gaze on the hillside before and above my head, knowing that when I reached the summit I would be able to survey not only my own house, its courtyard and stable but also the full length of the Florence road as it wound down towards Gallaza. Any new or imminent arrivals since my own departure would then be likewise visible. I was now among the poplars and passed through banks of deep shade, skirting occasional piles of wood, coppice cut for winter burning. Arriving, at last, at a rock projection which stood beyond the line of trees I clambered up the final few feet and, at its very pinnacle, turned to survey the valley.

Two horses. Standing by the gate to our courtyard. From this height I could make out a male figure who had entered the yard and was striding towards the line of buildings through which he would pass in order to arrive at the terrace. By the horses a further male figure stood waiting. Of the small carriage there was no sign either close to the house or on the Florence road which I could now see for a distance of some five miles until it disappeared into the haze of the afternoon. Recognition of either figure was impossible at this distance although it appeared from the speed with which the walker crossed the yard that he was in familiar territory. On the terrace I could see my father, plainly alerted by the arrival of the horses, approaching the wide doors which gave entry to the house. Both men entered the building from their respective sides at almost exactly the same time.

Cursing the fact that I had walked so far, I now began to run down the hill, through the poplars, past the vines and towards the bridge, now a mile distant across the river which glinted in the fierce light. Twice I fell; on the second occasion doing some damage to my right knee which, in my haste, I ignored. Neither man had emerged from the house either onto the terrace or courtyard but I could still see the figure which waited by the horses and could make out his general configuration with sufficient accuracy to ensure that he was unknown to me. It was clear, however, that he was of extraordinary stature, standing rock still between the two horses which he controlled with both hands. In an instant he was lost to view, cut off by the roofline of the house now becoming rapidly closer. By the time I reached the bridge I was quite without breath and, despite the urgency of the situation, was unable to run the final distance through our own olives to the foot of the terrace. As I climbed the steps I heard a voice which I recognised only too well and, in my joy and excitement, called from halfway up, 'Lorenzo! Lorenzo!'

As soon as I saw him, coming onto the terrace to meet me, I realised that the news was as bad as possible. His face was set like rock and his extended arms foretold immediately the necessities of comfort. I threw myself into them and, as I did so, saw beyond his back the figure of my father slumped at the table, his head in his hands.

'Lorenzo!' I cried. 'What has happened?'

Without answering, he held me for a moment and then, taking me by the shoulders, he guided me to the table on the terrace where my father had been during the morning. Placing me onto the bench he sat beside me, his arm still firmly around my shoulders.

'Fredo, you are going to have to be very brave...' I interrupted him and said, 'Is she dead?'

'No, Fredo, she is not dead but she is in great danger. She has been arrested...

'Arrested!'

'Yes, she has been arrested by the Salti and taken to the Stinche Prison. So far as we know she is unharmed and,' he said, stopping my question with his outstretched hand, 'nothing can happen today which is a Festival, no punishment of any kind is allowed on such a day.'

'Punishment? But what has she *done*?'

Lorenzo's answer was interrupted by my father who, through his hands, shouted, 'Nothing! Nothing!'

Leaving me, Lorenzo crossed swiftly to him and took hold of both hands, still compressed to his face.

'Gallupe!' he said softly. 'Control ... you must ... it is he that matters now. You must be a support for him.'

'But what *has* she done?' I said, rising from the table and going to stand before them.

Lorenzo looked up at me. 'Your father is right, Fredo, your mother has done nothing which could be described as wrong. But she was arrested in the Jewish sector. Christian women are not allowed in the houses of Jews, by law...'

'But she is...'

'Precisely, Fredo. She is and she is not. That is the difficulty that we have.'

112

My mother had, Lorenzo told me, gone to the house of Antonio Magliabechi in the Via del Corso. There she had, unwisely, dismissed the boy who was driving the carriage and told him to return for her at the same time the following day. Antonio was not at home but was attending to his business at the Medici Palace. My mother obtained admittance to the house by informing Otto that she was the wife of Gallupe Credi. Having waited for several hours, her patience exhausted, she set out, on foot, for the Jewish quarter to find the father whom she had not seen for over twenty years. It was, of course, an area of the city in which she had been raised and it was therefore with no difficulty that she eluded the various Salti, guardsmen and associated thugs who formed a loose ring about the area, prohibiting access and 'regulating' those who lived within. She was however seen by a member of the 'vigilantes', an unofficial organisation loosely linked to the Salti and encouraged by them to spy on the Jewish sector and anyone who might seek illegal entry or commerce in that part of the city. Thus she had been followed to the house of her childhood where she obtained entry with difficulty and against the protestations of a new housekeeper who of course was in ignorance of my mother's identity and, indeed, her very existence. Once she was seen to enter the house her pursuer made his way swiftly to the nearest group of Salti stationed at the far end of the street. There he informed them of a strange woman, who appeared by her dress and bearing to be a Christian, who had slipped into the Jewish sector and was, at that very moment, visiting a house not a hundred paces away.

My mother, meanwhile, had encountered considerable difficulties. When old Isaac, now totally blind, had been informed that his daughter waited upon him he replied that 'he had no daughter'. My mother's sudden forced entry to the room and her own pleading had no further effect on the old man in whom twenty years of obduracy may well have cheated a senile belief in his own false denial.

My mother's sadness was, of course, mitigated by her finding him unharmed and she allowed herself to be shown to the door by a deeply suspicious maid at which point, as it was opened, she encountered the area captain of the Salti. All this was later ascertained from the maid by Antonio Magliabechi who, on returning to his house and guessing the purpose of my mother's visit, had sent after her one of the messengers still available between the closed parts of the city. Isaac's maid had returned with this messenger to Magliabechi's house. The girl's distress when learning the truth of my mother's story was very evident particularly since she herself, on being questioned by the Salti, had repeated Isaac's direct disavowal of the woman who was now taken into custody.

Further enquiries revealed that my mother had been taken to the Stinche Prison (and here Lorenzo firmly took hold of my hand) on suspicion of prostitution. 'But,' Lorenzo told me, 'whatever the penalty *may* be for such an offence it could not be carried out today which is a city Festival.' Even while he, Lorenzo, was with us Antonio Magliabechi had made arrangements to enter the Jewish sector and speak, personally, to old Isaac. He would further arrange, on the following morning, for both Isaac and himself to attend at the Stinche Prison in order to prove my mother's true identity. The previous disownment of my mother would be blamed on Isaac's patent blindness. If any difficulties were raised by the Salti then he, Magliabechi, could be at the Pitti Palace within minutes in order to place the full facts before the Grand Duke. This would, necessarily, mean revealing the secret of my parents' wedding and, indeed, my own paternity. It *might*, Lorenzo said, affect their marriage and my own position but this was thought unlikely in view of my father's high standing and the venerable nature of the 'offence'. Even *if* Isaac remained unbending, said Lorenzo, raising an arm against my incipient objection, Antonio himself would go straight to the Stinche Prison to explain the whole story whilst, as an added safety factor, he, Lorenzo would attend at the Pitti Palace, together with Antonio's sealed note, to be placed before the Grand Duke. By this means every risk was annulled and every contingency met. The worst prospect was the disclosure of a clandestine marriage and a technical offence committed by entering the Jewish sector without a permit (which would undoubtedly have been granted, in time, had my mother's true identity been revealed).

During the detailed recital of these matters my father, who had plainly only received the most superficial information by the time of my arrival, recovered considerably. Would it not be advisable for him to go to Florence with Lorenzo? No, said Lorenzo, at present that was neither necessary nor desirable. *If* the Grand Duke required confirmation of Antonio's story then my father could be sent for, post-haste. For this purpose Mario should travel back to Florence and be available as an instant messenger. Travelling at speed, the journey to Florence took barely three hours and my father's testimony could therefore be obtained within the day. Furthermore it was obviously undesirable that I should be left alone at this time. In all it was better to trust to the influence of the great librarian whose abilities in this regard were now well proven.

Would not the patience of the Grand Duke, asked my father, be now sorely stretched by a further offence, however minor, committed by the Credi family? Undoubtedly, said Lorenzo with the first smile I had seen that day, but there were other factors at play. The last 'incident' had reawakened considerable public interest in the battle of Mongiorno, one of the only recent military successes enjoyed by the Medici family. The Grand Duke had seized upon this ground-swell in public opinion to repair his own sadly damaged popularity. Fresh stories, albeit exaggerated, had been circulated about the great battle and, indeed, today's Festival would contain a brief *opera seria* praising the Gods of valour and celebrating the fortieth anniversary of the victory (the fact that it was now forty-one was apparently unimportant). A happy result of this political contrivance was to elevate still further my father's popular standing. It was difficult to adulate a national hero on one day and to ... disgrace his wife on the next. Lorenzo finished uncomfortably and no one asked for any further elucidation.

So matters were decided. Lorenzo's confidence and the abilities of Antonio Magliabechi (which had, for me, now achieved legendary proportions) much increased my own expectations and I began to hope that this dreadful misadventure of fate would be swiftly resolved.

I was taken across the courtyard in order to meet the gigantic Otto whose monstrous face stared at me, impassive, as my hand disappeared into his distorted palm. Mario was summoned and was also introduced to the Turk whom he regarded with unalloyed horror and distaste. He was given clear instructions and, despite his evident unwillingness to do so, was despatched with Lorenzo and his companion along the road to Florence. It was late afternoon and my father and I watched them go, their three shadows lengthening across the valley, remaining visible even after they had turned the corner and begun the descent to Gallaza.

Chapter Nine

Before they left Lorenzo had taken me on one side and pressed in my hand a small bottle containing a red liquid.

'It is quite clear to me, young Fredo, that you have had little sleep for some while. Just remember that for all your natural worry and good intentions there is nothing that you can do save to ensure that you are fit and well when your mother returns home. Tonight when you go to bed (which must be *early*) you are to take the contents of this bottle. I have provided your father with a similar potion though I doubt whether he will take it. You will be unlikely to wake before tomorrow's sunrise which will bring with it, let us pray, a happy and memorable day.'

I required no urging towards bed that evening. I left my father sitting upon the terrace apparently calm at the prospect of concerted action. We embraced silently and I made my way across the darkened room to the single wooden stair. I had already prepared my candle and, as I climbed between the partitions of solid oak, its light reflected the patina of age and the English tapestries which hung from the balustrade above. Once inside my room I undressed, pulled on my nightshirt and knelt and prayed for the safety of my mother and those whose friendship now bore my confidence and hope. I climbed between the woollen covers of my couch, drank Bellini's draught, doused the candles and fell into a deep and serene sleep.

The window of my room overlooked our courtyard and it was a great commotion in that area which brought me, in part, back to my senses. At first I thought the dawn had risen but the rapid movement of the light together with the shouts below my window appeared, even to my drugged senses, as the flashing of a lantern. With great difficulty I raised myself on one elbow from which position I could hear the excited voices of Mario and my father although I could make out neither the detail nor the gist of their words. Silence was followed by darkness as both they and the lantern entered the house to the right-hand side of my window. I attempted to rise but as I did so the images of the room swam like dark water disturbed and I fell back into sleep.

When I woke it was still dark and although my first waking senses found a profound silence I was aware that my sleep had been interrupted by a terrible noise and I searched for its meaning as the blind grope for coins fallen from a bowl. I was close to sleep again when the shout jerked me into consciousness. A single word uttered at the extremity of pitch; my father beyond doubt. As I raised myself it came again, this time from beneath my window, and as it did so the light of the lantern reappeared, reflected against the ceiling and dancing like the waves. Making what haste I could I left my bed and crossed to the curtainless window from which I could see the whole of the courtyard and the gate to the road. My father was already by the gate wrestling with the latch and, as I watched, the bar came clear and the heavy gate fell in, appearing to push him backwards as the lantern swayed wildly from side to side. In that uncertain light I could see that he wore the clothes in which I had left him the night before. Plainly unsteady on his feet he grasped the corner of the door and propelled himself forwards in the direction of the road. As he did so he shouted the same word into the night and disappeared beyond the front wall of the house. In the one hand the lantern swung in sympathy with the disorder of his gait whilst in the other the muzzle of his carbine was held fixedly ahead, the stock resting on his shoulder as a man might support the carcass of a beast. I could no longer see his figure but his passage on the road could be marked by the light of the lantern still flashing erratically above the wall and moving towards the village, away from Florence.

I knew, of course, from that word precisely where he was going and even my drugged brain deduced his purpose but the reason for his rage was yet unknown to me. Had it not been for the laudanum I would immediately have deduced at least that much of the truth but now my only thought was to reach him before he himself could reach the far side of the town. My limbs remained leaden and curiously unresponsive to the necessity of action. I could find no flint with which to ignite my candle and the coincidence of darkness and near-narcosis retarded my progress to that of an infant child. Clothes could not be found. Buttons left fastened produced insurmountable barriers to fingers and brain. Shoes could not be found and the clasp of the door, itself a mere drop hinge, presented a problem of dexterity and coordination almost beyond my powers. It was in this condition that I arrived, staggering like a

117

drunk, into the wreckage of the main room in our house. Much had been broken. That which remained intact lay in disorder across the floor. In the grate a fire still burned and around it were scattered the charred remains of documents and clothes which I perceived at once to be my mother's. The acrid smell of burning and the reek of spirit alcohol pervaded the room. I became aware of a regular noise, a rat-tat-tat, without urgency or alarm, the steady methodical rhythm of the music teacher beating time. I swiftly found its source. On the floor beside the fire Lorenzo's machine demonstrated the perfect transfer of momentum beside the fragments of my mother's life.

Another sound had me starting across the room. This was the sound of an opening door, certainly that which led to the courtyard beyond the stairwell. Suddenly unafraid I approached the door of the room which had closed after my entry and pulled it aside. Framed in the outer doorway was the figure of Mario, a lantern guttering in one hand, the other still on the latch as one afraid to enter upon forbidden ground. I, of course, was framed against the candles which burnt behind me, shoeless and unbuttoned, my eyes as wild as a foal in pain.

'Mario!' I cried. At the sound he turned and fled across the courtyard, the lantern swinging by his side illuminating the stables, the still-open gates and, tethered immediately inside the courtyard, the horse which he had used on the journey to Florence. Whether it had remained in this position or whether he had even now removed it from its stall and prepared for flight I cannot say. In any event, even as I reached the house door, he was up into the saddle, the lantern placed with a servant's care upon the stone bench set against the stable wall, and he was gone into the night, the sound of hoofs disappearing along the road to Florence. Now, with some renewed control of my limbs, I struggled across the courtyard, picked up the lantern and, with growing apprehension, ran towards the village, unable to discern any light in the direction which my father had taken.

Soon I came to the road where it turned along the river, the town lying silent and dark on my right-hand side. The lantern was proving an encumbrance to speed and I placed it upon a wall close to the village square, thinking, with astonishing foresight, that it would serve to light our returning steps. Now trusting to my eyes and the light falling from a mean, early moon I plunged on breathless towards the village school.

At this point the poplars which lined the road impeded my forward vision of the houses which lay alongside. Thus I heard the sounds of conflict before I had sight of the slaughterhouse or the adjacent buildings.

First I heard my father's voice, the words unintelligible to my straining ears. I did not see him until I came within fifty paces. What I then saw occurred very quickly. My father was standing to the right-hand side of the road just inside the school gate. The lantern he had carried still burned beside him, throwing his figure into silhouette. Steadier now, and quiet, he stood with his gun raised to his shoulder. One leg was thrust forward and his head lay on the side of the stock, sighting towards the disabled wooden cart which I could now see, a dark mass at the roadside on my left. My own shout seemed to be simultaneous with the noise of the shooting.

Certainly there was more than one explosion although whether my father's musket was discharged, in truth, I cannot say. Later, so they told me, it was found to be empty of powder and shot which, of course, proves nothing. I only saw him jerk backwards through the school gates as though suddenly pulled from behind. The lantern must have been extinguished in the fall for the school yard was suddenly plunged into near darkness, the only illumination provided by a thin light proceeding from the slaughterhouse door.

I have no recollection of travelling those last fifty paces but I remember kneeling beside him and pulling his head across my lap. He was unresponsive as stone. That he was dead there was no conceivable doubt. His eyes were wide open, staring unblinking into the sky, and I felt blood coursing over my unbuttoned leggings although any sight of the wound from which it proceeded I was mercifully spared.

As I knelt there I heard shouts from the direction of the butcher's house and a further musket was discharged, although how close the ball came to my position I cannot say. I was then suddenly possessed with that stillness of mind to which I have already referred when I witnessed the attack on Giuseppe Manzini. There are those, no doubt, who will deem it incredible that a boy of fourteen years, confronted with the sudden and violent death of his father, drugged with laudanum and very probably under fire, could react with such coolness of purpose. Nevertheless it is true. I perceived, immediately, that flight was the only sensible option. For whatever reason or motive my father had died in the course of an attack on the Bomboni house. Even were I able to find the carbine, powder and shot, I had rarely used such a weapon and had but the scantest knowledge of its preparation. Even had I wished for revenge at that time – which I did not – the wherewithal was plainly beyond me and any attempt to continue my father's actions was necessarily doomed to failure. Acting precisely in accordance with these

119

considerations I returned the lifeless head to the earth of the school yard and, pressing my awkward frame into the smallest possible size, I rose and ran for the cover of the school buildings. No sound came from the butcher's premises, neither voices nor firing, and within seconds I was in the deep shadow of the school and concealed behind the corner which was formed by the buttress of the new wall. I did not look back but continued past the silent buildings to the furthest extremity of the school fence. When I had been in daily attendance I had not infrequently carried out errands by leaving in this direction, climbing the low fence and thus arriving immediately at the outskirts of the village through which it was possible to come to that point on the river bank where Giuseppe had nearly died. My bare feet made no sound on either the compacted earth of the streets or the cobbles of the main square which I crossed as closely as possible to the lower buildings whose eaves provided deep shadow now more sharply in contrast with the first signs of approaching dawn. I reached my discarded lantern, still guttering in the morning breeze. Soon it would be of no assistance in the gathering light and I abandoned it in favour of unhindered speed.

I arrived at our stable block, heaving and quivering like a shot bird. Despite my physical condition I was still in control of my senses and, on the journey from the village, had formulated a clear plan. I immediately entered the house and climbed the stairs to my room. I believed that I had no time to change my clothes but, with the haste of desperation, I strapped on my strongest boots and took up the German travelling cloak which my father had brought from Brunswick. I had a small supply of money, accumulated presents from Lorenzo and Patrick which I thrust into the pocket of the cloak. Returning to the stables, I saddled our piebald mare, the oldest, slowest and least reliable of our horses, and scrambled onto her back. She was, at first, unwillling to move at all but when on the road she turned instinctively and positively in the direction of the village, having taken no other route in the last ten years of her inactive and contemplative life. With growing desperation and anger I sawed at the reins, locking her head into a direction totally opposed to that in which she continued to proceed. Finally she halted and then, with stubborn resignation, retraced her steps towards the stable, where only the most violent physical and verbal exhortations drove her past the gate. Thus I was borne, deserted, blood-stained, and close to exhaustion slowly and with immeasurable reluctance along the road to Florence.

BOOK TWO

Florence

Chapter Ten

I know it sounds harsh, but I did not grieve for my father. Not even then. Of far greater import were the whereabouts and, indeed, the fate of my mother. The joys and achievements of my childhood, such as they were, were shared with Lorenzo and with Patrick.

There was, of course, an unbridgeable gulf between our ages; when he met his death my father was nigh on sixty years of age and he lacked the wild catholic enthusiasm of both my mentors. That he was *their* friend speaks much to his credit but of the strengths and virtues which earned that friendship and respect I saw but little. When I expressed this view, some years later, I was roundly chastised by Lorenzo who chronicled, with academic precision, my father's qualities, strengths and achievements upon which, so Lorenzo maintained, lasting reverence should be based. Well, perhaps. Yet even on that road to Florence I could not ignore or forget the fact that the circumstances of his death presupposed an indifference to my own welfare and safety. Of course I have forgiven him and, indeed, forgave him then, but grief is not susceptible to the dictates of rationality, however generous and profound.

The horror of what I had witnessed and, indeed, what I still feared pressed upon me like swaddling clothes and I hunched into the recesses of my cloak as a child searches for refuge in some forgotten warmth. The weather itself had turned, the blistering heat of summer suddenly replaced by a robust businesslike breeze that beat among the Tuscan hills. When the dawn was finally complete it revealed a high, grey sky.

The reek of dried blood now rose from my inner clothes and my misery was steadily increased by the aimless plodding motion of the mare, her head lowered towards the dust of the road. I had never ridden in this direction. Whilst I assumed that the road ran clear to Florence I had no knowledge of its deviations nor was I aware of the towns and villages through which it passed. Even distance meant little to me. I had, of course, been informed of the general nature of the journey and listened to Lorenzo congratulate himself upon a 'hard ride, three hours at most'. If, however, that description related to a brisk trot then my present progress would barely achieve the city in a full day. Nor did there appear to be the slightest prospect of improvement. If anything the mare's ambulatory pace was slackening as the distance from her manger steadily increased. I was contemplating abandoning the horse and proceeding upon my own feet when we came to a small hamlet which I now know to be barely four miles from San Casciano. Here there were signs of life as the peasantry began the business of the day. There was a small inn and, as luck would have it, an ostler feeding three travel horses tethered to a rail outside its stables. He was a lad little older than myself and the natural empathy of youth together with a substantial financial bribe persuaded him to add my mare to his charges. Having plainly regarded the northern boundary of San Casciano as the ancients perceived the edge of the world, my mare relished her meal with the satisfaction which attended the discovery of the Indies. Thereafter she contemplated new pasture with the joy of the explorer and, indeed, became almost skittish on the downhill paths.

None of these harmless analogies occurred to me at the time. My central preoccupation remained, of course, the events which had taken place in Florence. Plainly Mario had brought bad news; perhaps the worst. Even the contemplation of such a possibility brought childish tears to my eyes and I sank still further into the folds of my cloak. But why had it affected my father thus? Why the attack on the Bombonis? I confess that the obvious explanation did not occur to me. Either my poor brain was shocked to such a degree that I did not comprehend or it rejected an explanation so manifestly fraught with evil possibility.

After a further hour we came to the village of Gallaza and passed the spot, I do not doubt, where my father had struck Pasto Bomboni many months before. Soon the road began to climb again towards a line of hills beyond which, if my best assumptions were correct, lay the valley of the Arno and Florence. I was wrong. On reaching the first summit, further empty acres of Tuscany stretched out before me.

Notwithstanding my own position I was, even then, moved to pity by the miserable condition of the people and the land which I passed. Entire hamlets appeared to have been abandoned. The shutters and doors of the houses hung loose and jerked to and fro in the gusting wind. People on the road begged from me although my own situation must have appeared powerless enough to all but the most corrupted sight.

It was not until I was well down from the hills and practically at the next ridge that I realised I was being followed. The noise of my own plodding had exercised a mesmeric effect on my brain, particularly as we had traversed the level bottom of the valley which had encouraged a positively anaesthetic evenness of tempo. Now that we climbed the mare's pace began to stutter and I realised that I was not travelling alone. Unwilling to turn my head, partly through apprehension and partly as a result of the torpor which now governed my spirits, I nonetheless encouraged my horse to a swifter ascent. As though in mimicry the following hoofbeats also increased in timing and volume. Further speed was impossible and, if violence was to follow, not wishing to receive an attack from the rear I reined in my horse which required little encouragement to become entirely motionless. My pursuer, perhaps surprised by the speed of my stopping, now rapidly drew alongside and also came to rest.

My worst imaginings immediately became flesh. The man's face which looked down on me with unmistakably evil intent contained two quite different sides. The right-hand closer to me was that of any Tuscan peasant: a broad dark cheekbone set below a small black eye and alongside the angular slightly flaring Tuscan nose. The other side was scarred to the point of disintegration. The existence, or otherwise, of his left eye was concealed with a patch whilst the cheekbone and nose fell away quite flat like the side of butter which has been left lying on the churn. That part of his mouth pulled suddenly downwards to a jawbone the line of which was interrupted by an ugly step halfway along its ridge.

In normal circumstances such a face coupled with the malice that shone from the right eye would have filled me with terror. Now, however, I had reached the end of my sensible reactions. I had become base metal without resonance or refraction. He spoke first.

'Where are we going then, in such a fucking hurry?'

I regarded him with eyes as dead as stones. 'Florence,' I said without animation.

'Florence, eh? Well, well, and fucking nearly there too.'

I said nothing.

'Florence, you say. And what do I say? I say to myself young men going to Florence are going for a reason. Now, says I to myself, what can that reason be? And I thinks about it and I thinks maybe he's going to buy something. What with? I ask myself and I answers myself straight away, just like that. Money! That's what he's got. Florins and crowns is what he's got. And then I say to myself, what's going to happen if he doesn't get to Florence? And I say to myself, if he doesn't get to Florence he won't be able to spend his money! So he won't need it at all. So who better to take care of it than me?'

He was wearing a rough peasant's smock overlaid with leather and whilst he was talking his hand reached into folds on the left side and reappeared with a knife of the kind normally employed in trimming cloth. Holding this between us, pointed directly at my own stomach, he said, 'So I says to you, I says, hand it over at once unless you want your fucking guts all over that horse's head.'

It was not fear that rendered me immobile it was simply resignation. The terrible affairs of the night, the conviction which I now held that my mother was dead and the exhaustion of the never-ending journey had reduced me almost to stupor. My reaction surprised him and he looked at me with his good eye narrowed.

'No answer, eh? Too tired to talk, eh? Too tired to hand over the money? Well, let's help ourselves then.' So saying he leaned across and pulled open the front of my cloak. As he did so he recoiled, instinctively causing his own horse to shift impatiently below him.

'Dear Mother of Mary! Now what's happened to you?' Then after a pause, 'It looks like someone's been at you already.' Why I answered I do not know. None was required and safety lay in silence, but I said, 'The blood is my father's, he was shot this morning.'

He looked at me for a moment as if in disbelief.

'What's that? Shot? This morning? Where did this happen? We don't *shoot* people on this road.'

'He was not shot on the road he was shot in San Casciano.'

'In San Casciano? This morning! Who was your father, lad?'

For a reason I cannot explain, I told him. I did not simply tell him of my father's identity and the circumstances of his death but I told him that my mother was in peril in Florence and that, in a way I could not understand, the two were connected. As I spoke he replaced the knife in his clothing and listened with both hands on his saddle, shaking his head as though in disbelief. When I had finished he continued to move his broken face from side to side, muttering, 'Credi, Bomboni, Bomboni, Credi.' Then he looked at me, 'You're the son of Gallupe Credi. Well, well. Going to Florence. Well, well, well.' Then his mood changed. He looked up at the sun and said, 'It is well past noon. If you are to get to

Florence in daylight on that bag of worms we must make haste. I can come with you to the top of the valley.' As he spoke he once again reached within the folds of his cloak and swiftly withdrew his hand. Our conversation had released my leaden state and now I started backwards, expecting the production of a further weapon. Instead he brought out a linen bag, rummaged inside and produced a piece of sausage which he handed to me. After this came a stoppered flagon which he also passed into my unresisting hand. I did not want to eat but I did so at his insistence. The bottle contained spirit alcohol as rough as I have ever had. The warmth and power of the liquor surprised me and, although we journeyed in silence, my head sang and the desperate misery which had oppressed me now lifted as we climbed towards the ridge of hills.

Before we had gone a hundred paces my new companion reined in and brought us both to a stop. He had become, suddenly, tense, his body raised in the stirrups and his head set like a hunting dog's towards the bend in the road ahead. Almost immediately I heard the sound of a horse hard-ridden towards us and increasing rapidly in volume. To our right the hillside fell away from the road towards a small copse of young poplar. My companion hesitated no more. Grasping the mare's bridle and driving his heels into the flanks of his own horse he propelled us both into the shade of the trees. Scarcely had he done so when the rider passed unseen behind us and the sound of his hoofbeats swiftly receded along the road to Gallaza. When they had quite died away, to my relief he led us back onto the road and we continued our journey.

The clouds now did little to conceal the heat, which became thick and oppressive, heralding the storm. After a further hour we reached the top of the valley and my destination lay before me. At this point my new companion stopped his horse and said, 'There you are, Florence, I can go no further but the road is safe from here. Take care in that city, it is full of thieves,' and then, smiling at the irony, he added, 'In uniform.'

'Thank you,' I said. 'Who ...' But he shook his head and indicated that I should begin on the downward road. I know that he sat watching me for some time, his wide sleeves flapping in the insistent wind but it was not until I reached the first houses that I turned and saw that he had gone: and so I made my entry into Florence; city of Michelangelo and Galileo, Brunelleschi and Donatello, the Bargello, the pincers and the rack.

Chapter Eleven

I was awed by its deceit. The perfect harmony of colours when viewed from the hills was unaffected by the greyness of the sky; rather they became blurred like paint on a palette persistently overlaid and softened by the workings of the brush. The dust-green and red of the landscape blended with the ochre and terracotta of the roofs and parchment walls as though nature herself had worked the canvas, haphazard and in perfect order. Within the spectrum of colours the symmetry of the roofs provided sharp emphasis for the cupola of the Duomo and the pencil-thin folly of the bell tower probed the sky like an accusation. Even now it takes the breath from my old body like a cunning whore and, for that reason, I rarely even look. It is always a fraud, such beauty. Our senses are gripped by the courtesan whilst our reason and our pockets are violated by the bully and the pimp.

I entered the city itself by the Porta Romana. Before arriving at that famous gate I had been conscious of the increasing numbers of people crossing and recrossing the road as though engaged in some festival dance. As I entered, the press became alarming. Horses and carriages gave no guarantee of progress and my own beast, unwilling to move even on the open road, remained rooted for minutes on end in the face of the unyielding crowd. I was struck, immediately, by the range of costumes. I had been concerned lest my own condition, rough and bloodied as I appeared, would call attention to my presence before I could reach my goal. In the face of such diversity this notion now appeared laughable. Every form of costume was in evidence. Some men wore the *lucco*. Others peasant jerkins and leggings. Still more had the absurd ballooning trousers and stockings said to be popular in Northern Europe. Many women wore clothes (or rather did not wear clothes) in a way which, had they gone out in public in San Casciano, would have invited the hurling of stones.

128

In the piazza beyond the Porta Romana all manner of occupations were in progress. To the right-hand side there ran a substantial wall broken at intervals by iron gateways ornately worked and closed against entrance. Through the bars I could make out long formal gardens, striped with gravel paths and punctuated with fountains in play. Along the wall were set out a multitude of stalls. Many carried vegetables and fruits perhaps newly arrived through the very gate that I had entered. Other stalls displayed leather goods, carpets and clothes dyed to every conceivable pitch and colour. Around these the crowd was thickest. Of those who were not selling many begged, others performed dances, played instruments or sang songs whilst their collaborators collected in wooden bowls. Two I saw performing prodigious feats of strength bending iron bars or shattering rocks against their sweating foreheads.

I had been further concerned about the smell of blood that hung about me like a pall. This I feared might draw attention to my presence and even mark me as a criminal, inviting arrest. All such anxieties were groundless. The stench which pervaded the city allowed for no individual contribution. Everywhere the drains ran in the streets. Those which had previously been conducted underground to the banks of the Arno had long since been blocked and, wanting any system of maintenance or care, now burst upwards through the stones, bringing with them the reek of sewage and the certainty of plague. Beggar children, soaked in effluent, their eyes wide with supplication, pulled tirelessly upon my cloak, encouraged by my continued immobility.

Obeying the directions of a coachman by whose side I had been marooned for several minutes, I crossed the Piazza and turned into the Via Romana, making my way, so I was informed, towards the great Ponte Vecchio. As I passed the great façade of the Pitti Palace I observed columns of Medici guardsmen drawn up on the Piazza, their backs to the road, motionless as herons in their summer cloaks.

Thus I came to the beginning of the Ponte Vecchio and, obeying the insructions I had been given, turned to my right and followed the river towards a narrow secondary bridge over which, I was told, my unwilling horse could make its way. The Arno was now to my left and initially obscured by houses for a distance of some hundred paces. Thereafter the buildings of the Lungarno continued only on the right-hand side. Dilapidation was everywhere apparent. Evidently some attempt had been made to clear refuse from the vicinity of the Palace; here, however, it littered the streets in profusion. Piles of household rubbish were augmented by commercial waste into mountains of rotting matter, some of sufficient age to have sprouted their own growths of fungal decay. Despite the apparent crowding on the streets here many of the houses appeared deserted. Doors had fallen or been taken off their hinges while shutters hung aside as though in obscure gesture towards the passers-by. In many instances the rendering on the walls had gone, revealing the rough stonework beneath.

By the time I had crossed the bridge and reached the great church of Santa Croce, I was long past the seduction of art or architecture and it was with the relief of Ulysses that I turned into the Via del Corso and came, at length, to the house whose description had entered my child-hood like a benign fable which renders impotent the fears of the night. The house carried no number or sign but I would have known it by instinct alone. In fact my height on horseback took me to the level of the lower windows. Through these I could see bookcases of red cedar and, with a feeling of warmth and happiness, I heard, through the open casement, the raised voice of Lorenzo Bellini.

Confident that my horse would remain stationary wherever she stopped I tumbled from the saddle, scrambled up the three steps and beat upon the door. Within seconds it was opened and, using my final reserves of energy, I fell forward into the arms of Pasto Bomboni.

Chapter Twelve

The face which I saw when I first woke I did not know. And yet it was familiar. For all its grotesque moulding it contained no threat. The sharp eyes which gazed down either side of a monstrous nose seemed to contain nothing but compassionate enquiry. Even as the features came into focus I saw them smile as though in relief. The face then left my field of vision to be replaced, almost immediately, by that of Lorenzo Bellini. By that time my brain had recollected and recorded much more of my condition. The room was darkened but the ceiling above my head was white and bordered by an ornate architrave. The bed in which I lay was warm and comfortable. Linen sheets pressed against my chin and, as I moved my legs, I felt the soft constriction of a flannel nightshirt. Indeed, my physical well-being did much to mitigate the anxiety which flooded across my consciousness. As Lorenzo smiled down at me I said, 'Has he gone?'

'Bomboni? Yes, he has gone these last five hours. I think you fright-ened him as much as he did you. Indeed, my young friend, you frightened us all. When first we removed your travelling cloak we thought you had come by some terrible injury.'

'Why was he...?'

'Why was he here. It is a long story, Fredo. But first we must consider your physical needs. I suspect you are very thirsty. Here, drink this.'

He was, of course, quite right. Apart from a quantity of Acquavita, I had drunk nothing since leaving San Casciano. I raised myself upon one elbow and gulped down the liquid which he presented to me. It tasted faintly of oranges and, I detected, some herbal ingredient, slightly bitter to the smell.

'It is the laudanum I gave him which produces so great a thirst,' said Lorenzo, 'but I sensed also the reek of liquor rising from an empty stomach.' He was not talking to me but to the other occupant of our room who possessed the extraordinary face I had first seen on waking.

Now I could see this figure more clearly in the light of a candelabra which burnt on a desk close to a shuttered window. Of course I knew at once who he was and I felt, even then, a sense of uneasy surprise at the accuracy of my own previous imaginings, a fact I now attribute to the vivid cogency of my mother's description. 'I think you have never met Antonio Magliabechi,' said Lorenzo, 'but no doubt you recognise him well enough.' My future master made his crooked way across the room and took my hand, now free of the cup which Lorenzo was refilling.

I drank a second cup and, as I did so, the door of the room opened and the giant Otto entered carrying a tray. A plate of steaming tortelloni was placed before me together with sliced sausage and bread. I had little appetite but Lorenzo said, 'You must eat, Fredo, even a little. Do not be afraid of it. This ugly fellow makes the best tortelloni in Florence.'

I ate more than a little. As I started my appetite returned and, with the food and drink, my resolution increased once more. 'Lorenzo,' I said, 'where is my mother?' From the expression on his face I had no doubt of the answer and I said, 'She's dead, isn't she, Lorenzo?'

He nodded his head and said, 'Yes, Fredo, yes, she is.'

I found breathing very difficult for a short while but curiously felt no desire for the comfort of physical contact which he offered by his proximity and the grasp which he kept upon my arm. After a short while I said, 'How did she die?'

'Do you wish...?'

'Yes, Lorenzo, I would like to know the whole story, please.'

So I learnt the story of my mother's death, sitting in that warm bed, my friend and my master beside me, as a child might be told a tale before sleeping.

Some of it I knew, of course, from Lorenzo's visit to San Casciano the day before. This he recounted, laying some emphasis on the arrangements which had been made to secure my mother's release on the day following the Carnival, that day, indeed, which had just passed in such awful circumstances.

'You must remember, Fredo,' he said, 'that whilst Antonio was aware that your mother had been arrested (he was informed by Isaac's maid) he did not know the identity of the officer by whom she had been taken. The maid herself was in ignorance of this matter, nor did it seem of any particular consequence.

'Whilst I was with you at San Casciano, Antonio, as arranged, went to the Jewish quarter and saw your grandfather. Isaac has now reached that stage in his life where pretence and reality are a blended mixture into which he dips at random, producing haphazard convictions as to both truth and time. It is now his general belief that he never owned a daughter. Thus, for him, the pretence so often expressed has become a reality. Even as Antonio explained the terrible dangers which were involved he could comprehend neither their substance nor their relevance to him. Plainly, his support could not be obtained and so it had been agreed, you will remember, that Antonio would go to the Stinche Prison at least to ensure that no action was taken against your mother in any event before he was able to place the entire matter before the Grand Duke.

'Perceiving no advantage in delay, he left Isaac's house and made his way through the city, across the Arno to the prison which lies well to the south beyond the Porta Romana. As you are aware, it was Festival day in Florence which causes great chaos and congestion in the streets. There is also, I fear, much drunken violence and it was necessary for Antonio to take a long, circuitous route in order to achieve his destination at all. When he arrived at the Stinche he was admitted, after some difficulties, to the rooms of the chief jailer.

'He had determined, if possible, to see Vittoria before taking action, in order to ensure that his assumptions as to her journey were correct. The jailer informed him, however, with some reluctance, that your mother had *already* been taken to the Bargello. Of course, Antonio pointed out, immediately, that it was a festival day and, accordingly, no sentence or punishment could be inflicted. "Not inflicted but passed," said the jailer, and so it transpired.

'It is apparently necessary even in these days of official brutality for sentence on some edicts to be formally passed in the Bargello. Since your mother continued to insist that she was Isaac's daughter (which would have been a defence to the crime charged) the law requires her to be present at the sentence to state her case however futile that may be. Indeed, in her particular case Antonio was told that the defence was regarded as especially absurd since, while maintaining her relationship with Isaac on the one hand, Vittoria resolutely refused to give any details whatsoever of her present way of life, means of support, family or acquaintanceship. Antonio demanded to be told when this sentence was to be passed and was informed that the hearing of your mother's trial had been fixed for three o'clock.

'At that moment the time wanted several minutes of three but, the jailer told him, there were frequently long delays in the lists, particularly during the afternoon. Antonio, therefore, left the Stinche and made what desperate speed he could, against the crush of people outside the Pitti Palace, towards the Ponte Vecchio which provides the shortest route to the Bargello. As he left the jailer he had received a piece of information which caused him even greater fear and concern. The jailer observed that the particular officer engaged in this case frequently managed to have his cases heard early in the list through a mixture of threat and charm. "Typical," he said, "of a butcher's son." When Antonio asked for the name of this captain the jailer said, "Bomboni, the bastard".'

Lorenzo continued to tell the story whilst Antonio Magliabechi, my future master, sat watching us in the half-darkness beyond the candles. It had plainly been agreed that Lorenzo should be the narrator but I could sense the affinity between them and satisfaction at the accuracy of the recounting. Even now I recall its details as though he were rehearsing those events beside me.

Magliabechi took nearly half an hour to reach the Ponte Vecchio, his stunted crooked body no match for the excesses of a Florentine festival. When some fifty paces short of the great bridge he was aware of commotion and excitement amongst the crowd. The reason for it spread swift as rumour.

'Some whore's thrown 'erself off the bridge. Been sentenced to 'undred lashes for fucking some Jew. God, the Salti are mad.'

In the additional crush my master had been pushed to one side towards the Lungarno and from here he could see the figure of Pasto Bomboni followed by a number of Salti running along the broad riverside street towards the end of the houses from which an unimpeded view of the river could be obtained.

'I am afraid,' said Lorenzo, 'that she has not been found. Since her hands were bound she had no chance of swimming and the river, in any event, is in unusual spate. (She leapt from the centre arch of the bridge having, we think, feigned sickness to avoid the Salti on her left-hand side.) Sentence had been passed only slightly late, her partial account having been rejected. One hundred lashes is the standard sentence for a prostitute found with a Jew. Few are so found and they seldom survive.'

I was looking at Lorenzo with my eyes wide in disbelief.

'But Pasto Bomboni must have known . . .'

'Of your mother's identity? Yes, of course he must have known. He must have known that the woman he arrested was the wife of Gallupe

Credi against whom, of course, he bore an intense personal grudge. Your mother's refusal to reveal her true identity effectively disclosed to him the whole truth. Here was his opportunity to wreak revenge upon your family whilst upholding this wicked law. Your mother has foiled him in that respect.'

'So that is why my father went to the Bombonis.'

'Yes, Fredo, we know of all this now. Here is another gigantic twist of fate. You remember that we brought Mario with us to act as a messenger? He has a sister, married to a leather worker who lives just outside the Porta Romana. He asked if he could stay with her and, since it is easily reached and on the road to San Casciano, we agreed that he should do so. He had, in any event, taken a quite irrational aversion to Otto. When Antonio learnt the terrible news of your mother's death he returned here immediately to await my arrival from San Casciano. I did not arrive, with Otto, until after dark and we decided, of course, that the news should be borne to you and your father *by us*. We determined that we should first ascertain all the known facts including whether your mother's body had been recovered. This morning we scoured the city for news and, finding little, Otto and I set out on the road intending to gather Mario on our way. When we arrived at his sister's house we learnt that Mario, by some infernal act of fate, had been in Florence for the Carnival (against our express instructions) and had witnessed your mother's leap from the bridge. He also had identified Pasto Bomboni as her captor. Returning to his sister's he had agonised on the course which he should adopt and had finally decided, fatally, to bear the news himself. Thus much his sister told us but, seeing the evident alarm in our faces, she lied as to the time of his departure maintaining, entirely falsely, that he had made efforts to find us in Florence that morning. She told us, indeed, that he had barely departed on the road towards Siena. We therefore believed that he could be stopped before arriving at his destination. I instructed her husband to ride non-stop to overtake Mario whilst I returned here, immediately, to inform Antonio that there was, now, yet a further witness to Bomboni's conduct. How the man missed you on the road I cannot guess.'

'He did come past me but I was hiding. I believed him to be a bandit.'

Lorenzo raised his hands into the air. 'It is a truly diabolical list of coincidences. In any event, when I returned here I found Pasto Bomboni with Antonio. *He* had just arrived, alone, in order to "discuss" the position in which we were now placed. He was, at least, entirely frank about his own predicament.

135

'Your mother alive and punished was his greatest security against discovery. She *could not* reveal his part in the matter without disclosing her own identity and that of her family. He knew she would do no such thing and thus neither disclosure nor revenge could follow. Your mother's *death* was, however, a different matter. Her disappearance from San Casciano was bound to cause enquiry. For the purposes of that enquiry he had, effectively, lost his best conspirator. It was important to cover his ground as much as possible and, for that reason, he returned to Isaac's house in the Jewish quarter in order to "speak" to the maid. From her (she was by this time quite petrified) he learned of Antonio's visit to the house or rather the visit of a deformed hunchback who had enquired after "the lady" and had spent some considerable time with her master. Bomboni knows, of course, of Antonio's relationship with your father and immediately realised the danger which he, Bomboni, was in. He had, after all, knowingly arrested and accused the wife of a Hero of Florence (albeit a Jewess) and stood silent whilst her identity was unsuccessfully explored. If this was discovered, it would inevitably lead to his summary dismissal and, at very least, a substantial and possibly fatal period upon the rack.

'All of this he explained to us with the utmost candour. Indeed the minute dissection of the risks and the cold calculation of his own position were the most frightening things about his behaviour. Of remorse, regret or contrition there was none. Having set out the dangers to which *he* was now exposed he stated, quite blandly, that "it is therefore, of course, essential that no word of this is breathed by anyone". At this point both Antonio and I became very angry and indicated that we had no intention of doing anything to save his skin. He then looked at us with an expression as close to demonic as that which I ever wish to see and said, "Not *my* skin, you old fools, but your friend Credi. Since *he* is a Hero of Florence I have taken the trouble to look him up in your precious library at San Lorenzo — Godawful shit-hole that it is — but it obviously has its uses. Gallupe Credi was not married to any Jewess, he was married at Santa Maria Nuova at Cotona on May 15th, 1662, to a Christian girl called Ballinari. If that was the Jew bitch who jumped from the bridge then our Hero of Florence was never married at all. He has been living in mortal sin. What is more, even if he were prepared to expose himself to get at me what about his son, fat Fredo the fucking prodigy? Nice little bastard he would make with all that it entails. You see, my crookbacked friend, only *you* can possibly identify the whore we arrested (now alas gone for ever) as the wife of Gallupe Credi. Even

136

that, I fancy, would require the corroboration of your black pig of a manservant. How do I know that? I'll tell you. If she had come to *you* then *you* would never have let her go near the Jewish sector in that way because *you* could have used your fucking influence to get her in there anyway. Just like you did to get that maid out. No, you weren't here when she arrived. I would bet a bar of gold to a whore's knickers that the only person who saw her in this house was that arsehole Turk. Turks in Florence, so they say, make pretty bad witnesses particularly when their tongues have been slit down the middle. You don't have to tell me I'm right about that, I can see it in your ugly face. You need the evidence of our old hero boy or his son. *They've* got to get to Florence along a very dangerous road."

'Well, Fredo, I was outraged by this speech and I began to shout at him, unforgivable, I know. It was then that we heard the knocker on the door and you made your entry into the proceedings. As I have said, your arrival, considering the very last words he had spoken, gave Pasto Bomboni a very nasty shock. He became even more concerned when we immediately pulled back your cloak (to look for any possible injury) and found you to be saturated in blood.

'Irrational though it was we all associated your condition with his last threat, including Otto, who had heard most of our conversation with Bomboni. Bomboni realised immediately the conclusion that *Otto* had reached and, what is more, that Otto was about to kill him. He may have become a Christian zealot, our Turkish pirate, but he still carries a toledo at his belt. As he removed it and advanced on Bomboni I can say quite honestly I have never seen anything more terrifying. Nor, I think, had Bomboni, for he backed away down the library screaming that he was innocent of any attack on you. As he went he kept hauling books from the shelves and hurling them at Otto. Most of them missed but those which struck him merely bounced from him without discernible effect. Fortunately for Bomboni the library, as I think you know, forms a circle at the foot of the house. By the time they reappeared beneath the stairwell I had ascertained that you were unharmed, at least in the body. It was necessary to demonstrate this to Otto who, by this time, had Bomboni by the throat and was about to slit open his stomach.

'I think Otto received the news of your well-being with mixed feelings and I also think it is the last time in your life that Bomboni will be praying for your good health. Once he was released, and perceiving that he was in no further danger, however, he reverted to his evil self. To the warnings he had given he added the threat to boil Otto into *mumia* and then left the house. You, my dear Fredo, had been unconscious through it all, not surprising, in view of the catastrophes which had occurred.'

Of course I felt nothing. The first effect of grief is to stun, to anaesthetise the senses. With my hand still held tightly in Lorenzo's grasp I lay back and closed my eyes. I suspect that his potions contained more than water and fruits for I slept then and subsequently without nightmares to augment the destitution of my existence.

I have discovered, many times, that pain is essential to the process of grief. It is the outward manifestation of our healing. Slowly it came in waves and tides, beating and then receding in the face of the flat immovable rocks of normality, the stucco ceiling, the white walls, the dark lustre of oak furniture and the coming and going of Otto, silent through both sympathy and necessity. Lorenzo had prescribed bed-rest for a week but, within four days, I was around the house with something of the curiosity of youth. Generally, however, I kept to my room, eating from a tray and receiving visits from both Lorenzo and Antonio who administered to the mind with the skill of surgeons. Within two weeks I was able to formulate plans and to recognise, once again, my present position as part of a wider perspective.

Lorenzo had left to spend four days in Pisa and had broken the journey at San Casciano. By the time he returned, twenty days after my arrival, I was strong enough to discuss the state of our affairs with a measure of rationality. After dinner we sat beside the great window overlooking the canal, where my father had once sat long ago, the circle of light as warm to the senses as the soft autumn air. Lorenzo took wine and gave us his account of the news from the town of my childhood, now, for me, a place of grim foreboding.

'Fortunately,' he told us, 'the Bombonis are as unpopular as ever. The killing of your father is thought to relate to the incident at Gallaza and there are some, the Prefect included, who remember the attack on Giuseppe Manzini. It is widely thought that the Bombonis were responsible for some grossly provoking act the nature and truth of which has died with your father. No proof is possible as to whether your father's gun had been discharged. By the time it was found in the morning it was quite cold and, although there was evidence of powder, this could well have been the residue of age. For this reason coupled with the place at which the shooting occurred and the fact that your father had clearly been drinking Acquavita, no charges are likely against any of the Bombonis, although they remain under suspicion and unable to travel. Alessandro has, of course, attempted to maintain that it was his wife and Nicola who were armed with the carbines and this has caused, I gather, certain family dissent. Given these limited assumptions, it has been decided that there should be no denigration of your father's memory. He has been buried in the village church and it is proposed that there should be a service commemorating his memory as befits a Hero of Tuscany.

'The absence of yourself and your mother is causing, of course, widespread puzzlement and some concern. *You* were seen running through the town after the shooting and the general view is that you are both stricken with grief and have sought refuge in some holy place. (Which, in a way, you have.) The house and land have come under the jurisdiction of the Prefecture who will, I gather, continue that role for a year when all will be sold, the expenses paid, and the resulting funds placed in trust (the interest being applied in the municipal good, a surprisingly sensible arrangement). It is clear, however, that the time has now come to decide what steps should be taken in relation to Pasto Bomboni. Before you speak, Fredo, may I point out one salient matter which may not have occurred to anyone. Pasto does not know of the existence of Mario or, more important, that Mario is aware of the link between Pasto and Vittoria's death. He believes, moreover, that the only people who can incriminate him are the two of you, Otto and, possibly, Isaac's Jewish maid although she, of course, knows of Vittoria's identity only by hearsay and conjecture. We all know him to be an evil and cruel man. He is also becoming a powerful and ambitious one. It may already have occurred to him that his problems will be solved not only by your mutual interest in silence (that, after all, may change at any time) but by your total silence, the silence of the grave. That factor, in itself, would argue in favour of immediate disclosure of what you know to the Chief Magistrate, no matter how dreadful the consequences may be. Ultimately, of course, Fredo, the choice must lie with you.'

I spoke with some vehemence. 'I want *all* to be revealed! I want Pasto Bomboni to be . . .' I was interrupted by the soft voice of the librarian.

'May I,' he said, 'offer a word of advice?' I looked at him, keenly. Since my arrival in the house he had said little, confining his remarks largely to solicitations and news, in the most general terms, of the city and its doings. Now it was as though I heard him for the first time. 'It is *only* advice. There is a substantial, reasoning, brain on your young shoulders to which I would not presume to dictate. Let us, however, consider the position with care. First, if we reveal the truth of the matter

139

we *may* not be believed. Even if believed we may not have sufficient proof to establish Vittoria's identity. As Bomboni points out so elegantly the evidence of a heathen Turk, albeit a reformed heathen Turk, is not the best evidence in Jesuit Florence. But even if our evidence is accepted and believed in its entirety it does not necessarily mean the undoing of Bomboni. He is now an established and feared captain in the Salti. If he is clever (and there is no reason whatsoever to suppose that he is not), then he will maintain a simple fiction. *Of course,* he will say, the woman did *resemble* Vittoria Credi (although he has not himself lived in San Casciano for some three years). Furthermore it *never* occurred to him that the woman *was* Vittoria Credi. After all, she *denied* it by maintaining that she was a Jew's daughter. Vittoria Credi was no Jewess. At least, he never believed her to be so until this evidence was produced. Not, you understand, that he believed that this woman *was* the Jew's daughter. Quite the reverse. But he would *never* have believed that Vittoria Credi, the wife of Gallupe Credi could possibly, dishonestly, maintain the story that she did. So incredible was the idea that he had not even thought fit to mention the passing resemblance when the case came before the Bargello. He now realises, with the priceless benefit of hindsight, that it would have been wiser to do so. However, he is only relatively inexperienced in his rank and would certainly learn from this unfortunate incident. He may well mention that the Jew Isaac, himself, denied that he had a daughter of any kind. Were he to argue such a case I think it very unlikely that we would establish against him anything other than the merest suspicion. Of course it may be put to him that he had a motive. Gallupe Credi was, after all, the man who struck Bomboni at Gallaza. However, the answer he will give to *that* is simple. "Certainly, after Gallaza I bore him some ill-will. However *my* activities were entirely vindicated by the Grand Duke himself. What is more it was the impulsive action of Gallupe Credi which resulted, directly, in my own appointment as a Captain in the Salti. Thus, from the wildest of acts, good consequences may flow and, contrary to any allegations of ill-will, I regard the whole matter with the equanimity of spirit related to happy outcomes however unforeseen."

'I do not suggest that he will put it in those terms but that will be the gist of the message. This man is cunning as a wolf. If these responses have occurred to my innocent brain then Pasto Bomboni will have them engraved on his heart. Furthermore, the last person to see your mother was Otto. Even he barely knows her by sight having previously seen her only fleetingly in Florence. Who knows whether her appearance, by the time she arrived at the Jewish quarter, was not different? Any official enquiry authorised by Cosimo or his mother will readily accept the possibility of female artifice particularly when it is associated with what was, by all accounts, a clandestine meeting.

'Thus we establish that this was, indeed, the wife of Gallupe Credi. We *may* establish that she was the daughter of Isaac the Jew but we will almost certainly *not* establish that Pasto Bomboni knew her to be either. The disadvantages of revealing all, however, are incalculable. At present Gallupe has died a revered and stainless hero of Florence. His wife, whilst missing, will always enjoy the reflection of that glory. We cannot deny that both of them were guilty of a deceit both against the Church and, in so far as Gallupe was a public figure, against the people of Florence. The deceit that *they wished* to maintain now dies with them as they would have wished. If we embark on disclosure we will either reveal that deceit to the world or, worse still, establish that the *Christian* wife of Gallupe Credi was, for a reason best known to herself, visiting elderly Jews in a forbidden area of the city. In those circumstances her refusal to own her identity will be seen as the final proof of impropriety. She will therefore die dishonoured.

'As to *you*, Fredo, your well-being is, I accept, furthest from your thoughts, but both results would be catastrophic. You will either become the bastard son of a shamed family, thereby debarred from any university, public office or public influence, or you will become the son of a disgraced woman and a duped husband. Effectively the result will be identical.

'Finally, this. Pasto Bomboni has become a dangerous part of a terrible machine. Left to run unchecked it will destroy the genius of Florence and will enlarge itself until it runs cog to cog, wheel to wheel with similar machines now growing throughout the civilised world. The mixture between the Jesuit Inquisition, the bully boy and the Tyrant Kings striving to maintain their Divine status is one of dreadful power and potency. Against it we poor bookworms, squabbling philosophers and 'ologists of all descriptions are mere pygmies. *Direct* opposition is futile but *restraint* is possible. Pasto Bomboni is well aware of the weaknesses of our position but he cannot be *sure* that we would not succeed in revealing this crime. Above all he cannot be sure that a 'Mario' does not exist unknown who can provide further evidence of Vittoria's appearance and behaviour immediately prior to her death. She was, after all, the most striking woman. Thus we have a hold on him. We have all become, in a way, flies struggling in the same web spun by his own actions and your parents' deceit. As to the point Lorenzo makes, *of course* there is a risk. Of course he may well try to kill us all. The risk to Fredo is not the greatest. When all is said and done Fredo knows nothing and may give evidence of nothing save that his mother has disappeared. As for myself it is a risk which I will willingly bear. I am deprived of the ability to carry physical burdens. I regard this as a compensation.'

When he had finished I felt a little ashamed. Such meticulous reasoning had never entered my head.

'Who knows,' continued my master in a lighter vein, 'we might even use this power to save Lorenzo from the hot pincers. Or perhaps not. I sometimes wonder if a few quick nips might not do wonders for his insufferable conceit.'

Lorenzo shivered. 'Do not jest about such things. Even at this moment there are poor devils writhing in the irons and we can do nothing to help them.'

I was aware that my own contribution, indeed my own *decision* was now required and I said, 'I accept your advice, Signore Magliabechi. To do otherwise would be plain lunacy. I only regret that I was unable, myself, to apply such reasoning.'

This decision, once made, released a further weight from my mind and, for the first time since my arrival, a feeling of contentment, feeble and fleeting certainly, grew within me. I even asked Lorenzo, 'Will I still be able to attend Pisa?'

'Of course, but let *me* give some advice. The risks which I mentioned are real. I respect and acknowledge Antonio's view and your decision but, until Bomboni can be sure that we have taken this decision, you are not safe. In Pisa I cannot watch over you and, as Bomboni says, the roads are long and dangerous. I would delay your studies for a year. Little will be lost and I can provide some explanation to your professors. In the meantime remain in Florence. This city is dangerous but here there are close friends and allies at Court. Antonio is always bemoaning his lack of a pupil. They are all, understandably, repelled by his ghastly appearance. But there is no finer private library in Italy, probably in Europe, and the Medici library, for all the recent depredations, is still a lodestone for these funny bibliographers. He is not a bad master when you get used to his appalling habits and I can keep you both under some form of observation. What do you say, Antonio?' We both looked at my master, seated by the great windows, who simply smiled a crooked smile and nodded his bald head.

And so it came to pass. I became a pupil to the great Magliabechi. It did not last long but it was a Wonder.

On that night I left them drinking and eating olives by the window and retired to my bed. Two things occupied my mind. To consider the first I discovered the purse which I had brought from San Casciano. In it, as it has always been, was my letter from Patrick. I opened the tattered paper and read again the words of my tutor. 'Remember to forgive...' Yes, well perhaps. My fear of Pasto Bomboni which, I realised, had been with me since my earliest childhood had now wholly disappeared. In its place grew a terrible desire for revenge. Powerful and cunning as a serpent, it gripped my thoughts and my imagination in a coil which throttled at birth the infant desires to reconcile and absolve; I possessed my own power – I *knew* things about Pasto Bomboni that had nothing to do with my mother.

My second concern contained no such augury. But it preyed on my mind like a nagging sore. My father's description of Antonio's library which I had carried since my earliest recollections was perfect save in two respects. There was no screen. And there was no door with a filigree window.

Chapter Thirteen

The great library of the Medici, at present in charge of my own venerable apprentice Alberto and safely housed in the Medici Riccardi Palace, was then to be found in the vast cloisters of San Lorenzo and several nearby vaults. It is, and was, a wonder beyond telling. Room after room, shelf upon shelf, cabinet upon cabinet contained the documented, referenced and distilled wisdom of two millennia. It comprised books and manuscripts, tomes and scrolls, fragments and maps, charts and atlases, codices and text inscribed upon every movable surface on which mankind has made his unique and dangerous mark. It remained, as Lorenzo had said, the lodestone of the literate world. Thus did my master achieve his fame, his reputation and his vast acquaintanceship of illuminati, pantologists and charlatans littered across Europe like autumn leaves. They came from Russia and Spain, England and France, Holland and Austria, Sweden and Germany, Egypt and the Indies, picking their myopic way through the blood and pillage of warring Europe. And here they sat, the literati of nation states elsewhere locked like scorpions in deadly battle; here they sat side by side in the sepulchral gloom, their hostility limited to mutual condemnation of any minor noise or disturbance other than a restrained exclamation of academic delight. Some, the most privileged, and generally the least pretentious, were invited to the Via del Corso to admire my master's own collection and, occasionally, to sample Otto's exceptional cooking.

Under the tutelage of Magliabechi I joined the endless process of compilation, listing and cross-reference which had continued for two hundred years. I did so with a fierce delight and enthusiasm mixed with a mounting unease and apprehension.

The Medici library had been founded by Cosimo I. Thereafter succeeding generations of the family had contributed to its growth. The greatest and the worst of them, the Lorenzos and the Ferdinandos, the

Dukes and the Popes, had poured their usurer's gold into its augmentation. One by one they added to its vast store of parchment, leather
and wood. But as the Medicis had built it so now, at the end, they were
tearing it apart. Everywhere there were gaps. The reference rolls, so
meticulously scribed, now bore the ugly scrawl of deletion, correction
and erasure. Every week new lists arrived. They bore the Medici seal
and the unmistakable stamp of the Inquisition. They were lists of
individual works or manuscripts and sometimes merely the names of
authors or Schools which were to be collected, culled and handed to
the Society of Jesus for 'registration'. Needless to say they were never
seen again.

The very selection of the works said to contain heresy revealed a
bizarre intellect at play as though a lunatic had been asked to apply the
interpretation of the Scriptures he had learnt as a child.

The whole of Seneca had gone (no great loss, my master said); of the
seventy-two works of Democritus only two remained (incomprehensible
in isolation and apparently selected for survival at random or by lottery);
of modern philosophical essays little remained, their titles appearing
upon the weekly demands in haphazard contrast to the works of the
ancients. Descartes's essays had gone with the works of the Monothel-
ites, Spinoza with Herodotus and Leibniz in the awesome company of
Marcus Aurelius and the Iconoclasts. In the cabinet intended for modern
English work Hobbes's *Leviathan* (a rare manuscript I still possess)
remained in lonely isolation, a stark tribute to its irascible distinction
and its impenetrable scholarship.

All this involved us in a new form of bibliography. The art of cross-
reference, so often confined to the *accumulation* of new work, was now
immeasurably complicated by the depreciation of that which was already
contained on our rolls. Many cross-references now referred merely to
gaps on the shelves like signposts to the Void. One of the more skittish
of the junior assistants, a likeable lad called Carlo Bassani, regularly
altered the reference by writing 'See Grand Inquisitor' or 'Apply to
Ignatius Loyola' until discovered and severely admonished by my
master, 'You must find better work for your hands, Carlo, if you want
to retain the use of your arms.'

I confess that, initially, I was gravely concerned by what appeared to
be my master's acquiescence to this weekly attack on the library. It was
not long, however, before I realised that a deeper game was being
played and, at the same time, understood his annoyance at Carlo's little
acts of defiance.

The lists with which we were provided were plainly the composite work of a group or committee. Possibly for this reason they were replete with error, particularly in the transcription of Greek hieroglyphics. I quickly observed that *any* error however small resulted in a polite, even puzzled, failure to comply with the demand. Not infrequently my master would couple this with a supposedly helpful suggestion. 'Possibly you mean the well-known...?' He would then suggest a work of quite impeccable theological credentials, often, indeed, a Jesuit publication. This obviously caused considerable consternation on the unseen committee and it was often weeks before the original work reappeared on the list. Frequently a still further error in syntax could be found and, thus, many manuscripts remained upon our shelves indefinitely safeguarded by a mixture of hebetude, artifice and deceit.

Other methods were employed, one of which engaged us all in a silent and unacknowledged conspiracy. This involved a deliberate misunderstanding of the demand. Thus where the list required the works of 'Leonitius of Byzantium' we provided the works of 'Georgias of Leontini'. Similarly a request for any manuscripts of the heretic 'Leger' brought forth a history of the 'Port of Leghorn'. It was a game at which our young minds took considerable pleasure. When asked to assemble all our books by 'Hippocrates', Carlo provided the total known output of 'Hipponax'. Asked to find the 'Theological works of Proteus' I myself managed to unearth an obscure work on the victories of 'Phocas by Theodosius'.

All this plainly caused yet further consternation to our invisible witchhunters. Thus, despite the general feeling of dejection and despair caused by the steady erosion of the library, we were sustained by a youthful mischief spiced with intellectual challenge. Whether Antonio Magliabechi was as heedless of the dreadful dangers that we ran I doubt. I can record, however, that he took upon himself the total responsbility for the 'errors' which occurred, blaming everything from his eyesight to his incompetent height for the continued duplication of effort.

Not all the problems arose from subterfuge or sabotage. On one occasion, when removing a 'listed' volume of profane poetry by Nonnus, it completely disintegrated in my hands leaving only a pile of brown powder, the consistency of fine snuff – an eloquent commentary on the Florentine desire for heretical verse. In the case of this volume no deceit was called for and, when my master offered what resembled two handfuls of brown flour to the Jesuit monk, he sniffed at it like a cautious dog. 'Is it all here?' he demanded suspiciously. 'No,' said my master, 'I am almost certain that there is a residue of dust on the shelf. I am taking every precaution to ensure that it is not inhaled lest some poor unfortunate should be infected by heresy *per nasem*, likely to be very painful, wouldn't you think?'

This particular monk was no fool. 'It is well-known,' he said majestically, 'that there is no direct tract between the nose and the brain.'

'Really!' said my master, glancing round at the little crowd of assistant librarians who had gathered. 'How then do you account for the great Torquemada who maintained that he could *smell* heresy in any building where it resided?'

'Ah,' said the monk, his small eyes revolving around the group of wide-eyed, innocent faces. 'Ah.'

'Of course,' said my master helpfully, 'he was a Spaniard *and* a Dominican.'

'Absolutely,' said the Jesuit, relieved.

'Do you suppose, Brother Lucius,' continued my master in a tone of academic enquiry, 'that *only* Spanish Dominicans have a direct tract between the nose and the brain?'

'Ah, well . . .' said Brother Lucius.

'And, if so, do you suppose they are born with such a distinction or that it develops when they are finally ordained? Still, we must not keep you, Brother, from your duties. Do not forget your profane poetry.'

Attempts to find a receptacle for the powder, despite thorough searching throughout the library by all the assistants, proved, regretfully, unsuccessful, thereby providing a considerable problem in the transportation of the loose mix through the streets of Florence in the face of the gusting autumn wind. A number of 'helpful' suggestions were made including one by Carlo that it should be thoroughly wetted and turned into a ball. By this time Brother Lucius would happily, I suspect, have suffered the agony of the martyrs in order to gain release from the library and he was finally sent on his way clasping a spherical lump of wet mud in the way that English children fashion snow on the white days of Christmas. As he went the liquid works of Nonnus leaked through his fingers, providing an interesting but theologically lethal dribble along the streets of Florence, previously polluted by nothing more dangerous than the excrement of animals and men. The monk, also, of course, quite forgot the pile of manuscripts prepared, from the week's list, for 'registration'.

Then there were peculiar happenings.

After a short while I observed that a number of the volumes whose production to the Jesuits we had delayed, by one ploy or another, simply disappeared from the shelf or cabinet where they were stored. When it became clear that they could no longer be protected by the stratagem we had devised they reappeared, apparently unharmed, in their allotted place. Indeed, not infrequently, they bore the marks of cleaning and recent perusal (the first such attention some of them had received for several centuries).

I also noticed that the library at the Via del Corso was suffering depredations as though from some haphazard but persistent pilferer. It was not, of course, as extensive as the collection stored in the cloisters of San Lorenzo but it contained many works, particularly modern essays and manuscripts, which duplicated those belonging to the Grand Duke. It did not take long for me to realise that the volumes which disappeared matched those which were finally handed over to the monks.

As to this steady erosion my master seemed totally unconcerned. Indeed I found him on one occasion perched on wooden steps like a deformed bat carefully rearranging a shelf to conceal the absence of books which had recently and inexplicably departed from sight.

I, of course, realised that he was party to some plot to safeguard his own library but as to the whereabouts of the missing manuscripts I had no idea. Nor did I enquire, partly through a natural reticence and partly, I confess, from a deep and uncomfortable conviction that, during this period in the history of Tuscany, knowledge of any kind was a very dangerous commodity.

The sense of impending doom was deepened by the news of the death of Mario Cantoni, my father's erstwhile groom, who had witnessed my mother's death and undoubtedly ignited the anger with which my father contrived his own destruction.

The news of Mario's murder was brought to the Via del Corso by his sister who lived outside the Porta Romana and with thom, on that dreadful day, Mario had been lodging, supposedly to await directions from Lorenzo Bellini.

On the night his sister came I had earned my sobriquet. Lorenzo Bellini, himself, was back from Pisa and my master was entertaining a famous German doctor of medicine. On such occasions it was my duty and pleasure to play the page to Otto's eunuch and I fetched and carried plates and wine whilst gaining admission to my place at the table and enjoying toleration and occasional verbal battering from my adopted guardians. (Although this description was strictly incorrect since I was now fifteen years of age and, according to the customs of the time, a master of my own affairs.) I had, I recollect, delivered myself of some profundity on the subject of anatomy and had been kindly exposed as the ignoramus I undoubtedly was. Amid some good-natured jeering I was ordered to fetch more wine with post-prandial cheese and olives. On my return from the kitchen door I crossed the second room of the library to the table which was now habitually used for entertaining guests, set as it was against the great window and admitting the cool of the evening and the meditative lapping of water, conducive to peace and scholarly contemplation.

'Look at that dreadful flabberguts!' said Lorenzo as I came through the door. 'Really, Antonio, I don't know how you can bear to look at such a wobbling mass of flesh. I suppose it is because you're such a ghastly deformity yourself. This house is turning into a circus for freaks. You come to the door and get let in by a black gorilla with bent paws only to be confronted by you two. I tell you this library is safe enough from the Inquisition. No one but a medical genius with a strong sense of enquiry could stomach it for more than five minutes.' Lorenzo had uttered the words 'medical genius' in German and smiled at our guest who supposedly knew no Italian and had been nodding his head slightly in mute, apparently uncomprehending agreement. 'See,' said Lorenzo, in Italian, 'he agrees too and *he's* got the medical brain of a carthorse. But really, Antonio, what do you think he looks like?' By this time I had arrived at the table smiling indulgently at my godfather and preparing to pour out his wine.

'He looks like a little barrel,' said the German in perfect Italian, surprising us all.

'Ah...' said Lorenzo, momentarily discomfited, '"Botticelli". Yes, I agree, well that's what we'll have to call him. "Botticelli" – *"Boti".'*

And so it arrived. Long after the affairs of this chronicle, in Pisa, London, Paris, Rome, I was known as 'Boti' Credi, a compliment of a sort, I suppose.

We had finished with this joke and Lorenzo was assuring his fellow anatomist that the word 'carthorse' in Italian vernacular was a compliment of rare distinction reflecting vast strength and perseverance, when Otto arrived, announcing Mario's sister. Despite the weight and resonance of the iron doorknocker none of us had heard her, so timorous was her approach. She now entered the room with that universal contraction of the body, unrecorded in medical science, but well known

149

to any who have studied the arrival of the meek and lowly at the jocund gatherings of the Great.

We perceived at once that she was in distress and Antonio rose, took her arm, and guided her to the couch set in the alcove where the shelves of books turned to form the wall facing the windows and the canal. As he did so Otto leant and spoke into my master's ear, his eyes extending above the misshapen back like black sunsets over a burial mound.

To this point, despite the rumours I will reveal later, I had not in reality contemplated my master enjoying any relationship, however passing, with womankind. The awfulness of his deformity paralysed the mind before any consideration of sexual performance. So as he sat beside her and took her hand I experienced a shock of awareness the impact of which continues with me in my dotage.

She looked at us, seated round that circle of light in the red cedar library beside the window, the Florentine rugs at our feet and her eyes opened resembling the stare of a dead beast. She bit her lip before saying 'I am...'

'You are Mario Cantoni's sister,' said my master in a voice which would have calmed the sea. 'Do not be afraid. These are all friends.'

They made a strange sight sitting on the ottoman, the pretty sister with her wide eyes and breathless story, her hand willingly gripped into the clasp of the hunchback by her side. This was the account she gave.

Mario, her younger brother, was a fine boy but weak-willed. *Apparently* so strong, so independent, but in reality so influenced by others. She remembered her father in San Casciano telling him to avoid the butcher's children, not to become a part of them. They are *maligna*, he would say, *prepotenti*. But Mario would not listen until they had nearly drowned Giuseppe Manzini. Then he had been frightened, perhaps not enough. But he had obeyed his father and had obtained work with Gallupe Credi. He was so proud of that. Gallupe Credi, the Hero of Florence. He had been very happy. At her wedding and when she went away to Florence he had told her that one day he would travel with Signor Credi everywhere in Europe. 'He has already told me this,' he had said, 'when he is old and needs a good servant then I will go with him everywhere.' Then she looked at me and said, 'You do not remember me, Fredo Credi, because you were kept in your home. We thought of you as a different type of boy. *You* would think my brother was just a groom, a servant, but he worshipped your father, wanted to travel with him, to learn. He saw the books your father brought and, though he could not read a word, he knew the carrying of them was the work he

150

wanted to do. Mario told me you didn't seem to know your father. You had your red-haired priest. But Mario worshipped your father, in a way loved him and wanted to travel with him. But he was still a weak boy, a servant. After he became your groom he never approached the Bombonis. Never gave them his time. Do you know, Fredo Credi, what that means in a town like San Casciano? Can you imagine how reviled he was by the Bombonis and their friends? "Gallupe Credi's bum boy" they called him. But he stayed with your father whilst you and your red priest made your school for which he was then too old.'

At this point she did not cry but looked at me with a kind of contempt I had not previously seen. Now, as I sit here and write these lines, I reject her sentiments. I had done what I could. But I do not forget her eyes.

She continued. Then came the awful day when Mario arrived, unexpectedly, to stay with her. He told her the whole story. How his mistress had disappeared; how his master had sat for hours on the terrace waiting for her return whilst his son was off climbing mountains. Then *they* had arrived, Lorenzo Bellini (well-known to Mario) and the ghastly black monster who came with him. He had been ordered to go to Florence. By agreement with them he stopped at her house and waited there until the following day. Then, acting against his instructions, he went into Florence through the Porta Romana to the Pitti Palace and the Ponte Vecchio. He had never seen the city. He arrived back in the early evening, distraught beyond belief. He had seen Vittoria Credi, a prisoner of the Salti and wearing the sentencing board of a common whore! Then he had seen the Captain of the Salti was Pasto Bomboni! As they crossed the bridge Pasto had said something to her and she had stopped and spat at him, then, in the confusion, she had ran through the centre arch of the bridge and was gone into the river.

He kept on saying to her that he must tell his master – but he had been ordered to stay. Making the decision was very difficult for him and then finally he decided to go back, unbidden, to San Casciano. He told her to tell no one, but when Lorenzo Bellini and the black man arrived she told them *part* of the truth; told them he had gone but told them he had gone only within the hour. In truth he had gone the night before.

She sat for a moment in silence, staring at the rugs at her feet and then she continued.

'I had not seen him again until two days ago when he had come again to our house. He was changed – he seemed stronger but, somehow

151

... wrong. He had been living with our father in San Casciano. There was no money. He had no job. He had been drinking. There had been arguments, fights between them. In San Casciano they believed that the wife of Gallupe Credi had gone to a nunnery. But they were mistaken. *He*, Mario, knew what had happened. He knew that Pasto Bomboni had killed her. He knew, also, of the feud between his master and Pasto Bomboni after the fight at Gallaza. Pasto Bomboni had become a great man. He had heard that he had been promoted again within the Salti. He knew he was a great man in the city, and feared. But he knew also that Pasto Bomboni had killed the wife of Gallupe Credi. Now, he told me, he could have work and money. Why should he stay in San Casciano and be beaten by his father, with no money? Pasto Bomboni would give him money and he would make him a Salti. What he knew about Pasto Bomboni was enough. He would not tell him all of it, but would hint at it. He would get his job.

'I had begged him not to go to Florence. Begged him, if he had this terrible secret, I told him to come here, to Signore Magliabechi, to Gallupe's son. To Lorenzo Bellini. But he would not listen. "What can *they* give me?" he had asked me, "with their books. I cannot read a word. What work will they give me?" I said that he could travel, like his master, like Gallupe Credi. But he shook his head. "The books must be read before they are taken. I could neither read nor understand."

'So he went immediately to the city to find Pasto Bomboni, to search him out at the Bargello or the Stinche. To get his work and to get his money. He did not return that night (last night) nor had he come during today. Then, this evening, as it grew dark horses came.' She looked at us with those wide eyes as we sat in the circle of light. 'Two riders. One carrying a burden across his saddle. Both had cloaks but with no marks and their collars were up as though against a wind although the night was fine. They dropped his body in front of the house and rode away towards the city. They did not hurry but walked their horses side by side as though on a "promenade". Those who came to the house and who had seen such things before said that he had been drowned. But his face and neck are scalded, the skin peeling from the bone. His body also has been burnt and the arms twisted away from the shoulders at an angle impossible to make. On his chest there was pinned a notice, the staple driven into the flesh. It is here, I brought it.'

It was the page of a book torn from its binding. From my position at the table I could see that the characters which covered the page were Greek. On one side, crudely scrawled in charcoal across the lines of verse, was the single word *Omerta*. She handed the page to Antonio Magliabechi who examined the script.

'Pisides,' he said. 'From the library. He is closer to the Inquisitors than I thought.'

The girl had told her story and now she sat, watching us, her eyes as wide as a child's.

'Who would have committed this terrible crime?' The question was asked by the German, whose presence at the seat closest to the window had been quite forgotten during the narrative we had heard. No one answered his question but Lorenzo rose and spoke to the girl. 'Come,' he said, 'I will go with you to your home. Your brother must be attended. Also you must not travel alone.'

As she also rose my master spoke gently to her, 'Child, who else knows of these matters?'

She alone knew, she said. Her husband she had not told for fear that the information might involve a danger.

She left with Lorenzo and, shortly thereafter, my master also departed with his guest to whom he had apologised for the unexpected ending to our meal.

'You have seen,' he said to him, 'another side of our city, not discernible in the works of Donatello or the architecture of Brunelleschi.' Our guest, for his part, said little and I could tell that my master was troubled at his presence and the information he had unwittingly obtained.

I was left alone in the library where I closed the windows, cleared the remains of the meal and sat to contemplate this latest development in what now appeared, obscurely, as a convergent pattern of forces like the beams and buttresses of a great structure as yet indistinct in the coming dawn. Though what would finally emerge, cathedral or charnel house, yet remained in mystery.

My master returned within the hour, obviously concerned that the German should have heard so much.

'He is a brilliant man but by no means a trustworthy confidant. I have done my best to impress him with the unreliable nature of this story and the necessity to ensure its accuracy before any account or report is given. However I know that he is meeting Redi tomorrow, ostensibly to discuss the health of the Grand Duke, and I have no doubt that this evening's affairs will be passed at least into that inquisitive ear.'

'How can that harm us?'

'It may not do so at all. Redi has no purpose to serve in carrying this

153

information to the Grand Duke. No one appreciates better than Redi the puerile impatience of the royal intellect. Such a story as this, told at third or fourth hand, even if comprehended, would evoke nothing but irritable disbelief. No, the only danger lies in the knowledge Bomboni now possesses that his guilty secret is known by more than our small group. He plainly intended that Mario's death should act as a signal. Hence the message on the page of verse. However, by allowing our German friend to receive the whole story, we have already, in effect, disregarded his warning. Now that Bomboni has been promoted to "Commander" his power to silence all or any of us is much increased. I do not say these things to alarm you but it now behoves all of us to proceed with particular care. Whilst I retain the ear and favour of the Palace we are safe from official assassination but Bomboni's powers now obviously extend further than that.'

I was silent with my thoughts; contemplating whether to reveal the secret knowledge I possessed concerning the Bombonis. Before I could reach any conclusion Lorenzo Bellini returned, plainly shaken by his discovery.

'Well,' he said as he poured himself wine, 'I have seen men who have sustained worse injuries but not at the hands of their own species. Perhaps I have led a sheltered existence. I have done what I can to disguise the effects, if only to spare his family. The body is to be taken to San Casciano in the morning. It will be a terrible shock for his poor father but I have told the girl to hold her counsel. The father will be told that the injuries resulted from a brawl and so, it is hoped, will be spared both the grosser imaginings of his son's death and the compulsion to revenge it. Were he to make any such attempt he would, I fear, meet the same fate. Indeed we must all be careful.'

'You do not think...'

'I think that Pasto Bomboni is a frightened man. Evil beyond belief, but frightened. The injuries he inflicted upon that boy were the works of a man possessed but also a man in desperate fear. He must have had accomplices. That, in itself, poses for him a further risk. He would not have gone to such lengths if he did not believe himself to be in danger.'

'Is there *nothing* we can do?' I said, surprised at the vehemence of my own question.

'Short of committing a mortal sin I do not think so. Nothing that has happened today has changed the position save for the worse.'

We continued our discussion without useful conclusion until my master left us for his bed. He had, of late, been suffering from increased pain connected with his deformity and aggravated by the cool damp weather which marked the early months of the year. I had in any event, intended to speak to Lorenzo, to unburden myself of my secret and to inform him of the use to which I intended it should be put. He listened to me intently, occasionally flickering his eyes with surprise and shaking his head in a mixture of repulsion and disbelief. When I came to deal with my present intentions his mood changed to one of consternation and alarm. He raised a number of questions, which I answered, and objections, all of which I believe, I was able to meet. Finally he sat there, silent on the far side of the single lamp set upon the table, causing the polished surface to reflect like water on a moonlit night. I heard him sigh and watched him begin to smile a little, I thought, in resignation.

'When I assisted your head into the world I did not dream it held such machinations.'

'I simply obey my mentors. Patrick told me to forgive my enemies. It is time that I started to do so.'

'Let us hope they respond with something better than a musket shot.'

Once we had decided upon a plan of action we agreed that it should not be long delayed. Furthermore we decided, with some misgivings, that those parts of our intentions which directly concerned Pasto Bomboni should be withheld from my master. In doing so we extended to him the safety with which he sought to endow me. In a world ruled by the Jesuits through the agency of Cosimo III and Pasto Bomboni knowledge was a contagion.

By the time Lorenzo left the Via del Corso the dawn was breaking. The air above the city was clear and sharp, the sky that pale hard blue promising a rare frost on the hills to the north. Mist lay knee-deep on the cobbled street and the monumental fountain, silent and unproductive, rose like a wet and lonely rock to which the sculpted figures of cherubim clung like beleaguered mariners, improbably naked and overfed.

I stood at the doorway watching Lorenzo disappear towards the Piazza de la Signoria, his body visible through the folds of the cloak he had pulled tightly about him. I watched him till he passed the fountain, some hundred paces distant, and was about to turn into the house when a sudden movement gave me pause. A figure, which had plainly been immobile on the far side of the fountain, now emerged immediately behind Lorenzo. My initial alarm swiftly abated when I observed that it was a child, the head and shoulders barely emerging from the swirling mist as though swimming strongly after the doctor's retreating back. For this reason I stifled the cry which had risen to my lips and watched as the tiny pursuer reached Lorenzo, took hold of the bottom of his cloak and tugged energetically, causing Lorenzo's head to jerk backwards like a horse sharply reined before a jump. His own exclamation, indeed, would have concealed my own as he slipped and almost fell upon the wet and invisible stones. Immediately Lorenzo turned it was apparent that he knew the child and such remonstration as followed was brief indeed before he placed both hands on the infant shoulders and drew the boy (if male he was) towards the side of the street at which point they all but disappeared from my vision. In the stillness and clarity of the morning air I imagined that I heard a muffled conversation and I could just make out Lorenzo's stooping figure, the child all but concealed within the folds of his cloak. What I *did* hear, without doubt, was a short barking laugh and a sudden smacking sound as though someone had been struck vigorously about the face. Immediately afterwards the small figure detached itself from Lorenzo, who raised an arm in farewell and resumed his progress towards the centre of the city. The other then turned towards me and, adopting a strange scuttling form of gait, discernible in the mist by the irregular jerking of head and shoulers, made his or her way swiftly in my direction. For some reason I did not wish to be observed, less through fear than through the natural embarrassment of one who has apparently been secretly observing intimate events with which he has no conceivable connection. As it approached the child patently did not see me: its eyes being below the brim of a woollen cap pulled down to meet the top of a rough winter jerkin. Any further clothing was concealed by the mist.

So the figure advanced until it reached the gap in the houses, some twenty paces from me and immediately beyond the shutters, now closed, which protected the library casements to the left hand of the door where I stood. At this point the figure turned abruptly towards the river and was about to disappear along the side of our house when, equally abruptly, it stopped as though sensing the presence of an observer in its immediate vicinity. I was already aware, from this distance, notwithstanding the woollen cap, that the child's head was wholly disproportionate to the body upon which it now rested motionless and pointed like a good hunting dog in the direction of the river. Suddenly the head twisted in my direction and, for a moment, our eyes met before the tiny form disappeared between the houses like a rabbit into a burrow. I own, even now, to a sense of shock. I had seen too little to provide any sensible description of the face or its characteristics save to be aware of a grotesque element impossible to assess. Of one thing, however, I was certain. The face was not that of a child. It was that of an old man.

I climbed to my bed aware of a sense of nausea and exhausted by the accumulated events of the night. I was, let it be remembered, barely fifteen years of age, recently orphaned and in deadly peril of my life being choked from me by some dreadful process of pain. I was also, for good measure, engaged in a daily game of scholastic *bluffo* with the Holy Inquisition. The appearance of a child with the face of an ancient shrouded in the morning mist of the Via del Corso was, I thought, as much as I could possibly bear. Little did I know that my journey had barely started.

Chapter Fourteen

The following day I obtained leave of absence from my master and, together with Lorenzo, planned our departure from Florence due to take place the next morning at first light. The previous night I had intended to tax Lorenzo with the existence of the 'child'. With the morning sunshine, however, came doubts as to the accuracy of my observations or, indeed, whether they had substance at all. Besides, compared with the revelations of Mario's sister and the business before us the matter assumed but trifling, irritating insignificance and I held my peace.

Lorenzo was now forty-three years of age and, in deference to this fact and the ever-increasing lawlessness which rendered the roads impassable to single travellers (a fact of which I was, of course, well aware) he now employed a servant specifically to provide company and protection on his journeys between Pisa and Florence and his other, increasingly rare, visits to the medical schools of Europe. This servant was a burly and taciturn fellow previously employed by the University to stop fighting between the students and the townspeople. The latter harboured a collective and bitter resentment against the former who they perceived, with justification, were doing little to further the common weal beyond an inflation of their self-esteem by useless and drunken disputation and occasionally successful attempts at the seduction of local women. The student body of Pisa was now largely comprised of the sons of wealthy Florentine merchants whose riches the last Medici had conspired to augment at the expense of the increasingly desperate poor. These unsavoury *braggados* made no secret of their opinion that the inhabitants of Pisa and its countryside were rural blockheads whose function lay in the provision, alternately, of services and sport.

Such mutually inconsistent views inevitably resulted in violence, at first sporadic and later of a more serious and organised nature.

Alarmed by the growing anarchy, the authorities of the University and town met in noisy session, not wholly dissimilar in character from the mayhem it was designed to consider and cure. Some limited measure of agreement was reached and this, in turn, resulted in the decision to appoint an official custodian of the peace charged with separating the warring factions and pacifying both camps. Such a role demanded a mixture of force, firmness, tact and toleration for which the talents of Mikos Faccioli were wholly and completely unsuited. It will come as no surprise to anyone, therefore, who has knowledge of academic institutions from Athens to Oxford to learn that, from a field of many candidates, he was swiftly and emphatically appointed.

I say that he lacked all the talents for the job but, on reflection, that is not entirely true. He possessed a vast quantity of brute force; reservoirs of it. In addition he had a rough and ready seaman's charm and was cunning as a rat. The central problem was that he was partisan. He was the illegitimate son of an expatriate Greek who ran a bar at the dock-side in Leghorn. His mother, one of the port's many whores, rapidly abandoned him in favour of a British sea captain with whom she disappeared. He was thus brought up by his father and inherited a withering contempt for three things: women, the gentry and the power or effectiveness of rational discussion. Physically as strong as an ox he soon ran foul even of the port authorities at Leghorn and, at the age of twenty-five, made an enforced decampment to Pisa. There he applied for and immediately obtained the job of 'Tribunis Pacis' as previously described. As a solution it had an effect similar to hurling buckets of gunpowder onto a kitchen fire.

To make matters worse, not only that he was partisan but his partiality extended only to the faction, University or town, with whom he had most recently been drinking. This led to two further complicating factors. First his capacity to drink was prodigious indeed, virtually unquenchable. Secondly, when in drink he rapidly bcame explosively and cata-strophically violent. Not surprisingly there was considerable competition between the factions to provide the necessary alcohol, thus completing a circle of behaviour likely, at the very least, to have undesirable consequences for all those involved. Soon fighting between the factions ceased altogether and was replaced by a series of massacres perpetrated by Mikos on and against both sides.

Needless to say, all this prompted the authorities of University and town to consider terminating his employment. The difficulty lay in finding a method by which to do it. Events had now created their own momentum and it *was* true that some of the major trouble-makers had been amongst the early casualties. However, on the town side a number of innocent people had already been attacked and the University, starved of endowments, was now desperately anxious to avoid further depletion in its numbers, no matter how scholastically unpromising the slaughtered students may have been. Complaints to the Prefect were of no avail. No one was prepared to give any evidence not least because those in the best position to do so had also been, from time to time, the prime conspirators. Finally, at his own request, the matter was placed in the hands of Lorenzo Bellini, the Professor of Anatomy. Enlisting two of his best students, Lorenzo, early one evening, made his way to the *albergo* where Mikos most frequently commenced his drinking. The burly Greek was discovered in the company of several ill-disposed students who eyed the approaching Professor with distrust.

'Don't bother to get up,' said Lorenzo, 'I just came over to buy Mikos a drink.' So saying he placed a large flagon of wine on the table which the custodian of the peace downed with gusto. The effect of the draught was almost instantaneous and after Mikos had fallen senseless to the floor Lorenzo's two students carried him back to the Professor's rooms. When Mikos awoke he was without recent recollection and he felt very unwell. Recognising the well-known Professor of Anatomy, however, he allowed himself to receive treatment. After several days he felt infinitely worse and believed himself to be close to death. In this belief he was actively encouraged by his physician, one of the greatest of his century. Finally Lorenzo announced that there was only one further cure which he was prepared to try. However, Mikos must understand that all medicine required, ultimately, the blessing of God and whilst he, Lorenzo, would do everything in his power it was essential that Mikos should assist by prayer, genuine penitence and resolution for his future conduct. Mikos's prayers, Lorenzo told me, whilst lacking the beauty of the Psalms contained much of the power of Lamentations. In any event they were blessed with conspicuous success and, within a matter of days, Mikos made a total recovery. Before he was *quite* recovered Lorenzo spoke earnestly to him about his future. In view of his illness and the difficulties which the work entailed it was, Lorenzo said, unsuitable for him to return to his post at the University. However he, Lorenzo, now required a companion for his journeys and a factotum about his house at Pisa. If Mikos would consider such a post then it would have a mutual benefit. His strength would be well employed assisting and protecting Lorenzo whilst Lorenzo's knowledge would be similarly employed safeguarding the continued health of Mikos Faccioli. This arrangement worked perfectly. Mikos drank no more. Lorenzo did not forbid him to do so. Indeed whenever Mikos expressed a wish to start drinking Lorenzo positively encouraged him by providing a flagon of the best local wine. This invariably left Mikos feeling so unwell that it created an aversion generally effective for many months. For his part Mikos regarded Lorenzo with a reverence close to fervour. It was even said that he kept a pile of Lorenzo's discarded possessions which he guarded with the devotion of Argus. His intellect precluded his ever becoming a stimulating companion but he was dedicated to his master's welfare and trustworthy unto death and, as Lorenzo observed, that was worth more than a cartload of theology.

It was with Mikos that we set out on the road to San Casciano. Also with us was an assistant librarian from the Medici library, a tall good-natured lad called Fernando who, having tried unsuccessfully to engage Mikos in conversation, rode silently behind us. It was barely dawn and, as we passed through the Porta Romana our shadows extended a hundred paces along the flat land to the north-west. Lorenzo was bound for Pisa and, when our business at San Casciano was concluded, it was agreed that he should continue with Mikos, leaving Fernando and me to return, within the day, to Florence. It was, again, a clear cold morning and as we rode into the hills, our cloaks pulled about us, our spirits rose and we discussed the purpose of our journey as men would discuss the properties of the universe, engaged as matter but detached as minds.

The rise of Pasto Bomboni had, indeed, been spectacular. His reputation now extended throughout the city. Everywhere he was feared save by those in whom privilege and preference had conspired, long since, to stifle the cries of infant Pity beneath the applause for order, discipline and commercial opportunity.

Following his promotion two areas of law now fell within Bomboni's jurisdiction; the Jews and Suppression of Immorality. The second of these had now, if anything, become the more demanding. Since the Grand Duke Cosimo had been deprived of his French wife his own sexual activities had been totally curtailed. It was widely believed that, left to his own devices, he would have followed the example of his father, Ferdinando, and pleasured himself with the ladies of the Court. This simple expedient was wholly thwarted by his mother, Vittoria della Rovere, and the Inquisition who were now, effectively, in joint control of the government of Florence. Vittoria, a woman so ugly that, it was said, Sustermans had refused to paint her, had swiftly driven her own husband, the late Duke Ferdinando, from the matrimonial couch whither he had returned, intermittently and without enthusiasm, only to ensure the continuance of the Medici dynasty. It was during one of these fleeting visits that, much fortified with alcohol, he had succeeded in the conception of Cosimo. To be fair to Ferdinando, his aversion to his wife lay not so much in her odious physical appearance as in her humourless bigotry and intolerance, ceaselessly expressed in a diatribe of sanctimonious and petulant complaint. Denied the attentions of her husband her moral zealotry increased and it was well known that, shortly before his death, she had presented him with a list of those in Florentine society who, it was alleged, committed acts of sexual deviance. The Grand Duke had surveyed its contents for some time (it was a lengthy document) and placed it carefully upon the fire, remarking that there was one other whom he could, with certainty, add to the list and that person had no desire to perish at the hands of the Inquisition.

The death of Ferdinando, the succession of Cosimo and, finally, the catastrophic end of Cosimo's marriage to Marguerite Louise of France provided Vittoria with the opportunity she had so long desired. Cosimo was rigorously denied the opportunity of any sexual gratification and, within a short while, underwent the conventional reaction of the enforced celibate: that which was unavailable to him he lost no time in denying to everyone else. To this end an Office of Public Decency was established, staffed by the servants of the Inquisition and provided with the services of the Salti. A series of edicts had flowed from the Pitti Palace designed, so it was said, to re-establish the 'old' standards of Tuscan morality. *All* prostitution was now to be punished by public flogging and incarceration in the Stinche until such time as fines (of impossible dimensions) were fully paid. Incest, carnal knowledge with children and sodomy, on the scantist evidence or denunciation, invited public flogging followed by castration in the hospital of Santa Maria Nuova.

Many of the edicts betrayed the workings of a mind tortured by sexual fantasy. Priests caught molesting virgins in the confessional were to be walled up alive. (This last measure, it should be added, was the only part of the overall legislation which enjoyed a measure of popular support.) The great festival of May, the Calendimaggio, the most libidinous and Bacchanalian in the Tuscan calendar, was cancelled and forbidden, as was the wearing of ribbons and brocade.

It was with the enforcement of these laws that Pasto Bomboni upon his promotion was entrusted, a task to which he had brought in the past months considerable energy and vigour. It was widely observed, however, that the burden of this moral yoke fell unequally across the Tuscan back. Those whose commercial fortunes had flowered under Cosimo's stewardship, among whom the brothers Assinari and Castanelli were prominent, appeared to enjoy, if anything, lifestyles of conspicuous decadence. Officers of the Salti, it was also observed, appeared exempt from those laws (particularly relating to prostitution) which they so rigorously enforced. Inevitably, in such circumstances, money and immunity intermixed and the corruption of commerce was thus firmly imprinted upon the moral pattern decreed from the Pitti Palace. As Lorenzo succinctly put it, 'Free fucking has become the handmaiden of fraud.'

All this we discussed on the road to San Casciano. Riding briskly on a cool spring morning and, despite the wretched poverty of the land through which we passed, the hills of Tuscany set against the blue sky lifted our spirits above the foul and malignant subject of our reflections. We made good progress, arriving at Gallaza barely later than the hour at which I had myself arrived on my way to Florence seven months before. I could not but reflect on the difference in my circumstances. Whilst my worst fears on that earlier journey had been realised, I remained in mortal danger and the state of Tuscany had, if anything, deteriorated, yet now I rode with friends, was guarded and secure, and the purpose of my journey, whilst still a search for protection, engendered no feelings of helplessness or despair. We stopped briefly to enable the horses to be watered and to drink a little of the hot, spiced wine still popular, to this day, to invigorate the morning hours.

The sun was still low in the sky when we arrived at my birth-place and here, as pre-arranged, we parted company. Lorenzo went to the office of the Prefecture whilst I, together with Mikos and Fernando, rode through the town and passed the river bank where I had left my lantern as I fled. I noticed with some ironical amusement that it still stood, rusty and useless, on the stone ledge where I had set it down, a testimony to both the honesty and indolence endemic in the Tuscan soul.

Shortly afterwards we arrived at the school, now enjoying its morning break between lessons and surrounded by the noisy children of the locality, including, I have no doubt, the progeny of Poggibonsi. I alone dismounted, leaving my two companions sitting hunched in their travelling cloaks like crows in the branches of a tree, and entered the school at which my own gifts had been employed many months before.

163

Much I did not recognise at all. The squat low façade remained the same and the new buildings I had, of course, seen before but, once inside, little resemblance remained. The school now had four classrooms and the cramped area where I, myself, had taught and obtained my first glimpse of the secrets of womankind was now a place reserved for the rest, meditation and prayer of the Benedictine fathers. That is where I found them and, as I entered, they rose in greeting. Two of them were known to me as those who had immediately succeeded myself and Patrick following his departure. Then, I had spent some little time with them explaining the basis upon which we had divided our pupils and carried out our work. They in turn were, of course, aware of my father's death and my own disappearance. Word had also reached them of my present occupation in Florence and one of the others, a Florentine by birth, had worked in the Medici library under the tutelage of Antonio Magliabechi. For a short while therefore we made a happy group discussing my own progress, that of the school and its individual pupils some of whom, indeed, including the miller's son had already departed on the road to the University at Pisa. This topic of conversation brought me directly to my business and, without giving any reason, I enquired after the fortunes of Nicola Bomboni. She was still at school, the eldest pupil and one who, like me, was now entrusted with her own magisterial role. She still, at her father's request, concentrated on the study of mathematics and, in particular, that concerned with the computation of percentages and the clarification (or obfuscation) of figures. At this she had become particularly proficient and thus, whilst still barely fifteen, was in some demand among the tradesmen of the village to assist in their fiscal problems, a service which she provided at some benefit to her father. She was, they told me, much changed as though the perception of her value to others had awoken a sense of her own place in the Divine Scheme. Her brother, Filippo, was also much changed but this was generally attributed to a kick in the side of the head by a resistant beast whose throat Filippo was preparing to slit.

As they had described so I found her. Whilst her features would forever preclude *serenata* sung in her honour they were affected by her manner in a way which lent them a curious attraction and charm. In particular her smile invited immediate spontaneous response and her eyes, which had once swivelled and darted like pursued mice, now settled on their object with bright composure. Nevertheless she was confused and a little embarrassed to see me and after a brief reintroduction the Benedictines departed to the classrooms, leaving us alone in a room which held, for both of us, uncomfortable memories. I decided it was best to explain swiftly and without preamble the purpose of my visit. I had not expected to find her so transformed and, thus, the dialogue which I had mentally rehearsed bore little resemblance to that which in fact took place. Nonetheless she listened with care and attention displaying, only occasionally, reactions of distaste or disbelief. When I had finished, and made my proposal, she looked at me in silence and, I thought, with some form of reproach, and then she said. 'Do I have any choice in this matter, Fredo Credi?'

'Of course,' I said, and then added with an inspiration worthy of Patrick, 'of course, whether you allow yourself such a choice is another matter.'

She smiled at this in a way which, I confess, irradiated the room and, despite the nature of our discussion, brought to my adolescent loins stirrings beyond my power to curtail. Perhaps she observed this for her smile broadened and the light of irony danced in her eyes.

'Of course,' she said, 'I will do as you ask. I am well aware that you and your monstrous red priest saved me from a life of misery and I have, I think, never adequately repaid you.' And we both smiled in something close to the delicious complicity of lovers and briefly took each other's hands before we rose and, having made some explanation to the head Benedictine, left the school and crossed to the knacker's yard. We were only just in time, arriving as Alessandro and Filippo Bomboni emerged from the house and trotted down the path bent, no doubt, on Louis Bonelli's inn. Seeing me in Nicola's company clearly provided both father and son with a considerable shock. Alessandro, indeed, fell over attempting to carry out a manoeuvre somewhere between advance and recoil. In falling he clutched hold of Filippo who would, himself, have been borne to the ground had he not thrust his father from him. It was, indeed, only after ten minutes of intensive persuasion on the part of both Nicola and myself and, let it be admitted, after some reference to the presence of Mikos and Fernando that I was finally admitted into the Bomboni household, Filippo having been dispatched to the Casa Bonelli with a substantial pitcher. By the time he returned I was confident enough of my own safety to have relieved Mikos and Fernando of their sentry duties and arranged to meet them at the office of the Prefecture. The next two hours I spent within the Bomboni establishment in the company of the entire family. The physical conditions within the house I will not describe. In part they were as one would have expected and, in part, infinitely worse. In odd places there were signs of haphazard decoration (Nicola's work no doubt) which had about them an oddly touching aspect, like discovering a hair ribbon in the middle of the Augean stables. Once it became apparent that my visit entailed some mutual benefit the atmosphere became almost festive and I had difficulty restraining Alessandro from despatching his son for another monumental pitcher of wine. At the end of two hours, when all the necessary arrangements had been made, the entire family and myself left the knacker's yard and made our way through the village to the office of the Prefecture. The constitution of our party was greeted with understandable amazement in the streets particularly given the evident good humour which exuded from the butcher. At the Prefecture Lorenzo and the chief official were waiting with some impatience.

It was early evening before we completed our business by which time Bomboni's mood had changed to one of sullen irritation, whether due to a surfeit of wine or lack of it was difficult to tell. He concluded, however, his part of the bargain and even invited Bellini and myself to eat at the slaughterhouse which we gracefully but firmly declined. It was too late, however, either to return to Florence or to make the onward journey to Pisa and we spent a pleasant enough evening in the Albergo Niccolo nostalgically discussing my youth in San Casciano and speculating on the whereabouts of our red priest and his present employment, about which we in reality entertained little doubt.

In the early morning we set off for our respective destinations and, after an uneventful journey, I arrived at Florence together with Fernando well before noon. As we approached the city gates my spirits fell into melancholy. The works of the Office of Public Decency together with the worsening condition of the poor and the increase in random lawlessness conspired to produce an atmosphere of corruption and decay. Everywhere rubbish and filth accumulated on the streets. Beggars multiplied and what tattered commerce remained was regarded by the majority with the indifference of the forgotten and uninvolved. Recent edicts concerning the likely success of the coming harvest and the improvement in Tuscan trade had been received, in these areas, with sullen disbelief.

Before entering the Porta Romana I digressed from our direct route to visit the house of Mario's sister. There I spent a little time, provided her with some part of the proceeds from my father's estate which had been released by the Prefect and also entrusted to her safe-keeping one of the bundles of documents contained in my saddlebag; such security as I possessed I intended to spread as thinly as I was able.

When we entered the city my spirits began again to rise. Despite the evidence of universal decay the buildings retained their serenity and the irrepressible bustle of urban life seethed below the enforced austerity like the convolutions of young animals constrained within a sack. The Salti were everywhere. There had been a further increase in their number and the conspicuous and aggressive brightness of their uniforms contrasted with the drabness of the streets like sharp stones in mud. Following the path I had taken when first I arrived in the city we approached the Ponte Vecchio, turned alongside the river, crossed below the church of Santa Croce, turned into the Via del Corso and arrived at length at my master's house. I remained there only long enough to change my clothes and to transfer the contents of my saddlebag partly into the locker beside my bed and partly into the canvas sack which I used for the transmission of manuscripts. With this I made my way to the house of Vincenzo Viviani, the erstwhile pupil of Galileo and custodian of the astronomer's great works. We had met on a number of occasions since my arrival in Florence and, whilst he was aware that I shared the knowledge of his secret, no word of it had passed between us. Respecting this convention I simply asked him whether he would add my small bundle of documents to his 'collection' and, to this end, handed him a letter prepared by Lorenzo. Having read this he took the bag with meticulous care and averted eyes as one might receive a receptacle containing, for instance, the head of John the Baptist. I entertained considerable doubts as to the wisdom of entrusting such documents to his care but I had been persuaded by Lorenzo that, lurking beneath the exterior of the deer was the heart of the leopard. One of us was to be proved right in the near future.

Whatever his pardine qualities, I was, nonetheless, pleased to take my leave and make my way to the place of my apprenticeship in the cloisters of San Lorenzo. Here I met my master emerging with a pleasant-faced Englishman dressed in the travelling robes of their Church. My master introduced him as Gilbert Burnet, the Bishop of Salisbury, and there began one of the longest and most enduring friendships of my life. Wine had clearly, already, been consumed in some quantity as my master, though far from inebriated, was discussing the state of Florence with a loquacity which bordered upon the indiscreet.

'I have been telling Doctor Burnet,' he said as we fell into step and made our way towards the Medici Riccardi Palace, 'that there are two thousand three hundred oriental manuscripts in the Medici library. They are, indeed, the only manuscripts which we are apparently allowed to keep unmolested. That is obviously because there is no one in Florence who is able to read them. It is the apparent aim of the Grand Duke and his mother to create the largest and most incomprehensible library in the world. There is nothing so satisfying to minds such as those of Vittoria della Rovere than great works of science and literature which no one can understand. People fear nothing so much as that which they do not understand and fear of learning is precisely what she wishes to create.'

I viewed these pronouncements with considerable and increasing alarm. We were now close to the Medici Riccardi Palace and the Piazza was crowded. My master frequently excited attention by reason of his singular appearance but such views, expressed in public, were likely to result in a very different form of enquiry. Already, I fancied, there were three or four who kept pace with us for no better reason than to follow his words. I glanced at Gilbert Burnet who walked on the other side of my master listening to him and apparently oblivious to the risks that we ran. I have often observed since, that the English treat heresy as they do the unexpected defecations of their household pets. Although it is finally removed from the house it is first peered and poked at in the hope of ascertaining precisely what injurious matter has caused its unwelcome and maladorous arrival in their otherwise untroubled lives. In this habit they are unique in Europe and likely to remain so. Certainly, according to my observations, there is never any consideration given to thrashing the brute who has brought forth the excrescence and this leads them, unfortunately, to the supposition that all men possess so kindly, tolerant and eccentric a disposition. Many years later I asked the great Bishop whether, in that visit to Florence, he considered, even once, that my master risked having his arms torn from their sockets for expressing the views which he had. He admitted that it had never crossed his mind, thereby proving the truth of my clever analogy about dog shit.

As we turned to the front of the great palace matters became infinitely worse. A small but perceptible crowd had now gathered in our vicinity demonstrating by their affected indifference the fascination of my master's discourse. Across the Piazza, already bisected by the shadow of the palace itself, stood the dark face of the Jesuit Seminary, now the residence and headquarters of the Inquisition itself. As though oblivious to the attentions of the people about him, my master climbed the first three steps of the portico elevating himself barely to the height of the Bishop beside him. From this position, with his young apprentice (I now freely admit) endeavouring to merge into one of the stone pillars, he delivered the words which were subsequently to become famous in Tuscany and, indeed, the world.

'Here,' he said, gesticulating behind him at the great façade of Brunelleschi, 'letters were born again and there,' he continued, his arm now thrown forward in accusation at the impassive front of the seminary, 'there they returned to the grave.'

The Bishop dined with us that night. It is well known that he possessed one of the finest intelligences of his age. My own humble contributions to our conversation were received with a gravity and attention which neither elevated nor patronised their content. A measure of his greatness is to be found in the fact that, many years later, when I was proud to share his hospitality, he remembered almost to the word the stumbling opinions of a fifteen-year-old boy and, whilst not above teasing me with their ingenuous nature, he demonstrated by that recollection the true characteristic of the great; that no man and no idea seriously and benignly intentioned is worthy of anything other than respect.

When he had left, in Otto's company, I dared to comment on the affairs of the day.

'Master,' I said quietly.

'Yes, Fredo, you wish to upbraid me for my ill-considered outburst at the Medici Riccardi.'

I was, as always, startled to have my thoughts not only read but transcribed with such accuracy.

'Well, master . . .'

'Do not deny it, Fredo, you consider that it was ill-advised and dangerous. You are quite right and I regret it. I gave way to the most destructive force in the world. For twelve years I have restrained myself from *anger*. For twelve years I have followed a pathway of my own making, constructed from artifice and supported on lies. I have served the Grand Duke in order to mitigate, to delay; sometimes, as in the case of your own father, to protect the reputations of my friends. Without the influence that I had created by my own abasement he would not have survived the recriminations which followed his assault on Bomboni. We delay the taking of the books. Where possible I warn the Jews of fresh measures to be taken against them. The Ducal edicts are sent to the library for transcription. Thus I know what the law will be days, if not weeks, before it is passed. That, in itself, has saved lives. But I am a bauble, a plaything. Cosimo requires stature. He has little enough of his own making but he has inherited what is (or was) the greatest library in the world. He requires also the greatest bibliographer. Thus I survive the attacks on me by the Inquisition and the jealousy of his mother.

'This afternoon, the Bishop and I had been discussing the state of England. It is an open secret that men of all parties desire the end of the Stuart Kings. It is no secret that William of Orange has been invited to take the English crown. Already they speak of it as the Glorious Revolution. And why? It is because in England men of influence and power and wealth do not creep about in the servility of compromise; they do not sell their souls and their freedom for commercial monopolies; they do not tolerate the enforced poverty of their people, the bigotry of their masters and the persecution of the weak. For five years they tore each other apart not to establish a *form* of government but to establish a *direction* which their governments must take, an honourable path towards the public good. All this we discussed about *England*. But where is this in Tuscany, the birth-place of the Renaissance, the traditional protector of Science and Art, the greatest historical example of republican democracy buttressed by enlightened commerce and founded upon trade? It was when I walked into the street and simply *looked* at Florence that the anger became unendurable and I said things which, for all our sakes, would better have been left unsaid.'

None of this, I should say, was a declamation. He spoke the words almost in a monotone, the impediment in his speech, as always, lending emphasis without warning as though the poplars and hillsides of Tuscany were magically transposed onto some erratic score. I waited for him to continue but he was sunk in contemplation resting, as always, without comfort on the settle beside the great window.

That night I noticed that, unusually, he checked the shutters and the bolts before he went to bed and, as I climbed to my room, I felt myself to be alive with premonition. That evil, hardship and pain were involved I had no doubt. In a way I willed it upon me as a soldier longs for battle with the (invariably misconceived) belief that it will produce the final expiation of hope and fear alike.

Chapter Fifteen

I awoke in the early hours of the morning. No glimmer of light came through the shutters though my slow-candle still burned in its dish, illuminating the white mouldings above my head and causing the fruits and flowers within the decoration to dance and flicker as though in a morning wind. I knew, immediately, that I had been awoken by a sound although its identity and direction were lost in my receding sleep. I lay, staring at the ceiling and straining my ears towards the door of my room. This opened directly onto the balustrade which surrounded the stairwell and was the closest door to the stairs which led to the left of the front entrance.

As I listened I heard the noise again. Unmistakably a footstep on those very stairs but whether it ascended or descended was, of course, unknown to me. I remained rigid with concentration as a child counting the pause between lightning and thunder to ascertain whether the storm approaches or recedes. Seconds later I heard a further footstep, fainter now and plainly at the foot of the staircase.

My bedroom was immediately above the library and its windows gave onto the Via del Corso itself. I had discovered shortly after my arrival that the plaster and lathing which formed the ceiling of the library had been laid straight onto the underside of the oak floorboards of my room. In places tiny fissures had developed at the cracks in the boards, unnoticeable from below but evident in the darkness of my bedroom when the library was fully lit by its candelabra. This light then formed tiny rivers along the dark floor of my bedroom, mirrored in the white ceiling above. In the room itself it combined with the moving dust and formed a translucent image as though the finest imaginable lace hung, in irregular pattern, from wall to wall. I had also discovered, with a childish sense of mischief that, by applying my eyes immediately to these cracks, I could obtain a clear but strictly limited view of the library floor beneath. Since the library was in darkness none of these phenomena was observable around my bed. However, now I heard distinctly the cedar door below me, rarely closed, being pushed open and the faintest noise informed me that someone had entered the library itself.

I knew it was not my master. His disabilities ensured that his right leg was forever dragged after the other to be used, simply, as an intermediate prop for further momentum. Even with the aid of a handrail he could not have descended the stairs with such stealth. I had frequently heard my master about the house at night and it was abundantly clear that whoever was in the library, he or she was not its owner. As quietly as I was able I threw back the covers of my bed, swung my feet onto the floor and, crouching on the oak boards, established with my stroking fingers the widest of the gaps through which I knew it was possible to observe the central part of the first room immediately below. Attempting to judge the point where the deviation was greatest I lay full-length and peered downwards, pressing my forehead and cheekbone against the cool and polished surface of the black oak. I could immediately discern the light of a candle, flickering and moving in a line parallel to the front wall of the house and between the red bookcases invisible on either side. The man or woman who carried the light was also walking on the side of the room closest to the windows and was therefore excluded from my vision by the thickness of the wood and plaster below me. I contemplated moving to another vantage point parallel to that which I now occupied. At this stage, however, I dared not move since the light was now passing close to my position and, had the invisible person been but two paces to the right-hand side, he or she would have passed barely a man's length below me. I say that the figure was invisible but this was not strictly true. The candle was plainly held to the left-hand side of the body which, itself, was turned facing towards the street beyond the shuttered windows. I could clearly make out, therefore, the shadow thrown backwards across the library floor and could, indeed, discern the movements that were being made. With a sense of shock I realised that the unseen prowler was in the process of mounting one of the short box steps kept at intervals along the shelves. I could also see the distinct movement of an arm and realised that books or manuscripts were being taken from one of the alcoves set between the windows. As I watched the shadow foreshortened, indicating that the figure had dismounted the steps and the candle moved rapidly away towards that end of the room furthest from the entrance door. At this point I expected to see the light extinguished as it moved to the right-hand side, the only possible direction of travel, towards the great window and the canal. To my surprise, however, the light actually increased and became more stable as though the candle had been set, with others, upon a table. This was accompanied by a strange grating noise and then silence. The light remained burning.

Curiously, at that time, I felt little fear. At first, of course, I had imagined that the Salti were engaged in some attack on the house. But they did not travel alone and, once in possession of their warrants, would have little enough reason for silence or subterfuge. Emboldened by this conclusion I rose from the floor and contemplated action. I was reasonably sure that the door to the library, at the foot of the staircase, had not been closed. In the spring and summer months it generally remained, at least, ajar and was stiff and noisy in its final shutting. I was equally confident that I could descend the stairs in silence. Despite my ungainly body I was relatively light on my feet and the oak staircase was as solid as rock. Attempts to rouse my master or Otto would forewarn our visitor and, since I would initially be travelling in the opposite direction from the library, would provide him (or her) with a leisurely escape through the front door. Therefore, gathering up my resolve and the hem of my nightshirt, I slipped from my room and began slowly and silently to descend the stairs. When I reached the first landing and looked down directly to the marble floor below me I perceived that I had been right in at least one of my assumptions. The library door, to the right, was wide open and the light which I had observed from above was now faintly visible, falling gently and barely perceptibly on the red carpet which lay outside the entrance to the room. As I softly descended the final flight of steps I kept my eyes riveted upon this soft pool of light, increasingly fearful that, at any moment, a shadow would fall upon it, indicating a figure about to emerge below me. No such event occurred and, reaching the foot of the stairs, I crouched to barely the level of my knees and, leaning forward with infinite care, projected one eye beyond the fluted architrave which surrounded the doorway.

I could now see the full length of the room beyond, that same room which had so delighted my father before my own arrival into the world. At its far end I saw immediately the source of the light which I had observed, imperfectly, from above. A candle had, indeed, been placed upon the reading table by the last of the street windows. However, the main light emanated from the bookcases themselves or, rather, from a doorway set in the shelves which ran at right angles to the street and which were directly opposite the door where I knelt, some thirty paces distant. The far 'door' was in reality part of the bookcase itself and opened 'inwards', away from the library. The shelves of books could still be observed, at an angle, their bindings reflecting the light which came from a source in the corridor or room which lay beyond.

A mystery was therefore explained. Immediately I had come to the house, even in my distressed condition, I had noticed the absence of the inner door described by my father and, indeed, the screen which had concealed it. This door, with its filigree window was supposedly set into the bookcases in the corner closest to the canal. My fertile infant mind had, of course, quickly perceived the possibility of a *secret* door built to give better protection to the room which my father had discovered. When left on my own in the library I had, from time to time, inspected that part of the bookcase with considerable care. I had even removed several lines of books and manuscripts in order carefully to probe the woodwork beyond to identify any crack or break in its surface. There was none and I had long reached the conclusion that my father's account contained a measure of fantasy or exaggeration. Now, I deduced immediately what had been done. The whole wall of books had been brought forward to form a corridor behind them. A secret door had, indeed, been incorporated into the woodwork but it was at the *other end*, closer to the street. Thus, I reasoned from my crouching position, if I entered the 'doorway' of books, turned to the right down the corridor which had been formed I would arrive at the door with the filigree window now set in the wall a good arm's length behind the rear of the wooden bookcase. Since the library, in so far as it was visible, was empty of any human presence and since the part which turned towards the canal was patently in darkness I assumed that the mysterious book-taker had already passed through the secret door which, through idleness or inattention, he had omitted to close. I confess, now, that I was frightened but I was also unbearably curious and anxious to resolve a mystery which had occupied my dreams and imagination since my earliest years. As I straightened up I realised that my legs, unnoticed, had developed cramp in the awkward position I had chosen. I waited to enable the blood, once more, to flow past my knees and it was therefore with acute *agphispilli* in my feet that I crossed the floor of the library as a penitent treads on sharp stones towards the shrine of his God.

I did not think that I made any noise as I passed between the silent rows of books and the shuttered casements. When I reached the far wall

I noticed, immediately, and despite my nervous state, how cunningly the door had been constructed. Its outer edges comprised the upward supports of the shelving and the top of the shelving itself. The whole thing dropped backwards before it opened. It was carried on brass hinges and a running wheel, set into the back of the bookcase, held its weight as it swung. Sheets of glass had been inserted into the ends of the shelves, which became devoid of support as their neighbours came away. This glass was itself concealed at the edge by moulding and retained the books on either side. Beyond the door there was, indeed, a corridor which ran to the right and this was, itself, lined with shelves of rough construction and sparsely inhabited by books. Candelabra burnt in the passageway and, by their light I was able to recognise some of the volumes and manuscripts which had disappeared from my master's shelves in sympathy with the identical volumes appropriated from the Medici library. At the further end of the corridor, barely fifteen paces away, yet further light fell from an open doorway on the left-hand side. As I approached this aperture I could see that the door itself was set within an ornate frame and contained, in the middle of its upper panel, a window partly obscured by filigree carving. I felt a mounting sense of excitement and dread, my heart began to pound in my chest and my legs became numb above the raging pinpricks which still afflicted both feet. Then, as suddenly as those sensations arrived, they left me with that peculiar cold detachment that I have described before. I now approached the opening as though observing my own progress from a convenient vantage point, allowing appreciation of action and sensation alike.

Notwithstanding this onset of sang-froid I immediately started with the noise which reached my ears. It came from beyond the doorway whence I had heard, from the moment of entering the corridor, a light sporadic scratching. Now, however, this ceased altogether and I heard a single loud crunching and tearing noise which one's imagination might associate with the grinding of bones. This was followed by the sound of intermediate rasping and, thereafter, by the insistent light scratching which I had first observed. As I stood there this also ceased and again came the sound of sudden violent tearing. Shortly this also ceased and the scratching resumed. As this point I regained something of my courage, advanced the final steps to the doorway and, with less circumspection, peered into the room beyond.

It was much as my father had described: a tiny scriptorium. It was also lined with rudimentary shelves upon which volumes, books and manuscripts were scattered in haphazard profusion. In the centre of the room was a large desk in the middle of which a lamp burned, giving adequate light for study on both sides which were now occupied by silent figures bent industriously over their work. On the left hand my master, Antonio Magliabechi, sat in a chair liberally packed with faded cushions which supported the deformity of his back. He wore the clothes in which I had left him the evening before (indicating that his purported departure to bed had lacked its apparent conviction). In his right hand he held a fine quill with which he was writing with meticulous care. Between his downturned face and the table was an apparatus which I perceived at once to be a large magnifying lens, framed and attached to an adjustable upright bar, allowing a persistent enlargement of subject matter without the use of either hand. From his quill came part of the scratching noise which I had heard.

At almost the same moment that I looked into the room this studious calm was shattered by yet another rasping crunch which caused the librarian to glance quickly at his companion and utter a sharp and despairing remonstration. This second occupant of the room, seated at the right-hand side of the desk, appeared, at first glance, to be a small child. The chair was certainly a child's chair, although padded with cushions, and was raised to within inches of the desk height. Tiny legs swung over the edge of the cushions and the trunk of the body which was also hunched over the working surface was barely longer than the forearm of a man. The head, however, now turned slightly away from me, concealing the face, was of disproportionate size, resembling that of an adult, albeit of slight build. Before this figure was set a similar mounted glass beneath which another fine quill was clasped in the right hand. In the fingers of the left hand, now resting on the desk top, was a large green cucumber partly consumed and ragged at its upper extremity. It was plainly the violent biting and mastication of this vegetable which caused the noises to which I have referred and my master's evident irritation. At my master's reproof the child looked up at him and spoke. The words were indecipherable but the pitch was so low as to cause immediate astonishment. As he spoke he swung to the left, possibly intending to jump from the chair in the direction of the door where I stood. So swift and surprising was the movement that I remained quite immobile and we stared straight at each other for the first time.

A shock it must have been for him but nothing compared with that which it caused me. The face was that of an intensely ugly man in late

176

middle age. His dome-like head rose above his eyes even further, proportionately, than my master's. From the apex of this dome, however, a profusion of hair hung down to his shoulders hiding his baldness from both side and rear. Hair also sprouted from his cheekbones and in tufts along the line of his chin. His eyes were the only feature which approached normality, being green, wide-set and below exceptionally hairy eyebrows which lay across his face like the brushwood obstacles in a Sienese horserace. Below these a great bulbous nose hovered above a wide mouth from which, I noticed with a further sense of shock, protruded on either side two hideously enlarged teeth resembling the downward tusks of a boar.

For a number of seconds we sat observing each other to the accompaniment of the steady scratching of my master's pen. Then, to my considerable bewilderment, and without otherwise moving, he solemnly closed one eye in the international sign of jocular conspiracy and recognition. So doing he slightly inclined his head towards the bent figure of my master indicating, quite clearly, that if I wished to retreat from the room my visit would remain a secret shared. I was too surprised to do anything and, indeed, on observing this extraordinary face had instinctively straightened up to bring myself into a position fully visible within the doorway. Assuming from this point that I was not going to move, the grotesque face broke into a wide grin revealing still more of the tusks which protruded from his upper lip. He raised the cucumber, winked again and, in the stillness of the room, bit off a further two inches of the green tuber. My master's exclamation of annoyance was stifled as he looked up and saw me standing in the doorway. For several seconds there was silence save for the ruminative chewing. Indeed it was the dwarf who broke the silence. Having swallowed his mouthful he said in tones of some contrition, 'I'm afraid I forgot to close the door.' My master's response was to close his eyes in an exaggerated grimace of resigned annoyance and irritation. However, when he opened them they displayed his invariable good humour.

'It really is quite extraordinary,' he said, 'that the Credi family cannot keep out of my scriptorium. I have been to endless trouble and expense to ensure its privacy though why I should wish to cloister myself with this deafening display of gluttony I don't know. Well, Fredo, now that you are here, come in and all will be revealed. I have kept you in ignorance only for your own protection but now, I fear, you have become a conspirator.'

Thus bidden I advanced into the room and the dwarf, with a practised movement, propelled his backside from the chair to the desk, bringing the top of his head to a point barely a hand's-breadth below my chin. 'Welcome,' he said, 'to this forger's den.'

'This unreal object,' said my master, 'is Jacob Bonetti, universally known as "Bono". I obtained his services in much the same way that I acquired Otto's.'

My master then briefly recounted the strange life of his fellow scribe who sat on the edge of the desk, occasionally gnawing at his cucumber and generally smiling broadly at the improbable narrative.

At this time Bono was nearly fifty years of age. When my father first visited the Via del Corso he had been little above thirty and a new arrival at the librarian's house. Prior to that he had, for some years, been the property of Prince Mattias de Medici, brother of the then Grand Duke Ferdinando. During the Thirty Years' War Mattias had been one of the few successful Italian generals and, with the substantial booty obtained in the conflict, he had assembled a collection of grotesques and deformities of which Bono was a part. Mattias had purchased the dwarf from a Turkish merchant who had, himself, acquired him from pirates operating in the east Mediterranean. Before this transaction, which occurred when the dwarf was barely twenty-five years of age, he had travelled more of the civilised world than most men of full stature travel in a lifetime.

Some part of his early life was described to me that night sitting in the tiny scriptorium until the dawn rose and Otto disturbed us. Other parts were described during our subsequent journeys but here, in the briefest outline, is the story of Jacob Bonetti.

A Sicilian by birth, his native town was Licata, a fishing village on the southern coast. His parents were of normal stature and watched with increasing horror the stunted development of their only son destined, when born, to haul the nets, mend the family boat and provide subsistence during their dotage. By the age of eight not only was it clear that he was a dwarf but he had begun to develop the tusk-like teeth which earned him his early nickname 'Porcellino', the small boar. He also developed a prodigious appetite for certain fruit and vegetables including watermelons and cucumbers.

'This habit,' said my master, looking sternly at the remains of Bono's vegetable, 'is, of course, linked to his deformity. Lorenzo tells us that the lack of growth was caused by damage to the pituitary gland which leads, in turn, to a persistent demand for moisture, hence this infuriating eating. In the absence of ordinary food on which to gnaw, the teeth tend to grow longer and malformed. Needless to say this is not an explanation which concerns Turkish pirates (or, for that matter, those unfortunate enough to work in his company).'

Perceiving that their offspring, far from providing financial security, was likely to become a lifetime's responsibility, Bono's parents decided that they should rid themselves of their deformed son at the first opportunity. This was not as difficult as it sounded since, in those days, dwarfs were much in demand among the fashionable nobility of Europe. Indeed large sums of money were available to providers of suitable pygmies. Bono's greatest drawback, at the age of ten, was his illiteracy. He was certainly small enough to be fashionable and possessed an added attraction in his ability to consume forty cucumbers, twenty figs and twenty melons in a sitting. His boar-like teeth also gave him a certain *eleganza*. The difficulty lay in his lack of education. Enquiries made of merchants in Messina established that, whilst there was a substantial demand for dwarfs as pages, footmen or simply as exhibits and play-things, *clever* dwarfs were the order of the day. The fascination lay in the apparent contrast between the compression of the body and the burgeoning of the mind. The Bonettis' poverty allowed for no formal education and, whilst cucumbers and watermelons could be obtained in relative profusion, even their purchase placed an intolerable burden on the income of a Sicilian fisherman. One answer, of course, was the Sicilian custom of *abbandono*, the discarding of children in the mountains. Indeed Bono was close to such a fate when a happy solution was found in the shape of the plain and childless daughter of a local landowner and Don. This unhappy woman came upon the tiny child munching a cucumber on the outskirts of her father's estate. For it she immediately conceived a positively maternal affection and the Bonettis were thus relieved of the midget burden which threatened to crush their simple lives. A suitable sum was agreed and so the parents obtained their security and the son an elementary education at the hands of a tutor especially hired in Palermo.

The arrangement worked extremely well. The landowner, a mighty law-giver in the great Sicilian tradition, doted upon his daughter and his daughter doted upon Bono. The tutor from Palermo was treated, by contrast, with that universal contempt that Sicilians still reserve for those unable to do anything other than teach. He had a wretched existence, living in a large kennel at the extremity of the formal garden and produced on a daily basis to impart the joys of the classics to a melon-eating dwarf. This continued for five years until, at the age of fifteen,

Bono was pronouned literate and ready to take his place in Venetian society to which his mistress was destined in a final attempt to procure a husband.

Leaving the unfortunate tutor to cross the hills on foot, his services having been terminated, the family therefore set out for Palermo where they took ship for Venice, a voyage which lasted barely nine hours before they were seized by Turkish pirates. From the ensuing pillage, rape and murder Bono and his mistress were miraculously spared, an indulgence for which both could thank only their respective physical imperfections. Possibly considering such mercy a disgrace worse than death Bono's mistress hurled herself from the side of the Venetian vessel and was never seen again. It swiftly transpired, however, that Bono had been spared for a purpose. The pirates had their headquarters on an island to the south of Malta over which they shared an uneasy dominion with several other pirate crews containing the usual mixture of thugs, brigands, manic killers and disgraced members of the English nobility. One of these other crews possessed their own dwarf whom they had captured from a French boat a year before. The purpose of Bono's captivity was that he might be pitched against this midget in a contest which would provide some break in the unrelieved boredom of dog-fighting, cock-fighting, bear-baiting and the like.

At three feet nine inches the other dwarf towered over Bono by a clear foot and was thus handicapped by having one hand tied behind his back. For the other hand he was provided with a toledo while Bono was armed with a tiny shield constructed from the lid of a cooking pot and a spear normally used for impaling fish. At the outset Bono caused considerable consternation by refusing, point blank, to enter a contest with an adversary, whatever his size, who was so deliberately handi-capped. The other dwarf, an Englishman, for his part announced that he would rather die than be engaged in battle with an opponent so much smaller than himself. The likely result of this intransigence would have been the death of both of them had it not been for the fact that their respective contentions were endorsed by the rival pirate captains who had long been bitter enemies and contestants in the power struggle which inevitably seethed below the surface of any such mutual tenancy of a thieves' den. Harsh drunken words were exchanged, followed by blows. The first weapon was swiftly drawn and, in the ensuing bloody mayhem, many were hacked to pieces. (This last information came from Otto who, as pure coincidence would have it, was a fledgling member of the crew originally opposed to Bono's party.) In the chaos and carnage both dwarfs contrived to make their escape assisted, of course, by the ease with which their tiny forms were concealed.

Bono's companion was, he discovered, an extraordinary Englishman called Jeffrey Hudson and, whilst I initially doubted the accuracy of Bono's account, it was later precisely confirmed to me, during my years in England, by the abundant, if anecdotal, evidence about the life and works of this extraordinary midget. His sobriquet was 'Strenuous Jeffrey' and he had commanded a detachment of horse in the English Civil War. He was also an accomplished poet, lover and duellist whose opposition to the Parliamentary cause resulted in his banishment to France and, hence, his presence on the ship which was taken by the Turkish bullies.

The story of their escape and subsequent journey to England may be read in many chronicles although, since most of them bear the unmistakable authorship of Strenuous Jeffrey, Bono's part is not accorded the prominence which it undoubtedly deserved. Following the Restoration of the monarchy in 1660 he and Jeffrey had enjoyed several years of fame and fortune before the latter became involved in a duel. His antagonist, who did not know the dwarf's reputation, was an ignorant buffoon who treated the entire matter as a patronising joke. Thus he arrived in the early morning mist of Hampstead Heath together with his seconds and a pistol which was a disguised watersquirt. It must have been a matter of considerable astonishment, albeit short-lived, when the ball from Strenuous Jeffrey's pistol struck him between the eyes. This incident caused something of a scandal for which Bono, quite unjustly, bore a measure of the blame. He had been acting as Jeffrey's second and had thus been responsible for loading the pistol. His lack of stature had precluded his examination of the disguised watersquirt which was not, in any event, part of his conventional duties. Nonetheless he had been forced to leave England in some haste and, after a period of relative unhappiness and destitution which included being, once again, captured by Turks, had been 'purchased' for the collection of Mattias de Medici. Upon the death of the Prince, Bono's fortunes had, one again, fallen to the lowest ebb, his being near thirty years of age, racked by his congenital illness and subject to the resurgent bigotry of the times which increasingly branded deformity as the mark of the devil. In this extremity he was discovered by my master, close to beggary and sick nigh unto death. Thereafter the ministrations of Lorenzo Bellini had restored his health to the best possible extent and, for the past twenty years, he had enjoyed my master's protection and employment in return for which he had become, according to my master, the best midget librarian in Europe.

Some of this chronology I did not learn in the early hours of that morning but much of it I did. My master, once roused, was a voluble raconteur and Bono himself enjoyed little more than reciting his own exploits with his own peculiar brand of laconic emphasis.

Other mysteries were now explained by the dwarf, his extraordinary face animated with the pleasure of disclosure. It had, of course, been Bono, then twenty years younger, who had disturbed my father and caused his precipitate entry into this very room. In those days the door gave directly into the library and it was not for some years thereafter that the false bookcases had been constructed together with the secret door. Before my father's entry Bono had made good his escape through the opening into the ventilation shaft. The scriptorium, my master explained, had once been the access point to cellars below our feet which had provided dry storage for the barges which then used the canal. A ventilation shaft still extended from the cellars to the top of the house and was occasionally still employed by Bono to gain access to his own rooms where he had lived a happy and hermit existence for the past twenty years. The stairs to the cellarage had been destroyed when the stone floor of the room had been laid and the ventilation shaft now provided the only access and egress to the storage areas beneath us. Thus they remained inaccessible to any save a child or one of Bono's stature. Those who had constructed the shaft, Bono informed me, had helpfully provided a brick ladder as they did so. 'Although,' the dwarf continued, 'at my age I now prefer to use the stairs like everyone else, which carries with it, I fear, the danger of arousing inquisitive boys.'

'Why do you wish to remain so concealed?' I asked.

Throughout our conversations, or rather their narratives, he had continued to sit on the edge of the desk occasionally swinging his boots against it in jocular accompaniment to his theme. Now his mood changed and he said, 'I did not enjoy my life with Prince Mattias. This generation of the Mēdici are a cruel strain. I wore a collar like a Roman slave and performed for his guests. You may not be aware that small people like me are still traded across Europe like cattle. Also the Inquisition, even then, was growing stronger once more in answer to the religious bigotries of the North and the zealots on both sides place physical imperfection high in their demonology. I have no wish to be burnt or drowned nor, indeed, to be stretched. I have had the adventures of my life and I am content with my lot although the limited company which I keep could be improved from time to time as, indeed, it has been tonight.'

'He complains,' said my master, 'but he does not have to concentrate against the deafening mastication of cucumber.'

This observation led to my consideration of the work in hand, as to which I had restrained all enquiry with the studious care of the portrait-painter avoiding a wart. The peculiarity of the work was, however, apparent to even the most cursory examination. Both men were working with lenses of considerable power suspended, as I have already recorded, above the surface of the desk, thus magnifying the pages upon which they wrote. Beyond the lens each had a separate volume elevated to the near vertical by oak bookstands. I had not approached the desk to inspect the nature of the labour with which they were involved but, even from the point at which I sat, it was apparent that the pages upon which they wrote were half-covered by dense blocks of graphite ink.

'Well, Fredo,' said my master, 'now you are here you want to know what we are doing. Equally, I suppose, now that you *are* here there is no great harm in your knowing. As I have told you your ignorance was for your own protection, and, I suppose, ours. That consideration no longer applies. Also, even if you have not already guessed what is afoot you would do so soon enough. Come here, and I will show you.'

When I approached the desk I was able the more clearly to examine the manuscript which was standing on the oak bookrest on my master's side and, with a small frisson of shock, I realised that I had seen it before, not in the Medici library or that of my master but on the terrace at San Casciano. My master had begun his explanation.

'This work,' he said, gesturing towards the printed words, 'is ...'

'*Hypothesis physica nova*,' I said. 'Leibniz, I think.'

My master looked at me with considerable astonishment. No clue as to the author or the title appeared on the page which was set open. So great was his surprise that I could not resist continuing, 'He dedicated it, I understand, to both the Royal Society and the French Academy. He invented Differential Calculus and believes in a Holy War on the Egyptians,' I concluded, staring fixedly at a point on the wall.

'Well!' said my master, and I heard Bono snort with amused admiration. 'You are a permanent source of surprise to me, Fredo. Barely fifteen and already one of the world's greatest experts on heretics. Where does it all come from?'

I endeavoured to look suitably modest and non-committal whereupon my master said, with his usual perspicacity, 'I think I detect the hand of Lorenzo Bellini here, do I not?'

I must have blushed because he chuckled with delight and added,

'You are quite right not to attribute any credit to Lorenzo. He enjoys far too much of it already. In any event, over there,' he indicated the bound volume which stood on Bono's side of the desk, 'you will find the *Tractatus Theologico-Politicus*, a rather different kind of heresy from Baruch Spinoza, an excommunicated Jew *and* a heretic. Think how delighted the Salti would be to get hold of him! It is something of an irony that both the lenses which we are using were also made by Baruch and sent to me via your father as a present. He would be pleased to know that his practical scientific achievements were being used to protect his own heresies. Whether he'd take the same view of the German variety I doubt.'

'Protect them?'

'I hope so. Look through this.'

At his bidding I peered through the lens and was astonished to find that what appeared at a glance to be mere blocks of ink were, in fact, tiny uncut pages of writing and, even at that magnification, I recognised the unique character of my master's hand. Each 'block' of ink was, in fact, a copy of a page of manuscript. Closer examination through the lens revealed that the page had been finely ruled and that each of the tiny 'pages' occupied an area less than that covered by my three middle fingers placed together. Once cut and bound they would produce a whole volume capable of concealment in a man's hand. I looked up from the lens and became aware of the fact that both my master and Bono were regarding me intently from beyond the central lamp, their faces poised as artists prepared for approbation.

'It is remarkable,' I said, with some hesitation, 'but why . . .'

'Why?' said my master, suddenly a little testy, 'You need to ask that? We have known for twenty years that the libraries were under threat; that they would be decimated in the name of one religious or political bigotry or another. Once it starts in earnest it is too late. It is possible, of course, to delay them by the silly games that we play. We may trick them, deceive them (although I doubt it), we may even save the odd piece of unimportant and ancient rubbish which their demented selection process has omitted, but to *stop* them is impossible. The *only* answer is to conceal and to duplicate in such a way that the risk of discovery is removed. In this room and in the corridor outside are many of the volumes which have been selected for 'registration'. Yet this room is vulnerable as you, yourself, have demonstrated. Its existence is known to a number of people. Your father knew of its existence. In fact, it was his idea to change the position of the bookcases.'

'Did he know ...'

'About Bono? Oh yes, he and Bono knew each other well.' And the dwarf winked at me for the second time, a gesture on this occasion of mutual sympathy. 'Your father was, of course, bound to secrecy and that is why you, in your childhood, were aware of the mystery but not its solution.'

'Where are the ... new books?'

My master and the dwarf looked at each other and it was the dwarf who said, 'Down there.' As he spoke he stamped on the stone flags which stretched without break or interval from wall to wall. 'When they are finished they are cut and bound, placed in envelopes, sealed and waxed and stored below your feet.'

'There are,' said my master, 'beneath your feet near a thousand different publications of one kind or another all supposedly heretical. I have, of course, never seen it but it must be as close to hell as any Jesuit would wish to come. Bono, alone, has access to the cellar which he guards like some deformed Cerberus.'

Indeed, looking at Bono's grinning face, the analogy with the guardian of Hades was singularly apposite. The strange tusk-like teeth emerged on either side of his upper lip and my adolescent imagination had little difficulty sinking them into the calf of any would-be trespasser from the Bargello.

Now as I sit, in my dotage, bathed in the morning Tuscan sun and the enlightenment of the eighteenth century, that secret library of wax and paper inaccessible save to the child and the deformed and guarded by what Lorenzo described, rightly, as an army of grotesques seems as unreal as the coming of the Apocalypse. But then so does the persecution and killing of the Jews, so does the daily fear of the rack and the lash. Perhaps they will never come again. Perhaps the soft breezes of peace and toleration will continue to waft over Europe, barely stirring the pages of scientific discovery fearlessly contemplated on a million desks. Then few will believe what we did and even those who do will regard it as the eccentric preparation of the mad. But then they will sit upon the wonderful, green mountain in the middle of the landscape of hindsight. Theirs will be the cool perspective over the travellers of yesterday who can be seen making their stumbling way across that very landscape unable to see beyond the obstacles, obstructions and dangers and frequently driven by fear and apprehension into tortuous routes at which the Olympian onlooker, secure on his mountain, does nothing but wonder. But it was real enough then, the pain and the death and the fear, and it was not inconceivable *then* that those racks of envelopes sealed in their grease and guarded by their dwarf might not, one day, have been the sole surviving distillation of the genius of an age.

The extent of the dangers we ran was about to be suddenly and graphically increased on the very day following my momentous discovery. And, on that very day, in the midst of the turmoil, apprehension and fear I met and fell in love with Caterina. With the benefit of my own hindsight I now realise that this was the precise equivalent of a man surrounded by lions choosing, of his own volition, to skewer himself to a stake.

Chapter Sixteen

No natural light entered the scriptorium. None of us, therefore, was aware of the dawn until we heard Otto in the library and, in particular, a grunt of surprise undoubtedly caused by the open doorway in the bookcase. Within seconds his great black head had appeared around the door of the room and, on seeing me, a flicker seemed to pass across his forehead just above the level of his impassive and motionless eyebrows.

'There's no need to get so alarmed, Otto,' my master said, 'he found us himself as a result of this,' (he jerked a thumb towards Bono), 'coming down the stairs like a Cyclops, leaving the door open and making noises like the Great Flood with his cucumber.' Otto looked at Bono, who smiled disconcertingly and took another substantial bite from a similar vegetable he had retrieved from a box in the corner of the room which appeared to contain the entire contents of a market stall.

'Well,' said my master, rising, 'I came here to do an hour's work and I have ended up spending the night discussing pituitary glands and pirates. In two hours we will be expected at the library although I doubt whether we will get much concentration out of Fredo today. Still, we shall...'

As he paused we all heard the beating on the front door of the house.

'Lorenzo...?' said Bono.

My master shook his head. 'He is certainly in Pisa. Otto, come with me. Fredo, stay here for the moment.'

Within an instant he had returned. 'Salti. It is impossible to tell how many through the shutters but they are hammering fit to break down the door. Just in case they *do*, Fredo, remain here. We will shut you off from outside.'

He left the small scriptorium and, after the sound of his footsteps in the corridor, there came the same grating noise I had heard a matter of hours before in the safety of my own room. As the noise ceased so also did any sound from the front of the house and I realised that the combined depth of the bookcase and the volumes stored upon it formed a barrier virtually impervious to sound. Bono rummaged in a drawer at the side of the desk and obtained a short length of candle. This he lit from the lamp which, in turn, he extinguished. We were now in semi-darkness and I immediately made out a needle-thin shaft of light falling from the back of the bookcase opposite the door to the scriptorium. At this point, barely above head height, there was obviously a small hole in the wood unobscured by the contents of the bookcase on the far side. In the sepulchral gloom I pointed this out to Bono who nodded and disappeared into the corner of the room whence he returned bearing a rough pair of steps formed from two boxes and used by him, no doubt, to reach the shelves of his secret library. By mounting on the lower stair I was able to place my eye to the circle of light, reflecting as I did so, with surprising coolness of mind, that I seemed to be spending an uncommon proportion of my time peering through holes in wood.

The aperture through which I looked would barely have accommodated the tip of a normal quill. The wood, itself, was near an inch thick and, thereafter, my vision lay between two upright volumes which had fallen together over the space no doubt upon the removal of their neighbour possibly, I reflected, by Bono the day before. I had, therefore, a highly limited perspective as one might gain from observing a cathedral along the meanest of streets. Framed in this narrow triangle were two men. The one standing closer to me wore a light Florentine *lucco* and carried in his right hand a bound volume, his arm crooked about it in the unmistakable grasp of the scholar or cleric. He had small bird-like features and wore iron-rimmed spectacles upon which the morning light reflected, mirroring their surface and concealing the eyes. Notwithstanding this effect the whole cast of his head, thrust slightly forward from his stooping shoulders, revealed a querulous myopia which the lenses failed adequately to correct. Memory stirred within me like the rumble of a storm long past.

Behind him, and partly concealed by the folds of the *lucco*, was a taller, fatter figure dressed in the uniform of a captain of the Salti. His face at first appeared that of a man enjoying rude health but, even from my vantage, it was possible quickly to observe that the colour of his cheeks, a mottled purple, proceeded from inner disorder rather than the beneficial effects of the environment. However, despite his ugly demeanour he was oddly unthreatening, at least compared with the smaller figure before him who was now speaking towards an invisible audience to my right-hand side. As he spoke his head moved backwards and forwards in an oddly pecking motion and he raised the volume which he carried and tapped it with the fingers of his free hand as though in time with the movement of his head. To me neither this sound nor that of his voice was audible beyond the bookcase. The only aperture through which noise could have travelled was firmly stopped by the compression of my cheek and forehead. As I watched he ceased to speak and his bearing altered to that of a recipient rather than a donor of invective. Indeed, after a short while, he appeared to start backwards as though struck firmly between the eyes. It occurred to me, at this stage, that there was little to be gained by observing this half of a dialogue and, removing my eye from the hole, I replaced it with my ear. I heard my master speaking softly, swiftly, almost without intonation. I strained to decipher the words but was unable to do so, the sound being distorted by the crevice through which it came. At one point I imagined I heard the word 'grandmother' but dismissed it as unlikely. After a short while my master broke off and I heard instead a high-pitched squeaking voice, imperious like the morning jay. Still unable to ascertain the sense or meaning I replaced my eye to the aperture and was able to make out the same figure now crimson with apparent rage, his head jerking to and fro, causing his lenses to flash in the light which fell, with increasing strength, through the windows which faced the morning sun. Despite his menacing demeanour, the fact that I could hear nothing which was spoken caused me to feel curiously detached and even amused, as though watching a clever dumb show in which the the silent apoplexy provides always the greatest *divertimento*. I was therefore in a state of almost relaxed curiosity when the mime which I observed changed dramatically. Removing the book from under his arm the clerical gentleman raised it above his head and hurled it the length of the library towards the bookcase which formed my concealment. The leather bindings opened almost immediately and the released white pages fluttered wildly in descent like a shot bird. Immediately after releasing the volume the figure thrust out its right arm and, to my intense discomfiture, pointed directly at the hole through which only a tiny portion of my eyeball would have been visible upon the closest inspection. Not content with this single gesture of revelation he continued to thrust his index finger forward and back like a bradawl piercing leather. As he did so the volume of his voice plainly increased for, even in my obstructive position, I was able to hear the extreme pitch of the falsetto. I was so shocked by my disclosure that I remained, for a moment, rooted on the steps before I leapt backwards and scuttled into the tiny scriptorium where Bono, still seated upon the table, was thoughtfully chewing at a watermelon, a pastime which implied contempt for the Salti and all their works. He did, however, show some concern at my obvious agitation.

'They have seen me,' I hissed, desperately indicating the opening of the ventilation shaft which would, I suppose, have accommodated barely one half of my substantial buttocks. The dwarf's ancient face frowned at me in the candle-light.

'What?' he said. 'How could they?'

'He pointed straight at me, at the hole in the bookcase!'

The dwarf pondered this for a moment and then shook his head, bit into the watermelon and spoke through the pink flesh, 'He wasn't pointing at you, he was pointing at the space on the shelves.'

The obvious truth of this assertion did something to calm the rational man. However, within me, my heart continued to palpitate with the speed of the pursued. I had calmed myself, sufficiently, to contemplate returning to my post and was indeed halfway towards doing so when the grating noise began and the secret door swung inwards, allowing the morning sunlight to flow onto the books and shelves with which I was surrounded. To my immense relief my master entered first followed immediately by Otto. I could tell at once that he was angry by the jocular tone of his voice. 'They have gone, though not, I fear, with a happy and joyful valediction. In fact you could say that they were as wild as Turks, don't you think, Otto?' The black giant simply inclined his head and thoughtfully withdrew backwards into the library from which he had previously been excluding the majority of the light. I immediately followed him while my master spoke to Bono and, after a short while, emerged into the library alone. 'He says that he wishes to continue working. He also says that he feels a strong sense of impending crisis for which he wants to prepare. Otto will provide him with some more of his wretched fruit and also some food for us. After a sleepless night we are about to experience a difficult and possibly dangerous day.' I looked at him in some alarm and he continued, 'We have been ordered to the Pitti Palace. No, *not* by the Salti. They would take us to a very different place. I think that the summons is purely coincidental. As our Jesuit friend left a messenger arrived from the Court. They appeared quite surprised to see each other, which may provoke some continuing confusion to our mutual benefit. However, we are due at the Pitti at noon.'

'*I* am ordered to go?'

'Indeed yes, it is specifically *for you*. Cosimo has known for some time that you are my pupil, the son of Gallupe Credi, and now he wishes to meet you.'

I felt two emotions. The first, of course, was the kind of stomach-churning fear which would occur to any fifteen-year-old boy summoned to the presence of his Monarch, however benign a despot he might be. The fact that Cosimo and his mother had, from my early childhood, been synonymous with bigotry, intolerance, persecution, pain, torture and death did little to improve this natural reticence. The second emotion was more complicated and resulted, no doubt, from my state of fatigue. I felt as though I were gripped by some momentous force over which I had not the least control. As a sailor caught in rapids I was being pulled at increasing speed towards an unknown end; as a sailor I hoped for calm water but contemplated the void at least with the comfort and resignation of the hopelessly committed.

'Do not be alarmed,' said my master, intuitive as ever, 'I will be there and, also, the advantage of the inevitable is that it relieves the agony of indecision.'

The news of this summons had quite driven the morning's events from my mind and it was not until Otto returned bearing a cold dish of rice and tortelloni together with a small jug of the hot spiced wine (to which my master had become addicted) that I asked about the visit of the Salti.

'They were not all Salti,' said my master, forking a large quantity of the cold pasta beneath the huge beak of his nose, 'one of them was an infinitely more dangerous individual called Andrea Cortese.' At the mention of the name my recollection was suddenly complete.

'Of course,' I said, unnecessarily banging the table and causing my master to steady his jug of wine, 'Lorenzo was...'

'You have heard that story? Yes, that is right. He had Lorenzo arrested, or rather taken to the Bargello, some years ago. It was intended as a warning to us all. Interestingly enough, with me he employed precisely the same technique. Ingratiation followed by threat. He began by reciting my life and works from a book. I am pleased to say that I irritated him so much that he ended by throwing it across the room.' I smiled but my master did not notice. 'As a matter of fact, Fredo, his first complaint was about *you*.' I stopped smiling immediately. My master took a copious draught of his Barolo, pushed open the casement and continued his narrative whilst contemplating the flat expanse of the canal and the crenellated roofs which the sun now turned the colour of dried blood, across the flat expanse of the canal.

'"Signore Magliabechi," he said to me, "I am increasingly concerned at the calibre of your assistants in the library."

'"How very kind," I said to him, "You are going to send me some monks to assist them?"

'This plainly annoyed him, the more so as the purple-faced Salti captain began to snigger behind him.

'"I will send some monks to *replace* them if their work does not improve. It appears that they are wholly incapable of reading or understanding the lists with which they are provided."

'"Ah, I see. Well, I am afraid that is my fault and not that of my assistants. Since these volumes are required by the Holy Inquisition I have given strict instructions that the lists are to be obeyed *to the letter* and I fear that many of the lists contain works which cannot be precisely identified from the description which is given and...'

'As he grew angry I noticed, as Lorenzo remarked, that he fell quickly, and almost alarmingly, into the vulgar vernacular.

'"Do not fuck about with me, Signore Magliabechi, I am not here to listen to your crapulant whining about error. You know full well the little bastards are playing a game at which you connive. For a Jesuit, Signore Magliabechi, I have a lively sense of humour. When my list contains an order for the production of 'Leger' and I receive a dog-eared history of Leghorn I take it in good part. Some of my colleagues would say that there is a heretic at work but *I* know that it is just some little arsehole, his head filled full of shit, who is trying to be fucking clever at my expense. But I am sorry to say that even my tolerance has now been exhausted. As you may have observed this city is in the process of being cleansed. It is one of many areas in Christendom where enlightened rulers, assisted by the Inquisition and by my Society, are creating a secure fortress from which to attack the heretic and convert the heathen. My own responsibility is the destruction of heretical works and thus I play a small but vital part in this divine scheme to re-establish the true teachings of Christ and the authority of Mother Church. My part in this great Holy enterprise is not going to be buggered up by you or your bum boys in the Medici library. If you or they continue in this game then they will find that more than their arseholes will get stretched."

'I confess that my reaction was very similar to that of Lorenzo's. The crude violence of the language, following hard upon the unctuous

192

platitudes of the priest, left one numb as though suddenly plunged from the sun into a barrel of ice. Fortunately, unlike Lorenzo, I had been prepared by his very experience and, rightly or wrongly, I concluded that retaliation was the only appropriate method of response. I also, in a curious way, sensed an ally in the captain of the Salti who, for all his repellent appearance and transparent capacity for violence, appeared less than sympathetic to his twittering and foul-mouthed priest.

'"It must be terrible," I said "to live in the fear that you have." Well, it surprised him. More than surprised him for he actually stepped backwards as though I'd poked him in the eye. I took some advantage of this. "Digging out all these old manuscripts and books, most of them unread for centuries, some of them reduced to piles of dust, others providing a harmless shelter for worms and earwigs, many incomprehensible, most illegible and of such priceless significance that the Holy Inquisition itself cannot even write down their names without making more errors than a schoolboy with a running nose."

'I perceived, immediately, that this approach enjoyed the sympathy of our fat captain. I therefore decided that more was in order.

'"Is this *really* how your Society employs its best minds in the service of the Inquisition and Holy Mother Church? For I tell you it is laughable. It is like a young cuckold, crazed with jealousy, setting about every cripple and grandfather in the town to satisfy his own vanity while his wife's being poked at home." (The captain liked that enormously.) "And what is worse you make use of good soldiers. Brave men who should be fighting God's wars are, instead, used as nursemaids for milk-sops and bollockless eggheads who give them no better work than the baiting of Jews and spying on their grandmothers in case they become tarts." This last observation relied on a piece of gossip which I had fortunately heard two days ago. Apparently the Office of Public Decency, displaying a fine capacity for the insensitive, recently issued a directive to all ranks in the Salti exhorting them to special vigilance for sexual depravity, notwithstanding that the culprit came from within their own family. This, I was told, provoked a good deal of resentment and ribaldry upon the "who's screwing your grandmother?" lines. I could tell at once that it was a happy observation on my part as the Salti captain glanced at his two inferiors (standing uncomfortably close to me) in a way which clearly indicated a measure of agreement and support. Cortese saw it and flew into an uncontrollable rage ill-suited to the limitations of his own voice which squeaked like a rusty hinge. One of the Salti actually started to laugh at him which provoked the hurling of my biography.

(It was, incidentally, retrieved by the Captain when they left and, I was pleased to note, he rearranged it with a certain degree of reverence.) All in all I do not think that much ground has been lost but one thing caused me great concern. When he had lost control of his temper and his discretion he made it quite clear that they knew, or suspected, that books were being concealed and, indeed, pointed to the gaps which plainly now exist on my own shelves.'

'I thought he was pointing at me,' I said and, then, in answer to my master's raised eyebrows, "I found a spyhole at the back of the bookcase. It's over there.' I led him to the first room of the library and pointed to the space which had, on inspection, contained at least two volumes and into which as I knew, the adjacent manuscripts had fallen. In the middle of the triangle so formed a tiny black mark indicated the existence of the opening. My master smiled and said, 'It must have given you a considerable shock but may do something to cure your abominable curiosity.' Upon this note he turned purposefully towards the door as one about to embark upon a substantial venture. 'Come,' he said, 'we must set about this troublesome day. I have an appointment this morning on the Lungarno. I had intended to go with you to the library first but, if we are to be at the Pitti Palace by noon, then the library will have to await us. I will take you with me to the Lungarno. After this morning I do not want you wandering the streets on your own, particularly in the direction of San Lorenzo.'

I changed in my room with a growing sense of anticipation and excitement. It was widely rumoured that Antonio Magliabechi possessed a mistress. Indeed their relationship was the frequent subject of irreverent discussions among the apprentices and assistants at the library. Although I was a half-hearted participant in these conversations I had not, in reality, contemplated the sexual nature of their relationship until, as I have said, the visit of Mario's sister. The identity of his paramour was equally well known and was itself the subject of considerable amusement and speculation. Her name, or at least the name by which she was widely known, was Lisa Mascini. Now in her mid-fifties she had but recently retired from her 'career' as an actress with the Pratalino Theatre. She was a woman of immediate and striking beauty. She was short in stature, a fact which she sought to conceal by an untidy profusion of blonde hair heaped upon the top of her head and pinned below a red velvet *cuffia*. She also habitually wore shoes whose heels elevated her carriage to a highly precarious point at which she constituted a permanent danger both to herself and to those in the immediate vicinity of her substantial and jutting bosoms. When moving through Florence at speed (which she frequently did, being persistently in arrears of her own multifarious arrangements) she presented a prospect similar to one who has ventured unsuspectingly onto sheet ice and is endeavouring to retain balance by maintaining ever-increasing velocity in the forward plane.

Female actresses were, of course, banned in Tuscany as in most countries of Europe. She therefore adopted the artifice, common in the age, of assuming the identity of a man in order to play the part of a woman. This artifice was so well-known and essentially harmless that it had, for many years, enjoyed the connivance of the authorities. Indeed the only occasions upon which Lisa had even bothered to resemble her male self was on her journeys actually to the theatre. Even then she had done little but reverse her own corset in order, so she fondly believed, to distort her contours into a male configuration. Thus, in the theatrical changing rooms, whilst the leading boys and castrati were busily padding themselves forward she simply released her drawstring to the immeasurable delight of her fellow thespians. All this had ceased with the coming of the Office of Public Decency. Performances by female actors was, henceforth, to be regarded as analagous to prostitution and to carry the same penalty. It was widely believed that Lisa Mascini had, in any event, engaged in such alternative employment from time to time during those periods of inactivity to which the acting profession, in any age, is unhappily prone. Indeed her only daughter Caterina was reputed to be the offspring of a French count who had, for a period, been the official companion of Cosimo's estranged wife, Marguerite Louise. The birth of Caterina (rather than her conception) was, so it was said, at the express wish of this nobleman who had settled a considerable sum upon his erstwhile mistress and still, from time to time, visited Tuscany for no better reason than to gaze with paternal fondness upon his beautiful progeny. This last rumour, I was subsequently to learn, was wildly untrue but there was no doubt that Caterina was herself a considerable beauty, which I was soon to discover.

Lisa Mascini did little to discourage these accounts of her past life and, indeed, the more florid rumours and anecdotes were strongly suspected to emanate from her own mouth. She was, however, possessed of a tenacious instinct for self-preservation and, with the coming of the Office of Public Decency, she retired gracefully and finally from the stage, leaving behind an 'adoring and distraught' public (her own exact words), and embraced with ardour her employment as the mistress of Europe's greatest librarian, a post which she had, hitherto, occupied only on a part-time basis. Despite the financial security which this (together with her considerable and provident savings) provided she continued to occupy her house on the Lungarno, a notorious area of prostitutes, pimps, thieves, and members of the Salti who adopted the dual role of fornicator and flagellator with the effortless skill that has always been (and will always be) associated with those to whom the enforcement of public morals is ultimately entrusted. It was to this house, therefore, that we were bound as an interesting precursor to our audience with the Grand Duke and his zealot mother.

Thanks, in part, to the providence of my master and, in part, to the residue of my father's estate which was at my disposal I now possessed a reasonable wardrobe, at least for an assistant librarian. However, since I had never previously been in (or indeed close to) a bordello or a palace I had considerable difficulty selecting a suitable mixture of garments. Lest anyone should consider this a strange preoccupation for a young man surrounded by enemies and danger I would suggest that he (or she) carefully consider the histories of martyrs and take good notice of the extravagant care with which the majority of the condemned have dressed themselves for their final ceremony. I am afraid, however, that even to my seventy-fifth year I have a lamentable choice in clothing, an inevitable by-product, I fear, of my unappetising body. Dressing therefore, as I thought best, for Court and courtesan, I emerged finally in the absurd ballooning trousers of the modern fashion, clasped at the knee around red stockings stuffed into my librarian's shoes. The rest of my garments I now forget but I have little doubt that they constituted a similar medley. It is, indeed, a bitter reflection on the poverty of the times that people did not throw coins at me as I made my way along the Via del Corso, carefully avoiding the running sewage and the children who played, interminably, in its flow.

Once in the Piazza Beccaria we took a chair and crossed to the Lungarno on the Ponte San Niccolo. The summer heat was now with us and the stench which rose from the Arno penetrated the curtains of the sedan as though a solid, malodorous presence had pressed itself upon us. Once on the south bank of the great river the progress of the chairmen became even slower not, I suspect, through any crush of people but simply because the rotting matter which now formed the basis of the roadway rendered the surface as treacherous as glass. Twice the leading man fell, causing us to pitch forward against the wooden partition itself scratched and dented as a result of many such collisions. By the time we reached our destination the poor fellow was breathing heavily and venting oaths like a consistent Gregorian incantation. The knees of his stockings were both torn and bloody and the quantity of refuse which clung to the hose carried the certainty of future infection.

As my master paid him I inspected the street which, in the coming months, I was to know so well. It was a depressing thoroughfare save only for the villa which we were about to enter. Its white walls and green shutters had been newly painted and, of far greater significance, the short steps which led to the stones of the street were brimming with earthenware pots filled with lavender and carnations now in full flower. The same plants trailed from the window ledges whereby, as my master said, the visitor was enthused, even before his entrance, with the gaiety and warmth of his welcome.

'Where have you been?' said Lisa Mascini as she opened the door and then, seeing me, 'And what in God's name is that?'

'Now, Lisa,' said my master, ignoring the question and ushering me into the hallway beyond, 'we are not late and, in any event, we have been entertaining the Salti.'

'Bastards,' she said, without emphasis. 'What did they want?'

'Not very much. We exchanged some views on Greek literature.'

'How very, very dull. You know, Antonio, I have told you many, many times not to spend your life discussing Greek literature with the Salti. No good can conceivably come of it. You would be much better advised to spend your time here with me. Mind you, with the number of them who appear to live in the brothels down here I can't *think* how they get time to read.'

'Oh come, they're a remarkable body of men,' said my master, climbing the stairs which rose from the small antechamber, 'most of them can do several things at the same time, branding flesh, reciting Horace, disputing the merits of Iconoclasm. It's all part of the daily round. Come on, Fredo, don't listen to a thing she says, the poor old thing's quite addled. Oh, by the way,' he said, turning on the fourth step and raising his voice with exaggerated care as one would address a child or lunatic, 'this is Fredo Credi, sometimes we call him "Boti". He's the son of Gallupe Credi. You remember him, do you?' Without waiting for an answer he turned and resumed his slow crooked progress up the remainder of the stairs, leaving me confronting a smile as wide and wicked as an afternoon in May. She had the largest blue eyes I have ever seen in an Italian woman (with the exception of her daughter) and, as they looked at me, they danced with the light of experience, enthusiastically embraced.

'Fredo Credi,' she said, running a hand through the blonde chaos above her eyes, 'welcome, Fredo Credi. Lorenzo and your crooked master speak much of you. Also I knew your father.' Then, delighted at the expression which must have crossed my face, she said, 'Not well, but enough to place him in my geantology. Come upstairs. Lorenzo has only just said that he had not seen you.'

'Lorenzo is here?'

'You didn't know? That's the problem with being Antonio's pupil. You never learn anything. He came last night; they are all here, a more shrivelled bunch of conspirators it would be difficult to imagine.'

So saying, she took my arm in a grasp of unnecessary intimacy and led me, unprotesting, to the first landing. From this area a handsome doorway of figured oak let into a room which, I calculated, faced towards the Arno and, indeed, as I entered the sickly smell of the river was borne through the casements together with the morning heat. In order to minimise both, the shutters had been half-closed which gave to the walls a greenish tinge, almost sylvan in tone. The room appeared full, although, once I was myself seated, I counted but eight men. Vincenzo Viviani was there as was Carlo Dati, the writer. I recognised also Lorenzo Magalotti, the former secretary of the Cimento who had, on several occasions, visited our house in San Casciano prior to being banished, so it was said, by the Inquisition to Vienna. Lorenzo Bellini was there, sitting by the window and nodding his head while my master spoke urgently into his ear. As I entered the room he looked at me, continued nodding and gestured with his right hand that I should sit beside him. As I did so Magliabechi moved away to speak with two men whom I did not recognise but who carried the unmistakable stamp of Italian rank. Lorenzo turned to me.

'Well, how is our young Botticelli? I understand from Antonio that you have been creeping around the house at night and burying yourself behind bookcases, unwise at any time but at present close to suicidal.' I was about to answer him with some spirit but he smiled and raised his hand, 'I speak only in jest. I have long been in favour of your knowing our little secrets and now you do; or rather, to be more accurate, you soon will.'

Antonio was obviously the convenor of this gathering and shortly he started the proceedings with a peremptory cough.

'Signori, welcome. I regret to inform you that our friend in the Palace cannot be with us this morning. He is much concerned at the moment lest he should reveal his true sympathies. He has, however, provided me with such information as he can obtain from the Grand Duke. It is uniformly bad. There are to be further edicts concerning the Jews. They are now to be deprived of all their remaining rights as citizens and will thus become free targets for any bully boy, official or unofficial. A "pogrom" is thought to be inevitable though how serious it will be and whether it will obtain the active support of the Salti remains to be seen. It is important, therefore, that we warn such contacts as we have in the Jewish quarters though the steps they can take are necessarily limited. There is to be a new drive for the "registration" of books and the eradication of heresy. This I have already experienced at the hands of Andrea Cortese this very morning. The Office of Public Decency is to issue further exhortations on the reporting and prosecution of adultery, sodomy, incest and the like although, no doubt anticipating a poor harvest, the festival of Calendimaggio is to be reinstated with a special dispensation that, on that day alone, brocade and ribbons may be worn in public.'

Lorenzo shifted beside me, uncomfortable in the morning heat. 'God,' he whispered, 'the woman's as mad as a partridge.'

'As far as our friend is aware no more *specific* arrests are to be made although you will be aware that poor Luccetti has just been sent to the fortress at Volterra for a minimum period of forty years. In that place, in his condition, I would have thought it unlikely that he would last as many minutes.' This news, although plainly already known to some members of our gathering, provoked general murmuring and shaking of heads as though a pestilential wind had blown through the house.

'Finally, a "registration" is to take place involving all scientific instruments and paraphernalia including medical devices.' I saw Lorenzo start forward beside me. 'Yes, Lorenzo, I am afraid all your bleeding bowls and bollock-crushers are about to follow the books of the philosophers into the pit.' At this Lorenzo rolled his eyes, though whether at the news or the pleasantry it was impossible to say. My master continued.

'The time has plainly come to take more active steps towards concealment. At present we have deliberately revealed little of our own, individual precautions lest any of us are subsequently put to the torture. It is important, however, if there is to be a sudden purge that we are in a position to warn or assist each other. Furthermore there are certain collections and volumes of such unique value that immediate steps should be taken to protect them.' As he spoke these words my master, I noticed, looked directly at Vincenzo Viviani who, in turn, gazed unhappily out of the window.

A general discussion now ensued relating to certain works and collections of which I had not previously heard and also concerning Antonio's recent visit from Cortese. I was endeavouring to take an intelligent interest in this discourse when I felt a light nudge from Lorenzo and, following his brief nod, looked towards the girl who had just entered the room bearing a pitcher of wine, and a quantity of the dry salt biscuits now produced, as a monopoly, by the brothers Assinari. In all my experiences, thereafter, recklessly libidinous though many have been, I have never experienced a sensation which could be placed within the same category. As a lexicographer I can state, with certainty, that there is no word in the languages of southern or northern Europe, whatever their linguistic root, which has ever attempted adequately to describe it. Even the Germans, with their extraordinary habit of building words like a stone staircase in order slowly and laboriously to reach the summit of meaning, would require several pages of manuscript and still fail hopelessly on syntax alone. It was as though every puff of air and every drop of blood had been suddenly and efficiently removed from my body to be replaced with a fluid which invaded every touch and sensation, every sound and every sight, every thought and every perception. The feeling of her presence brought a suffusion of warmth immediately followed by an ice-like apprehension that she might, at any moment, disappear. This in turn was swamped by the radiant heat contained in the knowledge that she would then exist in another place accessible only by the universal nature of my adulation. 'Wine?' she said, pausing before me with her tray of glasses and decanters then, perceiving quickly that she dealt with a simpleton whose wide eyes, hanging mouth and blotched complexion stemmed from some congenital misfortune, she pronounced the words with exaggerated care and volume. 'Would ... you ... like ... a ... salty ... biscuit?' Faring no better with this approach, her features relapsed into a studied smile of condescension followed by a barely perceptible raising of the eyebrows as she turned towards Lorenzo Bellini.

'Yes, thank you,' said Lorenzo, pouring two glasses of Orvieto and seizing a handful of biscuits, 'I will take some for my young friend whom I expect to recover soon.'

I do not think he has ever been responsible for so inaccurate a prognosis. Sixty years later on a fine cool morning overlooking the most serene landscape in the world, I am still suffering.

She was *not* beautiful. Yet when she walked in the Piazzas or entered a room, male heads snapped round as though subject, suddenly, to some mystical cosmic force. I have watched it happen, sometimes with the smug satisfaction of the envied but more often with the dread of the insecure. Her mother, whilst manifestly and delightfully sluttish in demeanour, owned a fineness of feature quite lacking in her daughter. Caterina had wide robust cheekbones and a marked heaviness of chin as though both these characteristics were necessary to incorporate the vast blue eyes and the monstrous mouth suspended beneath her long aquiline nose, the only feature of sculptural significance. She had inherited her mother's blonde hair which, contrary to the fashion of the age (in so far as such things still existed in Tuscany), she wore loose about her shoulders. Like her mother she was short and her body well-endowed, her broad shoulders appearing to perform a necessary cantilever for her splendid breasts upon which so many eyes daily fastened in rapt admiration. Her buttocks were too large and her thighs pressed impatiently against the linen folds of her *soltana*.

Her character provided my most persistent problems. I reject the word 'unstable'. Her emotions resembled a high poplar subject to winter gales. And yet, to pursue the analogy, there was a part of her deeply rooted in the Tuscan soil, that part which required the nutrients to sustain the wild energies of her life, namely money and love. She devoured both; insatiably. I spent a good deal of my life in her high branches, swaying madly between ecstasy and perdition. The remainder I spent carefully tending her soil.

None of that, of course, was apparent to me in that moment, aged fifteen in the house on the Lungarno. The blood coursed, the head swam and I entered a kind of delirium wholly unsuitable to my surroundings and the urgency of the matters under discussion. As she left the room and my world dissolved into dust my attention was drawn, unwillingly, into the conversation concerning the great manuscripts of Galileo with the irritation similar to that which Alexander must have felt, when, having decided to conquer Asia, he was required to mediate in the squabbles of his eunuchs.

No one remained in any doubt as to the proximity of the danger. My master informed the meeting that he had now reached the inescapable conclusion that the attack presently mounted upon the libraries and their contents was not merely a Tuscan phenomenon.

'The bizarre mixture of the lists received from the Inquisition I had at first attributed to the obtuseness of a committee. Now I see this is not the case. A wider game is being played. Lists of proscribed works are circulating throughout Europe and, wherever the Inquisition regathers its strength, now largely in the hands of the Jesuits, the lists are amalgamated and the works upon them steadily destroyed.'

The discussion had previously centred upon methods of concealment and delay (although I noticed my master made no mention of the tiny manuscripts lying in the cellar of the Via del Corso). Now it concentrated upon the works of Galileo, and the bleating voice of Vincenzo Viviani filled the room like the sound of spring lambing.

'I really do not think I can bear this responsibility alone any longer,' he said in a series of nervous jerks. 'I know there are more modern works, developments, new revelations but if these originals fell into the wrong hands it would be catastrophic. They would be subject to any number of alterations and false interpretations which, without the originals, it would be impossible to refute. I do not exaggerate when I say that, with some ingenuity, we could be pushed back to the cosmology of the Dark Ages. I know that seems unthinkable but just reflect, for a moment, on how few men there are who could seriously refute such an attack. To the vast majority of mankind the stars might still be suspended from the heavens on ropes. It will take little to persuade them that any other view is nothing but a deranged heresy. We must not forget that man *wants* to believe he is the centre of his universe. Even the most enlightened of us have difficulty in conceiving otherwise.'

After this disjointed contribution there was an uncomfortable silence in the room, not infrequent when men of impeccable scholarship are impelled to the necessity for physical action. Characteristically it was Bellini who spoke.

'There is no doubt that the manuscripts must be removed from Vincenzo's house. When the searches start he will be a principal target.' At this bald pronouncement I saw Viviani experience an uncomfortable spasm, his eyes opening like those of a night owl. 'We must therefore decide,' continued Lorenzo, 'where they are to be stored and how they are to be moved. It is no easy task. They would cover half of this room to the height of Antonio's hump.'

As you may imagine this was greeted by a further uncomfortable silence. Whilst the meeting contained an impressive volume of intellect it was, let it be confessed, singularly deficient in the musculature necessary for such a task. Carlo Dati spoke in the vacuum.

'I know a landowner near Impruneta. He is an educated man, though half English and eccentric to the point of madness. He was a friend of the poet, Milton, in whose house we met. He was forced to leave England when his countrymen took leave of their senses and invited back the Stuart Kings. He had fought with Cromwell in Ireland and was therefore in some danger. He has taken his wife's name. She was a Tuscan girl, now alas dead, who was, I think, a cousin of Lisa's.' He glanced at Lisa Mascini, standing by the window, and she nodded in confirmation. 'In any event I know that Lisa and Caterina have been there from time to time. I'm sure he would help us if he knew of our purpose. At this time of year he cuts the first hay and his barns are full. They may well provide the hiding place we seek. Also, it occurs to me, that from time to time his wagons come to the city delivering that very commodity. They may provide a suitable, if somewhat undignified, vehicle for these great works. As to the means of loading them secretly I cannot assist you, Vincenzo. Unfortunately I, myself, have a bad back strain. The product, no doubt, of constipation.'

This information, delivered in the punctilious staccato for which Dati was well known, caused general relief in the meeting. It was agreed that Carlo, notwithstanding his physical condition, should take a carriage to Impruneta (barely as far as San Casciano) that very afternoon in order to ascertain the enthusiasm, or otherwise, of the expatriate farmer. Vincenzo, whilst plainly relieved at the prospect of discharging his awesome responsibilities, still remained concerned at the method.

'Even if this Englishman agrees to the plan,' he said in a somewhat querulous tone, 'how am I to load this haycart without attracting the very attention we seek to avoid? Also, Dati may have a bad back but I, for my part, have an extremely painful elbow.'

'I am very surprised,' said Lorenzo Bellini, smiling politely, 'that none of these physical infirmities has been brought to my attention. I am quite sure that, given a correct and careful diagnosis and the appropriate medicine, they may swiftly be cured.'

'Possibly,' said Vincenzo Viviani, regarding Lorenzo with a poisonous stare, 'but even were I at the apex of my condition I could not load these works, alone, in less than a day, by which time every bully boy in the Salti would be sitting in the cart.'

'That is true,' said Lorenzo seriously, 'which is why I, certainly, would give you every assistance.

'And so would I,' said my master, 'although, without wishing to add to the catalogue of infirmity, my own disability is apparent enough. However I have no doubt that Otto will be a willing assistant.'

I heard myself say that I would like to assist as well. I have since often reflected that, following the information supplied by Carlo Dati, I may have harboured motives ulterior to those of defending Academia but, given the confusion of my mind at that time, it is difficult to say. In any event, if there was such a purpose it was swiftly answered.

'You may count upon my assistance too,' said Lisa Mascini from the window. 'I would not miss this game for anything. It is many years since I have had a ride in a haycart. Caterina, I am sure, will want to join us.' So there it was again, the consummation of my blissful imaginings achieved, no doubt, by a measure of academic turpitude.

To my immeasurable disappointment Caterina did not reappear before the meeting ended and our conspiracy of scientists ushered forth into the polluted streets of the Lungarno. My misery was increased by the absence of chairs or carriages and I was therefore constrained to walk slowly beside my master, attempting to avoid the rotting matter on the roadway and suffering acute discomfort caused by my ballooned leggings which, at knee level, now cut sharply into the red stockings I had selected for my royal presentation. I fancied that we attracted a certain amount of attention as I minced towards the Ponte Vecchio beside the crab-like figure of my companion. We turned left into the Via Guicciardini and came to the first buildings of the Pitti Palace a full half-hour before the noon appointment. My master clearly enjoyed rights of access, at least into the outer grounds, and we passed through the first wicket gate and entered the extremity of the Boboli Gardens, the furthermost point of which I had first seen, exhausted and bloodstained, on my entry through the Porta Romana. The contrast with the streets of the Lungarno could not have been more marked. The gravelled paths, wide as carriages, bisected the green lawns like a geometric text. On each of the lawns miniature hedges and colourful displays of marigolds and lemon and orange trees surrounded monumental fountains of marble and stone. The midday sun was now of great heat and the water which fell upon the remote edges of the basins swiftly became steam adding to the perfect symmetry ethereal clouds of vapour. We stood for a moment, both, I think, entranced, when I heard my master's name being called from the direction of the palace and I recognised the approaching figure as Francesco Redi, the royal physician so maligned by Lorenzo Bellini. I had never met him but, on an occasion during my early days in Florence, he had been identified to me as he walked across the Ponte Vecchio.

'Antonio!' he called again as he came closer. 'I am pleased to have intercepted you. There is a matter which I need to discuss.'

My master made a small grimace in my direction and then, as Redi reached us, effected the necessary introductions.

204

'I know who you are,' said the physician, gazing at me from beneath a bushy set of eyebrows and dabbing perspiration from his face, 'I knew your father when we both attended the Cimento many years ago. He was a great man. I trust you will follow his example.' Despite my age and the awesome surroundings in which I was a stranger I felt angry at this wanton hypocrisy but I bit my lip and bowed at the compliment. 'I would like to talk to you alone, Antonio,' said Redi with significance and my master turned to me and said, 'Will you go ahead of me, Fredo. Do not be concerned. No one will accost you at this time of day. If you go through that archway and cross the courtyard beyond you will find stone benches in the cloister where you may wait in relative comfort.'

Thus directed, I bowed once more to Redi and made my way across the lawns, fifty paces or so to the stone archway set in the outer walls of the great Palazzo. As I went I confess to a feeling of steadily growing unease. Everywhere was deserted and the stillness was broken only by the distant chatter of the fountains and the air which danced in the midday heat.

I passed through the archway and saw, as my master had described, a large inner courtyard fully one hundred paces long and near that in width. Around its perimeter was a cloister formed in red marble, the interior of which, to my right-hand side, was entirely in shadow sufficient to hide any person or object beyond the row of arches. To the left-hand side the sun, now nearly overhead, imparted some light but, even here, the back wall of the cloister was in deep shadow although, at the far end, I could dimly perceive the stone bench of which my master had spoken. Inside the cloister the courtyard was bounded by a low box hedge and a gravel path. For the most part, however, the area was covered with a dense green carpet, camomile I suspect, and, in the centre, the inevitable fountain played.

I had reached a point halfway along the path when I heard the musket shot. Simultaneously marble splinters flew from a pillar immediately to the left of my head and I threw myself flat onto the ground before me. In this position I pressed my face against the gravel which, below its hot upper surface, remained damp from the daily ministrations of the Medici gardeners.

Only once before in my life had I been under fire and, on that occasion, my instincts had served me well, resulting in flight. Then, however, I had the cover of darkness, familiar terrain and the nearby security of the school buildings. Now I had none of these advantages and I lay without conscious decision motionless where I had fallen. It was a measure of my affliction that, at that moment, my thoughts were entirely filled with Caterina and the future imagined joys which would now, amost certainly, be denied me. In the renewed silence of the courtyard I heard the unmistakable rattle of a musket reloaded in expert hands and then, from the far cloisters, footsteps approached in a steady unhurried gait as though on a promenade. At first they sounded upon the gravel, then became muted on the soft herbal lawn. I even heard a short intake of breath as the musketeer passed, presumably, too close to the fountain's edge. Then, immediately behind my head, the footsteps once more fell upon the gravel, hesitated, then moved a little faster around the top of my body and came to rest before my open eyes. I saw a pair of black boots, highly polished but scuffed as though from recent riding. Between them and my face was the muzzle of a musket from which smoke still rose, in lazy ascent, in the clear, burning Tuscan air.

Chapter Seventeen

I closed my eyes and awaited my quietus. Silence followed. The water in the fountain rippled and a light breeze stirred the box hedge on my right-hand side. Then I heard behind me, with indescribable relief, the unmistakable dragging gait of my master. At the same time I heard his voice, raised in uncharacteristic alarm, from a point which I calculated to be just inside the archway.

'Grand Duchess!' he called. 'Your Highness...' He was interrupted by a voice, immediately above my head, speaking Italian with a marked accent, whether German or French I could not immediately define. It also sounded slightly drunk.

'Becci, *salute*! I suppose this belongs to you.' It was the second time that day that I had been referred to as an inanimate object and, to be frank, it was approaching the truth. My master was now very close and I heard him say, 'Yes, yes, Your Highness, he does indeed. He is my apprentice. I assure you that he is quite harmless and...'

'Oh, Becci,' said the voice with a tone of irritation, 'I wasn't aiming at *him*, I was aiming at the pillar. With these damned modern sights one can only see along the barrel. He just wandered into the line of fire. I say, why is he wearing those extraordinary trousers?'

The relief which flowed through me was total. The explanation seemed at least credible and, I imagined, those bent on murder did not usually concern themselves with the sartorial eccentricities of the victim. In any event my master avoided the question.

'Do you think he could get up? We have an audience with your husband in barely fifteen minutes' time.'

'Of course he may get up. I would quite like to have a look at him. He appears terribly overweight.'

Requiring no further bidding I scrambled to my feet, shedding gravel from my garments like hailstones. As I did so I found myself under the scrutiny of a penetrating green eye, its companion being concealed by a black velvet patch which fluttered slightly in the breeze. I was, I knew, in the presence of Marguerite Louise d'Orléans, Grand Duchess of Tuscany, the estranged wife of Cosimo, the cousin of Louis XIV and, by all accounts, one of the most remarkable women of her century. I already knew much of her history since it had, for years, provided the principal gossip in Florence, if not the whole of Europe. She had married the Grand Duke, with extreme reluctance, ten years before my birth in 1661 when she was fifteen years of age. It was widely known that she had been forced to marry at the insistence of Cardinal Mazarin, the most powerful man in France and an aspiring Pope. It was this ambition which had caused him to promote the marriage at a time when the Medici supposedly retained some influence in the Vatican. From the moment of her arrival in Tuscany she had loathed her husband and hated and detested his mother, Vittoria della Rovere. Despite bearing him two sons (the younger of whom, Gian Gastone, was my exact contemporary) she had ceaselessly connived and plotted to obtain her own return to France. This had taken numerous forms from persistent infidelity to a fraudulent contraction of smallpox. All this caused much delight among the city people who turned her into something of a heroine. Finally, twelve years before our meeting, she had persuaded both her husband and the French King to allow her return to France where she had been, for many years, a principal source of scandal. Indeed, when she departed from the Pitti Palace, it was discovered that she had stolen the vast majority of the Medici silver. It was also widely put about that she and my master had enjoyed a considerable friendship and his appointment as librarian had been one of her final acts of influence.

'Well, he doesn't look too stupid,' she said, removing the patch from her left eye and revealing a perfectly sound pupil beneath. 'It's these damned modern sights. You have to blank out one eye to get a decent bead. It's not too difficult but it does stop you seeing approaching librarians. Well, Becci,' she said, turning to my master, 'is my fat mother-in-law still in charge in the Pitti Palace?'

'I think that would be the general view,' said my master, smiling diplomatically, 'but it is an unexpected pleasure to see Your Royal Highness. I believed you to be in Paris.'

'Your intelligence is impeccable as always. I have been there for the last ten years. I have come to see my younger son. Why, I can't think. He's grown up just like his father, or rather his grandmother, dull, fat, bigoted, cruel and obsessed with the supposed ailments of his own

208

disgusting body. I shall leave at dawn tomorrow. Everyone knows that I am here but no one will admit it. Louis positively forbade me to come and then paid for my carriage. Cosimo actually *saw* me as he passed through his son's apartments and affected not to notice. I wish that he had always behaved in the same way. Still, officially, I am travelling *incognito.'*

The idea of Marguerite Louise passing unnoticed in any environment was extraordinary. Above her green eyes, upturned patch and wide forehead was an impossible profusion of dyed red hair set in ringlets which cascaded to her shoulders like Medusan serpents. She was little over forty at the time but, on closer inspection, she appeared somewhat older. Her long angular face, the colour of light oak and raddled with lines, was aged by an unlikely mixture of weather and dissipation. That she had once been beautiful could not be doubted. Whether she remained so depended entirely upon the set of her features. For when she smiled the great green eyes eradicated the imperfections like the sun reflected from a broken shield.

'Did you know,' she demanded of my master, 'that they had locked me up in the convent at Montmartre? Can you imagine it? Me! It was supposedly one of the conditions for going home but I never thought that they'd stick to it. I tell you, Becci, it was absolutely dreadful. Within weeks I had been hauled in front of the King for attacking the Mother Superior with a chopper. All quite untrue, of course. I had only *threatened* her with the chopper when she refused to allow me out of the building. Anyway it's been a lot better since. She died immediately afterwards (of natural causes, of course) and they had some difficulty replacing her. Now we've got a charming old girl who minds her own business. Not so many nuns though, the place has got a bit of a reputation. I'm afraid I shot one the other day. Similar sort of problem. These damned sights. Anyway, Becci, tell me about Florence. They're burning the Jews and books, I gather?' Despite the apparent callousness of her question her tone had lost all jocularity. 'There's no need to tell me. I know that it is true. My son told me with a certain amount of unpleasant satisfaction. It's the priests behind it, of course. All this claptrap about heresy, Order and Divine Right. It's starting in France. I am afraid that this so-called Enlightened Age may already have reached nightfall. Still, time will tell, I've never taken much part in it as you know. It all seems so *meaningless* and cruel. I just spend my time shooting small birds and librarians.' So saying she turned towards me and her smile reduced her to an age of mischief scarcely greater than my own. 'You know, Becci, he's not bad-looking when he holds his head up. Tell him to brush himself down before he sees the great Fat Gut. I suppose it's too late for him to change his trousers? Not that Cosimo will notice. He'll be far too preoccupied with his own health. Do you know,' she said to me, her eyes narrowing with amusement, 'that on our wedding night he was attended by a physician *throughout*? Can you imagine it? He gave vent to his passion with one arm thrust through the curtains of the bed so that his pulse could be permanently checked!'

I confess that I was somewhat embarrassed by this revelation but endeavoured to accord it the consideration it deserved by smiling with tight-lipped sympathy and imperceptibly nodding my head. This amused her enormously and she guffawed with laughter, at the same time poking my chest uncomfortably with her gloved finger. 'Well, Becci, I think you have chosen well with this boy. What's his name?'

'His name is Fredo Credi, Gallupe's son, and now, Grand Duchess, if we do not go we will be late ... he will be in danger of a public flogging.'

'Fredo Credi,' she repeated, 'Gallupe's son. I knew your father. He ...' She broke off, sensing, perhaps for the first time, the agonies of apprehension with which I was now gripped. 'But of course Becci is quite right, you must not be late. Get along, Fredo Credi, I am pleased to have met you. And take good care of this old snail. Like his body he is a triumph of hope over disaster.'

As we left her presence (I had not, to my recollection, uttered a single word) she and my master exchanged inaudible and mercifully short admonitions before we hurried to the end of the cloister and passed through a further, smaller archway into the palace beyond.

The magnificence of the Pitti Palace has had many chroniclers whom I will not seek to emulate. I dislike it still. My country upbringing rebels against a profusion of paint however great. But if you wish to experience the genius of Italian art laid out as though on a market stall then there is no better place to go. Here, in the first rooms which we entered, beneath the ceilings of Cortona one may admire the works of Raphael and Rosa, Rosselli and Manetti, Titian and Tintoretto, del Sarto and Veronese, Salviati and Bartolomeo, thrown the one upon the other in baroque confusion. None of this did I notice then as I flew past them, scattering gravel as I went, the crooked figure of my master painfully hauling himself forward in a grotesque *courante*. Here again the great chambers were strangely deserted save for the presence of attendants in the livery of the Medici who observed our progress with the indifference of stone. Finally we came to the Appartamenti Monumentali and were brought to a halt by attendants who barred the entrance to the antechamber beyond which lay the audience room of the Grand Duke. Here Medici guardsmen stood at the four corners of the chamber and, at the double doors themselves, a further four were posted. At a desk immediately before these doors sat a clerk bearing upon his *lucco* the mark of the Medici bureaucracy, itself once a model to the world after its creation by the young Machiavelli. Upon this desk my master laid the credentials which had accompanied our summons and the clerk, without speaking, rose and disappeared through a smaller door close to the corner of the room. Almost immediately he returned and, without speaking, indicated that we should take our places on the stone benches which lined the walls. Onto this welcome ledge I lowered my panting figure, aware, as I did so, of the ridiculous breeches which ballooned upwards before me.

In the silence of the room the minutes passed in slow procession. I began to feel a great weariness. On little sleep I had lived through a day unlike any in my experience. With the growing torpor my apprehension receded towards indifference and, even, a feeling close to irritation. I placed my head back against the cold stone and closed my eyes.

I was awoken by a considerable noise emanating from the double doors which were now opened outwards into the chamber where we sat. A substantial number of people were disgorged through the opening, all walking backwards, their heads bowed, as though simultaneously impelled into some lunatic fandango. I assumed, rightly, that they were leaving the royal presence. The method of their leaving was, for us, a blessing since the entire group continued thus across the anteroom and through the doors beyond. These were then closed, ensuring that those who had passed through could neither see nor identify those waiting for the royal audience in which, of course, we were included. The constituent parts of the retreating group, however, were alarming. They were about twenty in number. Two were plainly Medici officials who wore the emblazoned *lucco* similar to that worn by the clerk. Of the remainder approximately half wore the black robes of the Jesuits and the remainder the uniform of the Salti. Within these two groups I recognised the figures of Andrea Cortese and Pasto Bomboni. My master had, of course, made the same observation and he continued to watch the closed door, his face puckered with concentration.

'A merry bag of ferrets,' he said softly. 'Where are the rabbits, I wonder?'

The doors to the audience chamber were now, once again, firmly closed and we resumed our waiting. Time passed and, at irregular intervals, others arrived bearing summonses or supplications and, at the direction of the clerk, joined us on the stone bench against the wall. Among these later arrivals I recognised one of the brothers Castanelli who had been granted the monopoly in leather, dyemaking and sewage-collection. By the abuse of this power, together with regular bullying, they had become as rich as the Assinari, a fact well attested by the ostentatious vulgarity of his dress. With some discomfiture I observed the approving glance he cast at my own breeches. We waited.

Finally, nearly two hours after our initial arrival, the small corner door opened and a further clerk entered the room. He was, in every way, identical to the first save that he was able to demonstrate the power of speech. In a high falsetto he announced that the audience would now begin. In view of the unavoidable delay, he said, all those who had been summoned would receive their audience at the same time. This news caused me considerable relief since it afforded the clear possibility of merging unnoticed into the crowd. Not for the first time I cursed my pantaloons. However, beside Carlo Castanelli, I appeared positively monastic and this afforded some sense of security.

Immediately the clerk had finished speaking the doors were thrown open by two footmen and we were ushered into the royal presence.

The first, abiding and lasting impression was one of corpulence. Cosimo and his mother sat on a raised dais. There were two other seated figures. A scribe sat at a desk immediately below the ducal thrones and, on a separate but smaller throne, a little to the right and slightly below the Grand Duchess, was an ill-tempered scowling man of indeterminate old age who, I learnt subsequently, was Giuseppe Tarcone, the Chancellor, a man whose reputation for nepotism and the sale of offices was a legend throughout Italy.

All four figures were immensely fat. The Grand Duke and his mother both wore the fashionable ruffs around their necks, an unfortunate choice since they elevated the numerous chins and folds of flesh into a single pronounced balloon immediately below their mouths. The effect, as my master remarked later, was similar to the primitive sack distended by bullfrogs when approaching the frenzy of courtship. (It also, plainly, rendered speaking uncomfortable since the pressure of the flesh below remorselessly elevated the lower lip whenever the mouth was opened.) Above the chins both mother and son possessed the fleshy bulbous nose of the Habsburgs separating tiny, suspicious Tuscan eyes. When I was in England, many years later, I learnt that the great diarist, Samuel

Pepys, had described Cosimo, on a visit to London, as a 'most good and comely fellow'. When I subsequently taxed Pepys with this patent inaccuracy he admitted that he had never actually seen the Grand Duke but had relied on a painting by Sustermans which had been circulated prior to the royal visit. This I mention only to demonstrate the care which must be taken when approaching even the best of English correspondents.

Cosimo's appearance was in no way further enhanced by a peculiar contraption set upon his head. At first sight this appeared to be a sheep's bladder and, indeed, I subsequently ascertained that it was. This was draped across his shoulders and, by some means invisible, suspended on the top of his head. Above this was pinned the full-bottomed black wig which remains the only accurate part of the Sustermans painting. The bladder was clearly part full of some liquid for it heaved and wobbled slightly with every movement of the royal head. The source of the liquid was readily apparent. Behind him stood Francesco Redi, the physician, who had, several hours earlier, accosted my master in the Boboli Gardens. To his side, and plainly under his tutelage, stood a page with a pitcher of some steaming mixture. From time to time, at the instruction of Redi, the page raised one of the ventricles still attached to the bladder and poured in a quantity of the liquid through a small funnel. He then applied a wooden clip to the orifice and, taking the second ventricle, removed a similar clip to allow a further quantity of the liquid, now no doubt cooler, to flow into a bowl. Of this process no one appeared to take the slightest notice. (My master subsequently remarked that, whatever its *medical* efficacy, the contraption was unlikely to find a widespread commercial market for its inventor.)

Ranged alongside Redi were a number of clerks and dignitaries all wearing the Medici crest upon the *lucco*. Several guardsmen stood against the walls which were, again, covered in a profusion of oil paint and gilt frame. On the vaulted ceiling above our heads was a vast fresco of the enthroned Deity surrounded by billowing cloud, heavenly horsemen, cherubim, seraphim and a seated figure, only slightly smaller than the Almighty, which, despite a number of flattering deductions (and the absence of the bladder), was plainly identifiable as the Grand Duke himself. As we entered the room we were required to adopt a crouching posture, similar to that exhibited by those who had retired from it barely an hour before.

The general purpose of the audience was one of introduction. As names were called those who were thus indicated made the same formal address. This consisted of the words, 'I salute Your Royal Highness and crave leave to present (so and so) my ward/assistant/new *commesso*.' Carlo Castanelli thus introduced his new 'captain of security', a thinly disguised street thug engaged, no doubt, in the enforcement of the monopoly. To all of the introductions the Grand Duke and Duchess gracefully inclined their heads, the former causing the distended bladder to tremble and oscillate and, through its ventricles, to emit small frothy gurgles and puffs of steam.

At length my master's name was called. I bowed my head and heard him recite the established formula 'I salute Your Royal Highness and crave leave to present Frederico Szorzi Credi, my new pupil and apprentice for the care and maintenance of your great library.' To my horror this did not evoke the familiar and formal response.

'Ah, Signore Magliabechi,' said the Grand Duke, speaking with considerable difficulty, his bottom lip thrusting uncontrollably upwards and the ventricles belching quietly behind him. 'We had particularly desired to see your apprentice. We understand him to be the son of Gallupe Credi, the Hero of ... of ...' One of the clerks bent quickly behind him and spoke into the side of the bladder. '... Mongiorno. A great man. Intemperate perhaps but a great man. I hope he will follow his father's example.'

'He is a gifted and zealous pupil, Your Highness.'

'Let us hope that his zealotry extends to the pursuit and destruction of heresy. You must understand,' and the Grand Duke's eyes were now fixed like staples upon me, 'that the care of the great library does not just involve the dusting of books. In so vast a collection the devil will undoubtedly find his way. Many can collect ephemeral knowledge and place it in rows for the edification of fools but there comes a time when the Almighty appoints One to cleanse. That time has now come. We look to you as our agent in this work.'

My master answered, 'Your Royal Highness does us great honour and we will strive to serve such a cause.'

The Grand Duchess now spoke, her Northern birth betrayed by the flat hardening of the language. 'Yet we are informed that the demands of the Holy Inquisition are not met.' Total silence pervaded the chamber. Even the bladder became still. My master spoke.

'My Lady, your informant errs. No doubt through excess of zeal. That which the Inquisition demand they are given. I have indeed become concerned that the Jesuits' seminary must now contain the largest heretical library in the world. Small wonder that those so exposed may be driven into error.' A slight murmur of amusement ran around the chamber, swiftly stifled by the Grand Duchess whose face had set like rock. After a pause she said, 'Your apprentices and assistants would do well to bear in mind, Signore Magliabechi, that the penalty for the concealment of heresy is the galleys or the fortress at Volterra.'

My master inclined his head, 'None of them, my Lady, entertains any doubt as to the gravity of his task.'

Silence again fell in the chamber before Cosimo raised his hand and, following this bidding, the clerk called the next summons whilst I gazed down at my ballooning breeches, wretched with the sense of impending doom.

Shortly thereafter the audience concluded and we all backed solemnly through the doors and passed the antechamber beyond. As the second doors closed before us I sensed an isolation whilst our fellow citizens moved away from our path and we bore the royal displeasure, like leprosy, down the great staircase, through the gilded rooms and into the cloister beyond.

'Let us hope,' said my master as we made our halting way along the gravel, 'that Marguerite Louise has found another target or is at least using both eyes.'

In the event we gained the shelter of the outer archway unmolested by gunfire and made our way to the wicket gate which separated the gardens from the Via Romana. The Medici guardsmen were changing posts and it was necessary to wait a short while before the gate was opened. Outside, we turned and made our way towards the Ponte Vecchio, walking in silence until the Lungarno appeared. As we climbed the slope of the famous bridge past the odd assortment of butchers' shops and jewel traders which lined its sides a great sadness fell upon me. We were, of course, close to the point where my mother had leapt to her death and the contemplation of that moment, as always, provoked a flat melancholy not improved by the perilous nature of our present undertakings. Perceptive as ever, my master provided some instant light and hope.

'We must return to Lisa Mascini's tomorrow at noon. By then Carlo Dati will have returned from his English haymaker and we can, I hope, relieve poor Vincenzo of his burdens. Also, I fancy,' he said eyeing me across his crooked shoulder, 'you would not be averse to visiting her house in any event.'

I smiled at his intuition and my colouring must have risen for he said,

215

'Yes I see that I am correct. Take care, Boti Credi, that girl will break a large number of hearts.'

I said nothing and we descended towards the Piazza della Signoria, its brick concourse part black with shadow and part roseate in the evening air. A small breeze lifted the flags which flew on the old Medici Palace and also brought the stench of the Arno flowing between the buildings, a messenger of pestilence and death in which the marble and alabaster statues stood like immovable and vengeful gods.

We crossed the Piazza and, as usual, made our way along the Via de' Calzaioli. When we came to Orsanmichele my master stopped to examine the tabernacles of the Guilds upon which the statues of Ghiberti, Donatello and Lamberti paid sublime obseisance to the marriage of commerce and art from which the Renaissance was conceived. I waited, a little impatiently, while he peered against the light. I was, of course, far too young to observe art as anything other than a pleasant abstraction. After several minutes of motionless contemplation my master shook his head as though to dispel water from his scattered hairs and, to my surprise and without explanation, turned on his heel, recrossed the Piazza della Signoria and made his way along the Borgo dei Greci towards the great church of Santa Croce. He did not enter but skirted the right hand of the portico and came at length to the Pazzi Chapel, the most perfect example of symmetry and scale which has ever been created. 'To enter it,' he said much later, 'is the closest one can ever get to entering the soul.' At the time I regarded the comment as a florid eccentricity but have since, many times, marvelled at its truth.

The Chapel was deserted and my master sat hunched upon the stone step that runs between the ribs of the building which, themselves, arise among the Pietra Serena to support the perfect dome. No building has ever equalled its blend of peace and strength and the effect on any mind is still irresistibly narcotic. As I sat on the stone step furthest removed from my master I became slowly aware of a low humming which filled the vaulted space with the resonance of a plucked string. Mesmerised, I listened to the rise and fall of the cadence and became aware that I was listening to the steady pace of a Gregorian chant softly intoned and filling the building like warmth from the morning sun. When it finally ceased the echo hung beneath the dome and it impressed into the ear of the imagination. Where my master had learnt such a song I never knew. As to its significance, if any, I likewise remain in ignorance.

As we left the building my master turned and examined the portico of Giuliano da Maiano.

'That chapel,' he said, 'was commissioned by the great Pazzi family for their prayer and contemplation. On the year that it was completed Francesco de' Pazzi attempted to murder Lorenzo de' Medici by stabbing him in the neck during a Mass in the Cathedral. He failed, so the Medicis chopped off his legs, put a rope around his neck and threw him from the top window of the Palazzo Vecchio. Did you know that story, Fredo?'

I said that, of course, I had heard of the Pazzi conspiracy but had never contemplated how truly wicked the act had been.

'Oh yes, they killed his poor brother Giuliano de' Medici by mistake. The priests were involved in the plot, you see. Invariably a mistake to invite them, I am afraid. Come, I will show you where Giuliano died.'

It was apparent that our wanderings had not yet finished. The prospect of danger clearly made him active and, although I longed for the security of the Via del Corso, I followed him dutifully as he picked his way through the detritus of the city to the great pile of the Duomo and the bell tower of Giotto. As we entered, Mass was in progress and the singing filled the vast cupola with no more resonance than my master's chant. As he had promised, he pointed out the plaque which marked where Giuliano fell then, without delay, turned to leave by the main doors. Before we did so I glanced into the chapel on their right-hand side and, to my surprise, saw the unmistakable uniform of a Salti captain. I recognised at once the man whose heavy features I had observed from my hiding place beyond the bookshelf that very morning. He was standing in rooted contemplation of the 'Pietà', motionless save for the fingers of his right hand which scratched irritably at the end of his purple nose.

With no further diversions we arrived at the Via del Corso where Lorenzo Bellini was waiting. He was anxious for news of our audience with Cosimo and, whilst we consumed a plate of Otto's tortelloni, sitting by the great window, he listened, with some amusement, to our descriptions of the proceedings and, in particular, the medicinal apparatus employed.

Bono who, following my discovery of the scriptorium, now made free of the house, also joined our company and listened with delight to my account of the musket shot. He also, it transpired, had narrowly escaped death at the hands of Marguerite Louise when the latter, hunting in the grounds of Mattais's Palace, had mistaken the dwarf, who was wearing a feathered hat, for a giant bustard, a species long thought to be extinct in Italy.

Night fell and, arrangements having been made for the morrow, I bade my guardians goodnight and ascended to my bed. As I lay, hot beneath the linen sheet, my thoughts, of course, were of Caterina Mascini. My imagination was stubbornly unwilling to assemble her features, no matter how I strained my recollection. After a while I even left my bed, took up drawing instruments and attempted to portray her image from memory as though, by some primitive process, the creation of her likeness would relieve the pain of separation. But I have always been ham-fisted with a crayon and the end result bore an uncomfortable resemblance to Vittoria della Rovere in her ridiculous ruff.

The ecstasy of love, however, was matched by a renewed trepidation. The dungeons in the fortress at Volterra or the rack and hot pincers of the Bargello now held not only the prospect of slow and painful death but also the immeasurably more agonising prospect of prolonged or permanent separation from Caterina Mascini. As I drifted into sleep, a little happier in the knowledge of our imminent reunion, I reflected on my knowledge of women. Prior to the events of the day my experience, limited to my mother and Nicola Bomboni, had been, by any standards, minimal. In the past twenty-four hours four women had now transformed this sparsely populated stage. With the daughter of one I was now hopelessly and helplessly in love; another had been within inches of blowing my head from my shoulders, whilst the fourth had promised me a lingering death chained to an oar. It is an unhappy fact that all men apply to womankind the grossest of generalisations. On the breadth of my experience to date I decided that any steps towards such a process were decidedly premature.

Chapter Eighteen

When I woke the remorseless Florentine sun was already penetrating the shutters. From the slow candle which still guttered by my bed I deduced that the hour was late and from the library below me came the sound of a commotion. Voices were raised and I heard the library door, imperfectly oiled, swing repeatedly on its hinges. I rose and dressed in my librarian's clothes as swiftly as I might and met my master at the foot of the staircase. He was already dressed for the street and paused, only briefly.

'It has begun. I must go to the palace to do what good I can. Lorenzo will tell you what we know.' Then he was gone into the city.

I found Lorenzo and Bono in discussion, seated at a table in the main room of the library. I sat with them whilst Lorenzo relayed the news which had arrived only within the hour. In the early morning there had been a full-scale attack on the Jewish sector. The Salti were involved, supported by gangs of bullies enlisted in large part from the employees of the Assinaris and Castanellis. Associates of the del Rosso brothers, who held the flour monopoly, were also reputedly at work. Many atrocious acts had been committed and the city was live with rumour and conjecture. There was little pretence as to the observance of formality and legality. Some warrants had been issued for trifling offences but none of the victims had been brought before the Prefecture. Of the many reported incidents one was repeated with sufficient detail to ensure its accuracy. A party of Salti led by a 'Commander' had broken into the house of an old blind Jew. He had been hurled from the top floor of his house with a rope about his neck. His maidservant had been seen leaving with the Salti. She had not returned and her present whereabouts were unknown.

I felt no filial grief for my grandfather. I shared only the horror and anger for an act at once so cynical and cruel. Lorenzo spoke my thoughts:

219

'Save for ourselves and Antonio the witnesses to your mother's death have all gone. It is now also widely known and anticipated that, after the Jews, they will come for the books and Pasto Bomboni may employ that enterprise to silence us all. We can lose no time in our preparations. I have sent Fernando to warn them in Pisa but it is here that the first blows will fall. They will, of course, search for secret rooms and we cannot rely on the security of that bookcase. Bono will take such volumes and manuscripts as he is able through the ventilation shaft into the cellar, although it may be as well to leave something for them to find. There is some good news. Carlo Dati has already returned from his journey to Impruneta. Apparently his Englishman is positively buoyant at the prospect of joining our conspiracy and has already cleared an area in one of his barns to receive our manuscripts. They are such children, the English; let us hope that his reckless enthusiasm does not undo the whole thing. In any event, as good fortune would have it, he has a cart already in Florence which should have been unloaded and is ready to return to his farm. Dati has now gone to the corn market with a message for the driver though what they will make of him down there God alone knows. We are due to meet at Viviani's this afternoon to begin the removal of the volumes from the attic, which will be a labour of Hercules. The cart's driver is instructed to be there at dusk when we will load them, conceal them as best we can, and send them on their way. Once at the farm the great secrets of the Universe are to be concealed under heaps of pig shit or whatever other suitable commodity our farmer has prepared.'

Despite an irresistible enthusiasm for this adventure I, nonetheless, felt a pang of disappointment and dejection. 'We are no longer going to the Lungarno?' I said with as much indifference as I could muster.

Lorenzo looked at me and smiled. 'No, Fredo, we are not going to the Lungarno. There is now no need to meet Carlo Dati, who is to be allowed to retire from the scene to nurse his bad back. I am afraid that great conspiracies of this kind cannot accommodate every inclination.' He paused and I could feel my face burning with embarrassment and, I suspect, a little shame to have been caught red-handed in possession of such unworthy thoughts. I now entertained, once more, the prospect of a short, unconsummated life chained to an oar. 'However,' continued Lorenzo adopting his own tone of indifference, 'I understand that Lisa Mascini and her daughter, what is her name, I forget...'

'Caterina!' I blurted and blushed.

'...Ah yes, Caterina. I gather that they are to meet us at Vincenzo's to assist in the loading although, of course, I advised against so risky an undertaking for a girl of her age. I am not sure that I should not go and reinforce that advice,' he continued, 'but then I suppose she knows her own mind. Also I am afraid that it has been decided that you, Fredo, should accompany the cart to Impruneta. The presence of a boy and girl on board should do much to allay suspicion.'

'And girl?'

'Yes, Antonio thinks that the daughter, what is her name, Canda...'

'Caterina!'

'Yes, yes, that's right. Antonio has decided that she also should go to Impruneta if, of course, she agrees, but given the character she possesses it is thought unlikely she would miss such a journey.'

I was filled with a reckless, burning happiness. Dungeons, hot irons, racks, the galleys and the lash, I confess, disappeared like a receding nightmare in the brightness of a summer morning. Improbable I know, irresponsible, certainly; reprehensible perhaps but no one who has ever experienced a tenth of my feelings will doubt the truth of what I write. That so perfect a mutual journey would fit so conveniently with the execution of all our plans seemed an omen too powerful to resist. In a way that any lover will understand I had, of course, completely forgotten (or decided to ignore) the fact that the only brief conversation which had passed between us, far from carrying a hint of promise, had been calculated merely to convince her that I was a half-wit in ballooning pants.

It had been decided that normal procedures and daily tasks should, if possible, be observed. If we were, ourselves, the subject of scrutiny (which appeared possible) then strange behaviour would be likely to attract precisely the reaction which we hoped to avoid or delay. Thus I set out for the library in the cloisters of San Lorenzo and arrived only a little later than my usual appointed time. The city was live with tension. The Salti were everywhere. At every *piazza* or junction three or four could be observed lounging in their short summer cloaks, cudgels and toledos hanging below them together with the coiled ropes that formed the badge of their trade. The side-streets, however, were strangely quiet and the market before the Palazzo Vecchio was all but deserted.

When I arrived at the library the talk among the attendants and the assistant librarians was all of the attack on the Jewish quarter. Isaac's death was recounted again in some detail together with a measure of prurient speculation as to the fate of his maid. Other acts, equally vile, were recounted with the unfortunate relish of youth and I sensed, even in this oasis of light, a faction not wholly opposed to the horrors which had occurred. Prudently I kept my peace.

My master arrived shortly before one. If he was troubled by dejection or fatigue it was not revealed in his manner which remained as calm and studiously academic as ever. He corrected certain pieces of work, checked the references upon which we were working, examined the books which awaited the visit of the Jesuit monk and complained to his principal assistant about the dusty condition of the reading tables. He even found time to sit and gossip with a number of the foreign luminaries who remained scattered among the tables pursuing their studious paths in the characteristic oblivion of Academia.

Approximately two hours after his arrival my master announced his intention of visiting one of our storage rooms in the basement of the Medici-Riccardi Palace. He would, he said, require some help and I was, predictably, chosen to be his assistant.

We left the library and made our way, initially, towards the Medici-Riccardi. Thereafter we continued, without pausing, along the Via de' Pucci, the cupola of the Duomo revolving to our right-hand side. Soon we turned in that direction and passed before the façade of the Santa Croce moving steadily towards the increasing stench of the Arno and the Ponte alle Grazie immediately before us. We walked, deliberately, without haste, and my master told me of his morning's work.

'I went to the Pitti Palace but I was denied entrance, a state of affairs I had rather anticipated. My credentials have been withdrawn. The guard on the gate, whom I know well, was unable to give me any reason and appeared somewhat embarrassed. I learnt, however, that I was too late for the main purpose of my journey. Marguerite Louise had already left for France and, knowing the speed at which she drives her coachmen, she will now be well beyond the Tuscan border. Despite their separation, Cosimo is still infatuated with his mad wife and I hoped to use her influence. She is, also, the cousin of the King of France who still dotes upon her and treats her as one would a brilliant and aberrant child. It is ten days' hard riding to Paris so, for our purposes, she might as well be on the far side of the universe.'

Before we reached the river we again turned to our right and had thus avoided the centre of the city. Here even fewer people were on the streets, their absence due as much to the atmosphere of tension as to the oppression of the midday sun. Mindful of Lorenzo's words I had from time to time glanced behind us and, so far as I could ascertain, we were neither followed nor observed. So we came, at length, to the house of Vincenzo Viviani which had, for the past thirty years, concealed the great works of his master. We found a scene of intense labour and activity. Already the floor of the *entrata* was half covered in bundles and parcels of infinitely varying size. Many were wrapped in hessian, others in linen, still more in the strong vellum frequently used for the safe-keeping of charts and maps. The air within the house was full of a fine choking dust which caused those who laboured to cough and sneeze as though afflicted by the plague. With the arrival of myself and my master we were nine in number. We joined (and completed) an organised chain which stretched from the *entrata* to the attic above the third storey of Vincenzo's house. Within the attic Lorenzo was working under the querulous direction of Viviani himself. Below the aperture which led from this space Otto was stationed. This position found him at the head of the stairs and, with his massive arms, he was able to reach Lisa Mascini who stood on the first landing. Below her was her daughter dressed now, I noticed, in only skirt and bodice, the better to labour in the afternoon heat. Below her was one of the men I had been unable to identify at the Lungarno meeting the day before. Below him, close to ground level, I was surprised to see the figure of Carlo Dati working without apparent difficulty, on the last flight of stairs. Prior to our arrival the overall distance was such that some movement was necessary other than a simple passing of the individual burdens. By placing ourselves within the chain we were now able to obviate this procedure and, thus, immeasurably to quicken the flow. I endeavoured to insert myself, of course, below Caterina Mascini, but she waved irritably towards the upper level and, with that instinctive obedience I was to learn so well, I climbed to a position immediately below Otto and above Lisa.

We worked in silence for perhaps an hour before Lorenzo anounced that the final package was about to descend. Following its passage we all arrived at the lower staircase and contemplated, through the orange haze of dust, the documents which had unlocked the secret of the Heavens, now resembling nothing more than a soiled heap of cloth, wax and paper like some instrument of war shrouded to conceal its awful potential from an unsuspecting foe. Although of a considerable volume the total was less than Lorenzo had reported and, given its proximity to the street and the cart (which was yet to arrive), we estimated that the loading could be accomplished in less than half an hour. This would be the time of greatest risk of discovery and my master directed that two of our number should be stationed at the extremities of the street to provide warning of any approach by the Salti or their friends. Daylight was now beginning to fade fast and Vincenzo provided a pitcher of wine which we drank, in near silence, as we awaited the arrival of the cart.

It arrived, perfectly, as the tall buildings finally threw the street into deep shadow and, in the majority of houses, the green shutters had been pulled close against the night. However, on inspecting the vehicle, my first instinct was one of alarm. It had clearly been constructed well before my own entry into the world and, since that time, no human ingenuity had been spared in an effort to extend its useful life beyond that which its maker could possibly have contemplated. It was of the two-wheeled variety and the first and most obvious defect was the fact that the wheels were of substantially different size. It progressed, therefore, like a ship which has been badly holed on one side. Throughout the superstructure there was further evidence of parts that had plainly been seized at random from other carts presumably, and remarkably, in even worse condition than this. Strange wooden spars of irregular height thrust upwards from the sides, presumably to retain a still larger quantity of hay. The floor and lower sides consisted mainly of holes covered by patches for which every conceivable material, wood, leather, canvas and iron had been from time to time employed. Above this movable wreckage was a thin wooden plank suspended on two of the upward spars, which served as a seat for the driver. The two horses which now stood dejectedly in the traces appeared, if anything, older and in worse condition than the burden they propelled. Although they bore no signs of ill-treatment they clearly approached their daily labour with a lack of enthusiasm patent in every line of their bodies. It was in this chariot that I and my beloved were to be borne towards the hills of Tuscany perched on the greatest cosmic discoveries of this or, in all probability, any age.

The generally dispirited air was completed by the driver, a taciturn, surly youth with a single wall eye and persistently running nose whose monocular attention seldom strayed from Caterina's splendid breasts. He was, however, not entirely without virtues or uses. When the purpose of our journey was explained, at least in outline and, in particular, the necessity to avoid any contact with the Salti, he contributed a monstrous quantity of phlegm to the filth on the street and said, 'Bastard-shits', in a tone which demonstrated, unmistakably, that, in this important respect, we made common cause. I realised, as well, that his repellent aspect could only favour me by contrast in the eyes of my fellow passenger from whom I already felt a certain additional warmth and affection stimulated, no doubt, by the obvious peccant lust which radiated from that single eye.

Despite our misgivings as to the condition of the transport there could be no more propitious time for the loading and thus, forming another human chain, we began the evacuation of the packages through Vincenzo's door.

To guard against surprise by the Salti we stationed our 'invalids', Dati and Viviani, at either end of the street where they could be seen peering earnestly into the gloom, as unlikely a pair of sentinels against the hosts of Midian as one could wish to find.

In accordance with his master's instructions the driver had retained a quantity of hay for the purpose of concealing the packages at the base of the cart. This was now heaped to the rear end and I was employed in receiving the parcels from Otto whose reach and height enabled him to pass even the heaviest of our burdens clear of the crumbling wooden sides. Beyond him Caterina and her mother formed a bridge to the door of the house while Lorenzo and my master (mainly the former) collected the manuscripts from the floor, now entirely covered by a layer of orange dust. Our driver, meanwhile, occupied himself with the horses, ensuring that they had water and food, talking to them with the confiding tones of the physically infirm unwillingly thrust into an asylum of the mad.

In view of the proximity of the cart the work was swiftly accomplished and, with the help of our driver, we piled the remaining hay upon the new base which now rose in total some three feet from the original floor. It would not, of course, survive even the most cursory of searches but, by the time we had completed our work, to the casual observer, the cart appeared half-full of straw, no doubt unwanted at the market and homeward-bound to a southern farm. Following the completion of the loading I also quietly obtained from Vincenzo the canvas bag which contained the documents I had obtained in San Casciano and placed this too in the cart. Well before ten we were ready to depart, it being the universal view that our precarious subterfuge were best attempted in the hours of darkness. With some haste Caterina and I took our places on the pile of hay through which the corners of the packages and parcels formed uncomfortable lumps and protrusions. Wine, bread and cheese was provided for the journey, the driver was bribed, arrangements were made for my return the following day and, with muted farewells and good wishes, we lurched forward on our creaking journey to Impruneta.

Those who remained, now joined by Dati and Viviani, watched us from the centre of the street until we turned the corner, with considerable difficulty, towards the river. An untidy little group they made: a slut, a Turk and four scholars united in a strange defiance of forces which seemed so infinitely more powerful as every hour went by.

At first we rode in silence. Indeed we had little choice since any form of conversation would have been drowned beneath the deafening noise of the cart as it passed over the cobbled streets. The drunken angle at which we proceeded clearly placed a near-intolerable strain upon the single axle, steadily becoming distorted within the hub on the lower side. Thus, even at slow speed, a persistent screaming noise emitted from the tortured metal relentlessly ground within the ill-formed socket. To this melancholy wail could be added a hundred further gratings and bangs as the rotten structure threatened, by the minute, to abandon us together with the manuscripts of Galileo into the effluent which flowed interminably through the street below.

The first obstacle, nigh insurmountable it seemed to our wretched horses, was the Ponte Vecchio itself. Twice on the descent towards the Lungarno one of our horses slipped and would have fallen but for the support of the other; and thus by a mixture of fortune and decrepit partnership we reached the beginning of the Via Romana. There were few people about. Here and there, particularly at the entrance of the streets to the Lungarno, individuals or small groups of Salti watched our progress with amusement or indifference. When we passed the façade of the Pitti Palace one of the sentries shouted as us, words which I did not hear but which apparently required only an answering wave from our driver. Despite the noise and discomfort and the ever-present danger of discovery my hopes began to rise. Lying back on the hay and placing my head upon one of the bulky packages beneath, I could look up at the Tuscan sky and contemplate at least a full day beyond the oppressive walls of the city accompanied by my beloved with whom I had, by that date, exchanged perhaps three words, all without significance.

No sooner had I given myself to a world of fond imagining than I felt our pace slacken and, as it did so, I saw the driver's free hand reach backwards, flailing above my head in an attempt to find contact or attract attention. I drew myself up to a position immediately behind his back from which I had a clear view of the *piazza* and the Porta Romana beyond. The gateway itself was, unusually, lit by torches and, by their light, I could see the cloaks and hats of the Salti, six of them at least attending those who passed the gate in either direction. Drawn up on the city side of the wall, now some hundred paces distant, were three carts not dissimilar from our own and a coach and pair awaiting some form of examination before being released on the road to the south. The first I noticed was being searched with some care but, even while this process was underway, the second was waved through with nothing but the most cursory examination. The searching, therefore, was plainly random and disorganised but the very nature of our own cart could do nothing but attract attention. For what purpose these investigations had been ordered I neither knew nor cared. I realised, however, with ominous foreboding that I had never, before tonight, seen this gate guarded. Any attempt to turn the cart and retrace our steps into the city would attract precisely the attention we wished to avoid. It would, in any event, be necessary to proceed to the *piazza* itself in order to obtain sufficient area to manoeuvre our ungainly vehicle.

I confess now that, for a moment, I contemplated taking hold of Caterina and making good our escape from the back of the cart into the darkness. I record such an unworthy temptation because, of course, I was to resist it. Also I had formed the view that little trust could be placed in our wall-eyed driver whose coarse features and runny nose had imparted immediately an impression of malign imbecility. I was therefore surprised (and subsequently more than a little mortified) by the fact that he now provided the very means by which we avoided detection.

The change in momentum had also brought Caterina to her knees at the side of the cart and she now contemplated the approaching Salti with feelings, she later told me, identical to my own. At this point our cretinous charioteer leaned backwards, slightly averted his head, and spoke one word with unmistakable urgency.

'*Amore!*' he said and turned once more to concentrate on the undemanding task of bringing our beasts to a halt.

Caterina grasped his meaning well before I did and, as I blinked uncomprehendingly ahead, both she and its full significance were borne in upon me at the same time. She immediately brought to the task an enthusiasm and capability which, even in a moment fraught with the most dangerous possibility, I discerned had as much to do with experience as intuition. For my part, it was all improvisation but I did the best I could relying principally upon my imperfect recollection of the works of Plautus and Pascal. That which I lacked in training, however, I endeavoured to overcome with burning ardour. Thus the member of the Salti who brought his torch to the rear of our cart (having exchanged curt greeting with the driver) was confronted by a vision of frenzied if not entirely cohesive activity in the middle of which my partner's ample thighs were much in evidence. He emitted a grunt halfway between surprise and approbation whereupon Caterina jerked upright in the light of his torch, making a fine pretence at fluster. Her great wide eyes and half opened mouth had precisely the same effect upon our Salti as it had on the majority of men. His own eyes instinctively narrowed and the tip of his tongue could be seen running across his lips like the hind part of some live but partly consumed mollusc. This whole expression deepened visibly when she provided him with one of her finest smiles mixing, without effort, the loin-tearing mixture of helplessness and vulnerability which so belied the character beneath. For my part I kept my face well into the shadow thrown by the side of the cart, attempting, at the same time, to arrange my upper limbs in languid spread sufficient to conceal the areas of paper and hessian rendered visible by our recent exertions. With considerable relief I noticed a vulpine smile spread across the Salti's face and, in a word intended to convey an unmistakable double meaning, he said, 'Avanti!'

We all did. The driver's whip cracked over the heads of our horses and I, once again, fell upon Caterina who responded, I was disappointed to note, with steadily diminishing enthusiasm as we passed from the gate and made our way along the road to Impruneta. Finally, when the lights of the torches had wholly disappeared behind us, she pushed me away and, without ceremony, rearranged her garments to provide modesty and warmth in the sharp night air. Thus did the manuscripts of Galileo leave the birthplace of the Renaissance on the way to the cowshed.

If I had hoped (which I undoubtedly did) that this happy artifice would provide a sound basis for our future relations I was to be disappointed. Not only did she pay me little heed but, to my considerable distress, appeared to give increasing attention to our Cyclopean coachman.

'Well done, driver,' she said, attempting to pile what spare straw there was into the far corner in order to provide some comfort against the persistent rolling and battering motion of the cart.

'Fighting and fucking is all they know about,' he said with economic perspicacity.

'It *was* a clever idea though,' I said, wishing to be involved but aware, immediately, of the unpleasant and patronising note in my own voice.

228

Endeavouring to recover, I made matters infinitely worse. 'What's your name then?'

'Galileo,' he said smartly and, after a moment's silence, we both laughed (rather uncomfortably in my case) at the absurdity of denying information to those who serve.

'Then I shall call you Galli,' said Caterina, still laughing in a way which I found distasteful. 'This is called Boti,' she continued, making me wonder if I would ever achieve the dignity of a personal pronoun. '*And*, Boti Credi, I can tell you that you have just about broken my back on these damned packages.'

I made some suitably sympathetic noise whilst indicating that I had also done some passing damage to my knee. 'Ah well,' she said, 'let's hope it's not always such a bone-shaking business.' This remark, as you may imagine, impelled me to silence whilst causing uncontrollable frissons of anticipation to rack my body like the onset of the plague.

It was, indeed, becoming very cold. I pulled my thick travelling coat about me and wedged myself into the far corner, sulking a little as we made our slow progress, the axle screaming with pain, across the black landscape which surrounded our journey. Thus far we had taken the same road to San Casciano but, after a steady plod for two hours, we turned to the left along a thoroughfare so narrow as to be barely visible from the road, even in daylight, and one which our driver must have found by instinct. Poplars rose like giant spearheads on either side and the full moon now gave the landscape, predominantly olive grove, a grey and luminous visibility. Soon, above our heads and the noise of the axle, came a soft intoned purring which I realised was Galileo's snoring, interrupted only intermittently by startled grunts as the cart lurched on the uneven track. I half-rose to wake him but the girl said, 'Leave him, the horses know where they are going.'

After perhaps a further half an hour she said suddenly, 'Your father was a great man. He came often to our house in the company of Antonio Magliabechi.' She paused as though contemplating the breach of a confidence and then said, 'Sometimes he spoke of you, his only son in San Casciano. He said that his travelling meant that he knew you but little. It obviously made him very sad but he said you had an English priest who acted as your father.'

For some reason, possibly fatigue, I felt a sense of overwhelming self-pity. Tears burned in my eyes and I trusted myself only sufficiently to say, 'Irish.'

'That's right, an Irish priest with red hair. He was a hero, your father said, a great soldier.'

'I know,' I said flatly, the pity dying within me and leaving the familiar void.

I could feel her looking at me in the moonlight before she said, 'Did you ever want to be a soldier?'

'No.'

'I did,' she said unexpectedly, 'I would have been very evil and ruthless. I would have captured whole cities and burned them to the ground.'

After forty years of marriage and twenty years of still-grieving widowhood I can say that her assessment of her own potential was entirely accurate but then, in the darkness, I could not make out whether it was a jest and I said, 'My red priest was in a city which was captured and burned to the ground.' I felt her stir with interest and so, with some relief at finding so compelling a tale, I told her of Patrick and Drogheda. Somehow the journey and the ghostly light gave an added lustre to my story-telling (I was, in general, a poor raconteur), and she listened in silence, occasionally expelling air through pursed lips in something close to a whistle though whether of admiration or disapproval I could not tell.

For the remainder of our journey I told her of Patrick's life and privations in the Indies, his subsequent escape and his journeys to Europe and Italy. Many of these have already been chronicled, inaccurately, by others and perhaps, if I am spared, I may yet commit that extraordinary narrative to paper. It is, however, not the business of the moment save to record that, on the road to Impruneta, I enjoyed the telling and my listener continued to provide the rapt attention which I sought. Thus, through Patrick's adventures, I obtained a measure of status wholly undeserved but enthusiastically embraced.

The sky was beginning to lighten when we passed through the small town of Impruneta and the horses, of their own volition, turned yet again from the road to follow a narrow track between woodland and the occasional field of stubble, the cut stooks standing like untidy giants at irregular intervals of march. Galileo was now awake and, leaving the horses to their own devices, he hauled a hessian bag from beneath his seat and extracted a flagon of wine. After he had drunk from its neck he passed it back to Caterina who did likewise before handing it to me. The warmth of her mouth and the moisture of her lips remained upon the clay, adding some small compensation to the hard vinegar which burned down into the body.

At the end of the track we came, at length, to a collection of farm buildings, the general condition and nature of which strongly resembled the cart in which we sat. Ramshackle wooden barns, their roofs bent and deformed under the weight of persistent overtiling, surrounded a low stone building on which, in the past, some care had been expended but which now bore the mark of indifference and decay. It was nearly dawn and our surroundings could be clearly seen in the grey light. The sun, still concealed behind the layers of haze, already imparted a thick warmth which promised considerable heat for the day, and the persistent drone of a million insects mixed with the song of thrushes and blackbirds hidden, no doubt, in the dense undergrowth which pressed upon our path.

As we passed the first barn our driver reined in the two horses and, reaching beneath the seat, produced a length of wood with which he beat energetically upon a metal pot that hung from a protruding beam. In response to this signal the door of the farmhouse opened to emit a short burst of English oaths and a male figure of singular appearance. He wore an extraordinary collection of clothes rather as though he had stood beneath a trap-door from which they had been dropped in careless profusion. The outer layer was a Tuscan smock, well patched with leather, which concealed, in part, the black sackcloth and white collar of an English Puritan gentleman. Below this was a pair of peasant leggings which terminated in dramatically odd footwear. On the right extremity was a monstrous leather boot whilst on the left was a red slipper of the type normally worn by men of quality in the comfort and serenity of their own rooms.

He stood for a while in studied contemplation of our arrival and then, without a word, commenced a lurching progress towards us. Whether his uneven movement was caused by the disparate nature of his footwear or whether it was dictated by some disability was not immediately clear. (I did learn later that he had indeed sustained several serious injuries during Cromwell's battles in Ireland and his own, no less ferocious forays into the bordellos of London.) Notwithstanding his many peculiarities, however, the most striking feature of our host, observable as he came closer, was the manic staring expression which radiated from his eyes. During my time in England, I observed precisely similar demeanour in many of the people regardless of class or occupation. The French, indeed, have long identified this as a particular Anglo-Saxon *dérangement* which results in an irresistible impulse to take the most mundane of life's events and occupations and transform them into adventures of incalculable risk. In England it is regarded as no more than a passing eccentricity and, indeed, in many circles inspires deep admiration. In any other country it would almost certainly result in public burning.

The name of our host was William Howard and much of his life history I learnt in the rest of the day. He sprang from the junior branch of a family reputedly of considerable influence in English society. William's father, an impoverished landowner, had died in one of those hunting accidents, peculiar to the English nobility, by riding headlong into the overhanging branch of an oak tree. Quite why so many Englishmen are killed in this wholly avoidable way I was never to discover despite interested and polite enquiry among the enlightened gentry of that country. Nonetheless, it appears to provide many young men, like William, at an absurdly early age, with the twin burdens of social position and economic ruin. William's solution to his intractable problems was, I believe, also reasonably commonplace in his country at that time, immediately before the English Revolution.

Whether he actually shot his mother and sister still, to this day, remains a matter of conjecture and gossip. During his discourse that afternoon in Impruneta he denied it with considerable vehemence although the wild enthusiasm which danced in his eyes lent little support to his protestations. In any event, whoever perpetrated the deed, it is certain that both William's immediate female kin were killed by expert musket fire whilst sitting on the terrace of their country home. Following this unhappy event (blamed eventually upon Irish sympathisers) William was able to sell what remained of his estate, compound his mortgages and, with what remained of his fortune, enjoy a life of conspicuous debauchery in those parts of Paris and London which had always remained unchanged and unmoved by the theological, political and philosophical earthquakes of the seventeenth century.

William's conversion to the Puritan cause coincided, remarkably, with the final extinction of his fortune and credit. Nonetheless he embraced his new faith with the zeal of a convert unusually modified by the rough and cynical charm of the reformed rake. He joined the New Model Army at the first opportunity and rapidly became a cavalry commander of acknowledged brilliance and ferocity. His contribution to the military success of the Parliamentary cause was considerable and, following the war, he was personally selected by the Lord Protector to identify and exterminate the Levellers whose demands for Justice and Equality (not to mention arrears of pay) had become a persistent embarrassment to Parliament. The success of this operation led to a further commission and the command of a large part of the Parliamentary cavalry during the campaign in Wexford which accounted for his absence at the siege of Drogheda.

On his return to England the New Model Army was disbanded and William found his reward in a substantial Parliamentary endowment, a country house and a plain Puritan wife of private means. During this brief period of distinguished public life he was befriended by many including the blind English poet, Milton, at whose London house he had met Carlo Dati.

Wealth, however, brought its own downfall and it was not long before the major part of his second fortune had followed the first into the bawdy-houses of London whose continued existence in a Puritan Commonwealth represented a marvellous testimonial to the resilience of depravity and vice. However, when his second wife was found shot dead on the terrace of his new home, even the suspicions of the English magistracy were awakened. A Parliamentary commission established to investigate this singular tragedy, whilst accepting William's explanation based on the unreliability of modern firearms during cleaning, nonetheless indicated strongly that, should any further wives or mothers be found with musket balls lodged in their foreheads, a less happy result would be likely to ensue.

For the remainder of the Commonwealth William continued to enjoy a remarkable lifestyle encompassing familiarity with whores and poets, pimps and Puritans, generals and thieves, and not surprisingly he continued to accumulate a formidable body of enemies. Anticipating the chaotic end of the Parliamentary experiment and the imminent death of Cromwell, he seized what little remained of his wife's fortune together with such funds as he could steal or borrow and, overnight, disappeared towards the Tuscan hills.

At the time of our arrival I was, of course, aware of none of this chronology and, indeed, some part of the detail was only ascertained by me during my time at Salisbury. Its undoubted accuracy, however, may be attested by his behaviour during the day and night which followed.

As he arrived at the back of our cart his eyes fell first upon Caterina now sitting on a bundle of manuscripts and attempting to remove quantities of hay from amongst her flaxen hair. Even to my untutored eye it was immediately apparent that their past relationship contained something other than avuncular concern and affection. He regarded her with a kind of leering apprehension whilst she returned his gaze with a quiet stare of hostility and contempt. It is an expression I have often observed in women and conveys the devastating power retained by one who has seen the object before them in that most humiliating of male postures, without trousers or self-control. Our host spoke first in tones of somewhat enforced jocularity.

'Well, well,' he said, revealing a near-perfect Italian accent, 'wonderful things, Florentine markets. You send in hay and you get back heresy.' Then, turning his eyes towards me, he added, 'And who are you?'

The patent hostility of the question evoked a pleasing and unexpected reaction from Caterina who interrupted my own mumblings and provided our host with a swift and entirely accurate account of my pedigree. I realised, with some pleasure, that this clearly indicated that I had been the subject of discussion between Caterina and her mother. Since the ultimate source of *any* information about me must have come from my master or Lorenzo Bellini I could therefore assume with confidence that it would have placed me in a most favourable light. The speed with which I reached this tortuous conclusion (whilst Caterina was still in the process of providing my brief biography) must provide some clear indication of the extent to which my entire thoughts (nay, my entire being) was concentrated upon one target and goal, namely approbation by the object of my desires.

She gave as good an account of me as I could have wished, including the fact that I was directly descended from a Hero of Florence, the Achilles of Mongiorno. Whilst she spoke I felt myself observed by William Howard, his eyes alight with manic malignancy.

Whatever his views on my physical presence, however, we were plainly engaged on the same hazardous undertaking and, following my introduction, he appeared to regard me with a grudging acceptance, even taking my hand and hauling me roughly onto the courtyard where I sank up to my calves in one of the many heaps of putrified manure which littered the uneven stone. In extricating myself from this glutinous mess I observed, also, the reason for my host's eccentric footwear. Some distance away, closer to the house itself, an empty leather boot, the companion to the one which he now wore, protruded like the mouth of a giant fish from a similar heap of offal. Plainly at some recent time it had been trapped by the inert suction of the foul mass and had been there discarded through indolence or a disinclination to excavate it in such circumstances. Whilst I was pulling myself, with intense difficulty, from the quag Howard himself noticed the discarded boot and, with a grunt of discovery, advanced upon it and, exerting considerable strength, heaved it free, causing the stagnant pile to omit an inanimate belch and a renewed quantity of foul air which rapidly became dissolved in the permeating reek of putrefaction and decay. Having thus obtained possession of this item of footwear our host thrust it upon his left foot, discarding as he did so the red velvet slipper which lay, until the time of my departure, with an air of reproachful gentility on an unidentifiable heap of green matter.

Having thus attired himself for the work in hand Howard dismissed our wall-eyed charioteer and, with the air of the chief conspirator, showed us the hiding place prepared for the works of Galileo.

In addition to the house the courtyard was formed by two rough wooden barns, open-fronted and containing untidy mounds of hay and straw extending, in both cases, to the height of a small house. Approaching one of these, he pulled aside three bound stooks which appeared sufficient to bring down the whole tottering edifice. It immediately became apparent, however, that this particular haystack was a mere façade, incorporating within its bulk an open area ten paces in diameter and to a height which would accommodate one man standing upon another. Upon entering this chamber I realised immediately that it had not been created for the actual or potential reception of forbidden scientific work. It had a more basic purpose, namely the concealment of a substantial spirit still and numerous casks and barrels which contained, no doubt, the liquor so produced. Scattered on the floor in the immediate vicinity of the 'entrance' were a quantity of empty flagons and a number of broken vessels. Items of clothing, several of them obviously female, also littered the floor indicating, to the perceptive mind, the likely recent departure point for the journey which had involved the loss of the leather boot.

'There we are,' said William Howard, beaming with insane satisfaction, 'no better place to bury cosmology.'

In fact I could not but agree. The area was manifestly dry and warm and, subject only to the permanent risk of fire from the workings of the still, there could be few better places for our purpose in the whole of Tuscany.

Thus far our welcome had, I confess, been very different from that which I had anticipated. In particular the night's exertions had left me with a sharp appetite and, whilst standing in the courtyard, it was possible to discern, above the pervading reek of ordure, the stomach-gripping aroma of cooking bacon mixed with the sweet smell of hot oil and pasta; William Howard had plainly eaten already. Despite the poverty of the times it remained the invariable practice throughout Tuscany, upon the arrival of travellers, to provide them immediately with the offer of food, however Spartan. Our host gave no sign of such a gesture, spontaneous or otherwise.

We were not left, however, entirely without sustenance. Seizing three of the broken cups from the floor of the barn Howard filled what part of each he could with the contents of one of the flagons. This contained a substance the consistency and colour of weak milk emitting an aroma curiously similar to burnt gunpowder. These cups he handed to us with the admonition that it would provide us with 'strength for the job in hand'. The liquor had no discernible taste but provided a sensation like a land-mine being detonated somewhere slightly above the pelvic region. I remember noticing, however, as the tears poured from my eyes and my senses reeled that Caterina appeared little affected by her own portion which she drank in its entirety with a swift tossing movement of the head and a barely perceptible shaking of her golden hair.

Having thus consumed the only offerings, we set about the unloading of our precious cargo and its deposit within the interstices of the stack. Since the cart was drawn up relatively close to the entrance the work progressed at a brisk rate. Caterina worked from the cart, heaving the packages to me whilst I considered the supple movements of her body with the lust of the innocent and (I have no doubt) eyes like an owl's. The only impediment to our progress came from William Howard who accompanied every alternate visit to the haystack with a substantial draught from one of the many flagons, and thus proceeded at a steadily diminishing pace.

Despite their journey the packets still remained coated in layers of fine dust, the deposit of Vincenzo's attic, to which was now added the residue of the straw in which they had been concealed. This mixture soon covered us all, adhering in particular to Howard's black Puritan frock-coat like a fine silt through which the rivers of spilt liquor provided a fascinating pattern of alluvial lines, deltas and streams.

It was well before midday that the cart was clear and the original works of Galileo had been stacked without undue damage in a pile as high as my head behind the still and immediately against the barrels of liquor which represented, no doubt, the dedicated industry of years. By this time I was faint with hunger, exhaustion and the release of nervous tension accompanying the final replacement of the stooks and bales which served to conceal the various products of genius which lay within. I was, indeed, on the point of *demanding* food when the wall-eyed servant reappeared and announced, without enthusiasm, that bread, pasta and olives were now available on the terrace beyond the house. Our host received the news with the dull comprehension of the already-besotted and, clasping a flagon he had prudently removed from his store, tottered towards the house through which it was apparently necessary to pass to reach the promised victuals.

The interior of the dwelling amazed me. From its immediate surroundings I had anticipated, of course, scenes of Stygian gloom and squalor. The reverse was the case. Whilst lacking in decoration the interior walls were as white as chalk against which grey stone fireplaces provided monumental relief. The rooms contained a minimum of oak furniture and the only hangings in each of the areas I saw was the simple Erastian crucifix in stark contrast to the walls behind. The floors, which were stone and meticulously scrubbed, completed the impression of cool ascetic peace, forming an extraordinary contrast to the dishevelled and drunken madman who led us through the building to the terrace beyond. Here again the filth of the courtyard was entirely absent. Beneath a trellis of vines and clematis, a table had been set with bread and olives, tortelloni, ham and sausage. There was no wine or water, and accepting, with reluctance, a further glass of the Acquavita we fell upon the food and ate our fill beneath the lunatic, unblinking gaze of its provider.

When we had finished I made polite enquiry as to the length of time which our host had spent in Tuscany and, in doing so, released a monotonous flow of reminiscence upon which is based, in part, the life history I have already recounted. The table was shaded by vines but, nonetheless, was becoming hot in the spring sunshine and, at some stage in the interminable narrative, I must have fallen asleep in my chair for my next memory is of the early evening shadow falling across a terrace dim and silent save for a recurring hideous noise which I took at first to be the persistent snarling of a wild beast. So vivid was this impression that I remained motionless and fearful for some seconds until I slowly turned my head and discovered the sound to be that of Caterina snoring. She had obviously consumed further quantities of brandy and now lay in her chair, her head thrown backwards, her mouth open to the skies like an insistent fledgling on the approach of a mother bird. It was a posture with which I was to become totally familiar in the next forty years of my life, the toleration of which occasionally placed considerable strain on the boundless reservoirs of my love and affection.

Beyond her the upper figure of William Howard lay heaped upon the table his black frock-coat emitting puffs of dust and straw when stirred by the light evening breeze. I realised, with considerable consternation, that the time was long past for our appointed return to Florence. Of the squinting servant there was no sign and apart from Caterina's cacophony the house was as silent as the grave. I had no desire whatsoever to spend the night at Impruneta, a prospect which I viewed with considerable (and, as it transpired, justified) apprehension.

My fears rapidly became reality. Neither of my sleeping companions could be roused despite considerable shaking and admonition on my part. A brief search of the house revealed no sleeping servant and thereafter I spent an unpleasant and unproductive hour wading through the dung which coated the remainder of the farm. Indeed the sources of this excrement had now revealed themselves. Several morbid cows and a number of semi-wild pigs had appeared in the courtyard congregating around a new pile of refuse no doubt deposited there by the servant during my siesta. Of the man there was no sign and now, already surrounded by the murk of evening, I returned to the terrace whence the sound of my beloved echoed like a foghorn across the Tuscan hills. When I arrived beneath the trellis I found William Howard awake, clasping a refilled cup of liquor, his wild glazed eyes fixed upon Caterina in unmistakable contemplation.

By this time I was much alarmed. Our continued absence until the following morning would cause great consternation in Florence at a time when any precipitate action could lead to our downfall. I therefore demanded to know when the cart was due to return.

'It's not loaded,' said our host, employing the carefully enunciated monosyllables of the chronic drunk. 'Horses fucked. Leave tomorrow.'

I expostulated to no avail. I had no idea of the whereabouts of the cart, still less of the poor creatures who dragged it. In the midst of this frustration and anger I found myself gripped by a bizarre sense of unreality and, even then, I reflected that the struggle for the integrity of human thought had known many battlegrounds but none so peculiar as this.

At this point Caterina awoke with a noise similar to the death rattle of a bull and contemplated her surroundings with the quiet confidence of the mentally detached. On being informed of our position she expressed no concern save to indicate in a voice pregnant with significance that she proposed to make her bed on the haystack immediately adjoining the house. Since I had no wish to remain alone in the house with a man whose homicidal tendencies, instinctively perceived, had been clearly established by his own life history, I elected to use the other barn and thereby to remain in close proximity to the great manuscripts stored within it. Shortly after this the imbecilic Galileo arrived to announce that the invisible cart had been loaded and it was proposed that we should set out at first light.

Refusing a further mug of liquor I managed to obtain a flagon of water which I consumed with the relish of a castaway. Since night was now falling fast on this the strangest of days I proposed to our host that Caterina and I should make our respective beds before the darkness rendered any ascent onto the haystacks hazardous in the extreme. In a moment of surprising solicitude he pressed blankets upon us and, employing what little light remained, we climbed into our respective barns. The height of the straw on which Caterina was to sleep was such that a ladder was necessary for her ascent. This also was provided by William Howard and, from my own vantage point, I noticed with satisfaction, relief (and no little admiration) that, after she had climbed into the black interior of the barn, the ladder (in reality a rickety series of steps nailed to a pair of uprights) was prudently pulled up behind her. She, at least was now safe from molestation save by the most acrobatic of men, which excluded all those known to be in the immediate vicinity (including myself).

Within my own barn I settled and rearranged the straw as best I could, spread my blanket and lay contemplating the dark timbers some six feet above my head. They were clearly visible in the silver Tuscan moonlight which now permeated the courtyard and entered my own lodging through a gap, barely a child's height, which separated the eaves of the barn from the topmost layer of the straw. Possibly through excitement, possibly through some instinctive apprehension and possibly due to my hours of unconsciousness in the afternoon sun, sleep eluded me. I remained, tiresomely, on its very verge, my thoughts bordering persistently between conscious images and dreams. In this state I drifted between my master's house, the secret scriptorium, and the serenity of the Pazzi Chapel. The latter was now darkened in my imagination and contained untidy piles of manuscript and a rusty still which bubbled and belched with the expellation of spirit. This object itself then became transformed into the gigantic bladder of a sheep and then, again, into some awful instrument of torture behind which I could make out the grinning figures of Pasto Bomboni and Andrea Cortese. Bomboni carried a butcher's hook whilst Cortese intoned remorselessly from a leather-bound book the detailed facts and secrets of my own short life. As I listened, fascinated, to my own biography Bomboni impaled one end of the hook in the beam above my head which now appeared to project beyond a window from which, as I watched, a figure was hurled kicking and writhing onto the upturned steel.

Whether it was the horror of the image which jerked me fully awake or whether it was the noise from the courtyard below was impossible to discern and I lay, for a moment, uncertain of reality until the noise came again. It was the unmistakable squelching sound of a footstep in mud. This was followed immediately by another, indicating, clearly, the presence of two people in the courtyard below me. At first I lay, frozen, conscious of the sharp stems of the straw protruding through the blanket, my ears straining into the night. It was swiftly apparent that the footsteps did not approach my own barn but rather were making a strange, apparently impeded progress across the courtyard before the face of the house itself. As silently as I was able I raised myself upon one elbow, eased myself to the right-hand side and peered over the edge of the straw. I now had a clear view of the courtyard. Although I was unable to see the sky above me the night was obviously entirely clear and the invisible moon provided abundant light to discern what, at first, I took to be an extraordinary beast making its tortuous way through the swamp-like surface of the courtyard. Immediately my eyes focused, however, I realised that this was no prehistoric monster. What I had taken to be enormous skeletal vertebrae were, in fact, the rungs of a long ladder. The fore and hind quarters were, of course, made up by two men bearing the ladder at either extremity. The task for both of them was by no means easy. The object was plainly of considerable weight and much sturdier construction than that which Caterina had employed for her own ascent. The bog-like ground which they traversed caused them, perforce, to move at differing speeds whilst hauling each successive boot from the cloying mess with a belching sound which I reflected, even then, may earlier have impinged on my semi-conscious brain. Since their grasp upon the ladder dictated an even distance between them, any differential in speed was absorbed by a sideways movement, often involuntary and frequently threatening to bring the whole proceedings to grief in the surrounding quag. The fact that both men were similarly afflicted did not, apparently, tend towards mutual sympathy and the whole proceedings were accompanied by muffled curses and exhortations partly in a foreign tongue which I recognised immediately from my school-days as the incomparable sexual abuse of the English language. The object of the enterprise was, of course, immediately apparent. William Howard, with the assistance of Galileo, was about to storm the doubtful virtue of the woman I loved.

I held my peace, a fact which Caterina was to use to my intense discomfiture in the years that followed. I maintain, however, in my own defence that it was less through fear than a helpless fascination with the manifest incompetence of the operation which I witnessed. William Howard, it will be remembered, had by his own account been through many of the sieges of the English Civil War. I simply comment that, on the basis of what I saw that night, the New Model Army would have been lucky to storm an ale house let alone the walls of Drogheda. (It may, however, with equal justification be pointed out that not since the Battle of Crécy could any general have picked terrain less suitable for his assault.)

As I watched, the interminable crab-like procession continued to the foot of the wall of straw, stacked within the barn at the top of which lay, supposedly unconscious, the object of our mutual lust. With the benefit of hindsight it is possible to say that Howard should have been forewarned by the uncanny silence from that quarter, particularly having observed Caterina's slumber during the afternoon. To be fair again, I also was blind (or deaf) to the implications of this sepulchral calm.

Amid further muttered curses and imprecations the ladder was finally footed some considerable distance from the edge of the barn. The oblique angle was dictated by its length, the height of the haystack and the well-known principles of Pythagoras which those bent upon rapine ignore at their peril.

Having erected the storming ladder Galileo was stationed at its lower extremity and William Howard, still, I noticed, clothed in the black stuff coat of the Puritan scholar, began the ascent towards carnal bliss.

I was, by now, genuinely alarmed and was (I swear) about to cry out when the situation rapidly changed. Howard was, by this time, within feet of the dark opening comprising the top of the haystack and the bottom eaves of the barn, a point which three men might have reached by standing upon each other's shoulders. His head, indeed, was about to enter the dark interior when the whole top of the ladder suddenly moved backwards. From my vantage point I think I realised before he did that it was pushed by the makeshift ladder which Caterina had used to climb to her bed. Anyone familiar with Newton's principles (which Caterina certainly was not) will be aware of the comparative ease with which the apex of a hypotenuse may be moved into the vertical plane. Whatever Caterina's theoretical ignorance, however, her practical demonstration was flawless and within a second William Howard found himself clinging to the top of a vertical ladder now considerably further from the ground, whilst below him the figure of Galileo could be seen floundering in the thick excrement attempting to stabilise at least one point of his master's situation. It will be plain to anyone that, once the ladder had reached a near vertical plane, only the slightest exertion of force was necessary to cause its wholesale plunge in the opposite direction. Certainly this simple fact was apparent to William Howard and, whilst it is near impossible to make supplicant gestures whilst clinging to a ladder thirty feet above a sea of shit, he undoubtedly did the best he could. Indeed the length of time which he remained in this position, the two ladders locked together, might have given some cause for optimism on his part. Perhaps because of this he actually appeared to take one faltering step down to the next rung when there came a tiny jerk from the invisible interior of the barn and the ladder prescribed a graceful backward arc, Howard remaining attached until the last moment when he disappeared, fortuitously, into a particularly large heap of rotting dung close to the perimeter wall. Galileo, perhaps unjustly, fared little better; both feet being stuck firmly in the surrounding muck, he was inevitably pitched straight backwards to be pinned into the excrement by the rungs of the ladder which descended against his face. As I watched, Caterina's ladder was swiftly withdrawn into the dark interstices of her barn.

As the demise had been sudden so resurrection took a considerable time. Galileo was the first to free himself, emerging from the swamp with a noise such as the giants must make when eating vermicelli. It is a tribute to his loyalty (already in evidence on our journey from Florence), that he then spent a considerable time excavating his master from the fetid pit of his own making. Indeed the courtyard was bathed in the brilliant morning of the Tuscan spring before master and servant were able to make a slow and apparently painful entry into the doorway of the house, leaving behind the fallen ladder, a silent and melancholy testament to the pitfalls of carnality.

I had assumed, of course, that Caterina had been awakened by the arrival of Howard at the top eaves of the barn and had acted in the panic of the moment. It was only subsequently that I learnt (from her) that she had, like me, observed the entire approach of the would-be seducers and had awaited, therefore, with precise calculation the moment of maximum advantage. Such extraordinary sang-froid (not to mention downright sense of mischief) should, it might be argued, have warned me of the miseries I was to suffer. At the time, however, it elicited nothing but wondrous admiration.

Despite the coming of the early dawn the affairs of the night were far from over. Following the departure of William Howard and his servant I had barely spread myself once more upon my blanket in order to contemplate our next course of action when I heard further noises of movement in the courtyard. Returning immediately to my position of vantage I saw, with a quickening pace of the heart, the figure of Caterina emerging from her own barn and descending the ladder which she had plainly lowered immediately before. Reaching the ground, she grasped hold of the light wooden structure and, apparently without difficulty, bore it in the direction of my own haystack. She then, in a moment which I could scarcely believe existed and which, even now, causes spasms to tighten my wrinkled neck, placed the top of the ladder inches away from my straining face and, within seconds, appeared on the straw beside me. Immediately, she exerted that supple strength which drove me to delirium, hauled up the ladder and thrust it into the barn behind us. Observing my incredulous gaze she clearly thought some explanation was required.

'That bastard tried to . . .'

'I know,' I said, 'I watched it.'

We looked at each other for a moment and then, like children (which of course we were) at the conclusion of a successful game, burst into silent laughter.

Later when we lay side by side in a futile attempt to gain some sleep in the morning light, overcome with longing and dread I attempted the first fumbling advances of my sheltered life. At first she resisted with a kind of weary impatience (justifiable perhaps in the circumstances). Finally, however, with a gesture of resignation she gave herself to the business at which she excelled beyond all others and thus I achieved my manhood transported into bliss whilst suspended on dried grass above the greatest scientific texts that history will produce and several thousand litres of hard liquor.

Chapter Nineteen

My first post-coital sleep was rudely broken by the noisy arrival of Mikos Faccioli, servant to Lorenzo Bellini and former policeman of the University of Pisa. Having failed to rouse anyone in the farmhouse he now stood in the middle of the courtyard prudently balanced on the rungs of the fallen ladder, shouting my name with as much volume as his substantial frame could produce. He had already ascertained my position, assuming, wrongly, that the monstrous snoring proceeding from the barn came from myself. He appeared, indeed, a little surprised when my head was thrust from beneath the eaves whilst the snoring continued, unabated, behind me.

As I have already explained, at length, Mikos's formative years were spent in his father's tavern on the quayside at Leghorn. In addition to a healthy contempt for the formalities of rank it had provided him with a direct, if limited, mode of speech which he demonstrated immediately.

'Fredo!' he bawled. 'Where the fuck you been?'

Lengthy explanations were out of the question, and I condescended to the use of the patois. 'No cart,' I replied. 'Horses buggered.'

'You must come quick,' he said, shifting his weight to another portion of the ladder. 'It's all gone pig-shit. Everyone's nicked. Your master's in the Bargello. Dati too. And Viviani. Lorenzo's gone to Pisa. You must go quick.'

I know it is trite but there are undoubtedly occasions when the brain refuses to believe the evidence placed before it by the senses. In my later life I experienced similar sensations when informed of Caterina's frequent adultery. This was merely an early example. During the past hours I had encountered a happiness more profound than that I had ever known. The racks and hot irons of the Bargello, the cruelties of Pasto Bomboni, the dictatorship of the Medici and the oppression of the Inquisition had been removed to another part of the Universe,

244

beyond sight and understanding. To have them once again thrust before me in the vernacular of the dockside thug rendered me as insensible as stone. I simply stared at Mikos, willing him to disappear, whilst behind me the sonorous drone continued unabated.

At this moment the door of the farmhouse opened and revealed what, at first sight, appeared to be a moving heap of dried dung from which two wild eyes peered into the morning light. At the sound of the door opening Mikos Faccioli had turned to face the house and started back a full arm's length whilst clutching, instinctively, at the toledo which hung at his belt. Thus confronted, our Puritan farmer himself recoiled, the door slamming shut behind him. This bizarre scene contrived, at least, to return my senses and with them the feeling of terror and apprehension the message so clearly conveyed. Telling Mikos to wait I scrambled back into the darkness of the barn, woke Caterina and explained, as swiftly as I could, the dreadful news I had just received. Within minutes the ladder had been lowered and we both descended to join our messenger who had, himself, left the courtyard and was standing by three horses on the track which led to the road. Here, he provided such further information as he had.

Early the previous evening my master had, apparently, received information from his 'source' within the Pitti Palace. From him it was learnt that concerted action was imminent against those believed to possess heretical works. On receiving this intelligence my master had swiftly summoned those known to be at risk. Lorenzo Bellini and Mikos were, of course, already staying at his house whilst Carlo Dati and Vincenzo Viviani had arrived shortly after nightfall. Immediate departure from the city had been contemplated but there was much consternation at my own continued absence. In the event my master and Lorenzo refused to leave Florence until I had returned or until word had come that I was safe and well. With some reluctance the others had agreed to delay their own flight until the following morning and, because of the danger of the streets at night, all had stayed at my master's house, intending to depart at dawn. This, in the event, was precisely too late. Well before the first light of day the Salti had arrived in force, led by Pasto Bomboni himself. Their approach had been observed by Otto, stationed at the upper windows for precisely that purpose. Thus, by the time the door was forced, Dati and Viviani had already been taken into the secret scriptorium. Lorenzo, the youngest and fittest of them all, had made good his escape through the window above the canal although he had been injured in the jump. Indeed, all might have been well, had my master not attempted to remove a number of manuscripts from the library shelves before he himself passed through the secret door. Perceiving the danger in this delay, Otto and Mikos had, between them, put up considerable resistance at the entrance of the house and had, Mikos told us with quiet satisfaction, broken the skulls of several Salti before they were overwhelmed. Otto, he believed, had taken the thrust of a toledo in the throat and was certainly dead. Mikos, forced backwards through the library door, had, at the last moment, turned and fled, leaping through the great window after his master whom he found lying on the canal path below and whom he hauled to the relative safety of a house occupied by one of the many women to whom Mikos was a regular visitor. That Magliabechi had been seized he had no doubt. As he fled through the library barely five paces ahead of the advancing Salti he had observed the closing of the secret door after my master's crooked form, a movement which must have been apparent to his pursuers.

Upon Lorenzo's instructions he, Mikos, had obtained four horses from a livery in the Lungarno and, with the day barely broken, they had made good their escape through the Porta Romana, mercifully unguarded through negligence or design. From Carlo Dati, Lorenzo had earlier received instructions as to the whereabouts of the farm at Impruneta. Lorenzo himself had taken the road to Pisa to forewarn those who were sympathetic to our cause. He had instructed Mikos to find us, provide us with horses and to bring us with all speed to the University whence we might make good our escape, if necessary to Milan where Lorenzo numbered many friends.

'But what will happen to my master?' I cried, the agony of indecision already within me.

'In the Bargello, they kill him,' said Mikos flatly. 'Slow probably. Lorenzo says that Bomboni wants *you*. Gave me no reason. Said you would know.'

A sickening fear possessed me and I sat heavily upon the broken wall of the courtyard. No one spoke and, in the early morning air, the drone of insects seemed as a chant of lamentation. The fear, let it be said, was not entirely the physical premonition of pain although this, undoubtedly, played a part. Above all it was a fear of losing that which I had only so recently possessed, mixed with the certain knowledge that, in my canvas bag, lay the only means whereby my master's sufferings might be avoided or at least delayed. Upon this reflection I realised, with a fresh wave of panic, that the canvas bag had been left on the terrace

246

the night before. Without pausing to provide explanation I left my companions and, making what haste I could across the courtyard, entered the unlocked door of the farmhouse, passed through its white rooms and emerged onto the terrace where, to my intense relief, the bag remained below the chair on which I had slept. Clasping it to me I turned to confront, as I had half-expected, the manic gaze of William Howard, now barring my means of return. With a presence of mind of which I am still justly proud I said, in a tone as matter of fact as possible, 'Everyone in Florence has been arrested. You must keep the manuscripts. We will keep our silence.'

Whilst he plainly digested the consequences of this news I crossed the terrace, pushed my way past him, strode through the house and rejoined Caterina and Mikos waiting, with patent anxiety, by the farm gate. Neither needed any urging towards our departure and, mounting the horses which Mikos had brought, we set out along the road which, at that stage, led to Florence and Pisa alike. Caterina, I noticed, barely with surprise, rode like a man, the folds of her *lucco* falling to her knees and revealing the sturdy calves with which I now felt a delirious intimacy and of which, I realised, I could never again be deprived.

For the first part of our journey we rode in silence. I was, of course, preoccupied by my own dilemma. In addition, our progress was made slow and difficult by the state of the track over which we passed. Two nights before, our cart had created its own passage drawn by horses well used to the snares and brambles of country ways. Our new mounts were from a city livery, accustomed to the flat if fetid highways of Florence, and they disliked the permanent clutching vegetation which, on occasions, threatened to obscure our pathway entirely. Thus any discussion, let alone that which tended towards our predicament, was postponed by the necessities of travel and concentration. Indeed the sun was well risen and the day already hot by the time we reached the road between Florence and San Casciano, as familiar a highway as I could wish to find. Here the choice was stark and inevitable. To the left, through the village of my childhood, lay the high road to Pisa and, thereafter, the relative safety of Milan, Bologna or a similar refuge within the influence of Lorenzo Bellini. To the right, in two hours' riding, was Pasto Bomboni and all his works. The horses, for their part, fretted in this direction, unfettered by the agonies of circumstance and duty.

Predictably, as I now realise, it was Caterina who ended my indecision. 'I am going home,' she said simply, and nodding towards Mikos Faccioli she set off, at a steady pace, along the roadway to our right.

The fact that she bade me no farewell indicated of course (I now realise) that she had already assumed the imperious direction of my life from which it was, thereafter, never entirely released.

For his part Mikos Faccioli understood the ways of the world. He raised a laconic eyebrow in my direction, reined his horse to the left and, with a slight wave, drove the unwilling beast towards Gallaza, whose houses were barely visible in the valley below us.

For a time I remained motionless, watching my own shadow shortening across the olive grove before me, and then, by the simple expedient of releasing the reins, allowed my horse to make brisk pace after the figure of my beloved, still discernible between the poplars which pointed the route to Florence.

No sooner had I joined her than we fell into an earnest discussion of the decisions and choices before us. In later life I often reflected that we made a curiously well-chosen couple for the business in hand. Despite our youth we each possessed a wealth of experience widely different in nature but, for our purpose, complementary to the point of perfection.

She was, of course, concerned for the safety of her mother whose association with my master was well-known throughout Florence. I, for my part, possessed in my canvas bag a deadly secret which could save or destroy us all at a stroke. Its ill-considered use, however, could provoke precisely the catastrophe it was designed to prevent; tactical considerations absorbed my thoughts and, in so doing, diminished my fears.

Notwithstanding my new resolution, as we drew closer to the city, my hopes fell. The more I reflected upon my circumstances the more I realised the weakness of my position compared to the powers which opposed us. I realised now that the potency of the weapon which I possessed relied, almost entirely, on the reaction of Bomboni to it. It was, indeed, possible for him simply to ignore its existence and to risk the consequences, secure in the knowledge that the strength of his influence within the Palace and the Salti would preserve him unscathed. In these circumstances the method of its use became all the more important and, in my deliberations, I realised the unhappy fact that the person to whom I would most readily have turned for advice was that same man whose helpless danger I now sought to circumvent.

In order to enlist her assistance I had, of course, to inform Caterina of the nature of my plans and my possessions, which she followed with an incredulous stare entirely alien to her normal phlegmatic nature. We thus concentrated upon my own predicament. Hers I believed to be simple. She must, of course, go straight to the Lungarno in order to find her mother. Thereafter I anticipated, without question, that they would take a carriage for Pisa and the safety which lay beyond. As to my own course of action she apparently also entertained no doubt.

'It is quite essential,' she said after I had divulged my own secrets and she had spent some minutes in silent contemplation, 'that immediate contact is made with your master.'

'But Mikos says he is already in the Bargello!'

'Precisely so, and thus it is quite clear where to find him.'

I stared at her in frank amazement. I own now to a somewhat childish reaction of bitter reproof. It was, I reflected, all very well for *her* to thrust me into the lion's den whilst seated in a carriage on her way to the West. I was about to give utterance to these thoughts when, fortunately, I was interrupted.

'Of course,' she said, '*you* cannot get into the Bargello. You are yourself wanted by Bomboni and may be recognised. But *I* can.'

I started with both guilt and amazement.

'*You* can?'

'Of course,' she said flatly. 'The Salti are men, are they not?'

I was digesting the unpalatable consequences of this statement when she added. 'Besides they may well be bribed and it is indeed the right of those in prison to receive a visit from their kin.'

(When my beloved acquired her vast reservoirs of street cunning and artifice I never knew but one thing I know now is certain; had she been thrust from the topmost storey of Giotto's tower she would, by the time she reached the ground, have arranged the necessary helpless admirer of sufficiently ample proportions upon whom to fall.)

There was little else to be decided and, whilst the thought of my arrival at the city stopped my breath in apprehension, nonetheless we urged our horses forward and it was at a brisk trot that we finally crossed the ridge where I had first set eyes upon the birth-place of the Renaissance and descended towards the brutal realities of the future.

Before we reached the Porta Romana we took a detour to the house of Bellina Cantoni, Mario's sister, with whom I left one part of the packages I had brought from San Casciano. From her we obtained further information based upon the rumour and gossip now rife in the city. Certainly a large number of houses had been raided. Outside them bonfires had immediately been kindled onto which whole libraries had been heaped and consumed. It was said that a fire had also been started in the Medici library itself, though whether this was officially inspired or whether it represented a mischievous attempt to conceal the existence of heresy was by no means clear. There had been a number of arrests and it was widely assumed that many more of the intelligentsia were actively being sought. Antonio Magliabechi had been among the first to be taken and he was presently in the Bargello. The general mood in the city, she reported, was by no means unfavourable to the Grand Duke. It was widely believed that substantial quantities of heretical work had been discovered including volumes devoted entirely to necromancy. The Cimento and all its works were now totally discredited and banned. Furthermore it was widely put about that the present sad state of Tuscan commerce and the repeated harvest failures, not to mention the recurrent plague, were obscurely linked to such heretical infestation. The simple thus believed that the city had, literally, been bewitched. A more sophisticated argument maintained that the heretical emphasis on scientific research and exploration had diverted the best intellects of Tuscany from their obligation to provide the springboard for national economic recovery.

Even Pasto Bomboni, whilst still an object of fear and trepidation, had achieved a certain status from recent events. The official view, encouraged and propagated by Church and State alike, was that the extirpation of Jews and heretics was long overdue. The instruments of this process were thus endowed with the related virtues of moral guardianship and firm government.

On hearing this news I was afflicted by a dull sense of dejection and hopelessness with which I became familiar on many occasions during my life. It stemmed, of course, from the somewhat sanctimonious conviction that one's attempts to fashion and maintain the paths of intellectual enquiry tend to the greater good of mankind. When one observes that same species, cleaving with apparent satisfaction to the brutalities of ignorance and spite, a feeling of futility becomes inevitable.

That was not all. Various proclamations had appeared throughout the city extolling the virtues of those to whom the commercial monopolies had been granted. Thus the Assinaris, Castanellis and del Rossi were now, in the popular imagination, elevated from the role of exploitation to that of commercial probity upon which the future well-being of the Tuscan people entirely relied.

It was thus with a heavy heart that we set out in the mid-afternoon sun, and allowed our horses to make their own enthusiastic course towards the Porta Romana.

The gate was now guarded but attention was paid only to those leaving the city who were inspected individually and searched at random. Once we were through the gate nothing appeared changed. Against the wall of the Pitti Palace the same ragged commerce continued with irrepressible vigour. The hot squalor of the streets contrasted with the acres of the Boboli Gardens visible through the iron gateways to our right. The Salti were everywhere in evidence and, from time to time, we encountered the ostentatious carriages of the new merchants providing a near-jovial counterpoint to the surrounding dilapidation and neglect. As we neared the Ponte Vecchio our pace, as ever, slackened to immobility. For long periods we were caught in the press of people and vehicles and, as best I could, I listened to the gossip of the town. Nothing I heard raised the gloom caused by Bellina's account of the general mood. From even the poorest and most afflicted sources the same malignity appeared to flow, providing, to my young ear, emphatic evidence for the unhappy truth that it is amongst the most debased that the urge to persecute finds its strongest roots. My master's name I heard on several occasions, his supposed offences against the soul being linked invariably to the deformities of body and flesh. I also heard, with increasing consternation, a number of references to Caterina's mother, and whilst I could discern no sensible message the prurience of phrase left me in little doubt that the Committee of Public Decency had been at work. None of this I passed to my companion lest she should betray our identities and purpose by some ill-considered reaction, although I should have realised, even then, that rash incontinence was not numbered among her faults.

At a snail's pace we proceeded towards the great bridge and, immediately before it rose from the quayside, we turned right and, now free of the crush of people, made our way, with increasing speed, towards the Lungarno. At this pace we soon came to the house of Lisa Mascini where we stopped in silence and disbelief. The exterior had become a ruin. The pots and window-boxes of myrtle and carnations lay scattered before the doorway, their contents crushed with gratuitous violence into the sets and cobblestones of the street. Several shutters had been smashed open from the inside and now hung precariously on splintered louvres above our heads. The door itself had been broken in and could be seen in two pieces at the foot of the narrow stairs which I had climbed towards the doomed conspiracy barely a week before. Above the doorway itself a wooden sign had been nailed upon which was painted the signature of the Committee for Public Decency: 'PER PUTTANA.'

I remember fixing my gaze upon the house, not daring to glance at my companion but conscious of her motionless by my side. When I finally turned towards her she had not moved and her face was set like rock, her bottom lip clamped between her teeth. At that moment, from the opposite side of the street, we both heard her name being called and saw, crossing swiftly towards us, a female figure, plainly one of the 'ladies of the Lungarno' supposedly extinct in the Florence of Cosimo III. Reaching us she took hold of Caterina's saddle and spoke with the urgency of stealth.

'They came yesterday. Salti, many of them. She has been taken to the Stinche. There was nothing to be done. One of them was the new boss, Bomboni.' Having thus imparted her message she turned and disappeared with the speed of a hunted beast.

There was, of couse, no knowing what dangers still lurked within the shattered house. Whether the pillage had ceased or whether some members of the Salti remained, bent on theft, destruction or even ambush, could be ascertaind only by entry and, despite my feeble protestations, Caterina dismounted from her horse and entered the door of her home with the emphatic stride of promised vengeance. Her action left me, as usual, with no choice and I followed her in apprehension and dread.

Damage, like pain, is relative. That which is random and unavoidable, the fatal consequences of our lot, we endure, for the most part, with fortitude and even, on occasions, with a heightened sense of nobility and purpose. Where, however, it is deliberately inflicted with the conscious delight of the brutal and banal, our spirit is itself afflicted and enfeebled by our very membership of so foul a human family. Thus the man who bears with Stoic grace the agonies of accidental calamity becomes as clay in the torturer's hands; his own will being destroyed by the perception of his own species debased in the joyous infliction of pain. So it was with us. The extent and wantonness of the destruction was rendered infinitely more intolerable by the harmless, frail and ephemeral nature of that which now lay smashed about us. Every room was the same, reflecting a considerable degree of method.

If Caterina shared my feelings she expressed them not at all save for the fact that her bottom lip remained clamped between her teeth and her eyes moved across the wreckage with swift and careful investigation like the hands of the blind.

The condition of one room, overlooking the street, bore evidence of a particularly frenzied attack. The floor was littered with what I took, at first, to be the bodies of dead animals, cats perhaps. It was only on closer inspection that I perceived them to be wigs which had been swept from shelves which lined one half of the chamber. Heaps of clothing revealed this to be the dressing room of Lisa Mascini, the workplace and store-room of Tuscany's best actress, packed with the raw materials of artifice and thespian delight.

In a moment of bemusement and vacancy rather than any juvenile sense of fun, I picked up one of the longer wigs and placed it carefully upon my head. It was a fine specimen and catching my reflection in one of the many fragments of mirror glass now littered about the room, I was slightly shocked to observe the effect which it had upon my features. To this day I have little facial hair and this fact, together with my roundness of face and the golden ringlets falling to my shoulders, conspired to produce an effect not wholly without charm. Caterina had also noticed this transformation and I found her staring at me across a jumbled heap of bodices and corsets which had, no doubt, provided some passing entertainment to the Salti the day before.

I have little doubt that the idea came to both of us at the same time. I had already realised, without active consideration, that Caterina would no longer be able to visit the Bargello in order to establish contact with my master if, indeed, he remained alive. Her first concern and preoccupation must now be with her own mother, removed to the Stinche and awaiting, at the very least, the payment of the substantial fines now levied for prostitution. There was no doubt, however, that I could, if necessary, be disguised for the purpose and, whilst the prospect of entering the Bargello turned my stomach with fear, I confess that the prospect of losing my own identity provided an immediate sense of relief. Anyone reading this account will realise, of course, that the idea was utter madness. It simply indicates that the lunatic acts of the sane are no bad barometer of the desperation of the times.

We discussed the details at considerable speed whilst I, even then, enjoyed the intimacy which now existed and grew between us. In my canvas bag (which I realised, even now, with a sense of panic, I had left on the saddle of my horse) I had, in addition to the papers from San Casciano, three hundred florins in coin and a similar sum in a paper draft upon the Milanese Bankers (to whom I had been directed by Lorenzo). These sums represented a part of my father's estate withdrawn against contingency. To this sum Caterina was able to subscribe a further one hundred florins which she obtained from beneath a floorboard in the very room where we now stood.

The fine which secured release from the Stinche had, until recently, been fixed at one hundred florins. However, the bribe required to avoid public flogging (and the probability, thereafter, of infection and death) was, at least by reputation, double that sum. Small comfort could be gained from the undoubted fact that the jailers in the Stinche invariably allowed a decent interval between arrest and flogging in order that a suitable payment might be arranged. Conditions in the prison were reputed to be such that this very indulgence frequently proved more fatal than the lash itself. In addition, since this very arrest had been perpetrated by Bomboni it was at least probable that those in his command (and subject to his power) would feel an unusual reluctance to engage in the business of graft. These considerations, however, if felt, were not voiced.

Whatever the problems and difficulties it was essential that Caterina should not delay in the attempts to secure her mother's release. Since it is only in the most sophisticated of countries (such as England) that bribery may be accomplished by banker's draft rather than hard lucre it was necessary for Caterina to possess the greater share of our florins. Moreover, whilst it was doubtful whether Lisa Mascini's liberty might be bought, it was equally certain that Antonio Magliabechi's could not. Thus I retained for myself only fifty florins in coin, sufficient, should it be necessary, to take carriage well beyond the Tuscan borders to the North. In order to effect this distribution of money it was necessary for me to retrieve my bag from the horses which had remained, by some miracle, untethered in the street. We then set about my transformation.

It did not take long. A lifetime watching her mother at work within this very room had provided Caterina with a master's art. Among the wreckage she discovered the necessary hairbrushes, rouges, powders and dabs and, whilst she worked, in a fragment of broken mirror, I watched my young manhood disappear and a large-boned, heavy-lipped, wide-eyed but by no means unattractive young woman appeared in its stead. Not for the first time that day I felt a bizarre, almost elevated sense of the unreal. We were, after all, but children and the game we played had had its counterpart (albeit less skilful) in a thousand happy homes surrounded by family warmth and festive mood. The same impossible, inappropriate levity also gripped Caterina and she smiled in her work, her head held on one side and her tongue protruding between her teeth as though trapped in jest. Thus we played the coquette amongst the carnage of our lies.

The clothes proved more difficult. Lisa Mascini was, as I have said, a woman generously endowed but she lacked my girth and a succession of costumes, dresses and *luccos* retrieved from the heap in the centre of the room proved impossible to lace or button. Finally we had recourse to the ultimate and timeless art of corsetry. With some protestation I was encased in the most substantial of Lisa's nether garments, the plates of whalebone crushing against the whole of my ribcage despite, I reflected even then, my masculine deficiency in that construction. Standing behind me, her foot wedged into my lumbar spine, Caterina drew the cords with all the strength of desperation. I felt the contours of my body alter, my breath disappeared, whilst my eyes bulged and tears coarsed through the powder and the rouge. Even in this extreme discomfort I observed that the contraction of the garment had thrust much of my surplus flesh into an upward direction. As a result I now possessed as fine a cleavage as many I have observed with interest in the streets of the Lungarno, a fact which was to prove of considerable assistance in the near future. Before I could beg for relief Caterina had expended her own strength and, with a satisfied grunt, had engaged the final hooks. Moving to the side, she surveyed with displeasure my streaked and crimson face.

'My God, you look awful!' she said, in what I regarded, even then, as an unncessary commentary on the obvious. 'Now I'm going to have to do that face all over again.'

Before she did so I attempted once more to enter the largest of Lisa Mascini's *vestita* and, to my intense relief, succeeded with considerable ease.

The sexual contours and aspects of my body were now not dissimilar from my face once it had been repaired by Caterina's deft work. Certainly I was buxom but even I could see that, whilst Ilium would not burn at my bidding, my favours might well be sought by many men not yet reduced by age or disability to a total lack of discrimination. This fact was so apparent as to cause me immediate concern, which I voiced to Caterina. For her part she replied, rather testily, that the job were better well done than not at all and so I resigned myself as best I could (after so little practice) to the dangers of young womanhood.

My voice was a further problem. By then it was fully broken and was, if anything, deeper than normal. My attempts at falsetto were rejected out of hand by both Caterina and myself and, after numerous attempts, it was decided that I should retain my natural octave softened, insofar as possible, by volume and aspiration. This effectively reduced my utterances to something close to a husky whisper which, together with the remainder of my appearance, caused me still further misgivings. It was, however, the best that could be done and my accumulated pessimism and gloom was dispelled by Caterina who, perceptively, took me to her and kissed me in a manner which could have caused my whole being to expand were it not for the constrictions of the whalebone and cord.

Lisa Mascini's shoes were, of course, out of the question on many counts. My own boots, however, were fortunately those which are laced to the calf and which were, at the time, not unfashionable for both women and men. In any event little of them could be seen beneath the inner petticoat of my new clothes.

Despite my concern as to the success of my disguise I nonetheless experienced considerable trepidation when we finally left the house together through the broken door.

I excited no comment. No one pointed; no one stared. I realised that the only incongruity was my canvas bag, slung across my shoulder like a traveller's sack. Carefully, I observed the women whom I passed and adopted a more feminine clasp immediately below my protruding bosom and drawing the contents tight against the unyielding front of my corset.

Riding was, of course, also out of the question. The tunic I wore was tighter than Caterina's *lucco* and, besides, any attempt to straddle a horse's back would undoubtedly reveal on either side the masculine nature of my footwear and, above, my ample calves which, unlike my cheeks, supported a prolific growth of black hair. I thus abandoned my horse and my beloved, the former to find its own way home and the latter riding towards the Stinche Prison and thence, pray God, to Pisa and Milan. I watched her disappear towards the Via Romana with all the agonies of loss and apprehension, then turned and made my way towards the Arno and the Ponte alle Grazie beyond which lay the Piazza Santa Croce, the Via del Corso and what remained of my master's home.

Chapter Twenty

By the time I turned into the street itself I was almost accustomed to my new clothes. Even the corset had become tolerable, my body learning to fall against it as though against the wall of a carriage. Like many Tuscan men I was accustomed, on occasion, to wearing the *lucco*, and the skirting provided, therefore, little inconvenience. The unaccustomed construction of the petticoats caused some discomforts and indeed obliged me to mince, which was no bad thing since my usual ungainly stride would have provided a certain physical contrast to the light golden ringlets which bobbed and swayed across my shoulders.

Thus did I make my uncertain way to the end of the Via del Corso. No sooner had I seen the house than I also saw the Salti before it. Two of them, one on either side of the stone steps, lackadaisical sentries against, I suppose, an imagined army of bibliophiles, philosophers and cranks. They, also, had seen me, the first to do so having reached quietly across the doorway, pressed his companion's arm and nodded with eyebrows cocked in my direction. It was, of course, the hair which attracted attention rather than any evenness of feature. From a distance the perfect ringlets in the hard afternoon sun resembled the work of Botticelli. Having been thus observed, retreat was impossible and, summoning all my composure, I passed before their eyes conscious, for the first time, of the frailty of woman. I heard them chuckle behind me and, amazingly, felt a strange sense of irritation. I remained, however, unmolested and, with considerable relief, minced into the Piazza del Duomo. Uncertain of purpose I continued past the great Cathedral to the Baptistery observing, with scant interest, my dull reflection in the metal doors. It was very hot. The afternoon sun beat upon the stones and reflected from the bronze. I became increasingly uncomfortable. Perspiration ran below the corset and I felt, with alarm, the loosening powder on my cheeks.

Despite these difficulties I was determined to enter the house. From Mikos Faccioli's account there could be no doubt that the secret scriptorium had been discovered. Of infinitely more importance, however, was the secret which lay beneath it and the whereabouts of its pygmy guardian.

I did know of another door to the house which I had seen but never used. This gave directly onto the canal from, I imagined, the kitchens which lay beyond the library and from which I had been rigorously excluded by Otto from the first moment of my arrival. By retracing my steps and passing between the houses at the end of the piazza I could reach the canal towpath without difficulty but one immediate danger occurred to me. In the heat of the afternoon there were few enough people on the streets, indeed the wide piazza was all but deserted. It was therefore difficult enough to avoid attention in *any* circumstance. The canal path, however, was rarely used *at all* and my presence on it at this time would invite immediate enquiry and investigation by anyone posted there to guard the rear entrance. It was impossible to ascertain whether this rear door was guarded until I was on the path itself. By that time I would be fully visible to any sentry and, in my petticoats and bodice, incapable of precipitous flight.

In the end my own growing discomfort, and the steady disintegration of my face, proved the decisive factor. Action of some kind was imperative and none held more promise. I returned to the mouth of the Via del Corso itself and, thereafter, made my way down one of the many small alleys once regularly used by pack animals carrying casks of Florentine dye to the canal below. When I arrived at its banks I was conscious of its strong stench, something of which I had never previously been aware even when sitting at the great window in the library within twenty paces of the water itself. I learnt, subsequently, that this was due to the red cedar bookcases and panelling which absorbs odour like a sponge (a fact worth remembering by anyone contemplating the erection of a library by an open sewer). The source of this pestilential air was not only the canal itself but its banks and paths which were heaped and littered with the refuse of the houses on either side, representing, no doubt, persistent unsuccessful attempts to propel the offal into the water beyond. Through this morass I now picked my way, lifting the hem of my petticoats in prudent anticipation of future need. Of the Salti or other guardsmen there was no sign.

Although I had never before approached from this direction, the house of Magliabechi was not difficult to identify. The single great window, the height of a man, was clearly visible amid the jumble of green shutters (for the most part closed) set in the walls of roseate clay.

The door was, as I remembered, some twenty paces short of the window (from which, indeed, its small projecting porch was just visible). When I reached it I saw that an iron ring was set into the left hand close to the jamb. I found it stiff to operate but, by exerting force with both hands, I felt the inner latch rise and, half-expecting to find the resistance of bolts, I placed my shoulder against the woodwork and pressed inwards. It gave easily and I found myself, as I had anticipated, standing in Otto's kitchen. A strange place it was, bare of all furniture save for a single chair set by the open hearth over which hung iron pots and a quantity of knives, spears and ladles, providing the atmosphere of an armoury rather than a kitchen range. Everything appeared in order and undisturbed. Beyond the hearth a flight of stairs led sharply downwards and turned to the right from which a low passageway extended, presumably beneath the floor of the library itself. At the far end a similar, narrow stairway rose towards a door which I rightly anticipated opened beneath the staircase and under the balustrades. I was now within four paces of the main oak door which gave onto the street, beyond which, I knew, stood the sentries whom I had previously observed. Accompanied by what seemed to be a deafening rustle of petticoats I crept towards the library door and peered in. I had received, perhaps not consciously, some hope and encouragement from the lack of damage to the staircases and balustrades which, in my imaginings, would have proved the first target for destruction.

The sight of the library, however, eradicated all cause for optimism, or consolation. It was a different room that I observed. The bonfires, which still gave off a lazy, dusty smoke, had blackened the ceilings, architraves and pillars and so removed all source of reflected light. Furthermore the effect of tearing down the bookcases had been to reveal the decorations applied to the walls by, presumably, the lawyer from whom my master had purchased the house after the Great Plague. Even in its damaged and worn condition, partly concealed by the remaining shards of cedar, I was able to recognise the large mural as a poor copy of the 'Cenacolo' of Leonardo da Vinci. Surrounded by splinters of wood, the face of the condemned Christ gazed downwards through the gloom at the glowing embers of recorded thought.

The scale of the destruction was difficult, immediately, to measure. It was apparent that it had not been random. A number of manuscripts and books had been untidily stacked against the walls and below the windows which gave onto the Via del Corso. What proportion of the library they represented was a matter of conjecture, rendered the more difficult by the method, or lack of it, in which they had been arranged. The piles were sufficiently high, however, to partially obscure the windows themselves, thereby restricting, still further, the light which fell upon the wreckage within.

Crossing the library floor was, if anything, more difficult than my progress along the canal. The cinders were still hot and twice I had to stop in order to snuff out minor fires along the hem of my skirt. The danger of becoming a human beacon was compounded by the need for silence. The first of the library windows had been broken and its shutters, in all probability, formed part of the bonfire at my feet. Through this gap I could hear the soft conversation of the Salti, a persistent idle murmur in the heat of the afternoon.

The necessity to remain as far as possible from the windows precluded any examination of the books that had been spared, or even the means to ascertain into which category they fell. Either they represented those works deemed to be 'safe' and acceptable or else they were the very worst heresies for which the vagaries of instant burning were incompatible with the sins they contained. One volume only I could identify which had fallen from the pile and lay somewhat closer to the centre of the room at the end furthest from the street door. This I saw was 'New Experiments Physico-Mechanical Touching the Spring of Air and its Effects', by Robert Boyle. Recollection stirred within me like a pulse but as to its status with the Inquisition I was unsure, a reflection not so much on my own ignorance as the aberrant nature of the censorship applied.

I had now reached the secret door formed by part of the bookcase. It was open. Indeed it had been wrenched from its upper hinges and leant forward, twisted across the room and blackened by smoke. Beyond it the inner passageway was in darkness. I stepped through the door and allowed my eyes to become accustomed to the gloom. It was as well that I did so for here the floor was littered with the remains of the rough shelving torn from the walls as the manuscripts were removed. Cautiously I made my way towards the inner door containing the filigree window and turned into the tiny scriptorium. Here, again, a fire had been started and the acrid smell of burning was still strong in the airless space. The desks were intact but the chairs on either side had plainly been used in the conflagration. Beyond the desks the opening to the ventilation shaft formed a black square on the darkened wall just beyond my upstretched reach. On the desks themselves remarkably little had been disturbed. One of the suspended lenses had been smashed, or had broken in the heat, but the other was still in position, magnifying the end of a discarded hammer, used no doubt in the assault upon the bookcases themselves. Also on this desk, the standing candelabra had merely been dislodged and the three candles lay beyond it in a pool of hardened tallow.

Relying upon the meticulous habits of my master I removed the centre draw of his desk and, feeling within, located his flint and wheel. Before lighting the candles I took the precaution of closing the inner door to ensure that only the filigree window would reveal my presence (and that only to the concealed corridor beyond). The flint worked well and, once all three candles were burning, I was able, the more quickly, to proceed with my design. Risking the inevitable noise I dragged one of the desks to a position just below the aperture and was about to climb towards it when I observed a tiny parcel of paper which had, hitherto, been concealed beneath the foot of the desk itself. I recognised it at once as one of the minute tracts copied by Bono and my master and assumed that it had been hidden, in haste, on the fatal approach of the Salti. I immediately took it up and, holding it below the remaining intact lens, I saw it to be a tiny copy of Descartes's *Meditations*. In area it barely filled my palm and was less in thickness than my signet finger. I left it beneath the lens and climbed quickly to a point at which my head was level with the ventilation shaft. The surrounding area was much blackened with soot and I realised, with a sinking heart, that even if the dwarf had made his way to safety the fire within the room might well have choked off the shaft itself and anyone attempting to live within or below it. Forgetting, for a moment, my golden curls I thrust my head into the shaft and gave one loud emphatic shout.

'Bono! Bono! It's me, Fredo!'

The volume was quite unnecessary as the shaft acted as an echo chamber and my voice rebounded past me towards the daylight dimly visible above. After its departure there was silence. I waited for perhaps a minute and then tried again, attempting a lesser pitch and greater articulation.

'Bono! Are you there? It's me, Fredo!'

Again there was silence and I was about to withdraw my head, sick with despair, when I heard a scratching below me and, to my immense joy and relief, heard the dwarf's voice barely an arm's length away in the darkness.

'Fredo, get your head out of the hole. I can't see a thing.' I stepped backwards along the desk and, almost as I did so, a hand appeared on the bottom ledge of the aperture and, immediately thereafter, the hideous face of the dwarf, now rendered the more grotesque by a thick coating of soot, peered out into the candlelight.

What he saw, of course, was a buxom girl set out in fashionable ringlets and with a sharply protruding bosom. His mouth fell open with surprise, revealing the row of tusks protruding from his upper jaw. 'Bono!' I said. 'Thank God!'

Twisting his head to one side, he projected it through the gap and stared at me in the flickering light. 'Fredo?' And then, 'What the fuck are you doing in that?'

'Oh,' I said, instinctively touching my tresses and added, stupidly, 'It belongs to Lisa Mascini.'

'I don't care if it belongs to the Pope. Do you know what has happened? Everyone's been arrested, Antonio, Viviani, Dati everyone. They burnt the place out. I nearly died down there. Otto's dead.'

This last piece of information came to me as a sickening blow. That which had previously been an assumption of Mikos Faccioli (an unreliable raconteur) had now become dreadful fact. Its significance lay even beyond grieving. It was the first casualty of a war.

'You are sure? About Otto?'

'Yes, I'm sure. Fortunately he died quickly from what I could hear. They threw his body in the canal. I saw them do so through one of the canal gratings. Perhaps he is lucky.'

I stared at him before replying, 'What of the books, below?'

'They are safe. The Salti are not complete fools. They dropped lighted tar down the shaft to ensure that manuscripts had not been stored within it. That it was connected to storage cellars they did not consider. I just had to live with the burning pitch and keep quiet. But *why* are you in those clothes?'

At that point we both heard the noise at the same time. Softened by the door behind me, but clear nonetheless, came the grating sound of the bookcase moving on its broken hinge and immediately thereafter a footstep in the passage. Whoever approached, this could be their only destination.

We reacted at the same moment. Bono's head disappeared like a ferret into a burrow. Trusting to fortune and the elevation of my petticoats, I leapt from the desk and, with a presence of mind which, even now, I find impressive, cried out loudly to obscure the rasping noise as I dragged it into its former position. I then turned to face the door, noticing as I did so, the tiny tract still lying on the surface of the desk. To lift the pedestal and conceal it required too much time and, in any event, bending and lifting was beyond my capabilities in the rigid confines of my corset. My canvas bag was sure to be searched and no other hiding place was readily apparent. In desperation I considered the cleavage between my breasts but whilst apparently impressive it lacked both depth and substance. Finally, in a moment of desperation, the footsteps within a pace of the door, I lifted my skirts and thrust the *Meditations* of Descartes between my substantial buttocks. Barely had my clothing fallen into array than the door was pushed aside and two members of the Salti burst into the room, toledos drawn and at the thrust. In what I hoped was a gesture more natural than melodramatic I stuffed my hands to my mouth as though to stifle a further scream and shrank back against the desk, my eyes wide with fear, by no means entirely artificial.

Remarkably they both spoke together the identical phrase, 'What the fuck...' before one of them demanded, 'Who the fuck are you?' while the other scanned the tiny and empty room in a futile search for further intruders.

Still I said nothing and, indeed, had very little to say. As the surprise waned so the situation became the more pregnant with menace.

'Well, well, well,' said the second, his eyes moving between my ringlets and the hem of my skirt. 'Well, well, well. I've seen you before, my girl, not half an hour ago.' At this observation his companion nodded slowly in agreement.

'Didn't we just say, Franco, how much we fancied that?'

The second, plainly Franco, continued to smile and, with an elaborate gesture, scratched the lobe of his ear which I noticed, with a further flicker of recollection, was slit from top to bottom.

'Now,' continued the first Salti with different intonation, 'now then, first things first, we've got a job to do and we'd better do it so you'd better tell us how you got in here and what you're here for.' When I remained silent he said, 'I can tell you that you *will* fucking well tell us, one way or another.'

Without looking at the speaker Franco said, 'Let's have her over, now.'

You will not believe me, but as I stood there, in imminent danger of rape or worse, I experienced, again, that flood of cold dispassion which Bellini tells me is certainly caused by some chemical mechanism in the adrenal duct. Whatever its source it has served me well. I was suddenly possessed of a calm, cold calculation. I can remember feeling the *Meditations* suspended between my tensed buttocks and reflecting that there were not simply the obvious reasons for maintaining my chastity.

I think they sensed a new resolution for I appeared to have an abundance of time in which to say, 'I am the daughter of the Prefect of San Casciano. His name is Angelo Ballari. I have come to Florence to visit some friends and my father asked me to deliver official documents for the Medici library. They are in my bag. You can check them.'

It was a thin story but it gave them pause. It took them several seconds before they perceived its weaknesses. Speaking at the same time the first said, 'How the fuck d'you get in here then?' Whilst Franco said, 'Why didn't you take them to the library then?'

I prayed for intuition and it came, 'The library is shut. They said there had been a fire. Been one here too, by the look of it. I came in through the back door. I have been visiting this house since I was a child. I saw you two standing by the front door and became frightened. It looks as if I had good reason.'

I do not know how I did it, but I did. Every word is true. It came as cool and clear as an autumn morning and worthy of a Prefect's daughter. I was nearly out of danger, but not quite.

'What are you doing in here?'

'I was curious. When I saw the damage I was about to leave, through the front door, to tell you I was here. Then I saw the entrance in the bookcase. I had never seen it before when I came to the house.'

'What d'you scream for?'

'I heard you coming. I did not know who it was.' And then, risking all, I attempted what I hoped was a disarming smile, seeking assistance. It was a mistake. The eyes of the first Salti narrowed to slits whilst Franco pulled compulsively at the shreds of his ear. The first one spoke, 'Better search her. You look at the bags.'

I felt his hands run over me, gripped, as you may well imagine, by every form of apprehension. I need not have worried. The corset did it all and, when he reached my bosoms, I even heard a grunt of satisfaction and approval. In the meantime Franco had found the depositions bearing upon them the official seal of the Prefecture incorporating the crest of the Medici. I had gambled, of course, that they could not read and so it transpired. He passed them to his companion who inspected them closely, enacting the silent and futile conspiracy of the illiterate.

'What's this then?' said Franco, holding up the banker's draft. (Illiterate he may have been but a sum written in florins makes common comprehension.)

'It's paper money. For the Grand Duke. Collected taxes, probably.'

It was this which proved my salvation. Over-zealous interference with a Prefect's daughter might result in some trifling punishment, at worst the slicing of an ear, but interference with the revenue meant death. Telling me to remain where I stood they retreated to the passageway where I heard an urgent and whispered conversation. Shortly they returned, churlish, unmollified but convinced.

'You'd better get along then,' said the first, handing me my bag, into which they had replaced the sealed documents and draft, 'and don't go snooping into what don't concern you. You could end up in a very nasty mess.'

I ventured another smile and, whilst they stood motionless, minced from the room, desperately compressing Descartes as I went. I felt them watch me, sensing some residual approval no doubt concentrated on the tight, tense curvature of my behind. The street door was open and I negotiated the shallow steps with acute difficulty. Thereafter I tottered towards the Duomo, fighting off incipient cramp, my knees banging like cymbals beneath the folds of my dress. Immediately inside the great cathedral I sought out the first deserted chapel. It contained, I later discovered, a fine fresco of the 'Madonna del Popolo' by Giotto and, beneath its serene gaze, I removed the *Meditations* from my aching loins.

Its concealment was, of course, essential and I crossed from the south to the north sacristy looking the while for an appropriate crevice. It was not until I was within the sacristy itself that I found a suitable place. Here the walls were lined with inlaid cupboards of great age and beauty which had, like so much of Florence, decayed to the point of disintegration. Between them and the plaster of the wall gaps and fissures had opened, some wide enough to allow the insertion of a man's hand. Into one of these crevices I carefully pressed the tiny manuscript until it was invisible to all but the most inquisitive eye. Months later, when I retrieved it, I learnt from an idle curate that it had been in that very chapel that Lorenzo the Magnificent had fled to avoid murder at the hands of the Pazzi family. Historical irony of a high order.

It was now late afternoon. Near twelve hours had passed since the arrival of Mikos Faccioli in the farm at Impruneta. From the bliss of the early morning I felt separated by a lifetime. And yet nothing had been achieved. I felt, however, that events had now gained their own momentum. Curiously my successful passage with the Salti had left me with a sense of urgency if not infallibility. I therefore seized my canvas bag and my resolve and set out across the cool, sunlit Piazza in the direction of the Bargello.

As I turned into the Via del Pronconsolo, however, I felt my new confidence drain from me as though bled by leeches. The sheer size of the building was awesome. Its castellations and tiny windows combined to produce an atmosphere of unforgiving meanness of spirit coupled with the horror of unbridled power. I felt and loathed my own insignificance as one would scorn a cheap toy. For the first time that day I felt totally isolated: a lonely child in a hostile city carrying the burdens of Reason in the permanent shadow of Death and Pain. Tears of self-pity welled into my eyes and for a moment I was close to collapse before I brushed them angrily aside with the hard surface of the canvas bag I clasped before me. It was thus with a mixture of anger and despair that I mounted the stone steps towards the great oak doors and banged upon the wicket gate inset beneath the crest of the Medici. Almost immediately, a window set behind a grille opened inwards and angry, suspicious eyes surveyed my golden locks.

'Yes?'

My recent experiences had, at least, provided me with a story to tell and I said, 'My name is Angela Ballina. I am the daughter of the Prefect of San Casciano. I have come to Florence with papers for Signore Magliabechi. At the library they told me he was here.'

Above the eyes I saw the forehead pucker in disbelief.

'He can't take nothing *here*. Don't even know if he's alive.'

'I know he can receive nothing but I must have instructions where to take them. I simply wish to see him very quickly.' Then I added hopefully, 'I've got money . . .'

'Money ain't no good in this case, darling, this is a Church job. Heresy, treason. If I take money I'm as dead as mutton.' The despair on my face must have been apparent for he paused in the very act of shutting the window and added, 'Look, come in and leave 'em here. I'll see someone talks to him about it.'

It was the best I could do and, as the wicket opened inwards I stepped into the prison I had dreaded all my life. I found myself in a stone gatehouse. Doors opened from either side whilst, before me, some fifteen paces distant, a lowered portcullis barred the way to a courtyard of not unpleasing proportions in the middle of which a fountain played. The Salti, by whom I was admitted, was the oldest of his kind I had ever

266

seen. It was clear from his eyes, however, that the fire of his loins was not completely damped.

'Well, well,' he said in the hopeless tones of the aged rake. 'Aren't you a pretty one then? Now let's have these bits and pieces.'

I was lost. I could not part with my canvas bag or its contents nor could I provide him with nothing. My brain was now devoid of ingenuity and I felt, suddenly, completely resigned to failure. Yet, even as I reached this conclusion, I saw him stiffen with respect or fear and I realised that another person had appeared in the doorway behind me. I did not move but I anticipated the worst.

'Ah, Captain,' said the gatekeeper, 'this girl's come from San Casciano. Says she has papers from the Prefect for Magliabechi. Told her she can't see him. Said she could leave the papers with us.'

I heard footsteps behind me and seconds later I confronted a familiar face. It was the Captain with the strangely blotched and reddened nose I had seen standing before the 'Pietà' in the Duomo. I also realised, of course, that I had seen him at my master's house during the visit by Andrea Cortese. On no conceivable rational basis I sensed the presence of a friend.

'Well, you'd better fuck off then, hadn't you?' he said, demonstrating immediately the fallibility of instinct. I persevered.

'I have been entrusted with these documents. I must know where to take them.'

Something in my tone of voice clearly moved him. Whether it was the urgency or the strange purring tone it was impossible to say. He looked at me closely for a moment and then, quite suddenly, shrugged with the tolerance of the world-weary.

'Oh well, why not? You can't do no 'arm. Besides that, he's good as dead already.'

The ambiguity in this phrase stopped my breath. For a moment my head swam and I must have swayed for he placed a hand, by no means roughly, on my arm.

'Bit tender, are we? Ah well, country girls. Paolo, take her down to the bugger. He might as well see a friendly face before he coughs it.'

So, without even the necessity of a search, I was led through a gate set within the portcullis and across the courtyard beyond. On three sides it was bounded by a colonnade providing shade when required. Now, in the early evening, it was possible to make our way diagonally past the fountain towards a wooden, studded door set back in the stone wall. For this door my guide produced a key and we passed through into a short passage, lit by candles, indefinitely replaced above accumulated mountains of wax. After ten paces we descended into the gloom.

As Lorenzo Bellini had described it many years before, so it was. I will not dwell upon it. I saw no man in pain but I saw the instruments. Two racks stood side by side, silent like those waiting to witness some dreadful act. I, too, noticed the crude decoration on the wheels with an empty sense of despair and wonder. No one was in this outer room. We crossed it, however, to the beginning of a corridor containing the doors of cells and here a further Salti sat listless with inactivity.

'Magliabechi,' said Paolo without enthusiasm.

'Third cell, no key, just bolts.'

We travelled perhaps a further fifteen paces till we came to the third low door. Here Paolo shot back the bolts and we entered my master's cell.

Chapter Twenty-one

He had been provided with candles. Whether through pity or influence I did not know. Also he had a rough bench and desk. Otherwise there was but a stone slab thinly covered with straw and one blanket. He was unharmed. He rose as we entered and when I saw his crooked form I was nearly moved to tears. In the dim light there was no recognition and he smiled with polite amazement at the apparition which now approached. Paolo spoke first.

'Girl to see you. Some crap from a Prefect.'

To my intense relief he left us. Not before he had searched both me and the canvas bag and, having questioned the banker's draft and received from me the same reply, withdrew to his business with the other guards. From the talk I overhead in the corridor it concerned a financial investment of dubious propriety with the Castanellis whose leather monopoly was now an open scandal.

No sooner had I spoken than my master realised my identity. When the door closed he motioned me to silence until we heard the beginnings of the conversation. Then he took me in both arms and said, as I knew he would, 'Fredo. You fool. Why are you here?'

'Master,' I said, 'I have come to tell you of our plan. You must be aware of it in case anything is threatened before it can be made to work. I have...'

'Depositions,' he said. 'Yes, I know. I have known for a long time. Bellini told me; for this very purpose. Fredo, now listen to me carefully. The depositions have no value without *live evidence*. No, please do not interrupt me, I did read some of the lawyers' books I owned. The depositions are sufficient to bring *charges* but it is unlikely that Bomboni would even be arrested prior to his trial. If *live* evidence is not given then the depositions are worthless. No, *please* hear me out. It *is* true that a witness *must* testify in accordance with his deposition or risk the galleys but that does not overcome the difficulty of *actually obtaining their presence.'*

'But they will come. They have said...'

'Yes, they have said and yes, they will come. *If* they are able.'

A terrible truth was beginning to dawn. I exclaimed, 'But he would not ... Not his own family.'

'Of course he would. You have read the depositions. Do you think a man who would do that would stop short at murder?'

Despite my resolution I crumpled onto the stone bench, all hope gone. He came immediately and sat beside me, took my hand and continued to speak in rapid tones.

'We must not give up hope. There is one way and, now that you are here, it may be tried. I have attempted to get a message to Bellini and to you but, in my case, no bribery is possible. We must get word to Marguerite Louise. Yes, the mad Duchess. Estranged from Cosimo she certainly is, crazy she may be, but she remains his wife and is the cousin of the King of France. For a reason which no one understands Louis dotes upon her. Cosimo's greatest desire is to marry his awful sons into the French line. Thus he believes he will ensure the independence of Tuscany from Austria. If our mad Duchess does not agree to such a match it cannot take place. Thus her influence remains. Besides, Cosimo was always besotted by her and that has not changed. It is to her that we must appeal.'

'But she is in Paris!'

'No, she is not. When she went back to France (is it only four days ago?) she left me word that she was to stay at the Carmelite Convent at Aix. It is one of the two retreats to which she is, in theory, banished. The other is Montmartre in Paris. They say she has a lover in Aix, a defrocked priest apparently. She stays there for many weeks at a time and will doubtless be there still. Aix is barely five days' ride. *If* she will intercede on our behalf then the whole business can be done within two weeks. Time is not on our side. Daily I am closer to the rack. Vittoria della Rovere wishes to have me stretched. Bomboni, of course, will do it. Only Cosimo for the moment demurs but not, I think, for long.'

I looked at him, once more the pupil, and despite the dreadful danger in which we sat I felt a burden lift from my ringleted shoulders.

'Then I must go to Aix.'

'Indeed you must and, what is more, you will be safe and that will lighten my load. Now tell me where you have been and how you find yourself in this sorry state.'

Briefly I told him of my journeys and the information I possessed. Only once did he interrupt me to say, 'Take Bono with you. He is in great danger here and, furthermore, you will find him a valuable companion.'

When my news was exhausted and our decisions had been made we sat in the gloom, unwilling to summon our jailer, whose voice could be heard in heated debate, at the end of the passage. So we talked. My master, who had never before allowed himself such rein, spoke of his life and told me, indeed, that he had once *met* Galileo shortly before the astronomer's death.

'My father,' he said, 'had paid for some of his experiments and I was taken to his study as a treat. He was dying, of course, and had little sight but he found me amusing. He unhooked some of the spheres which he had supported to demonstrate the relative movement of the heavens and used them to play me at marbles. I beat him and when I did so he said, "There, my young friend, now you know more about the movement of spheres than any man alive."

'Now, my dear Boti, you must go. I will keep you in danger no longer. We must call for our friend.'

Yet as he rose and made towards the door we both heard a substantial commotion in the passage beyond. It plainly signalled the arrival of others and voices were raised as though in admonition. It ended in the unmistakable sound of a blow, followed by footsteps towards the door of our cell. I was now standing in the corner and thus, as the door propelled inwards, I was concealed by its width. I did not, however, require sight to recognise the voice of Pasto Bomboni saying, 'Right, now where's this tart from San Casciano?'

He entered the cell alone, splendid in the uniform of a Commander of the Salti. He realised, of course, where I was but took some time in turning. When he did so, at first, he frowned since he had doubtless expected to recognise any of the town girls who might have been sent on so improbable a mission. Taking up a candle he then thrust it closer to my face and advanced his own to within a hand's breadth. I felt his breath upon me as a smile, slow as lava, spread across his features.

'Well now,' he said softly, 'well now, what a lovely fat little tart we've got here. Come all the way from San Casciano, has she? Do you know I remember a *boy* in San Casciano. Fat as a fart. Dressed up as a girl. Sitting by the river bank. I *wonder* what happened to him?'

Moving at considerable speed he straightened and, as he did so, jammed a knee between my legs causing me to gasp and double with pain.

271

'Yes, oh *yes*, I wonder where *he* is now?'

Through the pain I heard my master speaking behind him.

'Bomboni...'

'You keep your fucking mouth shut,' said our tormentor evenly, 'I came to tell you that you've fucking had it. I now know what you've been doing. Yes, I do. That quivering arsehole Viviani has told me. You've been *copying* the books with that lens we found on your desk. They must be in miniature. God knows how many you've got but we're going to find them. You are going to tell us where they are. As soon as I get this news to our fat Duke he will have your bent back on that rack. And then, my clever friend, you will tell us where they are. But who would have thought,' he continued, turning towards me, 'that we would have two fish to fry? I wonder if this girlie knows where they are. Cosimo's not going to stop me putting the irons on *him*. All very, very convenient. Now I'm going to take her with me.'

Taking hold of my arm Bomboni pulled me backwards and then thrust me through the door. Beyond it four Salti, including the Captain, stood there, the tension as tight as a bow. Turning to one of them Bomboni said, 'Shut it!' and the cell door was slammed behind me. 'Find me a cell for this. I'm going to talk to it.'

We marched back into the main area of the cellar where a list was inspected and a number drawn. Thereafter we crossed to another passageway, similarly lined with doors, and through one of these I was pushed.

'Wait!' said Bomboni to the Captain when he followed me into the tiny space and levered the door to. 'Now,' he said, 'you and I are going to have a little chat.'

It was not any chemistry in the adrenal duct which kept away the fear. It was loathing. As I watched him I felt the hate grow till it pounded like a torrent against the front of my brain and I *felt* my eyes begin to glow like fire. Here an arm's length before me was the man who had blighted my childhood, imprisoned my friends and killed my parents as certainly as if he had impaled them upon a pike. Standing there in my petticoats and golden curls, pain radiating from my battered scrotum, I knew the time had come to fight back.

'Very well,' I said and, even then, he recoiled as though I had struck him between the eyes. '*Just* what I want too. I've got something very important to show you.'

As I fished into my canvas bag he grasped for his toledo and I said, 'No, don't worry. It's not a weapon. It's much worse than that.'

272

Finding the four packages I threw them to him one by one, the last three falling on the ground at his feet as he stared at seal and legend.

'What the fuck is this?'

I said, 'Open it. Read it. Don't worry about the seal. It's a copy.'

It was dark in the cell and his was the only candle, now set on the stone bench. In its flickering light I watched his downturned face as he read the tightly drawn lines of the Prefect's scribe. I heard his breath drawn long and even, as a man will breathe when engaged in some unending and arduous labour. Finally he looked at me and, in a single movement, ripped the paper across, the heavy wax seal cracking as he did so.

'The bitch.'

'Not just her. At your feet you will find the depositions of your father and mother and Filippo. It explains why you left the village so quickly. It explains a lot. For what you did to that girl they will castrate you in Santa Maria Nuova and bury you at Volterra.'

I felt his eyes upon me like a cold fire. Then suddenly he moved towards me and I anticipated a blow but his movement was simply a gesture, as though to release some pain. Then he said, 'They will have to . . .'

I had been expecting it and now I waited to hear from him the legal pitfalls rehearsed by my master. But he said nothing else and immediately I realised the significance. Until his family was dead Bomboni was not safe. He assumed that I was ignorant of the law and that I believed (as indeed I had) that the depositions were themselves sufficient. He said nothing therefore to warn me or them of the danger in which his family now stood.

'How d'you get them to do this?'

'Very simple. Either Alessandro or Filippo shot my father. I know it was no crime. He was the aggressor and I saw it. They were under investigation for murder. I gave my evidence in exchange for theirs. How did I know about Nicola? She told me. Why did she tell me? Because, together with Patrick Morahan, I saved her from your rotten family.'

Although I could not see his face with any clarity I felt him to be smiling. It alarmed me until I knew the reason.

'Right then,' he said, 'where are the originals? You can tell me now or with a hot poker up your fat arse.'

'I might well tell you if I am put in pain but by that time it will be too late. They are lodged in the city with a person who is wholly reliable and who has every reason to harm you. If I am not with him by nightfall, that person will take the originals to the Chief Magistrate. In this cell we cannot see the daylight but there must be very little of it left.'

I both felt and heard him draw breath. He said nothing so I continued.

'So let us understand each other. I know you cannot release my master because he is the prisoner of Andrea Cortese. But you *can* leave him unharmed. Now you will let *me* go. If I am followed I will simply not meet the person of whom I have spoken and the Chief Magistrate will have his evening disturbed by having to read this awful evidence. For as long as my master remains unharmed your secret will be safe. In order to ascertain that he is safe and well one of the assistants from the Medici library will call at the Bargello every day and must be allowed access to him. The same applies to Vincenzo Viviani and Carlo Dati. If it appears that they have been harmed in any way then the original depositions go straight to the Chief Magistrate to whom, incidentally, I will also reveal the identity of the woman whom you arrested in the Jewish quarter and who jumped from the Ponte Vecchio.'

I knew he was smiling again.

'Well, fat Fredo, you've worked it out very well. You could become a member of the Salti. Or even an Inquisitor. I wondered when your mother was going to be mentioned. Very well, it will be as you say. But you understand this, my fat friend, if these papers go anywhere near a Magistrate then your master and the other eggheads and arseholes in here will become slabs of raw meat. Do you understand?'

I understood perfectly and, unbeknown to him, understood a great deal more. With the power at his command it would be a matter of days before his family disappeared. With their passing the depositions would cause him but fleeting inconvenience. They would be vilified as forgeries or the product of deliberate, malicious falsehood. Whatever might be *believed* nothing could be proved and he *was* a Commander in the Salti. Thus, in the silence that followed, our contemplations were similar and our conclusions identical. I knew it. But he did not.

Nothing else was said. He turned and wrenched open the cell door beyond which the blotched face of the Captain could be seen in the flickering light.

'Take him ... her to the gate and chuck her out.'

As the Captain raised his eyebrows Bomboni continued, 'And, until further notice, Magliabechi is to be allowed one visitor a day provided he brings the scroll from the Medici library.' And then, to me, with exaggerated politeness, 'Will that be sufficient?'

'There is one other matter,' I said in my woman's voice, and I fancy I saw him wince, 'I would wish to have access to Magliabechi's house.'

The smile on his face would have frozen a serpent when he said, 'Of course. You will find, in any event, it is no longer guarded. Soon, I dare say, it will become a museum.' With that he turned on his heel and, followed by three Salti, whom I took to be his personal guard, he disappeared towards the room of the racks. The Captain watched him go with an expression, I fancied, not far from distaste. Again I felt a strange warmth towards his damaged face and I dared to say, 'Why do you stand and watch the "Pietà"?'

He looked at me in surprise and then grunted 'Doctor's orders. Says it will do my back good. And "these apaches"...' With that he jerked a thumb at his nose which wrinkled like a squeezed fruit.

'Does it work?'

'Course it fucking doesn't. These doctors, they don't know their arse from their eyeball. But what can you do? Once you start it, you've got to keep it up.' We walked in silence across the courtyard, through the portcullis and, with a feeling that I will not even attempt to describe, I was expelled into the streets of Florence whose dung-covered surface I have never been so glad to see.

The light was, indeed, fading fast and I took a chair, immediately, to the Porta Romana. I had no time to ascertain whether or not I was followed but relied on the power of the threat I had made. Once through the gate I paid off the men from the florins I still possessed. I then continued on foot to the house of Bellina Cantoni, Mario's sister. I found her in a state of considerable agitation and uncertainty; whether she would, indeed, have gone to the Magistrate with the depositions still remains a matter of conjecture. Here I discarded my women's clothes, accepting shirt, leather jerkin and trousers which had formerly been the property of our ill-fated groom. They were too tight, of course, but after the corset they were bliss indeed.

Bellina's husband, who had been without work for many months, I now provided with employment. I drafted a letter to be delivered, without fail, into the hands of Nicola Bomboni, warning of the danger she was in and advising flight. This I entrusted to the husband together with ten florins as payment and for the hire of a strong horse. I stressed the urgency without providing information and placed in him my trust. Again, I had little choice. It was essential that I left immediately for France and our only chance of rescue and relief. For me to travel to San

Casciano would entail the loss of at least a day. Furthermore I still had business in Florence.

Upon reflection it was clear that even Bomboni would require time to construct a plan and assemble the forces necessary to destroy his own family. If my master was right, any assistance from Marguerite Louise would be two weeks coming. Equally, I had no doubt that, once his family had been silenced for ever, Bomboni would proceed immediately to encompass the death of his prisoners by any contrivance. Their continued existence could only work to his disadvantage if the contents of the depositions were ever to be known. The course of the race, therefore, was clearly charted. The Bombonis must be kept safe for two weeks and every day was therefore mortgaged to fate.

We set out immediately to the nearest livery which was a little further from the city gate. Here we obtained our horses separately, in order, so far as possible, to obscure future enquiry. Whilst my messenger set out along the dark road to San Casciano I, with a spare horse in train, rode back towards the city.

The Via Romana was now all but deserted and I made good speed past the Pitti Palace and across the Ponte Vecchio itself. Leaving my master's house and the Via del Corso to my right I went immediately to the cloisters of San Lorenzo, the home of the Medici library. The library was, of course, closed and deserted. However I, like all the apprentices, knew several methods of entry. Choosing one, which involved little exertion through a low window, I passed through the darkened rooms to the assistants' desks. Here I left two letters, prepared earlier at the house of Bellina Cantoni. The first was for Fernando, instructing him to attend daily upon his master at the Bargello. The second letter was to Carlo Bassani whose remarks on the reference lists had caused my master such concern many months before. This high-spirited lad I directed towards San Casciano with a duplicate of the letter I had entrusted to Bellina's husband. Thus was I doubly insured.

Leaving, once more, by the window, I directed my horse towards the Via del Corso, arriving in a state of near total exhaustion a little before midnight. The door to the street was barred, a circumstance I found not unfavourable. I therefore had recourse, again, to the entrance on the canal and, once inside the building, this door I also bolted and jammed. Feeling my way through the house I passed, once more, before the plagiarised 'Last Supper' and re-entered the scriptorium. Here I lit the candles I had previously used and, moving the desk to its position below the entrance to the shaft, I climbed upon it and thrust my head into the void. As I did so I heard from below the faint but unmistakable rasp of a torn vegetable. I smiled with relief into the blackness.

He heard me immediately and, within seconds, was standing beside me in the scriptorium, his fangs set in a grotesque grin and the remains of a cucumber clasped in his right hand.

I was now, as you would imagine, quite faint with tiredness and I was able only to impart the outline of my story. He received it all with the composure of one who has seen infinitely worse times and finally said, 'You have my horse?' When I nodded he said, 'We must leave at first light and now you must sleep. I will wake you.'

Yet again I crossed the library floor, oblivious now to the burnt remains about me. I climbed to my room which I found, predictably, had been ransacked. The wooden bed was broken but the mattress of feather and down left mainly intact. On this I fell in a state not markedly different from that in which I had first touched its surface. I closed my eyes and entered a world from which all dreams had been banished by the nightmares of reality.

BOOK THREE

France

Chapter Twenty-Two

I woke like a man hauled from a deep shaft at the head of which, with the light behind him, was the grotesque and grinning face of Jacob Bonetti. As though from a great distance I heard his voice saying, 'Come on, my young friend, come on, we must begin.'

I sat up and observed the first light of dawn through my broken shutters. I had slept for barely four hours and my body implored its just rewards of rest. The demand could not be met. It was, of course, essential that we cleared the city gates by dawn. Even in my drugged state, however, I observed a remarkable change had come over Bono. He was now equipped for travel and wore, I have no doubt, the clothes in which he had once adventured across the face of Europe. Beneath a coarse travelling cloak, no more in length than one of my arms, he wore a leather tunic and jerkin open at the throat to reveal a shirt of fine cotton. Leather breeches disappeared into riding boots which would have fitted a child of six but, on their present owner, carried an assertion of confident, almost swaggering poise. At his belt hung a toledo (a paring knife in any other hand) and visible beneath the cloak was the butt of a tiny inlaid pistol, a present he later informed me from 'Strenuous Jeffrey' himself. Altogether it looked as deadly a package as one could wish to find. Beside him I felt totally ill-equipped, a circumstance for which he had come prepared. He buckled about me a fine toledo which I recognised, immediately, as Otto's. 'They fished this out of one of the Salti,' he said with satisfaction. 'Otto would have wished you to take it.' He also handed me a pistol, unloaded and rusty with age, for the sole purpose, he said, of 'demonstration'.

As we descended the stairs towards the door the dwarf collected, from the balustrade, the most remarkable part of his uniform. It was something between a helmet and a hat. Whilst plainly armoured beneath the felt it contained a wide brim and the crown sash of a *cavaliere*. From it hung a leather chinstrap which fitted precisely below his jaw and extended to cover the bottom half of his face. A rebate had been fashioned for the nose and, for his mouth, the leather had been pricked out to enable sound to pass. The effect was totally to conceal the cavernous mouth and enormous tusks.

When we reached the horses I saw that he had been busy. The saddlebags had been packed and from one emerged the ends of a melon and cucumber. I anticipated a noisy morning. In one of my own bags there was also food for the journey, bread, cheese and dry sausage. Into the other I decanted my canvas sack and, still weary of muscle, hauled myself into the saddle. I realised, when I had done so, that I had made no effort to assist Bono onto his pony but I need not have worried. From a standing start he sprang straight upwards, grasped the edge of the saddle, heaved, swivelled on his belly before landing upright with an air of apparent unconcern. Scorning the stirrups and, with a brief nod to me, he drove his heels into the pony's flanks and trotted briskly towards the cupola of the Duomo, now stark and beautiful against the clear morning sky.

We rode towards the north, crossing before the dramatic façade of Santa Maria Novella gleaming like polished ivory in the weak and early sun. Soon we came to a part of the city where I had never ventured and we passed, I realised, through the roads adjacent to the Jewish sector. Here, even at this hour, Salti guarded the streets and watched our progress with sullen indifference. At length we came to the Porta al Prato, the great mass of the Fortezza da Basso rising like a giant's dwelling well to our right.

Bono was, of course, both my companion and my guide. He had ridden these roads on many occasions, albeit twenty years before, and was plainly gripped with the dormant enthusiasm of youth. Enthusiasm, indeed, was necessary to maintain the spirits for the condition of the villages and the countryside to the north was, if anything, worse than that in the direction of San Casciano. Here men begged without shame and hollow-eyed children observed our passage with the apathy of habitual hunger and disease.

'Vittoria della Rovere should see this,' I heard my companion mutter as we passed through a particularly debased township. 'Even she might have some pity.' Personally I doubted it. I had seen her.

Where the road permitted we rode at a good pace, without pause. Where possible we cantered the horses and otherwise drove them to a fast trot. By midday we all required rest having, by my calculation, travelled nearly forty miles from the city gate. We therefore looked for suitable ground and, shortly thereafter, came to a small wood composed of poplar, alder and stunted oak. A stream ran beside the dusty road over which the trees provided ample shade. Here we tethered the horses to drink and graze whilst we found a clear area of the bank on which to lie and escape the sun now at its hottest above our heads.

As Bono dismounted I realised why he excited so little comment and attention whilst on horseback. Relative to a man of normal growth his legs were substantially shorter than the trunk of his body. When riding, his cloak fell to the stirrups and the height to which he rose above the horse's back, to the casual glance, could just have been that of a normal, if diminutive traveller. The extraordinary hat also served to increase his size whilst concealing his tusks.

Thus far he had been the best of companions. Loquacious to a fault he had recounted many of his exploits during his journeys in France and, indeed, whilst on this very road. Generally he paused only to devour one of his many vegetables or fruits, the chin-strap whilst he did so hanging unbuttoned to his chest.

I was, of course, anxious to proceed with all possible speed but, thus far, we had found nowhere to change the horses and some rest was essential. We therefore spread ourselves upon the grass, in which position I returned, immediately, to the deep slumber of the night.

It did not last long. A vast weight descended upon my chest and, as consciousness flashed upon me, I heard the rib crack. As my mouth opened to scream a hand was slapped upon it, constricting the air, causing me to choke and gag against it. Above me, through tears. I could see the dappled pattern of the alder and, framed before it, the head of the man whose knee now pinned me to the grass. The sun, beyond the trees, rendered him featureless save for a wild mass of hair which coiled and sprang as he shook his head.

'Now, *now*,' he said and, with a dismissive swipe of his free arm, he thrust aside the hand which I waved in futile gesture towards his face.

'Now, now! No need to get nasty. No one's going to get hurt so no one needs to get nasty. All that's going to happen to you and your little friend is a nice long walk back to Florence. So there's no need for anyone to get nasty.'

With desperate force against the restraining hand, I wrenched my head to one side. With swivelled eyes, I could just see the figure of the dwarf, his back uppermost, his face thrust into the soft spring grass by his captors. Unnecessarily, there were two of them and one was carefully inspecting the inlaid pistol indicating that Bono, at least, may have attempted a better show of defiance than I had done. Beyond them, two others were inspecting the contents of our saddlebags, the first discarding considerable quantities of cucumbers and fleshy fruit. All of them were roughly dressed, their hair as wild and ragged as that which fell towards my face.

My desperation needs no description. The loss of horses and money and the slow return to Florence was death for my master as sure as the falling axe.

Despite the pain which radiated from my chest I wrenched my head from side to side against the hard flesh of the palm.

'Now, now, *now*! There's no cause for wriggling. You'll only hurt yourself. All you want to say is that you don't want to walk. Right? Well, I understand that. I've even, you might say, got some sympathy with it. But you see, young fella, our need is greater than yours. If you knew how much, you wouldn't mind walking. But I haven't got time to tell you. They all say I talk too much anyway and they've got a point. I do run on, *particularly* if I've got a grievance. Not necessarily *my* grievance, you understand, but *a* grievance. It's all a question of seeing both sides. From your position now it's very difficult. I accept that. That's only reasonable. But there's no need to be *nasty* about it so just lie...' He broke off with a sudden yelp of pain. By regularly twisting my head I had worked my jaw apart and loosened his grip. Now I was able to sink my teeth into his palm which I did with as much force as I could muster. As he instinctively tore his hand away, I said, 'You *can't* take the horses.'

The fact that I did not cry out and the desperate insistence of my voice appeared to give him pause. As he turned to face his companions I could make out some of his features, rough-lined and belonging to a man of, perhaps, fifty.

'Can't? *Can't* take the horses. Now that's not logic, is it? *Can't* take the horses won't rhyme at all. *Shouldn't* take the horses. Now that's another matter. That's a moral issue. Not the same thing at all. Not an imperative.'

'We are going to France. To find help for my master, Magliabechi. He is in the Bargello. They are going to kill him.'

The features disappeared once more within the general silhouette as my captor stared down at my face.

'Ah. Errand of mercy is it? Got to get help. In the Bargello. Now you see what I mean by a *moral* question. All very unfortunate, I'm sure. But you see, young fella, it's all a matter of balance. Children dying. No food. Women dying. Men begging. Monopolies everywhere, given to crooks. Stripping the poor. It's a moral question all right. It's a dilemma.'

'Why don't you shut up, Giuseppe,' said one of the men by the horses. 'Just keep him quiet till the *capo* arrives. Then we can all fuck off.'

'Don't agree,' replied Giuseppe with a note of recalcitrance, 'this is a nice young fella. Rich no doubt but nice enough. Needs to understand the moral dimension.'

'Our need,' I said hopelessly, 'is *now* much greater than yours. If you leave us the money and the horses I will arrange that you are repaid.'

'*Repaid*, now that's not logical. You need to pay to be repaid and I've given you nothing, except a few words on the moral dilemma. That's not worth much. Some people think it's not worth anything at all.'

At this point we all heard the sound of a horse ridden along the road. The man with the pistol quickly left Bono and crossed to the far side of the dusty track, some twenty paces away. From this point he could, plainly, see further around the bend and, after a moment, waved to his companions, a clear gesture of relief. Within seconds the rider himself came into view, entering the shadow of the trees. Instinctively I exclaimed with recognition, causing Giuseppe once more and with reluctance to place his hand across my mouth.

'Now don't start getting *nasty* again. It's just the guv'nor.'

The horseman reined in and dismounted. At a leisurely pace he inspected our horses and the contents of the saddlebags which were displayed to him. Having done so he walked towards Bono, still pinned face-down on the bank. He paused, curious at the tiny body, then, slightly shaking his head, proceeded towards me.

My recognition was accurate. I could never have forgotten that face. Half a face it remained. A patch still covered the left eye whilst all around flesh and bone had disintegrated and flattened as though from some gigantic crushing blow. The right eye inspected me carefully, the head jerking forward with concentration like a pecking hen. With a slight gesture of his fingers he waved aside the hand which covered the bottom half of my face and then, in so far as it could possibly be so described, he smiled.

'Holy Mother of God. Fredo Credi. All the way from Florence.'

I started to say, 'Please don't . . .' but he held up his hand, his face set in a mask of irony.

'Please don't take the horses? Am I right? I dare say you have already said that to Giuseppe and he has given you a tedious lecture on the moral dimension. Am I right?'

Giuseppe and the men by the horses all laughed while I remained, as yet, unmoved.

'Let him up, Giuseppe, let him up. This is Fredo Credi, Gallupe's son.'

This caused a stir amongst the men around him who, as I rose with difficulty to my feet, now inspected me with greater interest.

'And this little fellow,' said the guv'nor, pointing at Bono, 'let's have a look at him too.'

Bono was hauled to his feet, his face smeared with earth, his eyes blazing with rage.

'Very cross he is too,' continued the guv'nor, 'I'd be frightened if I were you, Pepone. He looks fit to do you in. Now, Fredo Credi,' he said turning to me, 'I have already given you one chance. Please tell me why I should not make you walk to Florence.'

I told him all of it with as much coherence as urgency and the pain in my ribs would allow. As I spoke they gathered around and I became increasingly aware that, to some at least, the events, locations and characters involved were well-known. I finished, of course, with our present predicament and the certainty of my master's death. At the end of my tale, for a moment, there was silence.

'Well, Giuseppe,' said the guv'nor, 'there's enough to fill your moral dimension for a year or two. Very interesting. So Pasto Bomboni is going to kill his own family to save his own balls. Now how is he going to do that, I wonder? One thing for sure. He will have to be there himself and, as they will not go to Florence, he must go to San Casciano. How very interesting. Very interesting. Well, Fredo Credi, you and I have already met. These men, you may be surprised to hear, are all from the region of Gallaza. We are a long way from home. But in this business you've got to keep moving or you get caught and then you get flogged and hung on a tree. Of course you may keep your horses.'

As he said this there was a general murmur, though whether of assent or disapproval it was impossible to tell.

'And your money too. But remember, Fredo Credi. Remember what has happened. These are poor men. Good men but poor. Some have watched their families die. Do not forget, Fredo Credi. If your master is released he will still be a rich man. There is a miller at Gallaza called Gimone. He is our friend. Money given to him will reach us. Do not forget. Now I wish you Godspeed.'

286

The happy end of proceedings was interrupted by Bono who said, 'I want my pistol.'

'Ah,' said the man called Pepone, 'of course, my little fellow. Here's your pop-gun.'

As he handed it to the dwarf, in a gesture devoid of malice but full of condescension, he reached down and tweaked his nose to universal merriment and laughter. It appeared at first that Bono would accept this indignity and, indeed, he had half-turned when suddenly he swivelled and delivered Pepone a driving and totally accurate kick below the kneecap causing the robber to yelp with pain and bend, instinctively, to the injured part. As he did so Bono grasped Pepone's nose and heaved him onto the ground, as neat a trick as I have seen outside the *pugilato*. To considerable spontaneous applause the dwarf then stepped smartly to his horse, vaulted into the saddle by the method I have described and, without valediction, trotted swiftly on the road to France. In carrying out this feat he had, of course, scorned the vegetables and I in more circumspect frame of mind, gathered them into my own saddlebag before mounting. As I left I turned to my one-eyed benefactor and said, 'Who *are* you?'

'Ah, Fredo Credi,' he said, 'that's not the kind of thing you ask in this game.' He brought his hand down on the rear of my horse which, needing little bidding, set out after the receding figure in the absurd hat.

I am not an Englishman. So I will not bore you to tears with the interminable details of our journey and the eccentricities of foreign people. By mid-afternoon we crossed the border into the state of Genoa and, by evening, had left Tuscany behind us by forty miles. We were now on the coast road bound for Genoa itself, the great mountains of the Apennine range rising to our right. Night had fallen by the time we reached the town of Lerici where we obtained new horses, putting our own to livery for the return journey. We slept for six hours and then, again in the first light of dawn, continued on the road towards the French border.

The pattern of travel continued. At times, when the mountains approached the sea, the road was rough and the going heavy but we pressed onwards at the best possible speed. Sometimes I slept in the saddle. Dangerously so, on the mountain roads. Several times the dwarf awoke me, his hand grasping my arm to ensure my balance. At the beginning of the third day we crossed into France. Little enquiry was made of us as we did so. The mountains still hemmed us against the sea but I could not do other than remark on the change in the towns and the people themselves. The further we progressed from Tuscany the richer the land became. When we crossed the great river of Var the coastal plain became more fertile. Olives, vines and standing corn grew in profusion and the fat, sleek cows of Provence grazed and gazed with the indifference of the sublime.

When we reached the town of Fréjus we turned towards the hills. Following the Argens we climbed towards the nunnery at Aix. At nightfall on the fifth day we still wanted some ten miles of our journey's end and so we rested until daybreak when, in a sharp hour's riding, we arrived at the home of the Carmelites of Provence.

An iron bell chain hung by the wooden gates and when it was pulled a dulcet ringing could be heard within the walls and, after several minutes, the grille in the wicket was opened.

I enquired immediately whether Marguerite Louise remained within the walls and watched a shadow pass across the plain face of the Carmelite sister. Marguerite Louise was still in residence. Our names and identities were ascertained before the grilleflap was, again, firmly closed. It was a further half an hour before the nun returned and admitted us into the outer courtyard. Here we waited again until a further, senior, sister arrived to lead us into the buildings themselves. I could not but notice that both our companions appeared nervous and apprehensive, their eyes darting from side to side and scanning the many windows, doubtless for sign of movement within. We had now reached a further, inner courtyard where both sisters accelerated sharply through a colonnade, the marble pillars of which I noticed with sudden comprehension were pitted and holed at irregular intervals.

Finally, to the evident relief of our guides, we were shown into a small, bare antechamber and asked to wait whilst the royal cousin was brought. As they were leaving a shot rang out, sharply indicating, I suspected, that Marguerite Louise was in the near vicinity. Indeed she appeared almost immediately thereafter, a smoking pistol in one hand, a dead rabbit in the other.

'I didn't kill it,' she said by way of explanation, 'I've just brought it from the kitchens. They haven't the slightest idea how to cook in this place so I do it myself. Now what's this about Becci. In trouble, is he? I'm not surprised. I've told him many times to stop poking that woman Mascini. Quite unsuitable. Much too big for him as well. Hello, Bono. Haven't seen you since I winged you in Mattias's garden. Thought you were a great bustard. Quite recovered? You must be getting on a bit now anyway. How long do you lot live for normally?'

I thought it best to intervene at this stage. 'Grand Duchess,' I said, with as much firmness as I considered advisable, 'my master *is* in trouble. He is in terrible danger. It does not concern his relationship with Lisa Mascini.' I then embarked upon my story. I had, of course, rehearsed it a thousand times on my journey but, under the penetrating gaze of those green eyes, it became disjointed and slow. Almost immediately she raised her hand. An imperious command.

'It looks as though this is going to be a long business. I have a ... friend who is staying here as a guest of the Mother Superior. He knows your master, slightly. He may be interested and helpful.' She turned to the novice sister, clearly her attendant, who had followed her into the room and had sat silent during our dialogue. 'Run along and get my monk, there's a good girl, look sharpish.' As she spoke she waved the smoking firearm generally in the direction of the unfortunate girl who, wide-eyed with terror, fled from the chamber. 'Now,' she continued, turning to us once more. Don't let's talk about Becci until he arrives. What do you think of these sights? They're quite new and bloody useless. Disaster, in my view, is absolutely inevitable.'

Mainly in order to stop her pointing the weapon in my direction, I took it from her and purported to examine the top of the barrel. I was doing so with elaborate care when the door opened and admitted Patrick Morahan.

Chapter Twenty-Three

There are times when a man surrenders to joy unconfined. I embraced him with the fervour of a son (which, indeed, was not far from the truth). Our meeting was, of course, as great a shock for him as for myself. As it transpired he had been, until recently, in Amsterdam where news of Tuscan matters is as rare as English wine.

I now began my account in earnest. In deference to Patrick I commenced with the death of my mother, thus lengthening a narrative which took a full half-hour to expound. At the end I outlined the reasons for our coming and the suggestions that my master had made. To my consternation the royal cousin shook her head.

'I would like to assist, of course, but I really doubt that I can do so. Becci exaggerates my influence. Once it was great but Cosimo is now ruled by his ghastly mother. It is possible, indeed, that any intervention by me might have precisely the reverse effect. It *is* true that they believe me to have influence with the King but, equally, they know that the King of France is unlikely to lift a finger to assist a Tuscan librarian, still less if he is charged with the accumulation of heretical work.'

'They *say* he has heretical works,' I cried, 'but . . .'

'Do not concern me with the merits of the case, *please*. I do not care if your master has a forked tail concealed beneath his hump. I will help him, if I can, because during my miserable years in your God awful country he was the only friend I had. Now, Monsieur Credi, I am going to leave you with this mad priest. They have now finally defrocked him, a decision which, as you see from his clothes, he purports wholly to ignore. I must superintend the proper cooking of our next meal. Whilst I am doing so I will contemplate what may be done. We will eat at noon in my rooms. It is early, I know, but it makes the Mother Superior furious.'

I spent the morning walking the cloisters with Patrick, guilty at my

290

happiness whilst my master's peril continued unabated. His teaching had, indeed, finally brought excommunication and, as Marguerite Louise had indicated, it was a sentence he ignored. Since leaving San Casciano he had founded two further schools, both teaching entirely in the vernacular, a fact of which he was still inordinately proud. He had met the former Grand Duchess when visiting the convent at Montmartre shortly before his sentence. Their relationship had become, for a time, the scandal of Paris, hence his banishment to Aix.

At noon precisely we attended the royal chambers, set above the outer courtyard whence, I realised, the Carmelite sisters had directed their attention when first we were admitted. A substantial feast had been prepared partly, I understood, in our honour and partly, as it transpired, to celebrate our hostess's departure to Paris. I waited with impatience for the conclusions, if any, that she had reached.

After the cold meats and potatoes we were served a substantial ragout of rabbit, pheasant and duck. It was not until we were well embarked on this course, several flagons of wine having been consumed, that she came to the subject in hand.

'I have been considering our problem,' she said through a mouthful of rabbit. 'To ensure success, or even the chance of success, any pressure on Cosimo must come from the King himself.'

'But,' I interrupted, unwisely, 'the King is in Paris.'

'No. The King is not in Paris. The King is in Versailles. That is where the King of France lives. Now please be silent and let me continue. The first premise on which we must act is that the King will know *everything* that happens in Tuscany. Charles Colbert (who, in case you did not know, is the Secretary of State and *real* ruler of France) has more spies in Europe than a dog has fleas. Our use of factual matter must therefore be entirely correct. Second, we must assume that he will do nothing unless he perceives it to be in the best interests of France and, therefore, himself. Librarians, in themselves, do not interest kings. Therefore we come to the first question. What interest has France in Tuscany? The answer to that question is: very little. What interest there is is negative and is confined only to frustrating any ambitions on the part of Leopold of Austria. Incidentally, we may also assume that Leopold's interest is exactly the same, namely it is confined to frustrating any ambitions on the part of Louis XIV. Our first task, therefore, is to persuade Louis that the arrest of the intellectual flower of Florence is, in some way, connected with the advance of Austrian influence.'

By this time my head was beginning to reel. The concept that my master's safety was, in some way, related to the Wars of Succession had, until then, eluded my fifteen-year-old brain. She continued.

'I think that I have found a way in which it might be done. Everyone knows that it is Cosimo's fat mother who has ordered the arrests and persecutions. Colbert will know this or will find out in minutes. Now the matter which preoccupies Cosimo and his mother even more than the Jews and heresy is the marriage of my ghastly son into one of the ruling houses of Europe. By so doing they hope to secure some lasting influence for the dying house of Medici. Vittoria della Rovere, it is well known, favours a marriage to Princess Violante Beatrice of Bavaria, a woman rumoured to be almost as ugly as my son. That is not, incidentally, the reason for which she favours the match. She herself is part German and looks with sympathy upon their gloomy aspirations. Cosimo himself favours a French match, identity unspecified. All this will be known to Colbert. Here, therefore, we have a coincidence of interests. Vittoria della Rovere favours a German marriage and Vittoria della Rovere locks up the egg-heads. What we need to establish is a link between the two. This is what *you* can provide.'

This last observation was directed straight at me and left me feeling as weak and faint as any of the dreadful events of the past two weeks. The idea that I should attempt to play a part in the power politics of Europe had not, even of late, entered my head. She continued.

'You have been at the secret meetings between the old members of the Cimento...'

'Only one...' I began,

'One is quite sufficient. Colbert's spies will know, of course, of these meetings but, unless they are deeper in than is reasonably conceivable, he will not know what is discussed. If he can be persuaded that these meetings are designed to influence Cosimo towards a French, rather than a German or Austrian, match then it establishes a reason both to thwart the grandmother and advance the interests of France. It is of course *absolutely essential* that Colbert *himself* should come to this conclusion. If necessary in the teeth of disagreement from those who most wish him to reach it. Do I make myself clear?'

From my point of view the whole thing was as black as pitch. I could see a number of drawbacks, about a hundred to be precise. I spoke the first, in a voice breaking with alarm and apprehension.

'How do I speak to this Signore Colbert?'

'*Marquis* de Colbert – that is quite simple. You must come to Versailles with me. I am, in any event, due to travel to Paris in the morning. In view of the urgency we may leave this afternoon.'

I felt as though the whole of my body below waist level had suddenly been plunged into cold water.

'But ...' I began again.

'There's no "but". The little details we can arrange on the coach. With four horses, regular changes and some firm encouragement to the drivers we can be at Versailles in two and a half days. We will, of course, sleep on the coach. The Mother Superior can provide some of her inedible food. Allow a day to see the King and, if we are successful, we will have you back here within the week.'

'But by then my master may well be dead,' I said in utter misery.

'Of course. He may be dead by now. We must just hope that these Bomboni people manage to keep out of sight and away from this Pasto. I must say that they do sound a most peculiar family.'

Further argument was, of course, quite useless. After the meal Marguerite Louise left to superintend the preparation and victualling of the carriage, an operation which resounded throughout the convent and which brought, I noticed, a radiant glow to the faces of the sisters I met.

I received some comfort, as always, from Patrick who told me that, for all her apparent lunacy, Marguerite Louise was known as one of the best and most devious schemers in the royal houses of Europe. I could but believe it and, with the afternoon sun still beating on its roof, the coach finally passed the entrance of the Convent, containing within its substantial interior a royal Princess of France, a fat fifteen-year-old boy and a dwarf. Behind us rode four horsemen, each leading two further horses to replace the four which now propelled us forward at a speed beyond that which I would have imagined possible for human beings to travel and yet survive.

'Why in God's name are they going so *slowly*?' cried our benefactress after an hour's journey during which, by the best of my calculations, we must have travelled nearly thirty miles, leaving, I could see from the windows, a litter of carts, animals and peasantry in disarray by the road's side.

From time to time our pace did slacken, doubtless to negotiate bridges or avoid cattle being driven along the road. When it did so it drove Marguerite Louise to new heights of impatience, causing her to beat furiously on the partition behind the drivers, an example, I suppose, of the 'encouragement' to which she had referred.

Partly through the speed and partly due to my own exhaustion the French countryside became a blur of colour and image. At first, to the

293

right, the great Alpes Maritimes shuddered and shook beyond the woods and fields. On the second day the country became greener. In particular I observed vines in a profusion I could scarce believe. These were interspersed with extensive woodland, the roadside trees coppiced and pollarded, the wood stacked and bundled with peasant thrift. It is a road, of course, that I have travelled now many times and accumulated memory blurs the sharp images of youth but it was a rich country then. Fat and soft as butter. Subsequently, in my lifetime, France has fought too many wars, on too many fronts, with too many enemies. Like the bear, baited on all sides, she has become drained of strength and blood. Now they talk of poverty, hunger and unrest. They even talk of an 'English revolution'. Personally I doubt it. Frenchmen need kings more than any country in Europe. Killing them is not in their nature.

On the third day it rained. The road became mud and our progress slowed to barely a walking pace. No urgings could achieve more. The wheels stuck and spun. Twice we were forced to enlist gangs of peasants who, for scant reward, laboured at the wheels, knee-deep in the cloying ooze. At the end of that day we were yet fifty miles from our goal, the horses exhausted and no change available. We therefore stopped at the tiny town of Longueville. Marguerite Louise slept in the only inn while Bono and I remained on the upholstered seats, embracing the blissful lack of forward motion.

We left at early light and, by noon, we arrived at the great palace of Versailles.

Marguerite Louise had her own quarters, outside the palace gates in the Château d'Enchat. Here Bono and I were provided with a room from which I peered at the amazing world below. I swiftly realised that, as San Casciano was to Florence, so Florence was to Versailles. I had never seen such sights nor, indeed, had they touched my imagination, fertile though it was. Men and women wore suits of pure gold and wigs which towered above their heads the length of a forearm before curling downwards to bob before them like the nodding horses of childhood games. Shoes I saw with points so long that they were lifted and clasped to the knee by golden strings and silver bows. All faces disappeared behind powder and rouge whilst hands fluttered like caged birds in the elegant dialogue of the Court. We were enjoined to remain in our chamber and I required no bidding. Bono, for his part, fretted at the inaction and the apparent lack of cucumbers available at the market.

I confess now that the sheer distance of travel had, again, reduced Florence to the world of fantasy and dreams. As I gazed upon the bobbing wigs and lamé slippers, the dungeons of the Bargello and their Salti guardsmen inhabited a different galaxy a millenium away. I slept and dreamed of a girl, half-buried in golden straw.

Immediately upon our arrival Marguerite Louise had left for the Court. Being famous for eccentricity she had not changed the riding habit she wore throughout our journey nor had she covered the red hair which fell in untidy profusion onto her velvet shoulders. I watched her disappear into the crowd, parting it before her as a dog divides a flock of bobbing sheep. She was gone for a day, during which time we were attended by silent footmen and allowed the luxury of recurring sleep. No one commented upon her failure to return and we were as powerless as one could conceive.

On the morning of the following day, the fifth since our leaving from Aix, she returned, unchanged save for the light of triumph which danced in her eyes.

She sat before us, her legs straddled across a chair, gripped with the enthusiasm of a grand deceit.

'I have seen Colbert twice. Once last night and once early this morning. I told him that I had had a strange envoy from Florence. I told him it was some nonsense about a society called the Cimento, Bavarian marriages and the like. I told him I could make not head nor tail of it and that I thought a polite refusal would suffice. "Ah well," he said,' and she touched the points of her fingers in evident imitation of the Marquis himself. She continued with a voice as soft as fur, '"Don't let us be hasty," he said, "I have heard of secret meetings in Florence. Our Austrian friends may be ... involved." I told him, of course, that I thought it was fanciful. I relied upon my years in Florence and the fact that I had never observed an Austrian plot anywhere. "Now, my dear," he replied, "that may well be because you were so busy trying to avoid your dreadful husband. Often those closest to the ground cannot see the grass." That was last night. He asked me to return this morning by which time he would have made his "enquiries". When I saw him again he was quite convinced. "I believe there is more to this than meets the eye. Consider. What kind of madman, or woman, would lock up a librarian in his dotage, risking all kinds of trouble and unrest, for a few books? There is more to this and I think the answer lies in Bavaria. You say this young man has been to these meetings, hmmmm? I think perhaps we should see him." "We?" I asked and he said, "The King is interested in this. He likes Italy." So it may have worked. You have a private audience at three o'clock.'

The rest of the day I spent in a condition close to terminal fever. I had been advised to wear my travelling clothes and thus, at least, there would be no problem with red breeches. At a little after two we left Bono at the door of the Château and made our way through the press of people that surrounded the iron gates beyond which the gravel path and famous fountains led, via the circular staircases, to the palace itself. We had brought no attendants and thus we made a strange pair as we mounted the stone steps and, on production of our warrant, were admitted to the great halls beyond. Here we passed into the care of a valet and began the long perambulation to the royal apartments used, at that time, for private receptions. Since then I have been in many palaces. I can simply say that none has even resembled its magnificence and, beside it, the Pitti Palace was like Bonelli's inn.

We came at last to the inevitable antechamber, itself not dissimilar to that where my master and I had waited the pleasure of Cosimo and his mother. Here there was no pause and, our credentials having been produced, we were ushered straight into a room of remarkable and delightful simplicity. It was here that I, Fredo Credi, son of Gallupe Credi, sometimes known as Boti, entered the presence of the Sun King.

He was seated at a desk, plainly engaged in some other matter of state. Of his features I could see nothing beyond the full-bottomed wig which drooped, on either side, almost to the level of the veneer. Behind him, some five paces distant, was a plain marble fireplace and beside this, his hat reflected in the baroque mirror, was a second figure, clearly the Marquis de Colbert. This face I could see and it bore a polite smile of welcome, cold as fish. Disingenuous, I smiled in return, causing a slight pucker on one of the most powerful foreheads in Europe. Apart from the busy scratching of the King's pen there was silence. I waited, poised.

Without looking up or ceasing to write, the King spoke. 'What do we think of Bossuet?'

I had been prepared for anything, but this, as for some obscure reason the English say, 'went straight through the racket'.

'My Lord?'

'Sire. The name is *Sire*. But don't worry about that. Hundreds make the same mistake who should know a lot better than you. What I said was, "What do we think of Bossuet?"'

It was a test, of course. A trap probably. I realised this at once but, like the lobster, I was already in, comfortable but without the remotest idea how to get out. I hedged.

'He is a professor of theology.'

'Yes, yes. We know who he *is*. He did, after all, teach my son. The boy's a blockhead but that's not his fault. Bossuet's, I mean. Not his fault. I suppose the boy also can't help being dense as marble but he appears to *enjoy* it. Anyway, we know *who* he is...' At this point the royal head was raised and the wide cool eyes looked straight into mine. '... What we want to know is whether he's a fool or a menace.'

I had to answer. I can remember thinking, with all the concentration I could command, 'What would my master say?' I had only seconds to do so before I said, 'I would say he is neither.'

The royal eyebrows raised in mock surprise. 'Neither? Well, well. Have you read his works?'

'Yes, Sire. They are well known in Florence. We have *L'exposition de la Foi Catholique* in the Medici library and it has not yet been forbidden or proscribed.'

'Forbidden? Proscribed? You think it will be?'

'Yes, Sire, I think it inevitable.'

'Really! Do you hear that, Charles?' he said tossing his head in the direction of the other man, who remained impassive. 'They're going to ban old Bossy. *That* will upset him. But tell me. Why should his works be forbidden and banned?'

'He maintains that God's purpose is the happiness of mankind and that man perceives God, has proof of his existence, through his own happiness.'

'Yes? Can that be doubted? Why should that make him a danger to your Tuscan Duke?'

'In Tuscany the people are not happy, they are weighed down by poverty and disease, their lives are blighted and shot. If Monsieur Bossuet is right then their condition denies the very existence of God *or* they will perceive the *potential* for happiness and, thus, the existence of God. In which case the lack of *actual* happiness must lie at the door of their Princes.'

From the fireplace behind the King's head Colbert spoke, softly and with clipped emphasis, 'That is too simple. When he speaks of "happiness" he does not mean the joy of the pig in the trough. He talks of the sublime contentment and wonder to be found in Faith.'

'So it is said, My Lord, but if that be right then the central proposition is a tautology. If "Happiness" is "Faith" then, according to Monsieur Bossuet, we are proving God by faith in him. I do not prove the existence of a hat by saying it is on my head.'

The King was smiling. 'Well, Charles, what do we say to *that*? How do you *prove* your hat, apart from seeing it in the mirror behind you?'

The Marquis had also smiled and ignored the question. 'What we say to *that* is that it is as well to ensure the happiness of the people.'

The King was now looking at me closely. 'Tell me, the view you have expressed. Is it your master's view?'

'No, Sire,' I said, 'I think he would agree with Monsieur Bossuet.'

'Really! You were putting the case against him so well that I was thinking of banning him myself.' And the royal shoulders shook in some silent and private merriment, 'That really *would* upset him. You see, Monsieur Credi,' he added, becoming serious, 'we must play with you no more. I should tell you that I regard the works of Jacques Bossuet as the finest compass I possess in guiding this difficult ship.'

My relief was profound. I had, of course, read not a word of the great philosopher but, by the purest chance, had been present during a long and, at times, acrimonious discussion between my master and Lorenzo Bellini on precisely the subject in hand. My relief, however, was short-lived as the King continued, 'Tell me about this Cimento.'

At least for this I had been prepared. 'It is, or was, a learned society, dedicated to the investigation of method. Similar to the Royal Society in London or your own Académie Française started by Monsieur Colbert.'

'Ah ha!' cried the King, alarmingly. 'Colbert! You hear that, Charles? Your brother gets about, does he not?'

The Marquis said nothing but pursed his lips and stared fixedly towards the window. Even more alarmingly the King now looked at me, his eyes bright with amusement, and winked broadly, 'Charles did not like his brother and his brother did not like Charles. A circumstance which I found extremely useful. But I think,' he said seriously, 'Monsieur Credi, you have not told us the whole story.' When I did not reply he continued, 'Do not concern yourself, Monsieur, we know everything that happens in Tuscany. The whole of Italy for that matter. Your Society has been meeting in private, has it not?'

'Sire ...' I began but he raised his hand.

'No, do not deny it. I see already you are a clever boy, and loyal. I would not ask you to break whatever oath you have taken. But we *know* that you hold secret meetings and, furthermore, they do not just concern the fallacy of method. No group of men would risk the rack for such a purpose. We know that the Society favours a French marriage and that is why the fat Grand Duchess (whose name, for the moment, escapes me) has ordered all your brain merchants to be locked up.'

I realised, with some surprise, that he had paused in the expectation of some kind of admiring or astonished reaction. I did my best, shaking my head from side to side in what appeared, I hoped, to be a gesture of amazement at the efficiency of French spies. Otherwise I deemed silence to be the best policy and I was right.

'Well, Monsieur Credi, our cousin tells us that you have come to plead for my influence. Frankly, quite how much I have in the Tuscan Court is doubtful. It was certainly greater before Marguerite made such a hash of her marriage. No, no, I am not going to go into that again. But I have *some* influence and your Duke Cosimo is very keen to marry his son into the French nobility. Awful boy I gather. Even worse than mine. Still, I am not opposed to such a match if a suitable heroine can be found and we are not ungrateful to our friends. You will be pleased to know, therefore, that I have written to Cosimo – he is, in any event, a distant relative of mine – and urged clemency on behalf of a number of those arrested. Your master among them. I have done so on the basis of scientific advance. Golden age of enquiry … frontiers of science … some heresy inevitable … librarians of limited intelligence … lack Divine intuition of Princes, etcetera, etcetera, all that stuff. But just in case he misses the point I have also suggested, in the same message, that a French envoy should meet his Chancellor to discuss the marriage of his son.'

I did not know what to do. I had no training in receiving the grace of Kings. What I *did* do was entirely by nature. I fell on my knees.

'Now now, dear, dear,' said the King's voice above me, 'how very Italian. Most unwise. If people think you're going to fall down every time they do something for you they become less willing to help.'

I rose awkwardly and said, 'Sire, how is the …'

'Do not concern yourself with that. The messenger has already left this morning. That is not to say, however,' he added, 'that he would not have been recalled if you had failed our little test. I will tell Jacques Bossuet of your regard. He likes Italy. I dare say he will come and stay with you again in Florence.'

As I bowed, he added, 'I have arranged a carriage for you and your dwarf as far as Aix-en-Provence. My cousin here is as penniless as a Huguenot whore and needs her only carriage. She relies on money from your Duke which never comes. It's all a terrible trial for me. In addition, if you would be so kind as to take that Irish priest back to Tuscany I would be very grateful. He causes dreadful scandals wherever he goes.'

He was about to resume his writing and I, indeed, was halfway through a deep and awkward bow when he continued, yet again, 'Oh, yes. I meant to tell you that I knew your father. Quite well really. When I was much younger I used to go to Paris, incognito. Got in with a bad crowd, Racine, Molière, La Fontaine and other riff-raff. Your father was often there, collecting his books. He didn't know who I was, of course, but we got on very well. We enjoyed ourselves a lot. I'd keep clear of the Rue Saint-Honoré if I were you. You might find you owe people money.'

My last memory of him was a smile both weary and a little wicked whilst behind him the Marquis, still as a statue, also smiled in polite valediction.

Chapter Twenty-Four

To celebrate there was no time. As we left the palace gates I clasped my companion with the spontaneous agony of relief but she waved aside my thanks. 'Men will do anything if they believe they are being clever,' she said, and it is as wise a remark as I can remember.

The carriage was, indeed, awaiting us in the royal mews. Tuscan to my boots, I marvelled at such efficiency of purpose. It was therefore in something close to triumph that we returned to the Château, ready immediately for the return to Aix. Indeed it was not until I had half-concluded my account to Bono that I felt the first dreadful premonitions of doom. Euphoria at our triumph (and, to be frank, a measure of conceit) had obscured the reality of our position. We were a thousand miles from Florence. Even with the assistance of our royal carriage and assuming, fine weather, safe passage and the provision of suitable horses from Aix it was nine day's travel. It was now eleven days since we had departed the city. Our total absence, therefore, could not be less than three weeks and might well be more. The power of Pasto Bomboni was sufficient to contrive murder within minutes. As I looked at Bono's smiling face I was filled with the total certainty that we would be too late.

In the event it took longer. The rain came again, sheeting against the side of the coach, driving through the doors and windows. In the confined space the air was permanently damp and the upholstery became sodden. The roads turned to rivers of slush and mud in which, with agonising regularity, we became firmly stuck. On those occasions we joined the coachmen, the ostlers and any who could be conscripted from the surrounding country in the perilous business of retrieval, knee-deep in mud, lashed by the rain, straining and heaving against the spokes and springs. During one such operation, Bono, losing his grip on the rim of the front wheel, disappeared completely beneath the sea of mud. As the coach lurched I was, indeed, terrified that he had been pinned beneath it but he reappeared, a nightmare figure, his tusks protruding from the oozing mud, and hurled himself again at the unmoving spokes. By the fourth day we were barely a hundred miles from Versailles, exhausted, freezing cold, our clothes and bodies ingrained with mud and clay. We stopped at Orléans. We had no choice. The horses were done for, the front axle was near broken and our coachmen were close to mutiny. Two days we remained there while the rain stopped and the spring sun returned. Clean, in new clothes, the axle mended and new horses hired, we set off again on the interminable journey.

Bono remained in high spirits. Infuriating but infectious, he maintained a continuous wry and observant commentary on the state of the people and country through which we passed. He had a Sicilian's loathing for the French whom he believed to be soft, sensuous and stupid. On our route he stole and consumed enormous quantities of their vegetables, many far from ripe. He also revealed an immensely wide knowledge of heretical literature, theology and crude verse. He bore my impatience and lamentations with the phlegmatic tolerance of the reformed buccaneer, and in a sea of despair he provided laughter like a raft.

Despite the improvement in the weather progress was still very slow. The mud of the roads had hardened into deep ruts which gangs of peasants now laboured to fill and scrape, forming, as they did so, a further, sullen hindrance to our progress. In all, from the time of leaving Versailles, it took nigh on two weeks to reach the Convent at Aix. By that time I had the fever. Delirious, cold, drenched in sweat, I was afflicted by nightmares of terrifying clarity. When awake, I was prey to hallucination. Caterina sat beside me in the carriage, one hand in mine, the other bathing my face and forehead with a scarf so damp that water, cold as ice, ran past my eyes and over my parched lips. Sometimes I knew it was the dwarf who performed these services and, in rare moments of lucidity, smiled in weak gratitude before returning to visions of the Bargello and the rack. I was in this condition for three days before we reached the Convent. It was a further week before I was able to travel again. I could not have wished for better nurses but I was helpless to resist the length of care and convalescence deemed essential to my recovery.

When I was capable of doing so, I understood that Patrick had left for Florence on the day we departed for Versailles. I had half-expected him to go but I now had further cause for anguish and premonition.

Also, by now, my funds were all but expended. My banker's draft I had encashed at Versailles, suffering, in the process, the deduction of a scandalous commission. The gold which I had barely provided us with the meanest of coaches and a coachman to match, and from the condition of the horses it was plain that progress, again, would be slow to the point of torpor.

I was, however, still weak and ill and this produced a resignation bordering upon apathy. It was now nearly five weeks since we had left Florence on a journey anticipated to last ten days. Even that period might well have seen disaster. We had extended it four-fold. I became oppressed with guilt. Should we not have returned immediately to the city armed with whatever influence Marguerite Louise could exercise herself? Was the journey to Versailles, *in reality*, not for my own security? Misery gripped me. I could not eat and I sat on the uncomfortable boards of our coach, hollow-eyed in silence and despair. Had it not been for the ceaseless ministering and energy of my companion our driver might well have delivered a corpse, a task for which he appeared perfectly designed.

We slept in the coach itself; our financial circumstances allowed no other course. The days were hot and the nights were cold and it was not until six days after leaving Aix that we crossed the border into Tuscany, the timeless ochre and grey-green landscape falling about us like a cloth through which the poplars speared towards the still blue sky. I was home, all but, and, despite the wretchedness of my condition, the bitter anxieties which now flooded back into my aching head and the poverty and destitution of the people, my heart lifted and my eyes cleared. On the seventh day we could finally see the city from the hills at Pistoia and we began our long descent into the valley of the Arno. Still we continued our tortoise pace, rocked, cradle-like, to and fro as the city appeared to recede before our slow advance.

We finally entered the al Prato gate as the late afternoon sun stood, barely tree height, above the hills. The city appeared little changed, the woven smells of putrefaction and the evening cooking were bitter-sweet with plague and familiarity. We passed Santa Maria Novella and, minutes later, turned into the Via del Corso. I was weak with sickness, dread and anticipation but, as the carriage drew to a halt on Bono's behest, I lurched from it, forced myself across the uneven cobbles and stood before the door. The window to the library was still broken. Inside candelabra were burning and I imagined I heard the voice of Lorenzo Bellini, at high pitch, though whether through anger, fear or excitement

I could not tell. Close to fainting I grasped the iron knocker and beat upon the wood. Seconds later the door opened inwards and I, still clasping the metal ring, was thereby pulled into the house.

Chapter Twenty-Five

'He had been strung up by his thumbs,' said Lorenzo Bellini, helping himself to another glass of wine, 'the others were all dead too but their bodies were not displayed in such a fashion.'

'A dreadful thing,' said Patrick, 'a terrible crime.'

'I agree,' said my master.

'Well, I'm afraid I do *not*,' said Vincenzo Viviani. 'When I heard the news in my cell – two of the guards were talking about it in the passage – I did nothing but rejoice. He was the most evil of men.'

'Perhaps so, Vincenzo,' said my master, 'but that cannot excuse the sin. Besides, what of the others who were with him...'

'They were bent upon *murder*...'

'They were bent, I am afraid, upon their master's bidding. Therein lies the tragedy. The corruption of the age, a group of men (good men too, if Fredo be correct) reduced to slaughtering others, among whom might well have been their own relatives, even sons. The blame for that, I fear, does not lie with the members of the Salti. Blockheads they may be but they did not levy the taxes, sell the monopolies, order the persecution of the Jews or the burning of the books.'

He was sitting by the great window, overlooking the canal. Lorenzo and Viviani were seated at the table. Bono had long since retired to his bed. I sat upon the ottoman, fighting back the waves of sleep. Beside me Patrick was examining part of the new bookcase. Night had fallen, though it was still early. The lamp, on the table, proscribed a circle of light, not quite meeting that shed by the candelabra left burning by the carpenters who had, until the past hour, been engaged in the long process of reconstruction. The great window was open, and, beyond it, the sound of the water could be heard above the fretting of the shutters in their metal clasps.

'Well,' said Viviani, 'I respect what you say, Antonio, but I fear I cannot agree. The Pitti Palace and the Inquisition would be powerless without the service of these "blockheads" and no one is bound to carry out the evil act of another.'

'Then let us rather agree to differ,' said my master smiling, 'than to start bickering now. The *real* business is to persuade Fredo to go to bed before he falls off that ottoman.'

I was persuaded. They rose when I left, a faintly embarrassing gesture, but, before I had passed the 'Cenacolo', now mainly obscured by new shelves, I heard them resume their seats and their conversation. I lay in my bed watching the plaster fruit and leaves dance in the candlelight above my head. I was warm and, so Lorenzo had pronounced after minute examination, well. Fatigue pressed upon me as I assembled our present circumstances firmly in my mind, a fortress against nightmare and doubt.

Alessandro Bomboni had received both my letters the day I left Florence. He had refused, point blank, to leave the knacker's yard, demonstrating the extraordinary capacity of human beings to defend their own territory, however foul and unpromising it may be. Pasto, for his part, had lost no time recruiting a loyal bunch of thugs from within the Salti and, on the sixth day following our leaving, had set out with a group, twenty-strong, on the road to San Casciano.

They were waiting for him at Gallaza. Not a member of the Salti escaped. It was, apparently, widely known in Florence that the ambush was the work of a group of brigands, many from the Gallaza area, led by a man called Mario Corcho. Years before he had been badly beaten and mutilated by Pasto Bomboni and a group of bullies hired by the brothers Assinari. Indeed, he might well have been killed, had it not been for the intervention of my own father, a fact which had now passed into legend.

The news of the massacre had swept the city. Curiously, of course, it placed the prisoners in greater danger since the power I possessed over Bomboni died with him at Gallaza. For the sake of discipline, however, it had been necessary to promote a new Commander at short notice and this had fallen to a Salti captain with a bad back and a blotched nose. For a reason obscure to many he appeared not to possess the same driving enthusiasm for the infliction of pain and the burning of books.

Following the news of Bomboni's death, a mother and daughter were released from the Stinche Prison. Here they had both been incarcerated for nearly a week. The daughter had attempted to obtain the release of her mother by bribery which would have succeeded in any case but this, which fell under the personal aegis of the Commander of the Salti. Upon the news of his death those entrusted with the imprisonment of the women took the money with their accustomed zeal. (Also released, on the same bribery, was a maidservant, said to be Jewish.) Once free, Lisa and Caterina had made swift progress to Pisa where they remained under the protection of the University authorities, unlikely adornments to the academic groves. Lorenzo had seen them before his own journey to Florence. He had learnt of our adventures in Impruneta and commented to me with some evident amusement that 'my star seemed high in the Mascini firmament'. This produced within me a feeling as uncomfortable as any I had suffered in my fever, leading to total loss of breath and a reeling of the senses. Mother and daughter were to return on the morrow and, with that contemplation, my young body burned.

The Bombonis had, of course, remained safe and, indeed, Nicola had come to Florence after the death of her brother. She had, it seemed, formed an immediate attachment to Carlo Bassani, the assistant librarian who had carried the message of warning. Perhaps more to placate her enthusiasm than for any strictly academic reason she had herself been offered a junior post in the Medici library, the first of her sex ever to receive such a doubtful distinction.

The release of my master, Dati, Viviani, and others who had been arrested for similar heresies followed upon the arrival of a royal messenger from France. He, you will remember, had departed from Paris some twelve hours before our own leaving and had thus, by the narrowest of margins, proceeded ahead of the storms which swept across the centre of France. He had made the best of time and arrived at Florence three weeks previously. Preparations were already being made, it was said, for a marriage between Ferdinando and a French Princess of doubtful age and, hitherto, total obscurity.

As to my master's library, it had been discovered that the raiding Salti were accompanied by Jesuit Inquisitors armed with lists of supposedly heretical works. Following the arrest of the conspirators the entire collection of manuscripts and books had been divided into two separate categories, the innocent which were to be spared and the heretical which were to be destroyed. Having carried out their task the Inquisitors left the house whereupon the illiterati from the Salti, with predictable and military precision, burnt the wrong pile. The result was that my master was deprived of a quantity of works which, he freely admitted, only sentiment had prevented his burning many years before.

This, not inconsiderable, irony brought a smile to my face in the darkness of my room. The bed, now resurrected by the carpenters, was soft, the night warm and I felt myself begin to drift into sleep. As I did so I could still hear the insistent murmuring of my friends in the library below, their indistinguishable voices rising and falling away like the sound of men singing a long way off.

Postscript

Tomaso Albinoni is dead. I heard the news today. There will be no Opera. All that I have is a narrative, a book.

The whole thing has been, perhaps, a waste of time. But I *do* wonder, when I look at this pile of paper, why I *worry* so much that someone is going to burn it.

FOR THE BEST IN PAPERBACKS, LOOK FOR THE

In every corner of the world, on every subject under the sun, Penguin represents quality and variety – the very best in publishing today.

For complete information about books available from Penguin – including Pelicans, Puffins, Peregrines and Penguin Classics – and how to order them, write to us at the appropriate address below. Please note that for copyright reasons the selection of books varies from country to country.

In the United Kingdom: Please write to *Dept E.P., Penguin Books Ltd, Harmondsworth, Middlesex, UB7 0DA*

If you have any difficulty in obtaining a title, please send your order with the correct money, plus ten per cent for postage and packaging, to *PO Box No 11, West Drayton, Middlesex*

In the United States: Please write to *Dept BA, Penguin, 299 Murray Hill Parkway, East Rutherford, New Jersey 07073*

In Canada: Please write to *Penguin Books Canada Ltd, 2801 John Street, Markham, Ontario L3R 1B4*

In Australia: Please write to the *Marketing Department, Penguin Books Australia Ltd, P.O. Box 257, Ringwood, Victoria 3134*

In New Zealand: Please write to the *Marketing Department, Penguin Books (NZ) Ltd, Private Bag, Takapuna, Auckland 9*

In India: Please write to *Penguin Overseas Ltd, 706 Eros Apartments, 56 Nehru Place, New Delhi, 110019*

In Holland: Please write to *Penguin Books Nederland B.V., Postbus 195, NL–1380AD Weesp, Netherlands*

In Germany: Please write to *Penguin Books Ltd, Friedrichstrasse 10–12, D–6000 Frankfurt Main 1, Federal Republic of Germany*

In Spain: Please write to *Longman Penguin España, Calle San Nicolas 15, E–28013 Madrid, Spain*

In France: Please write to *Penguin Books Ltd, 39 Rue de Montmorency, F-75003, Paris, France*

In Japan: Please write to *Longman Penguin Japan Co Ltd, Yamaguchi Building, 2–12–9 Kanda Jimbocho, Chiyoda-Ku, Tokyo 101, Japan*

A CHOICE OF PENGUIN FICTION

The High Road   Edna O'Brien

Her long-awaited new novel of a lyrical love between two women. 'Contemporary and sophisticated ... *The High Road* is all that I wanted it to be ... the same emotional sensitivity, especially in the arena of sexual passion. The same authority of characterization' – *Guardian*

The Philosopher's Pupil   Iris Murdoch

'We are back, of course, with great delight, in the land of Iris Murdoch, which is like no other but Prospero's' – *Sunday Telegraph*. 'The most daring and original of all her novels' – A. N. Wilson

Paradise Postponed   John Mortimer

'Hats off to John Mortimer. He's done it again' – *Spectator*. Why does Simeon Simcox, the CND-marching Rector of Rapstone Fanner, leave his fortune not to his two sons but to an odious Tory Minister? A rumbustious, hilarious novel from the creator of Rumpole.

The Anatomy Lesson   Philip Roth

The famous forty-year-old writer Nathan Zuckerman decides to give it all up and become a doctor – and a pornographer – instead. 'The finest, boldest and funniest piece of fiction that Philip Roth has yet produced' – *Spectator*

Gabriel's Lament   Paul Bailey

'The best novel yet by one of the most careful fiction craftsmen of his generation' – *Guardian*. 'A magnificent novel, moving, eccentric and unforgettable. He has a rare feeling for language and an understanding of character which few can rival' – *Daily Telegraph*

A CHOICE OF PENGUIN FICTION

A Far Cry From Kensington   Muriel Spark

'Pure delight' – Claire Tomalin in the *Independent*. 'A 1950s Kensington of shabby-genteel bedsitters, espresso bars and A-line dresses … irradiated with sudden glows of lyricism she can so beautifully effect' – Peter Kemp in the *Sunday Times*

Love in the Time of Cholera   Gabriel García Márquez

The Number One international bestseller. 'Admirers of *One Hundred Years of Solitude* may find it hard to believe that García Márquez can have written an ever better novel. But that's what he's done' – *Newsweek*

Lolita   Vladimir Nabokov

Shot through with Nabokov's mercurial wit, quicksilver prose and intoxicating sensuality, *Lolita* is one of the world's greatest love stories. 'A great book' – Dorothy Parker

My Secret History   Paul Theroux

'André Parent saunters into the book, aged fifteen … a creature of naked and unquenchable ego, greedy for sex, money, experience, *another life* … read it warily; read it twice, and more; it is darker and deeper than it looks' – *Observer*. 'On his best form since *The Mosquito Coast*' – *Time Out*

Decline and Fall   Evelyn Waugh

A comic yet curiously touching account of an innocent plunged into the sham, brittle world of high society. Evelyn Waugh's first novel brought him immediate public acclaim and remains a classic of its kind.

FOR THE BEST IN PAPERBACKS, LOOK FOR THE 🐧

A CHOICE OF PENGUIN FICTION

The Radiant Way Margaret Drabble

To Liz, Alix and Esther, fresh from Cambridge in the 1950s and among the most brilliant of their generation, the world offered its riches...'Shows a Dickensian desire to encompass the whole of contemporary British life ... Humane, intelligent, engrossing' – *Independent*

Summer's Lease John Mortimer

'It's high summer, high comedy too, when Molly drags her amiably bickering family to a rented Tuscan villa for the hols ... With a cosy fluency of wit, Mortimer charms us into his urbane tangle of clues...' – *Mail on Sunday*. 'Superb' – Ruth Rendell

Nice Work David Lodge

'The campus novel meets the industrial novel ... compulsive reading' – David Profumo in the *Daily Telegraph*. 'A work of immense intelligence, informative, disturbing and diverting ... one of the best novelists of his generation' – Anthony Burgess in the *Observer*

S. John Updike

'John Updike's very funny satire not only pierces the occluded hocus-pocus of Lego religion which exploits the gullible and self-deluded ... but probes more deeply and seriously the inadequacies on which superstitious skulduggery battens' – *The Times*

The Counterlife Philip Roth

'Roth has now surpassed himself' – *Washington Post*. 'A breathtaking *tour de force* of wit, wisdom, ingenuity and sharply-honed malice' – *The Times*